Praise for Sean Dietrich

"*Kinfolk* is the Southern story you've been waiting for. I absolutely loved this delightful and heart-wrenching story chock-full of both laughter and tears. In a small Alabama town where everyone knows your darkest secrets, and where the Grand Ole Opry is a balm to the soul, we meet a cast of endearing and quirky characters you won't forget. *Kinfolk* is a page-turning delight with Dietrich's trademark humor and heart-filled insight. In this wild ride we call life, Dietrich has a special view and one he shares with wit and kindness in turn. When a young girl working at Waffle House and a sixty-five-year-old man whose life is falling apart cross paths in Park, Alabama, no one in their world will ever be the same. *Kinfolk* is a novel about second chances, deep love, forgiveness, and the power of country music—all wrapped up in a lyrically told story."

—Patti Callahan Henry, *New York Times* bestselling author of *The Secret Book of Flora Lea*

"Sean Dietrich has a lovely, seasoned voice that's anchored by his deep understanding of the charm and depth of the South. *Kinfolk*, the latest in his oeuvre, is a heartwarming and well-told tale with lyrical writing that's as rich as my mother's grits casserole. I'm left satisfied, uplifted, and perhaps a little homesick too."

—Boo Walker, bestselling author of *A Spanish Sunrise*

"Sean Dietrich is a master at creating Southern characters who are relatable in their brokenness, hope, and perseverance. Laugh-out-loud colloquialisms bring sincerity and realism to small-town life. *Kinfolk* spins both a heartbreaking and heartwarming tale about family, redemption, second chances, and the power of love that moves us all."

—Jennifer Moorman, bestselling author of *The Baker's Man*

"The legion of fans who have already discovered Sean of the South's heartwarming southern stories will be raving about this knock-out novel, and readers new to his work will find this tale strikes every perfect note. With relatable characters, comedic relief, sensory-rich descriptions, a dose of romance, and a fast-paced plot that keeps the pages turning, Dietrich has hit a home run with this one . . . a victory that would surely make The Incredible Winston Browne proud."

—*New York Journal of Books* for *The Incredible Winston Browne*

"Dietrich imbues plenty of Southern charm and colloquialisms in a read that will appeal to people of all genders, and especially to fans of small-town living. Readers who enjoy well-developed, realistic characters similar to those from Charles Martin and Lauren K. Denton will want to watch for more from this author."

—*Library Journal* for *The Incredible Winston Browne*

"Dietrich meshes mystery and romance beautifully in this moral tale about one man set on using what is left of his life to enrich the lives of others. Dietrich's fans will love this rip-roaring, dramatic inspirational."

—*Publishers Weekly* for *The Incredible Winston Browne*

"This poignant novel is about people, life, community, family, friendship, love, the day-to-day, even the mundane . . . Baseball fans and non-fans alike will enjoy this sometimes humorous, occasionally heartbreaking story about all that we hold dear, which gives us a timely reminder that we need to live in the moment, or life can pass us by while we aren't paying attention."

—Historical Novel Society for *The Incredible Winston Browne*

"Sean Dietrich has written a home run of a novel with *The Incredible Winston Browne*. Every bit as wonderful as its title implies, it's the story of Browne—a principled, baseball-loving sheriff—a precocious little girl in need of help, and the community that rallies around them. This warm, witty, tender novel celebrates the power of friendship and family to transform our lives. It left me nostalgic and hopeful, missing my grandfathers, and eager for baseball season to start again. I loved it."

—Ariel Lawhon, *New York Times* bestselling
author of *I Was Anastasia*

"Sean's writing is infused with the small-town South—you can smell the exhaust of the cars cruising down dusty back roads, and you can sense the warmth of the potluck meal on your plate. Make no mistake. [*The Incredible Winston Browne*] is a classic story, told by an expert storyteller."

—Shawn Smucker, author of *Light from Distant Stars*

"Sean Dietrich has given us an absolute treasure of a novel. Moving, powerful, and dazzling, *Stars of Alabama* is a page-turning wonder of a story."

—Patti Callahan, *New York Times* bestselling
author of *Becoming Mrs. Lewis*

"Dietrich is a Southern Garrison Keillor. Fans of the latter and former will be pleased."

—*Library Journal* for *Stars of Alabama*

"[*Stars of Alabama*] is a testament to inner strength, and the good that can come from even the worst beginnings . . . Historical fiction and mystery readers will find this to be a very satisfying book."

—*Booklist*

"Sean Dietrich has woven together a rich tapestry of characters—some charming, some heartbreaking, all of them inspiring. *Stars of Alabama* is mesmerizing, a siren's call that holds the reader in a world softly Southern, full of broken lives and the good souls who pick up the pieces and put them back together into a brilliant, wondrous new mosaic full of hope."

—Dana Chamblee Carpenter, author of the Bohemian Trilogy

"Set during the Dust Bowl, this pleasing, ambitious epic from Dietrich brings together unlikely allies all escaping dire situations . . . Though filled with preachers declaring judgment and prophecies of the end-time, Dietrich's hopeful tale illuminates the small rays of faith that shine even in dark times."

—*Publishers Weekly* for *Stars of Alabama*

"Mysterious and dazzling."

—*Deep South* for *Stars of Alabama*

"Sean Dietrich can spin a story."

—*Southern Living* for *Stars of Alabama*

"A big-hearted novel."

—*Garden & Gun* for *Stars of Alabama*

"Sean Dietrich's *Stars of Alabama* is a beautiful novel, mesmerizing with its complex characters, lush settings, and lyrical language. It is, quite simply, Southern literature at its finest."

—*Southern Literary Review*

Kinfolk

Also by Sean Dietrich

FICTION

The Incredible Winston Browne

Stars of Alabama

Lyla

Caution: This Vehicle Makes Frequent Stops for Boiled Peanuts

The Other Side of the Bay

Small Towns, Labradors, Barbecue, Biscuits, Beer, and Bibles

NONFICTION

You Are My Sunshine

Will the Circle Be Unbroken?

The Absolute Worst Christmas of All Time

The South's Okayest Writer

Sean of the South: On the Road

Sean of the South (Volume 1)

Sean of the South (Volume 2)

Sean of the South: Whistling Dixie

Kinfolk

SEAN DIETRICH

HARPER MUSE

Published by Harper Muse, an imprint of HarperCollins Focus LLC.

Published in association with The Bindery Agency, www.TheBinderyAgency.com.

Scripture quotations are taken from the King James Version. Public domain.

This book is a work of fiction. The characters, incidents, and dialogue are drawn from the author's imagination and are not to be construed as real. Any resemblance to actual events or persons, living or dead, is entirely coincidental.

Library of Congress Cataloging-in-Publication Data

Names: Dietrich, Sean, 1982- author.
Title: Kinfolk / Sean Dietrich.
Description: [Nashville] : Harper Muse, 2023. | Summary: "When a mysterious teenager shows up in Nub's life in rural Alabama, he learns that family, forgiveness, and kindness can be found in the most unlikely of places"--Provided by publisher.
Identifiers: LCCN 2023020837 (print) | LCCN 2023020838 (ebook) | ISBN 9781400235636 (paperback) | ISBN 9781400235643 (epub) | ISBN 9781400235650 (audio download)
Subjects: LCGFT: Novels.
Classification: LCC PS3604.I2254 K56 2023 (print) | LCC PS3604.I2254 (ebook) | DDC 813/.6--dc23/eng/20230605
LC record available at https://lccn.loc.gov/2023020837
LC ebook record available at https://lccn.loc.gov/2023020838

Printed in the United States of America

23 24 25 26 27 LBC 5 4 3 2 1

This book is dedicated to the little eleven-year-old boy whose father shot himself in the garage of his brother's house. The little boy who played music from age three. The little boy who eventually grew into me.

⮜ THE BEGINNING ⮞

This is the wrong way to begin a novel.

Novels are supposed to begin with suspense, romance, explosions, intrigue, boy meets girl, or a car chase. But this story does not begin with a car chase. Truthfully, the author wishes this story could begin a different way. But we must start at the beginning, or nothing that follows will make sense.

The man was forty-two years old. He was handsome. Smart. Funny. A farmer. A father. A Baptist. A pipe smoker who always smelled of Cavendish and sweat. He had red hair and long limbs, and his clothes were always hanging from his frame like a tunic.

He was trembling when he removed a 10 gauge from its canvas case. His heart was beating quickly, like a Sousa march. His hands were shaking. He wasn't unfamiliar with firearms. He was a gun person. This was his rifle. He knew how to operate it. How to clean it. How to disassemble it. The weapon was an extension of his body when he was hunting deer, turkey, or boar with his eleven-year-old son. He taught his son all about the safe handling of firearms. Sometimes his boy, Jeremiah, borrowed this rifle and went hunting on his own. His boy would come home with several squirrels or a coon. Maybe a rabbit or some quail. His son was always so proud of his kills, no matter how puny. Such a male.

He would miss his son most of all.

The man sat on the floor of the walk-in closet, cross-legged, beneath hanging clothes, nestled beside a stack of old *Saturday Evening Post* magazines, cradling the rifle, attempting to work up the courage.

His life was falling apart. But then, the whole country was falling apart. It was a heckuva year in America. Warren G. Harding was the twenty-ninth president. Labor uprisings were happening everywhere. There was a race massacre in Tulsa. China was now communist, and there were rumors of the same cancer spreading here. Babe Ruth hit his 138th home run. Everything was changing. Especially the tobacco industry.

Sixty-five percent of the country now smoked like riverboats. Tobacco companies were raking it in with both hands. But it wasn't enough for tobacco tycoons. Tobacco prices plummeted when companies started gouging the market and underpaying growers to increase net gains. Simply put: the modern way of doing business was changing. It was low-down and crooked. And it was making a lot of executives rich by killing the tobacco farmer.

This man was one such farmer.

He didn't even have enough money to buy his son shoes. He worked from dawn until eventide, yet his family lived on poke salad and hominy. And as of last night, he had defaulted on his mortgage. After the weekend, bankers in suits would show up on his front lawn, and they would haul his belongings away.

The shotgun smelled like gun oil. His back was positioned against the wall. The man closed his eyes and prayed for strength. Which seemed sacrilegious at this moment, to be asking God to help him do something that was so awful. But he didn't know what else to do. Maybe God would step in and stop him from this wicked act. Maybe a miracle would happen. Maybe his problems would go away if he just had enough faith. Maybe his transgressions would be forgotten, if not forgiven. Maybe God would figure out a way to save him from his own bad decisions.

Maybe.

"Please, help me," he said between sobs. "Please."

But nothing happened. No bright lights from on high. No angels with curly blond hair came to prevent him from doing the unthinkable. No sacred choirs. No nothing.

He'd tacked a note to the closet door.

DO NOT COME IN HERE, JEREMIAH. CALL THE SHERIFF.

He had also written a letter to his wife and son that he'd left on the kitchen table. The note included all the usual stuff. *I'm sorry. I love you. This isn't your fault. I couldn't take it anymore. I'm sorry for all the sorrow I caused so many people. You'll be better off without me.* Blah, blah, blah. But all his words sounded like a pitiful excuse.

Then, just to be sure his son wouldn't barge into the bedroom, he'd barricaded the door with a dresser. He'd walked into this closet, spread bath towels on the floor, and here he sat.

There was nothing left to do. No loose ends left to tie up. It was now or never. He was doing this for his family, really. It was all for them. With the father out of the way, the wife and child would have a chance at life. The man was doing the whole world a favor.

The man steadied himself with a few deep breaths. He positioned the rifle in his mouth. His big toe was in the trigger guard. His last words were muffled. But they were heard.

"Christ forgive me," he said as he wept.

The blast blew a hole into the ceiling, destroying the plaster above him, frightening birds from nearby treetops, probably forever. The perfect silence was ruined. He was gone.

It was Thanksgiving Day 1921.

And that is where our story begins.

BOOK
1

In Alabama, "Drive safe" is code for "I love you." There are different versions of this phrase, of course. But the words all mean the same thing. They all carry the same spirit. In central Alabama, one variation of this phrase is, "Be careful, the cops are out tonight." In northern regions of the state, people say, "Y'all be safe going home." Others might say, "Watch out for deer."

Either way, the specific words are inconsequential; they all convey the same meaning: *You matter to me. You're important to me. Keep your high beams on. Keep both hands on the wheel. Deer are homicidal.* Eavesdrop at any Alabamian get-together, from women's Bible studies to Veterans of Foreign Wars halls, from Boy Scout rallies to bunco games, and at the end of the night, you won't hear I-love-yous uttered. Not even among families. You will, however, hear the "drive safe" invocation used about fifty or sixty times.

Nub Taylor nudged open the steel door of the Legion Hall, his cousin Benny following close behind. The old sponges at the bar bid him farewell.

"Careful on the roads tonight," said one man.

"Be safe," said another.

Nub wished them all a happy Thanksgiving.

The ancient soaks returned the favor with a chorus of laughs and mumbles.

Thanksgiving. November 23, 1972. The world was going to pot in more ways than one. Violence and idiocy ruled the culture. The hit movie was *The Godfather*, which featured two hours of sustained gunfire interrupted only by boobs. Don McLean's "American Pie" governed the radio waves, a two-chord song that was approximately the same duration as veterinary school. Nixon was in office, so there was that. The Vietnam War was still in full swing, and everyone was either protesting it, protesting the protestors, or protesting Jane Fonda. Meantime, in Alabama, Governor George Corley Wallace, the same man who once shouted from podiums for "segregation now, segregation tomorrow, and segregation forever," was head honcho. The world was a mess. And now 1973 was on the horizon, and Nub wasn't nearly drunk enough to face it.

"Good night," said Nub.

The door slammed.

Nub and Benny began their trek across the parking lot. That night the parking lot of the Legion Hall was covered in a quilt of snow. The American Legion's annual Beer and Bird Supper was the highlight of their holiday year. Leigh Ann went to painstaking trouble to cook for the bachelors in town. She was the only one who would. The food was pricey, but worth it. For six bucks you got all the bird you could eat along with all the trimmings, including collards and hocks, dressing, and a homemade peanut butter pie that was good enough to qualify as adultery. After feasting, all the codgers played their annual tournament of Hold'em until they were either broke or naked. Or both. When the night was over, they were good to go for another 365 days.

Nub's and Benny's footsteps made crunching sounds in the snow crust.

"You really think there'll be a blizzard tonight?" Benny asked.

"The news said there would be."

Nub and Benny moved cautiously across the parking area, one step at a time. Benny walked with great difficulty. His recent stroke had left half of his face paralyzed, his left leg gimpy, his speech slurred, and his body off-balance.

"I ain't got no firewood at my house," said Benny.

Nub fumbled his keys from his pocket. "Well, now, there's a big surprise."

"I hate chopping."

"I'll bring you some wood in the morning."

"I don't want to put you out, Nub."

"Oh, but you're so good at it."

Benny clutched his cousin's arm. "What would I do without you, Nub?"

Nub threw open his door and helped his cousin into the vehicle. "You'd lie in bed and freeze to death in your own urine. Now get in the truck."

Benny crawled into the cab with a laugh and closed the door behind him. Nub climbed into the driver's side of his rust-colored F-100. The truck's front end bore a large dent as though it had run headfirst into a municipal dam and lived to tell. Nub fired the engine, then placed both hands over the warm air vents and tried to work feeling back into his fingers.

The two old men were silent as they watched flurries fall.

"When was the last blizzard in Park?" said Benny.

"What last blizzard?"

"We've had blizzards before, ain't we?"

"You're confused. You must think you're in Minnesota."

"I remember back in '21 we got eight inches."

"That's not a blizzard. Guys on the radio are calling for *eight feet*."

Benny stared out the window. The whole sky seemed to be filled with uncertainty. "Scary, ain't it? All that snow. People trapped in their houses."

"Sure is," said Nub, throwing the truck into gear. "We run the real risk of running out of beer."

"They're calling it Snowmageddon."

"I'll bet they are."

The vehicle rumbled with automotive emphysema as Nub eased onto the slickened roads. Mounds of snow, some two feet high, were already forming against the curbs. The trees looked like yogurt-covered pretzels. Before wheeling out of the Legion parking lot, Nub's vehicle grazed two trash cans, one mailbox, and a pile of cinder blocks.

"You sure you're okay to drive?" said Benny.

"I'm great."

"You had a lot to drink tonight."

"Thanks for noticing, Tammy Faye."

Nub flipped on the radio. Barbara Mandrell was singing "Tonight My Baby's Coming Home" as they motored past the happy houses on Camellia Drive, Fillmore Street, and Sycamore, where flocks of cars with out-of-state tags were congregated in driveways, about to get snowed in for the holiday weekend. The exiles were back in town. Nub flipped the station to a weather forecast. The radio weather people were all chewing the same cud. They said temperatures were going to sink lower than they ever had in Alabama history. Eight feet of snow. Worst storm in history. Chicken Littles, every last one of them.

They motored through the portrait-perfect streets of Alabama's smallest county. The snowcapped world looked like a Norman Rockwell.

Park, Alabama. Population 1,302. Ash County, the smallest county in the twenty-second state. A county about half the size of Maryland. With no major cities, no major landmarks. No notable citizens unless you counted one third baseman who played for the Cubs in 1915. It was Podunk, USA. Once upon a time, everyone knew where Park was. Passersby had to drive through the town on Highway 31A to get to Birmingham. But now there were bypasses. A new interstate had been built. Park became a no-name place like all the others. Wilsonville. Meadowbrook. Brantleyville. Just words on interstate signs.

When they neared Fifth and Bellville, Nub braked at the four-way stop. Before them was the largest home in the city. At one time, Park, Alabama, had been six hundred thousand acres of peach orchards. This house had been the overseer's home. Today it was where Nub's heart lived.

He gazed out the window of the truck.

The Greek Revival pillars, the gracious windows, and the wide porch were magnificent. Several cars were parked in the driveway; a line of them snaked down the street. The place was thumping tonight. Everyone in the western hemisphere was at this house celebrating the holiday. Everyone except him.

His daughter, Emily, walked past the window and he felt a sharp pain beneath his sternum. Her red hair was pulled back. Her slender, pale neck showed.

"You're spying," said Benny.

"So what?"

"So, spying ain't friendly."

"And?"

"And we didn't have to eat at the Legion. We could have gone to Emily's for dinner."

Nub lit a cigarette. "We aren't wanted in the big house."

"She invited us fifty times."

"She was just being polite."

"She's your daughter, Nub."

"Thanks for the reminder."

Emily's living room faced the street. Through the monstrous windows Nub saw his ex-wife, Loretta, sitting on the sofa, legs crossed, wearing her sphincter-like facial expression. His grandson, Charlie Jr., sat in the corner, looking sullen, like all teenagers do. Nub saw a bunch of other people he didn't recognize, who were probably Episcopalians, just like Emily. She had converted from a Baptist and become a 'Piskie when she married because now she could afford it.

Emily's chimney was pumping plumes of purple smoke into the darkness. Everyone inside was having quite a time.

Nub muscled the gearshift into first and drove onward without speaking.

"You're not going to go wish her a happy Thanksgiving?"

"No."

Benny shook his head. "Too poor to paint, too proud to whitewash."

Nub hated this holiday. It was the worst day of the year.

"I'm sure she'd like to see her father on Thanksgiving."

Silence in the truck cab.

The stereotype of absent fathers is that they are careless and selfish. But sometimes the opposite is also true. Sometimes absent fathers care too much. Sometimes they're drunks. And sometimes drunks know they're drunks. Sometimes, contrary to what you've been told, drunks don't want to screw up your life. So they stay away.

They reached Clairmont Avenue, where they had a clear shot of the water tower in the distance. The tower was lit by newly installed exterior lights and bore a fresh coat of powder-blue paint. The tower had been painted as of this morning. Nub knew this because he and Benny had been the ones who painted it. Eighty-three gallons of blue paint it had taken, and it had taken them three weeks dangling in nylon positioning harnesses, some 140 feet off the ground. They finished two weeks behind schedule. The tower looked nice except for the Big Mistake.

When Nub was painting the town's name, he had forgotten to paint the right leg of the R. Namely, because he had been hammered at the time. He spent most of his life that way. Thus, the letters on the tower read "PAPK." He planned on fixing it, but with the blizzard of the century approaching, it was simply too dangerous to go back up there. The town would remain Papk until further notice.

Nub and Benny were the unofficial maintenance men of Ash County. They were the county grunts. The ones who hung Christmas decorations each year, cut the courthouse lawn, painted fire hydrants, and built stage sets for the community theater production of *The Music Man*. One year Benny even played Mayor Shinn.

When the truck pulled into Benny's driveway on Chestnut Drive, Nub threw the gearshift into Neutral and yanked the parking brake. The motor idled like a guy choking to death. Benny didn't wait for Nub's help. He kicked open the door and attempted to ease out of the truck himself. But he failed. The old man floundered out of the cab, falling face-first into the snow. Nub swore, then jogged around the vehicle to help his cousin off the ground.

"You big dummy," said Nub. "You should've waited for me."

"I can do it myself."

"Clearly."

Nub's cousin struggled to get his feet under him and brushed himself off. "I'm stubborn, Nub. Family trait."

The old man's lip was bleeding; there was snow on his

face. He braced himself against Nub's shoulder and caught his breath.

Nub used his hankie to wipe the blood from Benny's mouth. "Open your mouth, dummy. You got blood all over your teeth."

Nub spent the next few minutes cleaning his cousin's face and fixing his hair.

"Happy Thanksgiving, Nub."

"Bah humbug."

Nub clapped his cousin on the back. This was followed by a brief but exhaustive demonstration of the Smoker's Cough aggravated by laughter. Then they beat each other's shoulders aggressively, the way men do.

"I'll bring wood over tomorrow," said Nub.

"It's too much trouble."

"Tell me about it."

Benny clapped Nub's shoulder one more time.

"Watch out for deer going home, Nub."

But Nub Taylor did not go straight home.

He sat in his truck, parked outside the Greek Revival house on Fifth. Snow heaped on his truck hood. The first pangs of a real blizzard were upon them. If it wouldn't have been so novel, it would have been terrifying.

His radio was playing a rerun of the *Grand Ole Opry* over crackling speakers. Roy Acuff played his fiddle. Minnie Pearl's voice came through loud and clear, live from the Ryman Auditorium in Nashville, Tennessee.

"*I'm just so proud to be here,*" Minnie Pearl said in her exaggerated Tennessee accent. Her trademark line. She said it every week, and it never got old. Nub was an *Opry* fanatic.

He turned up the volume and smiled. Then he took another sip from his half-pint bottle.

Emily was in the kitchen window, washing dishes. She wore all black. Black was her favorite color, always had been. This used to worry him. Only weirdos, freaks, and New Yorkers wore all black.

He was remembering too much this evening. Such as the way Emily looked when she was five years old, missing her front teeth. He remembered when her mother used to French braid her hair. He remembered the way she looked when she was a teenager, lovelier than other girls her age. Emily had always had an unnamable quality. Even so, there had always been something serious about her, a solemnity just beneath the surface, a worry beneath every smile. Sadness beneath every laugh. A sadness he had put there. He was just following in the family business.

He started to take another drink.

No sooner had he raised the liquor to his lips to finish off the bottle than headlights rolled in behind him. Nub cussed and tucked the bottle beneath the seat.

The headlights stopped behind his truck. He recognized the car. Ash County's lone sheriff cruiser was a Toyota truck, tiny, like a roller skate. Only uglier. The Toyota was all the pitiful sheriff's department budget could afford. Toyotas were cheaper than Fords and Chevys, even if Toyotas were an affront to patriotism.

Nub waited for the door to the police vehicle to open. He knew that the guy getting out of the county vehicle was going to be either Deputy Gordon Burke or Danny Black. If he was lucky, it would be Danny, who liked to drink. If he was unlucky, it would be Gordon, who was a deacon. He waited to see which schmuck was behind Door Number Three. The door finally opened and Nub watched a figure emerge. It was Burke. Gordon

Burke. A guy who looked like a cross between Teddy Roosevelt and Colonel Sanders. He was doing the cop walk. Either that, or Gordon was severely constipated.

Gordon rapped on Nub's window. Nub rolled it down.

"Happy Thanksgiving, Nub."

"Gordon."

"Mind if I ask what you're doing parked in the middle of a four-way stop?"

Nub nodded at the house across the street. "It's my daughter's house, that's what."

Burke smiled. "I know who lives there. But what are *you* doing here? You're blocking traffic."

Nub made a big show of looking around. "What traffic?"

"This is a city street. You can't stop in the middle of the road."

"I'm celebrating the holiday with my daughter." Nub nodded toward the house.

Gordon let a beat go by. "Do you need a ride home?"

"No, I don't *need a ride*, Dudley Dipstick. I'm sitting in a perfectly good truck. Now leave me alone."

"Nub, I don't mind taking you home. It's no trouble if you're not in the condition to . . ."

Nub flicked his cigarette past the officer. "If you got something to say, just say it."

Gordon sighed. "Nub, please."

Nub changed the subject. "How's Elaine?"

"She's fine."

"How're your girls?"

"They're good. They're all good." The officer pushed his cowboy hat brim upward. "How about you climb into my vehicle? It's warmer there. We can park your truck at the courthouse; you can get it in the morning."

"It's Thanksgiving, Gordon. Why aren't you at home with your girls?"

"What's it look like I'm doing, Nub? I'm working for a living."

Nub stared at the house in the distance. "There are things more important than work."

Burke ignored Nub and opened the vehicle door. "Come on, old man. Let's go home."

Nub yanked his door shut. "Who are you calling old? You're only one year younger than I am."

"Nub, I'm not going to stand out here and argue with you. It's too cold, and I'm not letting you drive this vehicle."

"Why not?"

Gordon rested his hands on his duty belt and sighed again. A mass of vapor came out of his mouth and nostrils. "Nub, please get in my car. I'm asking nicely. You've had too much to drink."

The truth was, Nub hadn't had nearly enough.

"Sorry, Gordon, I don't ride in Japanese cars. Not since Admiral Isoroku Yamamoto tried to blow me up."

"You weren't in Pearl Harbor."

"I was in the United States Dadgum Navy."

"Congratulations. I was in the United States Army, Nub. Are we going to see who can pee the farthest now? Get in my car or I'm going to *put* you into my car."

Nub cranked up the radio to an obscene volume. Minnie Pearl's voice sounded like a Columbiad cannon. Burke reached into the cab and turned down the music.

"I mean it, Nub. Come on. Let's go."

"Gee, Officer, will you let me play with your handcuffs too?"

Gordon leaned onto the door. He leveled his eyes on Nub, boring a hole into the front of his head. "My patience is getting brittle in this weather."

"Is that your cop voice?"

"Get out of the vehicle, sir."

"Faithful Deputy Burke. Keeping the streets of Park safe from deviants like Nub Taylor, driving his Japanese Radio Flyer." Nub reached beneath his seat and hurled the almost empty schnapps bottle out the window. It shattered on the pavement. "God bless you, Deputy Do-Right, and the horse you rode in on."

"Nub. You're making this hard. This doesn't have to be hard."

Nub stepped on his clutch, threw his gearshift into first. His engine screamed loud enough to throw a rod.

"Everything is hard, Gordon. You ought to know that."

"Out of the car, Nub. Now."

Nub stuck out his tongue.

Then he stomped on the gas, sprayed a rooster tail of gravel onto Gordon's Toyota, and sped away. A piece of stray gravel cracked Gordon's windshield.

And—*boom*—there's your car chase.

CHAPTER

Nub sped forward on County Route 19. The red and blue lights on Gordon's Toyota were spinning behind him. The siren was howling. Nub was driving in the wrong lane, sometimes on the shoulder, and occasionally on people's lawns. He couldn't tell where the road began and ended with all the snow on the ground. Gordon was hogging Nub's bumper. Nub could hear the Japanese engine screaming like a mosquito on amphetamines.

"Let's see how fast your little toy can go," said Nub.

He turned up the radio and mashed the pedal as Minnie Pearl sang another tune. A car in the oncoming lane honked at Nub. Nub swore at the vehicle. He felt adrenaline coursing through his blood, which was a nice feeling on Thanksgiving. It felt better than feeling sorry for himself. Still, the adrenal glands could do nothing to counteract the alcohol in his bloodstream.

Nub veered to the right lane momentarily, trying to find the highway beneath the prairies of snow. He was driving by feel now. His truck hit a curb, obscured by the snowdrifts, and he felt the wheelbase lift from the pavement briefly, then crash onto the solid earth. The car bounced so hard that Nub's jaw hurt from the impact. He swerved again. Another oncoming car honked its horn. Nub honked back and began to laugh, although he wasn't sure why this was funny. The car was speeding toward him. Nub swung into what he assumed was the right lane to avoid the vehicle and almost ran into the ditch. The truck tires rolled over the rumble strip and he almost lost control, but somehow he managed to get back into a lane. Albeit the wrong one.

Another car was heading toward him. A Chevy. He punched the gas pedal even harder. His wheezing truck struggled to pick up speed. The needle climbed from eighty to ninety. From ninety to a hundred. The American-made engine was redlining. The Chevy swerved out of the way and Nub's truck shot by.

He glanced in the rearview mirror. Gordon's truck wasn't keeping up. Gordon was half a mile behind him now. Nub felt a wave of satisfaction wash over him. He cackled with delight, still gazing into the rearview mirror. But he never should have taken his eyes off the road.

Because Nub lost control of the wheel.

Immediately, the night air filled with the screams of squealing Goodyears. Then came the impact. He heard twisting Dearborn steel. The shattering of a windshield. The bleating of his own cries.

And his world went to black.

When Nub awoke, six men in medical uniforms were standing around him. His ears were ringing. The truck cab was covered in dark blood and snow that fell through the open windshield. Alcohol-thinned blood poured out of him like water. His cold clothes were matted to his body. He could taste copper. Music from the *Opry* was still playing on the radio. Happy sounds, which was a curious soundtrack to hear under the circumstances.

The night air was filled with sirens, lots of them. He kept drifting in and out of consciousness.

"What happened?" he slurred to his rescuers.

"Sir, I need you to stay completely still. You're injured."

"What happened to me?"

"Please, sir."

Nub was pulled from the vehicle by many hands. Strong, capable hands. Angels maybe? Or maybe the devil was dragging him off to his prepaid condo on the Lake of Fire. They placed him onto the snowy curb, flat on his back. They shined lights in his eyes. They cut open his clothes with pocketknives and scissors. He had no idea what was happening. He was too wasted to tell the paramedics his name. His speech was too slurred for them to understand him.

"Emily," he muttered.

"How's that, sir?" said a young deputy taking his pulse.

"I said 'Emily'!" he screamed.

"I can't understand you, sir. Please, try to hold still."

"Emily!" Nub was weeping now.

The medics restrained him and placed him onto the stretcher. They carried him away, and Nub got a brief view of the damage he'd caused, although the world was spinning too wildly for him to focus on anything. Emergency flares were burning on the highway. Water was blasting from an unseen crevice in the ground. The street was flooded in six inches of water. Fire trucks were everywhere. Cop cars surrounded the scene. People stood around gawking. And the snow fell. Snow upon snow.

"What'd I hit?" he said.

The medic asked him to repeat himself, then he answered. "You hit the water tower, sir."

"The tower?"

"Sir, I need you to remain still. You might have a broken neck."

"I want my daughter."

"Are you listening to me, sir? You could cause real harm to yourself if you keep moving around. We're going to put you into a brace."

"Emily."

"Sir. Do you understand what I'm saying to you?"

Then Nub began to vomit. He could feel himself losing consciousness again. They turned him onto his side, and he emptied the contents of his stomach onto the snowy gravel. When he finished puking, his world began to get dim.

Then the medic shouted, "A little help over here. I'm losing his pulse!"

"Emily," he mouthed. But no sound came out.

"He's not breathing!"

CHAPTER

~ 3 ~

Waffle House did not close on Thanksgiving because Waffle House never closed. Waffle House was like the Vatican, only with better hash browns. Nobody on staff at the Waffle House had a key to the store, not even the manager. Because there were no keys. The doors never locked. Waffle House just went on and on. Sort of like disco.

Working for Waffle House was not a job, per se. It was a calling. The shifts were grueling. The customers could be impatient. The pay was so-so. You did not get holidays off. No benefits. No incentives. Few promotions. No employee of the month awards. No bonuses. You were always covered in grease. You always smelled like pork products. You had nightmares about pecan waffles. You had to be a special kind of person to sign up for a job at Waffle House. This special kind of person is called a *masochist*.

Tonight there were more people in Waffle House than you would have expected on a national holiday. Park was under a severe weather warning this Thanksgiving night, and yet because it was situated right off the new highway, the place was packed with interstate travelers, most of whom had weary looks on their faces. Some of these people had toddlers who were engaged in finger painting the windows with jelly and fresh boogers. Truckers were seated at the bar, men stranded thousands of miles from their homes, grounded because the sky was falling. Men who would be sleeping in their truck cabs tonight and bringing in the holiday with a hip flask. Men who looked so lonesome they could cry. In the back of the dining room were a few college-age kids horsing around in the booths, playing grab-butt with one another, trying so hard to be noticed by the opposite gender. Trying so hard to stave off the insecurities of youth. A guy in a business suit was doing paperwork in a binder. The place was crazy.

Minnie had been slinging food all afternoon and evening, standing at the grill. The sign over her stove read "Good Food Fast." During the last ten hours she had cooked an entire hog's worth of bacon, fried enough eggs to bring the poultry industry to its knees, and served enough chili to give the state of Alabama irritable bowel syndrome.

At age fifteen, Minnie Bass was the youngest Waffle House cook in the entire organization. Although Waffle House didn't know this inasmuch as Waffle House didn't know she was fifteen. On her application, Minnie had told Waffle House management she was nineteen years old. Minnie could get away with such lies because she was six foot five. Nobody ever would have looked at Minnie Bass and guessed she was fifteen. When you looked at Minnie Bass, you saw a linebacker with a cherub face.

"Pull three, drop three," the waitress said to Minnie.

Minnie nodded. "Pull three, drop three."

"Drop two in a ring. Drop one scattered."

Minnie repeated this.

Waffle House speak.

This meant three orders of bacon and three orders of hash

browns. Minnie scooped three orders of hash browns onto the flat top and placed two into steel rings and scattered the other. There was something gratifying about being a cook in a place like this. Something empowering. At any other job, you were just a laborer. A worker bee. A faceless employee with a name tag. But at Waffle House, if you were a cook, you were somebody. At Waffle House, a cook was the only one who knew how to make hash browns. The cook was the only one who knew the intricacies and quirks of this particular commercial range stove—every range stove had intricacies and quirks. Without the cook, this place was nothing but a room with a bunch of chairs. It was the cook who made it Waffle House. If a waitress showed up late for her shift, for example, the restaurant would struggle along, but it would keep going. If a manager called in sick, the world would keep spinning, and sales would still be made. But if the cook didn't come in, it was game over for the Waffle House.

Outside, in daily life, Minnie was a middle school dropout, a loser with a boyfriend who treated her like garbage and a mother who drank all day. But in this tiny building, just off the interstate, Minnie was in control. She was someone.

She scooped ribbon-cut potatoes onto a hissing flat top. She placed orders of bacon onto the grill, then weighted them with heavy grill presses. She cracked eggs into hot skillets one-handed. She stirred grits. She assembled patty melts. She was elbow-deep in breakfast orders when the door to the establishment opened.

Two sheriff deputies entered.

The temperature inside the eatery dropped by several degrees as a wintry draft filled the room. Carol, one of the waitresses that night, told the deputies to sit wherever they wanted, but these men informed Carol they weren't customers. They needed to speak with—they looked at their notepads—Minnie Bass.

Minnie turned to look at the men.

"Are you Minnie?" said an officer.

The officers were wearing khaki uniforms and cowboy hats. Black boots. Duty belts. Winter coats. They were not local men. Their arm patches said "State Police."

Minnie stopped cooking and approached them. "I'm Minnie."

They asked if there was somewhere they could talk.

"Can't right now," Minnie said. "I've got orders on the grill."

"We'll wait."

The officers sat in a booth.

When she finished plating her orders, one of the officers asked again if there was somewhere private they could all go. He asked nicely, though his tone didn't really sound like he was asking. So Minnie led the men into the back break room and she took a seat on a large sack of waffle mix, back propped against the wall. Arms folded. She was not happy about the interruption during a holiday rush. She was in work mode.

"What's going on here?" she said.

The two men pulled up chairs. One man sat backward in his chair, trying a little too hard to be informal. He removed his cattleman's hat and began turning it in his hands. Something about this simple gesture made Minnie's pulse quicken.

"Can someone please tell me what's happening?"

She stood.

"Sit down, Miss Bass. Please."

"I ain't got time to sit down," she said. "People are out there waiting for their food. It's Thanksgiving."

One of the officers closed his eyes and took a breath. "It's your mom, Miss Bass."

Minnie just looked at him. "What's she done now?"

"Your mom, she's . . ."

The officer paused.

"Yes? What about my mother? What did she do?"

The men glanced at each other. There was something they didn't want to say. By the looks on their faces, it was something *really* bad.

"Is my mother hurt?"

One of the deputies rubbed his own face. "Uh, no. Not exactly."

"Please tell me what's going on."

The room was filled with nothing but the sound of refrigeration compressors and thrumming kitchen equipment.

"Miss Bass, we don't know how to tell you this . . ."

"What? Spit it out."

"Your mother. She took her own life this afternoon."

Eleven miles away, Emily Ives was in the bathtub. The room was filled with steam. The mirror was fogged. Her company had left for the evening. Hallelujah. All day she had been using the promise of a hot bath to reward herself for enduring the misery of kith and kin. Now, here in the tub, Thanksgiving was officially over. There was still work to be done, of course. Her kitchen looked like a nuclear holocaust. But she would deal with that tomorrow. Right now she was tired. She was overworked. She was oversocialized. Her hands hurt from cooking a Thanksgiving feast for eighteen people.

She wet her violent-red hair by submerging herself in the water. Emily's holiday had always been like everyone else's. She spent the occasion primarily around people she couldn't stand; with distant family she disliked; with her mother's snobby friends, whom she didn't know or *want* to know; and her late husband's in-laws, who were Episcopalian, ungodly rich, and all about as much fun as a poke in the eye with a cake fork.

But this is just what you do on Thanksgiving. Thanksgiving is not about being happy. The holiday is not about mirth and beauty and the warmth of gaiety. Thanksgiving is about fulfilling family obligations and being miserable the way the good Lord intended.

She took a few deep breaths and placed her toes on the edge of the tub.

Emily squirted a generous portion of soap onto her washcloth. She began scrubbing her neck and upper arms, pondering conversations she'd had earlier in the evening. She replayed each passive-aggressive remark her mother made about Emily's housekeeping, about her cooking, about her hairstyle, about her figure, about her parenting abilities, about her home decor.

She didn't really enjoy her mother's company. They were friends, sure, but they had so little in common they might as well have been different species. Her mother was the kind of person who reorganized closets for fun. Emily was the kind of person who felt closets were the only place a mess was permissible.

Emily was a widow. After her husband, Charlie, died, her mother swooped in and tried to effectively replace Emily's husband. And for the most part, Emily had let her mother rule the roost. But Charlie had been gone for eight years now, and her mother was still the queen. Wasn't it time to move on?

She stopped scrubbing when she got to her armpits.

She felt something.

Emily raised her right arm and inspected her breast. She probed the tissue, moving all around. She felt a knot. A golf ball embedded deep beneath her skin. She got out of the tub and went to the mirror. You could see the lump when the light hit it just right. Emily moved closer to her reflection until her nose was inches from the glass. There was a lump in the other breast too. She was about to examine other parts of her body but was interrupted when headlights came glaring through the bathroom window.

Who would be coming to her house at this time of night? She stood on the toilet and looked out the window to see her mother's Oldsmobile pulling into the dark driveway. Great.

Within moments, there was a knock at the bathroom door. A hard knock.

"Emily?" came her mother's voice.

"I'm not dressed."

"Emily, come out here."

More knocking.

"Hold on, Mama," said Emily, wrapping herself in a towel.

"Sweetie, hurry up and get dressed. Something awful has happened."

Knock, knock, knock.

Emily opened the door. Her mother's mascara was running.

"What's wrong?" said Emily.

"It's your father."

∝ 4 ∝

The Ryman Auditorium used to be a church. Of all things.

The building sat smack-dab in the belly of Nashville's bustling city. It was a pretty building. The edifice featured modest brickwork, stained glass windows, and a low-pitched roof. Nobody considered it a church anymore. They called it "the Carnegie Hall of the South," "the New York Met of Appalachia," or "the Opry House." Most just called it the home of the *Grand Ole Opry*.

But at one time it was the Union Gospel Tabernacle. A serious house of revival. Camp meetings were held there. All-day gospel singings. Healing services. Weddings. Funerals. Holy Spirit hoedowns. Jehovah jamborees. People got filled with the Holy Spirit in that room. They talked in tongues. Some clucked like chickens for Jesus. But clucking didn't pay the bills. Almost overnight, the Ryman went from being a house of prayer to a place leased for public events. A local radio program moved into the Ryman on June 5, 1943. And it was all downhill from there.

The Ryman's altar was transformed into a stage. The room was desanctified. People sang cheating songs and drinking songs. Record-industry floozies, encased in translucent shells of Aqua Net hair spray, pranced around a stage, flipped their skirts, and used sex to sell what passed for country music.

At the age of twenty-nine, shortly after arriving home from the Pacific War theater, Nub, along with his band, was invited to play the *Opry*. At the time, the doctors told Nub he had shell shock, whatever that was, but Nub didn't trust doctors. *"Doctors don't know everything,"* he always said.

Doctors had convinced his mother to send eleven-year-old Nub to an asylum after Nub's father had swallowed the business end of a 10 gauge. Doctors told his mother that he had to be suffering from psychosis when he suddenly stopped talking and quit eating. His mother took him to Walton Hospital for the Insane in Florida. He spent a year there. He was never the same.

Still, after the war, Nub definitely had *something*. It was even worse than when his father died. He couldn't sleep at night. Sometimes he felt frightened for no reason. Especially when he heard loud noises—for example, fireworks. He started drinking like it was his profession. Soon he was divorced. His daughter was forbidden to see him. His ex-wife had demonized him. His whole life fell apart. He contemplated more than once doing what his old man had done. In fact, he had tried three times to end his own life, but he was too chicken.

So he went back to work at a paper mill. It was a crappy job, but it was something to do. In the evening hours he played music for a living.

Nub could play anything with strings. Music had been his childhood escape. It was also a cureless compulsion. Ever since he saved up to buy his first guitar. He would never forget the ad in the back of a *Popular Mechanics* magazine that read "Five Cents a Day Buys a Gibson!" His band had a weekly gig at a beer joint called the Oasis, just over the county line.

They spent the evenings playing two-steps, waltzes, and fiddle tunes for audiences who often possessed a grand total of six teeth. And Nub made a serious attempt to drink the state of Alabama dry.

One night a group of nice-looking men walked into the Oasis wearing matching three-piece suits. Green neckties. Fancy shoes. One of the men had on a silverbelly cowboy hat. They were polished men. They were well-groomed. They looked like movie stars. Nub was playing mandolin in front of a cheap microphone when the men entered the building. The men in suits stayed for two musical sets. They drank the Oasis's watered-down beer. The men did not converse with one another. They did not break smiles. They watched. Nub was starting to think they were gangsters. Or maybe lawmen. Or both. But when Nub's set was over, one of the suits introduced himself as Mr. William Monroe. Monroe was friendly and complimented Nub's playing. He asked Nub if he and his band would be interested in playing on a little radio show they did in Nashville on Saturday nights.

"We call it the *Opry*," said Mr. Monroe.

"Bullspit," said Nub, who was half drunk at the time and did not use the word *spit*. The *Opry* was the most famous radio show in the known solar system.

"If you're Bill Monroe, I'm Rita Hayworth."

Monroe just looked at him. "You don't look like a Rita."

"Prove it," said Nub.

Monroe did. Monroe's band got onstage and played one tune using borrowed instruments. Monroe played Nub's mandolin for nearly three minutes. When he finished, Nub could have sworn his mandolin was smoking. Before Monroe left, he wrote Nub's phone number on a matchbook.

Four weeks later, Nub's band drove up to Nashville in

Nub's '20 Packard with a bass violin strapped to the roof, scheduled to play before five hundred thousand listeners via WSM 650 AM. The band couldn't afford hotel rooms, so they paid for a campsite at Radnor Lake, just outside the city. Fifty cents a night. They brought pup tents and Boy Scout mess kits. They ate supper out of an iron skillet and practiced their music by the glow of a campfire. They were barely able to sleep that night.

When they arrived at the Ryman Auditorium, Nub's breath caught in his throat. The place was the Taj Mahal. Gleaming tour buses were parked around the auditorium. Ten-gallon hats were everywhere. The four Alabama hayseeds entered the tabernacle and marveled, staring at the colored windows, pitched ceilings, half-circular balconies, and uncomfortable oaken pews lining the sanctuary. "I can't believe we're actually standing here," said Nub's cousin and guitarist, Benny.

It was nothing short of incredible.

When showtime got closer, the audience began filling the pews. It was hot in the Ryman, so people were perspiring through their clothing. Everyone had matted hair. Sweat puddled beneath their haunches. Old women pumped paper fans, doing little to cool themselves but successfully spreading body odor around the room.

That night Roy Acuff was hosting the show. Roy stood behind a Green Bullet microphone wearing a gilded suit, playing his fiddle, singing "Great Speckled Bird." Minnie Pearl told the audience she was "just so proud to be here!" Backstage, Nub met Ernest Tubb, who was drinking a bottle of Dixie beer, clad in a baby-pink suit, fanning himself with a Stetson. Hank Snow was standing beside Tubb smoking a cigarette. He offered a smoke to Nub. It was a Camel.

Hank Snow smoked Camels.

"Where'd you get that beer?" Nub asked Tubb.

The cowboy pointed through the stage door. "Tootsie's."

Enter Tootsie's Orchid Lounge. Across the alley from the Ryman was a bar. A famous one. It was more than a beer joint. It was a rite of passage for performers. Everyone went to Tootsie's, where beer cost a quarter. It was highway robbery, but you only went to the *Opry* once.

Nub's guys entered the watering hole with smiles on their faces. A jukebox was playing something by Tex Ritter. Nub sat at the bar. He ordered beers for the guys and drank his in one swallow. Then he ordered another. Then another. It was a long-established fact that Nub's off switch was broken when it came to alcohol. He started drinking at age thirteen, shortly after his stint in the asylum.

Thus it was that Nub Taylor's final memory of Nashville was lying on the curb outside the Ryman, puking all over his brand-new suit. His bandmates tried to lift him from the pavement, but the deed was done. The stage manager found someone else to fill the band's slot. A young, attractive woman stood in the backstage doorway of the Ryman and watched Nub's friends peel him from the sidewalk and escort him down the lane. The girl said as they passed, "What a shame such a nice-looking man like that had to go and pee himself." These words would never leave his brain.

This is what Nub was thinking about when he woke up in the hospital.

"Dad?"

It was a female voice. Emily?

"Can you hear me?"

He opened his eyes to see a sterile white ceiling. He was nauseated. The universe was spinning, and he wasn't certain he was fully in it. Tubes were running into his arms. He heard a rhythmic beeping noise. His mouth was dry. He tasted an antiseptic flavor. His eyes focused on a young redhead seated beside him. He could see that her face was tearstained. "Emily?" he said.

But it was only a nurse. And her hair wasn't actually red. It was brown.

"Calm down, Mr. Taylor," said the nurse. "You are going to be okay."

Nub tried to speak, but his voice was too dry. All that came out was a crackle.

"Emily."

The nurse approached his bedside.

"Emily's not here," the nurse said, looking down at a clipboard. "Although she *was* here. But that was a few days ago."

He focused his lazy gaze on the nurse. "Days?"

She started to take his pulse. "You've been out awhile. How are you feeling, Mr. Taylor?"

He tried to form a sentence, but his brain was too sluggish. Daylight shone through the windows and pierced his skull with pain.

"I asked how you were feeling, Mr. Taylor."

"I'm just so proud to be here," he said.

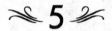
One hour and nineteen minutes south of Park, Alabama, a guard tapped a knuckle on the steel door in cellblock C in Draper Correctional Facility. The knock made a thudding sound within the corridor. The postage-stamp windows of the modern cell doors were soon filled with curious faces. Prisoners were straining to see out; some were beating their doors with hard objects, making loud noises. It was not unlike a large kennel.

Sugar could hear the racket from inside his cell.

He closed his Bible, stood from his cot, and extinguished his cigarette. His nerves were shot. Being in prison meant having time to think. Too much time. Too much thinking wasn't good. He stretched his lithe body. His institutional-blue chambray uniform was crumpled, hanging off him. His hair was messy. Whenever he caught his own reflection, he was surprised at how much older he looked. Shug smoothed his thinning hair in the tiny mirror on his wall, a looking glass no bigger than a postcard; it was the only company he had in this cell. He straightened his collar and thought he looked just like his dad. His old man had been a man with heavy hands and a quick temper. Not the kind of man you wanted to resemble.

Another knock on the door.

Two guards were glaring at him from behind the glass-and-chicken-wire window. They knocked again. It was a knock with authority behind it. Not like the knocks from a friend who visits your back door, asking to borrow a cup of flour. No, this was *boom, boom, boom. Come to the dang door. Right now.*

The door's iron slot opened. Shug placed his hands through it. They cuffed him and then he stepped backward. The massive door swung inward. One of the guards and Sugar shook hands awkwardly, then pulled each other in for a clumsy hug. The guard clapped Sugar on the back. It was the hug of two friends. Old friends. Friends who used to turkey hunt together. Turkey hunting is the hardest kind of hunting there is. Turkeys are smarter than humans, more clever than cats. When you hunt turkey with a guy, you become close.

The guard's name was Graham. When Shug and he were kids, they all called him "Graham-ma."

"You look good, Shug," said Graham.

Sugar knew he was lying, but he was grateful for the lie. It meant he still cared. And tenderness was a scarce commodity in here.

"You too," he lied back.

"They're ready for you," said Graham. "How do you feel?"

Shug shrugged.

"Have you been memorizing the scriptures I told you?"

He nodded.

Graham touched his arm. "I was sorry to hear about your wife."

Sugar did not respond.

He was placed into leg cuffs and a belly chain. Two guards accompanied him down the sterile white hallway, beneath the buzzing lights overhead. The prison looked more like a sick ward than a penitentiary. Like a place where people were *actually* rehabilitated. Which was laughable. Prison was not rehab. Prison was like a never-ending bout of the stomach flu. Sugar had lost at least forty pounds in prison. Maybe more. His hair had lost color too. It was gray at the temples and sort of burnt umber now. His face had lines on it. His pallor looked like he was dying.

Prison years were harder on the body than regular years. The stress was so great that a man aged four times faster than he did outside. The odd thing was, it didn't feel like time was moving faster inside this place. It felt as though it were merely creeping by. But the body tells a different story.

Sugar was fifty-one. He looked like someone's grandfather.

"How's your kid doing?" said Graham as they shuffled forward.

No answer.

Prison is especially hard for a man who is different. The last thing you want to be when you're in prison is different. Prison is all about people groups. Blacks against whites. Hillbillies against Townies. Strong against weak. The more you fit in, the safer you are. If you're different in any way, you're manure. Standing at six eleven, Shug was larger than everyone else, and broader. To the unbaptized, this might have seemed like an advantage, but it was not. Not in Draper. Being big meant Sugar had a bull's-eye on his back. Guys with a point to prove were always trying to take him. He was constantly attacked. Constantly assaulted in the showers. Constantly winding up in the infirmary. Shug tried to get relocated with the sex-offenders and other criminals who were housed separate from the general population for their own safety, but his lawyer hadn't been successful. But then, it wouldn't have made a difference anyway. In the end, prison was prison.

Graham spoke. "Okay, listen up, Shug. The man who will be sitting on your right is your ally. Name's Kahn. From Huntley. He's sympathetic to you. I talked to him a little about you. He knows your case."

Shug nodded.

"The chairman's a different story. He's got a broomstick shoved up his you-know-what. He's the one with thick glasses. He knows you were involved in organized crime. He knows big things went down. He knows what happened."

Shug nodded again.

"Don't even think about using the word *self-defense* or you're screwed. You're *rehabilitated*, remember? Full admittance of all crimes. Full responsibility. The whole deal. Show some remorse. Cry if need be."

It had been fifteen years since Shug had stolen a lot of money from some very dangerous men. At the time, he had just gotten out of the military, just arrived home from being stationed in Korea. He was screwed up from what he'd seen. He got a job at a steel plant in Jefferson County. He drove fifty-three miles to work each morning in a piece-of-crap Ford that was barely holding together. It was weird, suddenly being an ordinary civilian after all he had seen and been through. You didn't just go to Korea and then come home and cut the grass. To earn extra money, he started working as muscle for a very private organization. An organization that did not, technically, exist. An organization that channeled its liquid assets through a rainbow of businesses to hide the income's less than legal origins. An organization with money.

One night things went terribly wrong. Shug's weapon went off. A man died. It was an accident, but Shug had been the one holding the gun. Shug and Willie got away, but only briefly. One Saturday afternoon two state troopers had shown up at

Shug's door and offered him an all-expenses-paid vacation with meals included. He was convicted of manslaughter.

The fact that he'd been granted a hearing had been somewhat of a surprise. Class A felonies usually required twenty years served before a parole hearing, but somehow his lawyer had convinced a judge to grant one at fifteen. Maybe luck was on his side.

They arrived at a door. The guard stood to the side. His friend straightened Sugar's collar one more time. "You hear about that blizzard?" asked his friend.

"Blizzard?"

"Bad blizzard in Ash County."

"I don't hear about anything in here."

"Park got hammered. Some places got eight feet. They still don't have power."

"A blizzard in Park?"

"I'm sorry I brought it up. You need to focus right now." His friend slapped his shoulders and looked Sugar in the eyes. "Talk about finding salvation, getting saved, forgiveness, repentance. Quote Scripture and all that crap. Talk about your service in Korea."

"Okay."

"Whatever you do, be careful. Guys have gotten denied for stupid stuff. Lighting a cigarette at the wrong time. A cocky look. Trying to be funny. Just act like a whipped puppy."

Sugar smiled weakly.

In many ways, he was afraid to get out of prison. He knew they'd be waiting for him. He knew they'd pursue him. The Organization was all about getting even. They were all about honor among themselves. They would be ready to make his life a living purgatory. They would be ready to kill everything he held dear and make him watch. Even so, he was homesick.

He missed the outside world. He missed the woods. He missed the holiday ham his mother used to cook each Christmas, which was a far cry from the meatloaf the prison served on Christmas Day. It was like the kitchen went out of their way to make it taste like wet socks.

"I have faith in you, Shug," said the guard. "I've pulled all the strings I can, called in every favor, kissed every tail. Try to relax. Be yourself. Guy like you, you can get out on good behavior. We'll be hunting turkey soon."

Sugar nodded.

The door to the room opened, and Sugar shuffled into the room for his parole hearing.

By four o'clock that afternoon, Sugar Bass was a free man.

When Minnie was a little girl, her mother used to sing a song before she tucked her daughter into bed each night. Every night, without fail. It was one of the first songs Minnie ever learned. It was a corny tune, but kids don't know the difference.

> *Love before her,*
> *Love behind her,*
> *Love above her,*
> *Love beneath her.*
> *Love on the crown of her head,*
> *Love on the soles of her feet,*
> *Love way down in her heart.*

There were hand motions to go with the lyrics. Minnie would touch a different part of her own little body for each part of the song. "Love before her," she would touch her tummy. "Love behind her," she would touch her little bottom. "Love above her," Minnie would reach her hands way above her head. "Love beneath her," she touched her toes—or at the very least her knees. "Love on the crown of her head," Minnie would place both hands on her head. "Love on the soles of her feet," Minnie would grab her tiny foot. "Love way down in her heart," at which point Minnie's mother would kiss her and tickle her.

Minnie thought about this as she lay in her hospital bed. She had been in this hospital for three days after passing out and hitting her head on the Waffle House floor after the deputies told her about her mama. When they couldn't get Minnie to wake up, Ash County medics brought her to Baptist Memorial. The hospital room was a double. An old man lay in the bed next to hers. He was snoring loudly. And Minnie was thinking about that song her mother used to sing.

Love before her. Love behind her.

It was late. A matronly nurse sat beside her bed, absently reading *Better Homes & Gardens* by lamplight. The lady's beehive hairdo was topped with a white paper hat. Why did nurses wear paper hats? Come to think of it, why did Waffle House cooks wear them? Minnie looked at the hospital bed where the old man was sleeping. He was making so much noise she could feel her teeth vibrate.

The nurse lowered her magazine. "Oh good, you're awake. Would you like something to eat?"

Minnie felt her stomach churn at the mention of food. She was famished. The doctor said she'd passed out because of low blood sugar, but he had yet to explain what this meant. Neither had he explained what a "subdural hematoma" was, which she also had.

"Yes, ma'am," said Minnie. "I'm pretty hungry."

The nurse gave a warm smile. "I'll be right back."

The nurse left the room.

Minnie thought about when her mother last sang this song to her. She would have been maybe ten or eleven.

The police said they found her mother's body in the closet

and that they had to use her dental records to identify her remains. When Minnie asked when she could return home, the deputies told her she couldn't. Minnie's mother had been eight months behind on rent, and the landlord was booting her out. And so it was, within minutes of waking up at the hospital, Minnie had been approached by a social worker who informed her that she was now homeless. She would be entering foster care. Things just got better and better.

Minnie sang softly to herself. And she began to weep. The sound came through her chest. It made her head thrum and dulled the pain a little. Her mother was gone. Her father was dead. She had no family. No people. She was officially alone in this large world.

The man in the bed beside her stirred. He spoke to her in a gruff voice. "Excuse me. Do you mind?"

Minnie just looked at him.

"What?" she said.

The old man's face was bruised and purple. His head was wrapped in bandages. He looked bad. Very bad. "I can hear you. Some of us are trying to sleep here."

"Sorry."

He rolled back over onto his side in a huff. She went silent for a few minutes and her mind began to drift, her head against the pillow, eyes pouring tears. The county was going to pay for the burial because the Bass family was broke. She started humming again.

The old man jerked himself bolt upright. He got a good look at her, and this time she could see in his fiery face that he was supremely ticked off.

"Sorry," she said, wiping her eyes. "I keep forgetting."

The man locked eyes on her. "Well, here's a wild idea for you: don't."

Then he rolled back over. He was quickly asleep again. Soon she could hear him snoring lightly.

Her mother had been a tortured woman. She dated anyone and everyone after her father had died in the war. Every month it was a new boyfriend. Every day it was a new bottle. Minnie's silence lasted a total of twelve minutes before she started humming as softly as she possibly could. She hummed because it reminded her of the good that existed within her mother. And suicide left no goodness in its wake. She could practically see her mother's face when she closed her eyes.

The old man barked, "Nurse! Nurse!"

The nurse came bustling into the room. "What's going on?"

"This kid won't stop singing."

"I said I'm sorry," said Minnie. She dabbed her eyes with her hospital blanket.

"I want to be moved to another room."

"Calm down, Mr. Taylor," the nurse said.

"I'm sick of playing *Name That Tune*. Get me out of here. Now."

The nurse shook her head. "I can't move you, Mr. Taylor. I'm sorry, but this is one of the only rooms in the hospital with power. We're running on generators tonight, ever since Snowmageddon. Would you like some Jell-O?"

"No, I would not *like some Jell-O*. I would like to get out of this godforsaken hellhole."

"Wouldn't we all," said the nurse as she left the room.

This time Minnie pushed her head into her pillow and tried to focus on something else. So she counted. Minnie was a famous counter. It was an obsessive habit. Her brain gravitated toward all things math. She'd always been this way. Before long, she had counted all the ceiling panels in this room twice. There were ten rows of seven on her side of the room. The old man's side of the room had eight rows of six. Altogether there were 118 panels. The prime factors of 118 were 2 and 59. If you added 2 and 59 together, you got 61. Which was prime. So she'd done all she could do there.

She counted other things too. There were nine overhead lights in the room. Four lamps. There were 412 floor tiles. There wasn't anything special about 412. She resorted to counting the freckles on her arms and had to stop when, thankfully, the nurse arrived with the food. She was hungry enough to eat a small lapdog.

The nurse placed trays of food on the patients' swivel tables. Supper was two slices of ham doused in yellow gravy that resembled congealed phlegm. Since the plastic silverware was flimsy, Minnie ate with both hands.

The old man stared at her.

"Well, aren't you a regular Emily Post?" he said.

Minnie ignored him.

"If you don't slow down, you're going to choke."

Minnie kept ignoring him. She washed down her ham with a carton of milk, then she got to work on her mashed potatoes and corn bread. She started in on her green beans and used a remaining hunk of corn bread to clean her tray to a mirror polish. All that was left was her apple cobbler.

"I don't know the Heimlich maneuver," he said.

Minnie pinched another hunk of bread and wiped her plate.

"I'm just saying," said the man, "that you're on your own if your apple cobbler goes down the wrong pipe. Don't blame me if you die right here, in a hospital of all places."

The man grabbed a carton of cigarettes from the nightstand and tapped the carton against his palm. She noticed his hands were trembling so badly he could hardly hold the carton. Her mother got like that sometimes in the mornings.

"What's the Heimlich maneuver?" she said.

"Keep inhaling that food and you're about to find out." He lit his smoke and took a deep breath. "What was that song you were humming?"

"What?"

"Singing. I'm talking about singing. What was that song?"

"Just a song."

"You ever hear of Kitty Wells?"

"What's that?"

"It's a who, not a what."

Minnie said nothing.

"What're you in for?" the man asked.

"Don't know yet. Doctor said I got the sugars. I got a hematoma."

He nodded.

"What about you?" she asked.

"I'm here because I'm an idiot."

The old man pushed his swivel table with his tray of untouched food toward the girl. The table rolled across the aisle between their beds and came to a halt in front of her. She just looked at it for a few moments.

"What'd you do that for?" she said.

"Because you're hungry."

❦ 7 ❦

Dr. Ruark looked at Emily apathetically. There was no mercy in his face. No sweetness. Ruark had black irises that seemed to swallow the pupils. Shark eyes. Ruark had been the doctor who delivered her. He was a dry man with the personality of mayonnaise.

Ruark did not use flowery language to explain his diagnosis. No softening of the blow. He was old school. Doctors from his generation were not here to mollycoddle you. They didn't pass you boxes of tissue and give you emotional support. If you needed comfort, you went to a preacher. If you wanted to cry in public, you went on the *Donahue* show. If you wanted facts, you came to your family doctor.

"Breast cancer?" she said.

He nodded. "Aggressive ductal carcinoma."

"Aggressive?"

"This will kill you, Emily. That's what I'm getting at."

Emily felt her insides get cold.

"I don't want to mince words. I've known you too long. This disease will not move slowly. You need to be prepared for that."

Her blood stopped. Her hands were ice. She couldn't breathe. The room was swallowed by the faint sound of the doctor's ticking clock.

"Did you hear what I said, sweetie?" The way he said *sweetie* sounded foreign to his lips.

"There has to be some sort of treatment."

"There isn't. Not for this."

"How about radiation? My aunt had radiation."

He shook his head. "I'm afraid it's too late for that."

"What about chemotherapy?"

"What about it?"

"Isn't that an option?"

The man heaved out a breath. "If it were, don't you think I would've mentioned it? How long do you think I've been doing this?"

"What?"

"To tell you the truth, I'm surprised you haven't seen me until now. Haven't you noticed anything unusual going on in your body? Don't you pay attention to your breasts?

"At this stage, your cancer has likely metastasized into other organs. It's spreading. You're a scientist, Emily; you know how this works. Your lymphatic system is probably struggling to keep up. In my opinion, a mastectomy would be a waste of your time. Chemotherapy will just ruin any time you have left. Radiation will destroy the quality of your life."

She could not believe what she was hearing. "I don't understand."

The doctor straightened some papers on his desk. "Your biopsy is not good. That's all there is to understand. You're going to have to make some hard decisions. Bottom line: you're going to have to accept this."

None of this was making sense. It was like trying to make ten dollars out of four nickels. What was going on here? How had life shifted so quickly? One minute she was teaching biology, raising a kid, cooking a Thanksgiving feast. The next minute Dr. Ruark was using words like *cancer* and talking about *"time you have left."*

"Are we talking years?" she said.

"Impossible for me to say. This isn't my specialty."

"But I feel fine."

"You said earlier that you were fatigued. You said you were tired a lot."

"I'm a high school teacher and a mother. I'm always tired."

The room began to spin even faster. The doctor replaced his glasses and led her to the reception area. Dr. Ruark had the gall to tell her to have a nice day before she left.

Shug felt awkward in his old suit. He was sitting in the back seat of a Chevy Impala. Looking out the window. Constantly tugging on his sleeves. Fifteen years ago he had come to court in this same tan suit, which he'd bought from a secondhand store. It was his first and last suit. He'd never wanted to own one before. Never needed one. But his lawyer said he should have a suit because suits improve the odds of overturning convictions. The jury, it turned out, could convict guys in suits just as easily as they could convict guys in jeans.

When the driver reached the Ash County line, Shug instructed him to stop by beating a hand on the roof. Prison habit. The Chevy slowed to a halt.

"You don't have to beat on my car, pal," said the driver. "Just tell me to stop."

"Sorry. Please stop here."

"Here?"

"I can walk the rest. I know the way."

"It's nine o'clock at night."

"So?"

"So it's dark, and this is the middle of the woods."

Shug opened the door and stretched his long frame. He was skin and bones. His belt was on the last hole; his trousers were falling off him. Once he had been thickly built. Now he was a skeleton with a size 30 waist.

"This isn't *nowhere*," Shug said. "Not to me."

He stared into the thick forest, not far from where he had been raised. The sky was the color of a Steinway. The heavens were peppered with brilliant stars. It had been 5,572 days since he'd seen stars. All he'd done inside was count the days.

"This is home," said Shug.

"You'll freeze out here."

"I could think of worse ways to go."

"I have orders to drop you at the motel."

"The motel is two miles from here. I need the exercise."

The driver seemed to be thinking it through. "You realize, if you don't get to that motel, you're violating parole and it's back in the can."

Shug slammed the door. "Do you think I want to go back?"

The driver relented, muttered something about not getting paid enough. Then the Chevy drove away, taillights winking out in the distance.

The walk was glorious. Walking. Breathing. Existing. It was the art of being alive, something you could not do in a federal correctional facility. Shug heard the sound of a distant train. He heard the empty hiss of a breeze, fingering its way through dead branches. He walked along County Route 19, duffel bag slung over his shoulder. It had been over a decade since he'd held this duffel bag, a leftover from his army days. He spent two tours in Korea with this bag, carrying it over his shoulder, following the meandering Yalu River on foot, on countless midnight walks with his company. He had been an Explosives Ordnance Disposal Specialist. Uncle Sam sent him to North Gyeongsang to blow stuff up.

He walked two miles until he came to an interstate cutoff with a large, lit-up gas station, a Scotty's Motor Inn, a Waffle House, and an interstate. It was all brand-new. None of this had been here fifteen years earlier. He felt a pang in his heart when he saw the Waffle House. He knew from letters his ex-wife sent that his daughter worked there.

He checked into the motel and left his duffel bag in his room. He stepped outside, lit a cigarette, and went for a walk.

The strangest addition to the landscape was the interstate. It was too much to take in. He wandered onto the concrete overpass, meandering along the busy shoulder, narrowly avoiding vehicles as they whizzed by. Motorists leaned on their horns when they passed. And it occurred to him that, even though millions of dollars had gone into creating one of the most elaborate road systems known to humankind, none of this highway was designed to accommodate foot traffic.

Another car shot past him and almost hit him.

He jogged across the bridge, out of oncoming traffic. He made it to the parking lot of the Waffle House, where he paused to catch his breath. He was in pitiful physical shape. Some guys spent their time in prison working out and lifting weights. He spent his reading Dashiell Hammett and Bill Shakespeare, trying not to get shanked in the exercise yard.

He pushed open the door to the Abode of Waffles. The dining room was mostly empty except for a few guys in the corner. The place was warm. Hank Senior was singing overhead, as though time had stood still in this room. A waitress reading a magazine barely looked up when he came in. He suddenly found himself nervous at the thought of seeing his little girl.

"Have a seat anywhere," the waitress said as if by reflex.

He looked at the woman intently. Was this his daughter? No. This woman was too old to be his child. And much too short.

He sat in the empty booth and ordered coffee.

"Ain't got no coffee," she said. "We got tea."

"No coffee?"

She shook her head. "We're the only place that stayed open after the storm. We didn't get power back on until yesterday. I got plenty of tea."

He handed the menu back to her and told her he'd take some tea and some tomato juice if they had that. "Is Minnie Bass working tonight?"

"No." The woman touched the tip of her pen to her pad. "What do you want to eat?"

"Just give me whatever you have."

"You're in luck," she said, tucking the pad into her apron. "That's our special tonight."

The cook at the grill got busy. Shug admired the way the man worked his flat top. He wondered if this man had trained his daughter to do the same. The pleasing sizzle was a wondrous sound to his ears. The waitress brought him hot tea along with a tall glass of tomato juice.

Shug held the juice for a few moments, staring at it. The stuff looked thicker than oatmeal. It had been a long, *long* time since he'd consumed tomatoes in any form. He drank the juice the way some men shoot bourbon. He closed his eyes and sighed. Then he looked at the glass absently. "Oh wow."

The waitress gave a quizzical glare.

He looked at her. "Sorry. It's been a while."

"You want another glass?"

"Yes, please."

No sooner had she returned with the glass than Shug noticed two men enter the establishment wearing suits and long, black wool coats. Black gloves. Black everything. Dressed in the kind of way people from Park did not dress. They locked eyes with Shug.

"Sit wherever you want," the waitress said.

The men sat in the corner. They kept their hats and gloves on, never looking away from Shug. When one of them locked eyes with Shug, the man drew an index finger across his own neck.

CHAPTER

≈ 8 ≈

The *Park Advocate* reported that Nub's truck had hit the water tower so hard that the impact damaged municipal plumbing beneath the pavement. A waterworks specialist had to be called from Birmingham to survey the damage. The city had to wait several days for crews to arrive because of the blizzard's snowdrifts and lack of power. When the snow finally melted, the town was on a boil-water notice.

Clairmont Avenue shut down while work crews repaired the damage. An Alabama Department of Transportation crew removed surrounding asphalt so that specialized workmen from Tennessee could repair the water mains. Civil engineers had to be consulted. Ironworking specialists joined the party. The city had to rent not one but two crawler cranes to repair the tower. A mechanical engineer was hired. Then an electrical engineer. Then a water sanitation specialist was put on call. Entire crews of utility workers were brought in. Electrical linemen. Journalists. It was a big, hairy, fetid mess.

But the downtown merchants had it the worst. They were projected to lose big bucks in the weeks ahead since roadwork would be blocking all downtown shops during the height of Christmas-shopping season.

So Nub was a popular guy.

On the afternoon he had been released from Baptist Memorial, Deputy Gordon Burke had been waiting for him in the front seat of the county's Toyota cruiser. The Toyota idled quietly, like a lawn mower. *"What do you say, Nub?"* Burke had said. *"Take a free ride in a Japanese car?"*

It was a long, silent ride home.

In any other city Nub would have been put in jail after being released from the hospital. But this was small-town Alabama. The sheriff's department fined him and that was about all. Then the city hired Nub to repaint the tower so he could actually pay his fine. But when Judge Pittman sentenced Nub to psychotherapy twice every week to "deal with his drinking problem," Nub was so mad he saw double.

And so it was that Nub entered the Ash County courthouse with his proverbial tail between his legs to begin paying off his fine. This morning the courthouse skeleton staff consisted of Judge Pittman and Marie, the county clerk. Marie sat behind her horseshoe desk with an unamused look on her face as she watched Nub walk through the front door. She was hanging Christmas decorations on the front of her desk. Little red balls and garland.

"Marie," he said. "You look resplendent today."

The old woman's face didn't change. "Where'd you learn such a big word?"

"I get around, Marie."

"Is that what you call it?"

Nub smiled. Because what else could he do? He removed the checkbook from the pocket of his Carhartt and started making out a check to the City of Park like he would be doing once every two weeks until he died. Marie watched him carefully. At one time, Marie had been the prettiest thing in Park Union High School. That was hard to believe now, as Marie wore the most awesome head of gray helmet hair ever seen, bringing to mind Aunt Bee after a very long night.

He tore the check from its booklet and leaned onto her desk. "Run away with me, Marie. Let's stop this charade. You know we're both crazy about each other."

"One of us is definitely crazy."

"We can ditch this place, go to Honolulu, drink fruity drinks, watch the natives dance. Leave this sleet and snow behind us."

She raised an eyebrow. "I don't look good in coconuts."

"Then don't wear any."

She took the check from his hands but did not smile when she read it.

"You made the check out to Papk?"

"I think it has a nice ring to it."

"You're just full of fun, aren't you?"

Nub smiled his bruised face at her. "Winning friends and influencing people, Marie."

He took a seat in the waiting room, and while he was reading a women's magazine that predated the Hoover administration, a familiar face entered the courthouse. He looked up to see the girl from the hospital.

Minnie Bass's crow-black hair was pulled back. She wore no jacket, only a T-shirt. She clutched herself like she was chilly. Her pale, bare arms were marbled from the cold. On her feet were Chuck Taylors that had once been red but were now covered in duct tape and stickers and were barely holding together. They looked like size fifteens or sixteens. Her bare toes were showing through the scuffed canvas sides of the shoes. In a few words: she looked poor.

The young woman sat in the chair beside him. Nub caught a whiff of her. She smelled bad too.

"Well, well," he said. "If it ain't the one-woman choir."

She said hello.

He nodded to her feet. "Your toes are sticking out of your shoes."

She didn't answer.

"Pretty cold out there to be walking around with bare toes showing, if you ask me. Your mama ought to be ashamed, letting you leave the house like that."

Minnie did not reply.

Nub read from his magazine for a few more moments before tossing the magazine aside. "Look, I owe you an apology."

"For what?"

"For anything I might have said that was unsavory the last time we met. I've had a pretty hard week. I don't expect you to forgive me, but I just wanted to put that out there."

No answer. The girl just continued to hug herself and shiver.

"What grade are you in?"

"Ain't in no grade."

"You dropped out?" he said.

"I work."

"Good for you."

Silence.

"How old are you?"

"Fi-teen."

Nub was one of those guys who knew no personal boundaries. In another world he might have been a successful brick salesman or a Tupperware magnate. He removed a cigarette from behind his ear, wedged it between his lips, then clicked open his lighter. "Where do you work?"

"Waffle House."

"On the interstate?"

She nodded.

"How tall are you?" he said.

"Six five."

"You scared of ceiling fans?"

"Huh?"

It took a few moments for his remark to hit home, but it finally did. She laughed slightly. Nub felt like he had scored some kind of point. He was about to say something else when they were interrupted by a pimply young man in a suit. The court psychologist was staring at Nub. "Mr. Taylor?"

"Pardon me, miss," he said. "I have to go talk about my *feelings*."

She nodded.

Nub stood and removed his oversized Carhartt. He gave it to her. "Here."

The young woman looked at him for a beat. Her eyes were big and beautiful. Her face was sculpted, reminding him of a Renaissance painting by some famous artist.

"What's this for?" she asked.

"It's cold, sweetheart."

She stared at the jacket.

"I don't want your jacket."

"I didn't ask what you wanted."

"It's too small for me."

"I'll pretend not to be offended by that remark," he said, draping the jacket across her lap. "If it's too small, give it to the Salvation Army. That's where I shop."

CHAPTER

9

Emily's late husband, Charlie Ives, was a jerk. There was really no other way to say it. He had always been a jerk. He had probably come out of the womb being a jerk.

Charlie Ives had been privileged, born with a silver spoon lodged in a familiar crevice of the body. His parents were old money, which was the worst kind. Charlie grew up believing he was a cut above other human beings. Superiority was in his DNA. He treated girls like garbage. He treated people who worked for him like third-world serfs. He treated his clients like toddlers.

A jerk.

And yet Emily had fallen in love with him. She wasn't even sure how it happened. They'd gone to school together but had run in different circles. She was a science nerd in cat-eye glasses. He was a jock. They had nothing to do with one another for the first part of their educational careers. They were different animals. Then she went to Auburn to study trees and he went to the University of Alabama to chase skirts and drink directly from kegs. But somewhere around college, Emily blossomed from a gawky teen into a full-fledged woman. She started wearing formfitting undergarments, and guys in her college classes started paying attention to her, sometimes even rushing ahead to open the door for her. Such things rarely happened for biology majors.

She graduated with a degree in xylology, then she went to work for the American Longleaf Council as an intern, studying trees. She got to travel. She got to meet interesting people. Her life was going great.

But then he happened.

She and Charlie were reintroduced at a party in Park. He was twenty-two, already on his way to becoming a promising young attorney in his dad's firm. He had a job in Montgomery, working at the capitol. Charlie Ives was going places. Everyone knew it. He was Park's most eligible bachelor. Girls would have lined up just to listen to Charlie Ives burp over the phone. Handsome? Good God, yes. But it wasn't just his looks. It was something else about him. Something in his mannerisms. A characteristic born of deep confidence. The kind of sureness that only money and lifelong Episcopalianism can buy.

The thing about Charlie was that he didn't care whether you liked him or not, which is of course why all the girls did.

He had fallen in love with her first. He wanted her because she did not want him. And Charlie was not used to losing. Charlie never lost. So he wooed her. He bought flowers. He gave her things. He hired a musical group to sing her a song in a restaurant. He told her she was pretty. He employed the oldest tricks in the book, using status to impress her, and she took the bait. He bragged about how he'd met the governor multiple times, played golf with the president once, and had supper with the prince of Monaco. He told her about the lake cabins his family owned in Virginia, North Carolina, and Upstate New York. The irony was that Emily used to despise girls who cared about stuff like governors and Monacan princes. But each moment she spent around Charlie changed her.

The first thing that changed about her was that she started putting in a lot more time picking her outfits, not because she was worried about how she looked, per se, but because she was worried about how *others* thought she looked. After all, she was with Charlie Ives now. That carried a responsibility. Hordes of women in Park would have given their right kidney to be on his arm. These women would judge her silently. They would pick apart each ensemble she wore. They would criticize her hairstyle. Her figure.

So Emily started getting her hair done in Birmingham. She spent money on nice makeup that wasn't drugstore junk. She started wearing contact lenses. She quit her job with the Longleaf Council so that she'd be in Park more often. No longer was she hiking through the woods with a clipboard, collecting tree specimens, studying the exotic properties of sap. She was making herself worthy of Charles William Ives II.

Emily married Charlie Ives at Saint Mark's. There was a horse-drawn carriage at their wedding. He bought her a Buick. A nice house. A food processor. She had dinner with the governor a few times. She actually met the prince of Monaco.

She was blind. Love is blind. It doesn't matter what the truth is about someone you love; you see what you want to see in them. She knew he was a jerk, yes. But she chose to see his good qualities. Charlie could be thoughtful, for however long this mood lasted. When he liked you, you were the sun and moon. You were life itself.

A few years later she gave birth to Charlie Jr. The young couple moved into his parents' old house on the corner of Fifth and Bellville. She hired an interior decorator. She got a job at the high school teaching biology.

Nine years into their marriage, Charlie Ives died.

His death was labeled a freak accident by the *Advocate*. But it wasn't a freak anything. Charlie's boat battery died while he was fishing on Lake Jackson. He docked the skiff at the cabin dock in shallow water and used a plug-in charger, attached to shore power, to recharge the battery. Charlie hooked jumper cables to a 120-volt plug, grasped the leads, leaped into the water, and waded toward his boat. Holding two live wires in his hands.

He made Emily a thirty-six-year-old widow. He left her with a kid to raise and a six-bedroom house. A house that, right now, was hosting yet another party.

Life as an Ives was all about parties. It was what you did. It was who you were. Currently the mansion was alive with social energy, crashing against the walls like breakers on the shore. There were people everywhere, holding drinks, eating from trays.

This particular party was an annual thing the Ives family held for the Iron Bowl game. Charlie's father had started the tradition. Downstairs, sixty adults and twenty-some kids were nestled in different sections of the house, drinking sodas, beer, and wine, eating corn chips, slopping up onion dip by the metric ton, ruining her carpets, laughing too loudly, and trying hard to impress each other.

Normally during a social event, Emily would be playing the role of June Cleaver, refilling sodas, restocking chips. This afternoon she was locked inside her bedroom, crying on the floor. She had no one she could share her diagnosis with. No friends she trusted enough to confide in. You didn't go around blabbing your business in Park, Alabama, especially when you were an Ives. The residents of Peyton Place gossiped about everything. If you were to die in Park, Alabama, people would know what color your underpants were at the time of your death.

Emily didn't want anyone to know about her illness. Namely

because she felt a deep sense of shame over it. It was inexplicable, but she felt as though she had done something to deserve this disease. As though her cancer were a result of her own failures. Punishment.

A knock on the bedroom door.

"Mom?"

Emily sucked snot back into her nose and used her homemaker voice. "What is it?"

It was Charlie Jr. "We're out of Coke, Mom."

"There's more in the garage."

"Nuh-uh. I just checked."

"I just bought a whole new thing of Coke, sweetie. It's in the garage."

"I didn't see it."

"That's because you're not looking."

"I looked, Mom. I didn't see it."

Her son couldn't find his own butt cheeks if the directions were tattooed on his palm. He knocked on the door again, louder this time. "Mom! Please! I can't find it!"

"Go look again!" she screamed.

"Okay, jeez," she heard Charlie Jr. say. Then she heard his footsteps as he stormed away.

She could have told her mother about her cancer. But Loretta Barnes was about as warm and fuzzy as a routine colonoscopy. Loretta didn't have time for dying. Her mother would have tried to help but only made things harder.

Likewise, Emily could have told her father about her problems, but that would have been a waste of energy. Emily's father had been involved only intermittently since she was seven years old. He'd been drunk since well before then. There wasn't an event he didn't ruin. Like the time he mooned the Baptist preacher, Brother Ron, at the neighborhood barbecue. The preacher had to be revived with cold water. Or there was the time he showed up to her high school graduation trashed. He sat beside her stepfather, Daniel, and spent the whole night talking about the torque of a Chevy Bel Air. Her father was so loud that everyone inside the gymnasium, including the graduating class of 1946, could hear her father's opinions on Chevy's 409-cubic-inch big-block V8.

Then again, at least her father had come to those events. Because as time went on, he started skipping out on everything. At some point he quit caring about her altogether, and he just stopped coming around. He did not attend birthdays, dinners, or special occasions. He did not show up on Christmas, Thanksgiving, Fourth of July. Nothing.

After his accident, she'd sat in the hospital with him, watching the battered man with broken ribs and a fractured skull slip into severe alcohol withdrawal symptoms. She was sure the man would die, but Nub never died. He always pulled through. Like a cockroach.

She leaned backward and sobbed.

"Mom!" came the shout from the other room, accompanied by a knock on the door. "I honestly can't find the Coke!"

Her tears turned into roiling anger. She stood, straightened her hair and her clothes in the mirror. She contemplated tearing open the door and cussing out her own son. Or maybe she'd run away forever. Then again, where would she go? And for how long?

Instead, she walked into her bathroom, clicked on the light, and leaned into her own reflection. She dabbed her eyes, fixed her mascara, and retucked her blouse. She drew in a few sharp breaths and nailed a smile to her face.

"Aggressive ductal carcinoma," she whispered.

Aggressive ductal carcinoma.

CHAPTER

≈ 10 ≈

Nub and Benny were on their way to the Legion to watch the Iron Bowl. They were in Benny's truck, a 1939 half-ton Ford, which Benny hadn't been able to drive since his stroke. Nub's truck had gone to be with Jesus a week ago. Nub sat behind the wheel. He was missing some hair from a place where the doctor had dealt with his skull fracture and installed seventeen stitches. But otherwise, he was good to go.

He turned off Clairmont and onto Long Avenue, trying not to pay attention to the water tower in the distance, which he had already defamed in more ways than one. He turned off Long and onto Rodgers. He downshifted and waited for the clutch to catch. Benny's truck had been on the skids for the last thirty years. But amazingly, his truck still ran, and this qualified as some sort of divine intervention that ought to be investigated by, at minimum, *Guideposts*.

When they got halfway down Rodgers, Nub saw Minnie Bass. She was walking along the snow-covered sidewalk, about to cross the street at the four-way stop, clad in a fast-food service uniform. Striped apron. Striped bow tie. Paper hat. Minnie Bass was carrying two grocery bags against her chest and bore the trademark posture of the impoverished. Slouching shoulders. Bowed head.

"Ain't that your new friend?" said Benny.

"It sure is."

She was wearing his old Carhartt. A group of young men were surrounding her. The teenage boys were keeping pace beside her and laughing. Horsing around. One boy was flicking her ears. Another was trying to trip her as she walked. One of the boys was Phillip Deener, a local troublemaker.

"It looks like those boys are picking on her," said Benny.

Nub rolled down the window. They were calling her the Jolly Green Giant. They were laughing to beat the band. Minnie walked faster, trying to get away from her tormentors. She was half jogging. Nub waited for the girl to lash out at them. She could have crushed them all with one swipe of her arm. But she didn't.

When she was about ten yards ahead of them, Phillip Deener picked up a rock and pitched it at her. Nub watched in disbelief as the stone sailed through the air and struck Minnie on the back of the head.

Minnie dropped her groceries. Canned goods rolled on the pavement. Her paper hat fell off.

Nub slammed his brakes. The truck came to a skidding halt. Then before he could get out of the truck, Phillip Deener threw another rock, and this one hit Minnie in the forehead. Nub gritted his teeth so hard he may have heard one of his molars crack.

"What're you doing?" said Benny.

Nub kicked open the door with enough force to take down a wall.

"I'm going to tell those kids about Jesus."

The woods looked different from the way they had fifteen years ago. Shug hiked through the dense forest near Ambassador, on the outskirts of Ash County, frequently pausing to glance behind him. Making sure he hadn't been followed.

The light of dusk was piercing through the treetops, shooting blades of sunset colors in all directions. As a boy, Shug knew every sapling and patch of jimson weed in these woods. But now he was a foreigner here. These trees were no longer young and naive looking. Neither was he. The trees were mature, scarred and gnarled, even. Just like him.

When he emerged from the woods, he was standing on his grandmother's land. Or at least what had been his granny's land. Her home had been demolished long ago to make way for a new subdivision. Brick homes had been erected in the distance. Flat rooflines. Bay windows. Ranch homes. The people who lived in these modern-looking homes mostly commuted to Birmingham. They called this a bedroom community. Whatever that was. It was no longer the sticks. This was ugly suburbia.

He disappeared into the thicket again and hiked through the woods for another four miles until he emerged in a clearing. A shack was in the distance. A faded gray building, leaning sideways.

He could have taken the dirt roads to get here, since that was the official route to this place, but he didn't want to be seen. Two men had been following him all week. The men were not attempting to hide the fact that they were tailing him. The men followed him in their white Cadillac, always idling nearby. They followed him to every meeting with his parole officer. Every trip to the supermarket. Every walk back to the motel. This afternoon he'd managed to sneak out of his motel room and evade them. But barely.

This shack hadn't changed much over the years. Shug's childhood homeplace had fallen into disrepair, but it was still basically the same ugly home. The gray wood siding was falling off. The roof was brown with inch-thick rust. Every window had fallen victim to some kid's brand-new BB gun. Doors were missing. The back porch looked like it had suffered the after-effects of a hydrogen bomb.

Shug stepped into his old home.

Weirdly, things inside weren't all that different. Everything was covered by decades of dust. Most of the furniture was gone, but some pieces remained. A chair here, a nightstand there. He entered into what would have been his old bedroom. His boy-hood dresser was still here, but that was all. Atop the dresser sat his tin model of the *Spirit of St. Louis*. The same model that every child in the United States had after 1927. It had been his most valuable possession as a boy. He sat on an old chair and a cloud of dust filled the air. He held the old tin plane in his hands and wiped the dust from the cockpit windshield. He smiled. Then he put the plane back onto the dresser in the same place it was before, as though he were maintaining some kind of shrine.

Shug walked to the closet. He opened the door and was pleasantly surprised to find a few articles of clothing still there. The gray trousers he wore when he graduated gram-mar school. The coat he wore to his mother's funeral. He was amazed these few artifacts had survived abandonment.

He bent low to the floor and opened his duffel bag. He removed the hammer he'd bought from the hardware store and used the claw to pry up a single floorboard. It took a lot of banging and scraping. He hoped nobody was nearby to hear the noise.

The floorboard came loose. When he lifted the board, the surrounding planks popped off easily. The floor of the closet became an empty cavern, plunging into darkness. He reached into the hole and felt around cautiously until his hand hit cold metal.

"Gotcha," he whispered.

They never saw Nub coming. His opening move was to hurl a full beer can at Phillip Deener like a major-league right-hander. The aluminum can hit Phillip Deener's chest so hard the kid was knocked off his feet. The Deener boy landed on his everlasting aspirations, hitting the sidewalk with a jarring *thud*.

Anger welled from a place deep within Nub's breast. He launched into a verbal tirade and got in the boy's face. He shouted so loudly, spittle came from his open mouth.

The boys started running away from Nub in all directions, but his temper had risen to inexhaustible heights. He went back to the truck and retrieved two more full cans of Pabst. He threw the cans at Phillip Deener. One missed its target. The other skidded on the sidewalk and sprayed geysers of suds, then lodged under the boy's foot. Phillip stumbled forward onto the pavement and face-planted into the sidewalk. His chin was scraped and bleeding.

"I'm telling my dad!" said Phillip.

"Titty baby!" shouted Nub.

The said titty babies ran away, although *sprinted* might be the more appropriate word.

When the sidewalk cleared, he and Benny approached Minnie.

The girl's forehead was bleeding. She was sobbing. Nub wiped her eyes with his hand. She was gasping between sobs, unable to speak. It was a little-girl cry. The kind of weeping a child does when she falls off a bike. The kind of cry that suggests the whole world is falling apart.

Nub pulled her into himself. It was instinct, really. The hug was the kind of fatherly impulse he thought had died thirty-odd years ago. He held her tightly. The girl squeezed him back and wept into his bony shoulder until he nearly started crying too. Her blood saturated his shirt. They stayed like that for a while.

"Are you okay?"

She just kept crying.

Then he released her and asked if she was dizzy. She said she was. He asked if she felt nauseous. She said she did. He held up two fingers and told her to follow the fingers with her eyes. Thanks to the United States Navy, Nub knew the signs of head trauma.

"Please let us drive you home," said Benny.

"No, I can walk. I'm okay."

"It's no trouble. Really."

She pulled herself together. "I'm fine."

"Why were those boys teasing you?"

"One of them used to be my boyfriend."

"You were *dating* one of those mules?"

She nodded.

"Let me drive you home."

"No, thanks."

Minnie was already leaving. She gathered her scattered groceries from the sidewalk and trotted across intersections until she disappeared. Nub and Benny were left alone on the pavement.

Nub and Benny climbed back into the truck.

"You shouldn't have pushed that boy," said Benny.

Nub just stared out the windshield.

"And you shouldn't have thrown a beer at him either," Benny said. "You could've really hurt him, you know that?"

Nub threw the truck into gear and squealed across the pavement. He gave no reply because he didn't want his cousin to notice that he was crying.

Shug removed a steel box from the gaping hole in the floor of the old cabin. He placed the box on the floor, beneath the light of the window. He was winded from the effort it had taken to pry up the floorboards. He wiped the sweat from his forehead with his hankie.

Shug stared at the box for several minutes. He paused his breathing for a moment to listen for movement outside, for rustling leaves, the sound of an idling Cadillac. The last thing he needed was a visitor right now.

Years ago he'd purchased this watertight box from the army surplus store. He knew all about these boxes because he'd used them in North Korea. They were impenetrable—made for carrying valuable cargo. Fifteen years earlier, he and Willie hid this box here.

He felt a wave of sickness come over him. What if this box wasn't watertight? What if there was a defect? What about moths? Moths were hellish creatures that could squeeze into impossibly tiny spaces and reduce anything into confetti. What about mold? What about rats?

The lid unlatched and came off with no problem.

The contents of the box looked just the way they had when he'd left them. The box was filled with small red wax cylinders. Long ago he and Willie had melted down the wax casings from eight giant wheels of hoop cheese to get this wax. They had spent two days dipping tin Kodak film-developing canisters into the wax to seal them.

Sugar Bass reached into the box, lifted one of the objects into his hands, and inspected it carefully. He used his Barlow pocketknife to slice open the waxy casing.

Fifteen years, three months, and nine days of being stuck inside Draper Correctional Facility, 5,572 days, approximately one-fifth of his life, all for the contents of this case, which he had stolen from the most powerful family in the Southeast. He would most likely die for the contents of this box. He knew that.

The wax casing fell to the ground until he was left with a tin can marked "Kodak Film Tank." He used his knife blade to wedge open the lid. And he quit breathing when he saw it.

As it turned out, $813,000 still smelled just as good as it ever had.

CHAPTER

~ 11 ~

Nub was an Auburn fan. His daughter had gone to Auburn. His father attended Auburn. His mother was born in Lee County. He had a pair of tiger slippers someone gave him for his birthday.

To be an Auburn fan was to be the perpetual underdog. For Auburn fans, this meant that you annually had to endure a constant stream of abuse from blood-lusting University of Alabama fans. And the abuse was worse this year, since the University of Alabama was favored to win. Alabama's Coach Bryant was undefeated, the winningest coach in history. Sometimes people invited Bryant to weddings simply so he could change the water into merlot.

Auburn didn't have a chance in a frozen-over hell.

But then, that was part of the magic of the Iron Bowl. Because sometimes the underdog actually had his day in this annual face-off. Sometimes justice was exacted. Sometimes the unthinkable happened. Which made this game the most exciting event of the season; the air was always filled with promise.

But tonight there was no promise in the game. Not for Nub Taylor. Nub kept looking at the traces of blood on his shirt. Minnie's blood. He kept thinking about the young woman. He kept remembering the way she smelled whenever he was around her.

She smelled bad. Most girls usually smelled—well—girly. Emily always smelled like perfume and bath powder. But Minnie Bass smelled like hard work and bacon grease. Like sweat. She smelled like an adult. Like a blue-collar job.

"*Ain't in no grade. I work.*"

The Legion Hall erupted in shouts over each touchdown. Applause filled the room. But Nub wasn't facing the TV screen. He was lost in thought. The tavern was choked with a tobacco fog so thick that there was no need to light a cigarette. All you had to do was breathe. But he was miles away.

"Come back to earth," said Leigh Ann.

Nub was jolted from his daze. He looked at the woman behind the bar. She was waving a hand before his face. "Ground Control to Major Tom?"

"Sorry. My mind was somewhere else."

"I'll say. You just missed the biggest play of the game."

Leigh Ann was pretty. Early fifties. She had a youthful quality that made her look like more than a barkeep. Her halter top didn't hurt either. "I was asking if you heard who I booked for the pool tournament this year."

"What?"

"I just booked Roy Acuff. He's going to give a concert right here in Park."

Nub gave no reaction, except to push his beer away.

She made a big production out of being surprised. "Is this the same man who once danced on the bar wearing a lampshade as a hat?"

"I never did that."

She just looked at him.

"It was a cardboard box," he said. "Not a lampshade."

"I thought you'd be excited. You love Roy Acuff. I thought you always listened to the *Opry*."

Nub shrugged.

"Nub's had a rough day," said Benny.

"Stick out your tongue," said Leigh Ann. "I want to see if it's measles."

"I hurt a kid today."

The crowd exploded in cheers. Someone scored. The place was coming unglued. Nub didn't care.

"He's telling the truth," added Benny. "He hurt the Deener boy."

Leigh Ann leaned onto the bar. "Phillip Deener? Am I missing something here? Isn't Phillip Deener in high school?"

"Yep."

"What could've possibly happened between a high school kid and a senior citizen?"

"Tell me something, Leigh. Did they ever make fun of you in school?"

"I was the skinniest girl in my class from kindergarten until ninth grade. They called me Clothesline." She confiscated one of Nub's onion rings and ran it through a mound of ketchup. The woman managed to eat the onion ring in a way that seemed immodest.

"What about you?" she said. "They ever tease you, Nub?"

Benny laughed. "Nub's five three. What do you think?"

Nub cut his eyes at his cousin. Benny stifled a chuckle and turned to face the television again. Nub was technically five two, but he let it slide.

Leigh Ann smiled. "Hey, personally, I love short people. They're more down to earth."

"What's happening to us?" Nub rubbed his tired eyes. "This country is getting meaner. What are we becoming?"

"What do you mean?"

"What I mean is that we're falling apart. Movies are all violence. Music is all about sex and drugs. They killed two Kennedys and a King. We're fighting a war we're not winning. We're a culture of bullies."

She shook her head. "Where is this coming from?"

"I blame the TV," said Benny, absently watching a perfume commercial.

"I don't think this world has changed," said Leigh Ann. "Things are the same as they've been since ancient times; we just hear about all the bad stuff now. Welcome to the age of television."

Nub shook his head. "That's not what I'm talking about. I'm talking about how cruel we have become." Nub jabbed two fingers onto the bar top. "Today I saw kids bullying an innocent child. They threw rocks at her. Made her bleed. Broke my heart. Just because she's different. That shouldn't happen in this town."

"A lot happens in this town that shouldn't."

Leigh Ann stole a few more onion rings. They were both quiet for a moment and pretended to watch the game.

"There's a lot I can tolerate," said Nub. "But I won't tolerate meanness in a man. I won't do it."

"We've always had bullies, Nub," she said. "They had a colosseum in Rome. They still practice bullfighting in Spain and Mexico. Sometimes the bullfighter gets killed and people actually cheer for the bull. How's that for meanness?"

"That ain't the point."

"Only a hundred years ago in America, executions were still attended by the general public. People brought their kids to public hangings. Are those the good old days you're talking about, Nub?"

Nub placed his money onto the counter. He'd had enough philosophy class for one evening. "Where'd you go to college?"

"Roll Tide."

"Figures . . . I'm tired of bullies," he said, sliding off his stool. "I'm tired of everything tonight. I'm going home."

Leigh Ann leaned onto the counter. Her hair fell into her face a little. "Do you think I'm a bully, Mr. Taylor?"

"You're the biggest bully of them all."

"It doesn't mean I don't love you," she said.

"Well, that makes one of us."

Nub dragged Benny out of the Legion before the game was even over. The night sky was blue-black. The world seemed cold and unfriendly. But smugly satisfied with itself. Auburn was losing. Nine–zip.

Emily sat on the bumper of her Buick, parked in her driveway, staring at the sky. She was smoking a cigarette. Emily hadn't smoked in almost nine years.

Charlie hated smoking. He had made her quit. He had said smoking made women look cheap. His words hurt her deeply, but she never said anything. The thing is, most biology majors smoked in the 1950s; it came with the territory. The only people who smoked more cigarettes were English majors who read Jack Kerouac and sewed leather patches onto their tweed jackets. A biology degree was among the hardest degrees to earn. You had to learn unfamiliar vocabulary, Latin words, and obscure mathematics and figure out how it all worked together. Xylology was even harder because trees were another language altogether, with its own set of jargon. This area of study required long hours with your head in a textbook. Which required a stimulant of some kind. Coffee only went so far. Cigarettes went further.

But she gave it up for Charlie. Then one day she learned that he'd had an affair with Lillian Smith, the kindergarten teacher. The woman was a human chimney. Something about this hurt Emily even worse than if her husband had been sneaking around with a nonsmoker.

She took up Pall Malls again that same evening.

The sound of the game was coming from inside. The shouts of dozens of inebriated partygoers who used her home as a place to establish their caste in Park's pecking order. Emily was probably the only resident in Park, Alabama, without any interest in football. Instead, Emily watched the moon, waning crescent. It looked as though it were a giant sugar cookie suspended in the sky, with a big bite taken out of it.

It was bitterly cold. She folded her arms to keep warm, then heard a rumble coming down the street. She knew that automotive sound.

Two headlights in the distance appeared, slicing the darkness. It was the only vehicle on the road. She almost went inside to hide from the oncoming motorist, but she didn't.

The truck wobbled down Fifth, making more noise than a marching band. The front end of the truck was smashed inward sharply. The hood was creased in the middle slightly but had evidently been reshaped with a hammer so that there were now pockmarks all over it. The suspension sounded like a tambourine salesman riding over railroad tracks.

The vehicle stopped before her house and the window rolled downward. The driver was handsome, older, with two surgically sharp blue eyes.

"You don't have nearly enough body fat to be out in the cold like this," said the old man.

She waved. "Nice ride, Dad. I like the dents."

"Yeah, Benny and I are talking about souping her up and painting flames on the doors."

Emily waved to Benny. "Hey, Uncle Benny."

"Hi, punk," Benny said.

"You're not at the Legion?" she asked the driver.

"Can't slip anything past you."

She faintly smiled. "You're not watching the game?"

Daughter and father held their stare.

"Nothing much to watch," he said. "Auburn don't have a shot at winning this one. I've seen enough defeat in my life. I don't like paying good money to be miserable. I get enough misery for free."

"That's the spirit, Dad."

"Why are you outside, kiddo? Your party's in there."

"It's my party, I can cry if I want to. Besides, I wanted to wreck my lungs, just like you. Where are you two going?"

"Home. We're old. We're tired. We need to drink our Geritol before we turn into pumpkins."

He flicked his cigarette into the snow. It was a simple gesture, but he did it so easily. So comfortably. Sometimes Emily was envious at how comfortable her father seemed in this world.

"Why aren't you wearing a coat?" he said. "You'll freeze out here."

"I don't wear coats."

"That doesn't sound like my Emily."

"That's because I'm not your Emily."

There was nothing else really to say to that, so she stepped on her cigarette, picked up the butt, then picked up his butt, too, to make a point. She bid him good night and turned to walk inside.

"Say good night, Gracie," he said to her.

She smiled without turning. "Good night, Gracie."

Emily heard his truck jostle into gear. Before he drove away, she called out to him without facing him, "Watch out for deer, Dad."

Nub rolled across the highway, cutting past hayfields and cattle pasture, tearing across the nightscape. The Iron Bowl was playing on the radio. It was third down. Auburn was down by sixteen points. The game was basically over. There was no way Auburn could win it now.

"Emily looks good," said Benny.

Nub nodded slightly, lost in thought.

The sleet was drifting onto the dark earth. It looked like he was driving through the deepest part of the ocean. Tiny bits of ice moved past his windows like microscopic fragments of ocean life drifting past a submarine porthole. When he was in the navy, they had traveled over the western Pacific. The lowest point on planet Earth was in the Pacific, called the Challenger Deep ocean trench. As a young seaman, Nub had spent many a night staring over the stanchions of the USS *North Carolina* wondering what was beneath that colorless deepwater. Maybe creatures nobody had ever seen. Maybe ocean life nobody had ever conceived. Maybe monsters. Then again, what classified a monster? Maybe the monsters didn't think they were monsters. Maybe they thought they were just regular creatures.

He veered onto the interstate and headed toward Ephesus and Ambassador.

They drove for a few more minutes until Nub saw the glow of the Kmart sign in the distance. He took the off-ramp and eased into the mostly empty parking lot, which was roughly the size of an average school district. He threw the truck into Neutral and yanked the brake backward.

"What're we doing at Kmart?" asked Benny.

"Just stay here and listen to Auburn lose. I'll be back."

Nub hopped out and began plodding through the slushy parking lot. He entered the store through pneumatic doors, then wandered the linoleum aisles, serenaded by anesthetic Muzak that sounded like all the musicians had received frontal lobotomies.

An employee in a red vest reminded him that they were just about to close. He asked the kid where the shoes were. The kid took him to the shoe aisle, and Nub was overcome by the vast selection. An entire wall of shoes. Too many different styles to take in. Too many colors.

"We have more shoes on the next aisle," said the kid.

"You have more than this?"

"Let me know if you need any help."

Nub browsed both aisles of shoes. Sneakers had come a long way since his childhood. When he was a kid, shoes were made of stiff leather. They cut into your feet and made your heels bleed until, finally, the shoes were broken in, at which point they ceremoniously fell apart and it was time for a new pair. That was the way the good Lord intended people to buy shoes.

Although, truth be told, Nub didn't know much about shoes. Growing up, he never wore them. Nub's father had not been able to afford shoes for his son. And after his father shot himself, leaving Nub and his mother penniless, shoes became a myth in the Taylor household. To this day, Nub had inch-thick calluses on his feet that wouldn't go away.

After a few minutes of searching, he found a pair of red Converse Chuck Taylors. He selected a size fifteen. Men's.

Biggest size they carried. When he got to the register, he bought the shoes and a dozen packs of Pall Malls. The cashier was a young man who looked like a freshman in high school, pimples and all.

"Big shoes," the kid said.

"Yeah," said Nub. "I wouldn't want to walk a mile in them."

Nub followed I-65, riding in the slow lane, until he reached the Waffle House. The eatery was a beacon in the Alabamian night, beckoning huddled masses. Lemon-yellow roof. Checkered multi-square sign. Cars galore in the parking lot. A few semis parked nearby. He pulled behind the building.

"What are we doing at Waffle House?" said Benny.

"Benny," Nub said, facing him. "Anyone ever tell you that you talk too much?"

"No."

"Well, I'm telling you now."

"We can't all be as quiet and well-behaved as you, Nub."

"You know something? You're *this* close to pushing me too far."

Benny shrugged. "Why are we parked by the dumpster? You going to rob the place?"

He turned to Benny again. "Benny, are you familiar with the Fifth Amendment?"

"Dang right I am. Government ain't taking my guns away."

"Stay in the truck."

Nub grabbed the shoe box and exited the vehicle. He walked around to the front door, then stood before the windows and peered inside. He could see Minnie's large frame standing at the stove. She was cleaning the grill with a wire brush. There was a white bandage on her forehead. A paper hat perched on her head. Striped apron around her waist. He watched Minnie gather a pile of skillets, then walk to the back room. He caught a glimpse of her dilapidated shoes.

Nub entered the Waffle House and placed the shoe box on the counter. Two truckers at the bar looked at him funny.

"Please make sure your cook gets this box," Nub said.

The men just stared at the box.

"Nod and say okay," said Nub. "It's kind of important."

"They look like shoes," said one guy.

"You must work for NASA," said Nub.

"No, I work for Liebert and Sons trucking company."

"I'm shocked. Just make sure she gets them."

The men agreed.

Nub left the store and stood outside the restaurant, in the tar blackness, waiting. After a few minutes, Minnie emerged from the back room. He saw her approach the counter. The truckers explained what had just happened. Minnie took the shoe box and opened it. She removed two bright red canvas shoes from the tissue wrapping. Nub watched her face light with genuine surprise. It wasn't a full-on smile, but it was worth a lot to him.

The girl held a giant shoe in one hand and covered her mouth with the other. Nub smiled so big he began to cry. Hot tears fell so freely he almost couldn't pull himself together. After several minutes, he crawled back into the truck.

"The game's over," said Benny. "Auburn won. Seventeen to sixteen."

"You're kidding me," said Nub.

The air truly was filled with promise.

CHAPTER

~ **12** ~

The small church was in the nearby town of Ambassador. Way out in the sticks. A tin roof. A steeple that was a little off-center. A sign that said "Mount Lebanon Church of God." The churchyard was overgrown, and the abandoned playground out back looked like a personal injury lawsuit waiting to happen. Nub eased into the parking lot, killed the motor, then checked his watch. They were late.

"Ain't never been to no Church of God church before," said Benny. "You think they handle snakes?"

"Maybe."

"I hate snakes."

"I hate church."

They stepped out of the vehicle and noticed how the other latecomers were dressed. Men were wearing suits. The women looked as though they had never cut their hair. Others were wearing prairie dresses, resembling Laura Ingalls Wilder on anabolic steroids.

"Holy cow," said Benny. "I feel underdressed."

Nub fixed Benny's necktie and patted his cousin's hair into place. Then he told Benny to spit out his gum.

"My gum?" said Benny. "They won't care if I chew gum."

Nub yanked Benny's necktie like a leash. "I can't believe

we're having this conversation. This is a funeral. Spit out your gum, or when they start passing around the copperheads, I'm telling them about the magazines you keep under your mattress."

Benny spit out the gum.

When they entered the chapel together, all eyes were on them. There must have been a few hundred people. Country people. Pentecostal people. People unafraid of exotic reptiles.

An usher gave Nub a bulletin. "Thank you for coming today," he said.

"Proud to be here," said Nub.

The usher started to respond but stopped himself, then guided them down the main aisle to a pew. Benny thanked the man and tried to tip him a dollar for his trouble. The man merely looked at the cash, turned, and walked away.

"Why is everyone all matchy-matchy?" said Benny.

"How should I know?"

"Notice anything about the men?"

"No."

"Long sleeves. They're all wearing long sleeves. We're the only ones wearing short sleeves."

He was right. The people in this room were dressed for a senior promenade, whereas Nub and Benny were wearing button-downs and Sansabelt polyester pants that made them look like the poor man's Fred Mertz. Nub's necktie featured a hand-painted, half-naked hula girl on the front. The hula girl's bare midriff was exposed, her bosom strategically covered by a removable floral lei. There was a string you could pull to make her dance. It was the only tie he owned, courtesy of the United States Navy.

"I feel like everyone is watching me," said Benny.

"That's because they are."

The service was nothing like Nub had ever seen before. It didn't feel like a funeral. It didn't even feel like a church. It felt like a concert. There was *a lot* of music, along with shouting, some dancing, and plenty of tambourines. Everyone in the congregation seemed to know the words to each song even though there were no hymnals or lyrics. The choir leader would occasionally shout something mid-song, such as, "Everyone sing, 'I believe!'" And the choir would then respond with, "I beeee-lieeeeve" for approximately forty-five minutes, until the leader shouted something like, "Lemme hear you sing, 'Thank you, Jesus!'" whereupon the choir would sing, "Thank you, Jeeeeeee-zusss!" until various individuals passed out from either Holy Spirit fever or extremely low blood sugar.

Two mornings ago, the *Park Advocate* had advertised the funeral of Celia Bass. The name looked familiar. The obituary said Celia Bass was Minnie's mother. Nub called a friend at the courthouse, Adam Christie. Adam told Nub that Celia Bass had locked herself in the back seat of her Buick and shot herself with a hunting rifle. A 10 gauge. Nub almost dropped the phone. He didn't say goodbye or thank you to Adam; he just left the phone dangling off the hook. He walked into the closet upstairs where his father had done the deed five decades ago and stayed there until the next day.

The funeral had been going for two hours—two agonizing hours—when the preacher removed his jacket and necktie and preached for another hour. Then Minnie took the stage and sang the song Nub had heard her sing in the hospital.

Love before her,
Love behind her,
Love above her,
Love beneath her.

Love on the crown of her head,
Love on the soles of her feet,
Love way down in her heart.

There wasn't a dry eye in the house. She had a muscular voice and great control. Nub couldn't believe that this child was able to sing at her mother's own homegoing service without breaking down into a puddle. When Nub's father had died, Nub didn't speak for nearly three hundred days.

When the service finished, everyone went to the graveside to watch the coffin sink into the earth. Minnie stood beside the casket and wept without reserve. Then everyone returned to the church fellowship hall for the repast. Nub had never heard of a repast before, but he soon learned it was an all-you-can-eat buffet. Although calling it a buffet was slightly inaccurate inasmuch as there was enough food here to feed the Chinese People's Liberation Army.

The Church of God folk, Nub learned, were professional eaters. Nub and Benny availed themselves of acres of casseroles and congealed salads. One young woman introduced Nub to smothered oxtail, a dish so rich he wondered how (and why) he had gone his entire life without hearing about it. Benny went back for thirds and fourths. There was crackling corn bread. Collards with hocks. Corn bread. Creamed corn. Purple hull field peas. White zipper peas. Crowder peas. Corn bread. Candied yams. Smothered pork chops. Corn bread. Fried coon. Corn bread. Sweet potato pie. Also, corn bread. Throughout the meal, Nub kept his eye on Minnie, who sat with a group of elderly parishioners. People approached her and extended their sympathies, but Minnie never offered more than a word or two in response.

Afterward, he and Benny went outside for a smoke break

and found themselves answering many awkward questions from other churchgoing smokers who were curious as to how two men with bad hair and synthetic fiber pants, who were clearly not Pentecostal, knew Sister Celia.

"Sister Celia," Benny said between drags, "was just that kinda lady. Made you feel like you'd known her your entire life."

People nodded thoughtfully but looked confused.

"I never knew Celia," said Nub. "But she was the mother of a friend of mine."

"Do y'all really handle snakes?" asked Benny.

The conversation died a quick death and Nub and Benny returned to the feast.

When they had their fill of cholesterol and corn bread, Nub and Benny left the dining hall. On their way out, they shook hands and hugged necks with all their new friends. One woman offered to prophesy over Nub right there. Nub had no idea what this meant, so he declined the offer by saying, "Maybe next time."

They passed through the sanctuary and found Minnie sitting in a pew up front. Alone. Nub sat down beside her.

"Hey there, Waffle House," he said.

"Hey."

A black-and-white photograph was propped on an easel. The woman in the photo looked so alive. Full of youth. She held a baby in her arms as she posed next to a Dodge Dart. A 1960. Good year. He supposed the baby in the photo was Minnie since the baby was among the largest he'd ever seen.

"Thanks for coming," Minnie said.

"Wouldn't miss it."

She smiled.

"That was a pretty song you sang," he said.

Minnie held her foot outward. "Thanks for the shoes."

Stickers adorned the new shoes. The toe rubbers were covered in colorful varieties of hearts and bananas and ponies. The shoes already looked well worn.

"You got a real thing for stickers."

"Twenty-seven on each shoe."

"Why twenty-seven?"

"Twenty-seven is a cube."

"Do what?"

"There are twenty-seven lines on a cubic surface. Twenty-seven is a decagonal number, and astronomers and scientists think that dark matter makes up approximately twenty-seven percent of the known universe."

"Everyone knows that."

She looked at her shoes again.

Nub said, "How'd you learn all this stuff if you ain't in school?"

"I read."

Her black hair looked like it was made of silk. It was so dark it had a violet sheen to it.

"Where's your old man?"

"He died in Korea."

Minnie swung her feet. A kid to the core.

He almost told her about his own father's death. But this would have been cheap and self-serving under the circumstances. Nub knew from experience that, at funerals, it was a grave mistake to attempt to relate to the grieving. Even if you could, even if you had a story worse than that of the bereaved, it was rude to share it. And yet that's what everyone does instinctually. Everyone comes through the funeral receiving line, shakes your hand, and offers some idiotic proverb. "Let go and let God." "He's in a better place." "Life is for the living." "Your father was a good man." The same clichés had been circulating for thousands of years.

Nub only patted her knee.

The young woman searched his face for a moment. "We were going to have taco dip casserole," she said.

"What?"

"Taco dip. I bought the ingredients for taco dip casserole that night."

"Oh."

"It was my mother's favorite thing I made for supper. It's got lots of cheese. A whole block of cheddar, and a bunch of spices and stuff."

He rested his hand on hers and recalled the shirt his father died in. Blue. It was blue.

"I miss her so much," she said. "I can't believe she did it. It don't feel real to me."

"It never will."

Before anyone could say anything else, they were interrupted by an elderly woman with cropped hair. The woman walked down the church aisle like she was on a mission. She asked Minnie if she was ready to leave.

"Leave?" Nub said. "Where's she going?"

The old woman ignored his question and touched Minnie's shoulder. "Do you have all your things packed, Minnie?" she said. "We need to head out soon." The woman made a show of looking at her watch.

"Where are you taking her?" said Nub.

The woman tilted her head in a canine way. "I'm sorry, sir. I don't believe I know you."

Nub stood. "That's funny. I was just thinking the same about you."

"Miss Bass is going to the Catholic Children's Home." The

woman glanced at her watch again. "And we really need to hurry, Minniford. I didn't expect this service to go this long. You people must have sung fifty or sixty songs."

Minnie stood. Her cheeks were slick with tears. The place on her forehead where the rock had struck her was scabbed over.

"The Catholic Children's Home?" Benny said. "What's that?"

"I'm sorry, sir. Who are you again?"

"We're concerned citizens, that's who," said Nub.

The woman turned to Minnie. "You have ten minutes, dear. Let's be quick." Then the woman walked back down the church aisle.

Nub gave Minnie a parting hug before she left. He followed her out to the parking lot and watched Minnie Bass's towering frame crawl into a nondescript black sedan. The car rolled onto County Route 19, and the car's taillights got smaller on the horizon until the lights were tiny red lightning bugs in the distance.

"She's all out of family," said Benny in a soft voice.

"Aren't we all," said Nub.

CHAPTER

$\sim$ 13 $\sim$

Eighty years ago, Appalachia had been covered in chestnuts. Once upon a time, the chestnut had peppered the entirety of the Southeast like crabgrass. It was the quintessential American tree. Ubiquitous. Unremarkable. Invasive, even. George Washington planted them at Mount Vernon. Thomas Jefferson had them at Monticello. Ben Franklin used them to build his outhouses. By 1904, the chestnuts were dying of an unknown cause, termed "ink disease." It was a fungal blight. Within a few decades, four billion American chestnuts were wiped off the continent. It took maybe forty years for the most abundant species in the Southeast to suffer complete extinction.

But then, that was how life worked, wasn't it? Life keeps changing and you can't stop it. You can't stall it. You can't do a thing about it. You just live your life on this earth like an innocent bystander, subject to the whims of selective extinction. Like a tree. The American chestnut species was officially declared extinct in the 1950s. The tree joined the ranks of the woolly mammoth, the saber-toothed tiger, the megalodon shark, the dodo bird, and chivalry. And that was the last word on the matter.

Until last year.

Last July, a local old man in Park named Ollie Adams

claimed he found an American chestnut. He also claimed this tree measured fourteen inches in diameter and was growing on his uncle's land, which was adjacent to Emily's father's land. Most people, of course, thought this was ridiculous. Nobody believed him inasmuch as Ollie Adams was regarded to be full of a substance that is plentiful to most barnyards and hog pens. But Ollie proved his critics wrong. Ollie cut down America's lone American chestnut with a chain saw and dragged it into a city council meeting. The naysayers fell silent. The tree lay in the middle of the floor like a cadaver. Ollie stood proud before it and said, *"If that ain't a chestnut, I don't know what is."* Everyone gathered around the tree and agreed that, yes, it had definitely been an American chestnut, all right.

News spread faster than the Bangkok flu. State environmental representatives traveled to Ash County to verify the chestnut's legitimacy. The tree was most definitely a *Castanea dentata*, and apparently this particular regional variety was resistant to blight. Within a week, state officials were hiking into the woods to study the stump. They were tree surgeons. Tree doctors. Tree researchers. Xylologists, dendrologists, grad students from SUNY College of Environmental Science and Forestry, biologists from Washington, DC. One international tree expert had flown in all the way from the Humboldt University of Berlin. The scientists found two *more* healthy chestnuts growing near Marcus Vaughn's place, land that also adjoined the Taylor farm. Both were bigger than Ollie's kill. One chestnut was nearly two feet in diameter, about the size of a washtub.

It was a cold December afternoon when Emily walked through the woods of Ash County with a clipboard. The sun was lowering. She passed state workers wearing white jumpsuits, dressed like they were about to be launched into outer space. She passed men taking soil samples, dutifully collecting bark specimens from the bases of nearby saplings. All tree scientists look like Grateful Dead fans. These two were no exception. The men hadn't shaved since the earth cooled.

She waved at them, but none of the men even acknowledged her; they were too shy. She knew their type well. Most scientists, in general, were afraid of the opposite sex. She could feel them watching her as she walked away. Once upon a time, this might have flattered her. But today their stares only gave her a stabbing pang of regret. Flirtation was a game reserved for the living.

Emily knew these woods by feel. This land, this dirt, these trees, they were in her blood. Long before her parents divorced, she had lived in these trees. Her mother would turn her loose in the mornings, and Emily would stay outside until she heard the evening call for supper.

She had climbed most of these oaks. She knew these trees intimately. It was because of these woods that she loved trees the way she did. It was because of these trees that Emily Ives had become interested in the new, thrilling field of conservation after she graduated. Namely because a broad stripe of optimism ran through the conservation community. Back in the fifties, she and her fellow aspiring science majors were going to save the world. They were going to change the planet. Save the whales. Protect the owls, the ponderosa pines, the sea turtles, dolphins. Everything.

She got her first job out of school with the American Longleaf Council and fought to preserve old-growth forests in the South. She had minor adventures, plodding through the Carolinas, the Appalachians, and even the Everglades. She hiked impossible distances alone in the mountains, tagging trees, researching dubious diseases that nobody else cared about.

And then she gave it all up when she got married and settled for the job of biology teacher to a bunch of high school kids who drew dirty pictures in their textbooks.

She placed a hand on a nearby ash tree. The bark was littered with telltale D-shaped exit holes, evidence of the emerald ash borer. The beetle would eventually send the ash species into extinction. Same as the chestnut.

When she was sure nobody was watching, she paused to light a Pall Mall. Earlier that day she had found twelve cartons on her front porch. She had no doubts where they had come from. She plodded onward, boots splashing through cold puddles. And as she walked through the sun-choked forests of her youth, she saw the chestnut in the distance, roped off like a sacred shrine. A few men were standing around the tree. She stubbed out her cigarette and approached the tree. The thing was marvelous, like something from a storybook.

Emily greeted the men.

"You the local biology teacher?" one man asked.

"One of them," she said.

The man shyly smiled at her. "You don't look like any biology teacher I ever had."

"Ah, but you do."

The wind was taken out of his sails immediately, but she was grateful for the flirtation. It made her feel less dead.

The men lifted the boundary ropes and left her to her own devices. They tramped away through the woods, and she was alone. With the tree.

She walked around the chestnut to get a better look at it, staring into the tangle of branches. It wasn't a big tree for a chestnut, only a baby tree in the arborology world. Probably forty-some years old. Around her age. The tree was slender, small for its species. It still had an entire lifetime ahead of it.

The bark was smooth and gray. The long, canoe-shaped pendant leaves were undeniably American chestnut. She touched the tree and tried to feel its quiet power.

"How are you, Betsy?"

Emily had named the tree.

"You look very healthy today."

Betsy chose not to reply.

American chestnuts have an average life span of five hundred years. They can grow upward of a hundred feet, rivaling the longleafs in their size. A chestnut's diameter can reach five feet, about the size of an average Cadillac. Their foliage can become so thick that animals sitting beneath the boughs during rainstorms remain dry.

She ran her hand along the bark of the tree. "You're a good old girl," she said to Betsy.

She peered upward into the tree's network of limbs.

"I'm dying."

It was the first time Emily Ives had ever said those words.

CHAPTER

~ 14 ~

Nub and Benny assumed their regular bar stools. The Legion was busy this afternoon. They sat among the millworkers, the cattlemen, the clock punchers, the Peterbilt drivers, and the surly old beer swillers who refused to go home to angry wives. Nub held a cold glass against his temple and closed his eyes. He was buzzed, but not nearly enough. He wanted more booze. He wanted to be completely numb. Then again, he didn't know exactly what he wanted. Everything seemed a little off. He wasn't sure what he was feeling. He wasn't hungry. He wasn't tired. He wasn't awake. He wasn't sober. He wasn't totally drunk. He didn't feel like talking to anyone. He didn't feel like thinking.

Overhead in the bar a song played. "Brandy" by Looking Glass. The song was the worst thing to come out of the 1970s except for, possibly, the Chia Pet. He wished someone would unload a rifle into the speakers and put an end to the garbage. Then again, it could've been worse.

They could have been playing John Denver.

Leigh Ann came to refill their glasses. Her hair was pulled into a ponytail, revealing a beautiful and girlish face. The ruffled tube top she was wearing showed off her shoulders. The old geezers loved her for those bare shoulders, and she had the midriff of a ten-year-old. To them, she wasn't just a barmaid. She was the prettiest thing in town. Leigh Ann performed a valuable service for the oldsters in this village. She flirted with them, batted her lashes. She was sassy and smart. And this made old men feel less invisible.

"Y'all need anything else?" she said.

Nub wasn't paying attention and didn't answer.

"Hey," said Leigh Ann, pointing to the little polka dots on the wooden bar in front of him. "What's wrong with you, Nub? You're crying."

Nub wiped his face with his hula girl tie. "I just wish someone would turn that radio off, that's what's wrong with me. I can't stand this crap."

"I've never seen you cry."

"I'm not crying. It's pollen."

"In December?"

"I have a very sensitive nose."

She reached underneath the bar and turned the radio to a different station. Soon Red Foley was singing "Tennessee Saturday Night."

"Thank you," he said.

"Are you gonna tell me why you two are so dressed up?"

Nub drew in a deep breath. "We went to a funeral."

"A wild and crazy funeral," said Benny.

"Who died?" asked Leigh Ann.

"Celia Bass," said Benny.

"Oh," said Leigh Ann sagely. "I heard about her. Suicide."

Suicide was an alien term to most people. To Nub, it was a word as familiar as his own name.

Nub looked at Leigh Ann. "Can I ask you a personal question?"

"You always do."

"You ever feel a connection with someone? Someone special, someone unique, but you can't seem to figure out why you feel that way about them since you have so little in common?"

Leigh Ann rested her eyes on him and her face softened. She placed a hand on his shoulder. "That's sweet, Nub, but you're way too old for me."

She laughed. So did a few other guys at the bar.

But Nub didn't. He put cash on the bar and left Benny on his stool. He was done here.

Leigh Ann called after him, "Hey, I was only kidding, Nub. You know you're the only man for me."

He waved her off.

"Nub, don't leave. It was just a joke."

Nub shouldered open the steel door and trudged into the parking lot. He walked to Benny's mangled Ford and leaned against the fender, watching the choreography of a winter sunset at play. Cattle trucks bounced across the railroad crossing. Ed's Feed and Seed still had a few rusted F-100s slumming in the parking lot. The paper mill's recovery boiler in the distance was outlined in red obstruction lights. The smokestack was spouting emissions into the air that made the world smell like severe flatulence. The train was whistling in the distance. The water tower still said "PAPK."

> *Love on the crown of her head,*
> *Love on the soles of her feet,*
> *Love way down in her heart.*

He was another year older, another year poorer. Poor in spirit. Poor in family. Other men had spent their lives accruing love, children, memories, and joy. Nub had spent his life doing . . . doing what precisely? He wasn't sure. Jack squat. He had no relationship with his daughter. His ex-wife hated him. So did every other woman who had ever been unfortunate enough to get close to him. So did half the town.

Benny startled him by tapping him on the shoulder. "Can I borrow a buck?"

"What for?"

"Pinball."

"No. I'm about to go home. Get in the truck. I'm tired."

Benny shook his head. "I'm staying here."

Benny never stayed at the Legion without Nub. Benny never did anything without Nub, not since they were two years old.

Nub ran a hand over his face and massaged his eyes. "What're you gonna do, Benny, walk home?"

"Cal said he'd drive me."

"Great. Well then, why don't you get Cal to loan you the dollar since he's such a Samaritan tonight?"

"Can't. Cal said if he loaned me a dollar, I'd never appreciate its true value. He told me to ask you."

Nub reached into his wallet. "Cal has a point." Nub handed Benny two fives. "You realize how much you owe me now, you big dummy?"

Benny looked at the cash and smiled. "Nub Taylor, you're a good man."

Nub stepped into the vehicle and slammed the door. "You really need to get out more, Benny."

It was sunset. The world was red and gold. Shug looked into the cavernous grave at Celia's coffin. A pauper's coffin. The wood was finished, but only slightly. It was dull, like the finish you see on a baseball bat. A light coat of lacquer, that was it. There was no scrollwork, no flowery molding. Just a plain box. Pine. Cheap pine at that. The kind of pine they used for pallet wood. It was a poor person's grave.

He had been standing at a distance during the funeral service earlier that day. He'd heard his daughter sing farewell to her mama. He had watched the emotion overtake his daughter as she stood at the graveside. It was the first time he'd ever seen her. She was marvelous in every way.

He had almost cried like a toddler when his eyes found her. But then, Sugar Bass didn't cry, not anymore. It wasn't that he didn't want to. It was that he lacked the upper octaves of emotion. Soldiers do not cry. Neither do inmates. You hold it in. If you cry, you are already dead.

The gravediggers were standing nearby, waiting for Shug to finish his moment of reflection. They weren't rushing him, but they seemed ready to get this show on the road.

Three other men were standing a ways back, their white Cadillac parked close by. They were leaning against a tree. Shug was too tired to care right now.

The strangers never took their eyes off Shug. After several minutes, Shug took two steps back and told the gravediggers to go ahead and cover his ex-wife. One of the gravediggers crawled into the seat of the Bobcat backhoe and used the duty bucket to scrape a massive pile of red dirt into the gaping hole. The falling dirt made a loud *thud* on the lid of the casket, then the operator used the back side of the bucket to tamp down the earth atop Celia's grave. The whole thing was done in a matter of minutes. And just like that, a human body was buried, six feet down, gone forever. In less than a few hundred seconds.

When the burial was finished, the backhoe motored away and the men with shovels followed. Shug remained at the graveside and placed a small object into the freshly packed pile of dirt. It was a small model plane. The *Spirit of St. Louis*. He tucked fresh earth over the figurine and put a hand on the moist dirt.

"Don't you worry, Cece," he said. "I'll watch out for our little girl."

On his way out of the cemetery he passed the men from the white Cadillac. The suits were motionless as he walked by, smoking cigarettes. They followed Shug only with their eyes.

"Long time no see, Shug," one of them eventually said.

"Welcome home," said another.

Shug just kept on walking.

"You sure got a pretty daughter," one man said.

The phone rang.

It rang again.

And again.

And again. But her father wasn't answering. Emily almost hung up, but she didn't. It was three in the morning; she should have hung up. But something prevented her.

Ring. Ring. Ring.

Nothing.

She was seated on the aluminum sofa glider on her back porch, moving back and forth. The cord from her kitchen phone was stretched to capacity, snaking through the open sliding glass door, following her into the covered porch area. She wasn't sure why she was calling him this late, except that maybe she needed to hear his voice. It would calm her down. Nub Taylor's voice had that unique effect on her. He could bring her back to center. She was about to hang up when . . .

Click.

"Yeah?" said Nub's voice.

He sounded surprisingly awake. Sharp and alert.

She did not speak.

"Hello?" he said again, perturbed.

She opened her mouth to say something, but she wasn't able to find the words. Nothing came out. Then Emily started crying. She covered her mouth so she wouldn't make any sound, but it was no use. She could hear herself sobbing.

"Who is this?" he said.

She still couldn't speak. She only cried quietly. Finally, she gathered herself together and took a long, silent drag from her cigarette.

"You're smoking again," he finally said.

Emily wiped her face with her sleeve. She felt a smile crawl onto her tearstained face.

"No, I'm not."

"Yeah, me neither."

She laughed. "You shouldn't have bought me these things. You trying to encourage bad habits?"

"Honey, I am the Monet of bad habits."

She laughed again.

"What's up, punk?" he said.

"Did I wake you up?"

"I don't sleep."

She started to say it. She started to tell him everything, but her voice got stuck.

"What are you doing up at this hour?" he asked. "Watching the test signal on the TV?"

"I don't sleep either."

"You've been crying."

"No, I haven't."

"Your nose is clogged."

"Pollen."

"Yeah, it's been bad this December."

She sniffed her nose loudly.

"You need me to come over?"

"No. Oh my God, no, Dad. It's three o'clock. I'm just tired. I think I just . . . I don't know."

"You must be hard up if you're calling me."

"I'm sorry I bothered you."

"You could never bother me."

Emily opened her mouth and tried to speak again. The words were right there, stuck in her voice box, ready to come out. The spirit was willing, but the flesh was weak.

"I'm sorry I called, Dad."

"I'm not."

"Good night."

"It's morning."

"Well, you know what I mean."

"No, actually I don't."

A long silence.

"I love you, Emily."

"Okay."

And she hung up the phone.

The Birmingham Catholic Children's Home was squalid. The room she was sleeping in was plain. Ominous. Sad. Barren. There were no pictures on the cracked plaster walls except for a very spooky picture of a blond, decidedly Catholic-looking Jesus. Why did Jesus always look like a cross between a California surfer and a Ken doll?

Minnie spent the entirety of the day counting tiles in

the communal bedroom. There were twenty-two beds in this particular room. Eleven on each side. Iron cots. Pancake mattresses. She could feel the springs digging into her backside as she hummed the theme song to *Bonanza*. There were 2,912 linoleum tiles on the floor and 2,611 ceiling tiles. Three flights of twenty-one steps to get to the third floor. There were nine floors in total, ergo there were 189 steps. She wanted there to be something special about 189, but there wasn't.

Both rows of eleven teenagers were snug in their beds, dressed in pajamas and nightgowns. They all kept their distance from Minnie, as though she were an untouchable. Life was all about the rank, and the others were trying to figure out where she fit in the rank and file.

Minnie walked into the bathroom; she slid on her mother's old gown. Pink with white flowers printed on it. The fabric still smelled like her mother. Still smelled like her old house. Like her old life. Like her childhood. Like all the things she had lost. When you lose someone to suicide, their clothes become religious relics.

She looked at herself in the bathroom mirror. The gown was too short on her. It barely covered her bottom. Her mother had been a much smaller woman than she was. She had inherited her height from her father's family, her mother told her. And that was about all she knew about him. His name was Clarence. He died in the Korean War. He was a war hero of some kind. He blew up bridges with dynamite or something like that. And he had been tall. *"Your daddy was big enough to build a barn all by hisself,"* according to her mother.

Minnie walked the hallway toward the bedroom, past rooms filled with adolescents. The orphans all glared at her. Some were younger than she was. Most were about her age. She was at least three feet taller than everyone in this place, including the nuns.

When she arrived at the bedroom, four girls were sitting on Minnie's bed, rummaging through her belongings. Her suitcase was slung open and her clothes were strewn on the floor. Her new Converse shoes had been confiscated by a girl whose hair was in braids. The girl was peeling off the stickers. Another girl was already wearing Minnie's Carhartt jacket.

Minnie said, "Take off that jacket."

The girl in braids ignored her and put Minnie's shoes on her small feet. The shoes looked like water skis on her feet. The girl sauntered toward Minnie. She was small. Wiry. Tough. She wore a look that said she had been in more fights than anyone else in the room.

"Take those off," said Minnie.

"I can see your butt in that nightgown," said Braids. She pushed Minnie and her toadies all laughed.

"How tall are you?" asked another kid.

"Can you breathe all the way up there?" said another.

"Fee-fi-fo-fum," said another.

Minnie shifted her weight and pointed to the shoes on the girl's feet. "I said. Take. Them. Off. *Now.*"

The girl with the braids met Minnie chest to chest. Actually, it was more like chest to belly button. The wiry girl placed a finger on Minnie's sternum and poked. "If you want these shoes, Big Butt, you're going to have to take them off my feet."

Minnie was happy to oblige.

≈ 15 ≈

The gymnasium at Park Union High was a fire marshal's worst nightmare. The bleachers were filled to capacity. Nub couldn't remember which basketball team Union was playing tonight because he didn't give a rat's fundaments about basketball. He hadn't followed high school sports for well over fifty years. And even fifty years ago, he hadn't cared much about basketball. The game was too fast. Nub was a musician, not an athlete. It wasn't that he didn't like sports; he loved them. But only when beer vendors were present.

But then, he was not here because of athletic interest. He was here because Charlie Jr. was starting tonight. And ever since Emily's late-night phone call, Nub had been worried. He knew his daughter better than she thought, because she was just like him. Something was going on.

"There he is," said Benny as they edged across the crowded bleachers. "There's Charlie Jr." Benny waved at Charlie Jr. wildly.

Charlie Jr.'s tank top hung like a parachute on his wire-thin body. Charlie Jr. did not wave back. He looked embarrassed. The boy wore a common facial expression Nub was used to seeing on his family members. The coach was still on the court, pep-talking his players who stood gathered around him and nodded at whatever he said. "There is no *I* in team," "Can't never could,"

"If you believe it, you can achieve it," blah, blah, blah. The sinewy boys of Park Union High School's boys' basketball team were all limbs and bones. They did not exactly portray Class 4A dominance. The Park Union High basketball team looked as though they could use some hearty dinners, quality time in the sun, and a round of basic inoculations.

"Hey, Charlie!" shouted Benny, pumping his arm in the air. "Charlie Jr.! It's us! Uncle Benny! And your granddaddy! We're here!"

The kid slinked into his shell.

"Keep it up, Benny," said Nub. "You're really winning him over."

It had been years since Nub had been inside this gymnasium. When Emily was a majorette, he came to games now and then. One game in particular stood out in his memory. Emily had just broken up with her boyfriend, Mickey Burns, who had evidently cheated on her and called her a terrible name. During the fateful game, long ago, Nub had taken the opportunity to find Mickey's locker in the empty hallway, whereupon he jimmied the door open and urinated inside the locker. He was caught in the act and promptly asked to leave the premises. He was helped to vacate the building by a gaggle of concerned fathers before he was even able to zip his trousers. It was ugly. Nobody had forgotten it. People rarely forget the antics of a drunk.

Tonight Emily was seated with a group of teachers positioned in the nosebleeds where she could keep her eye on the wayward youth in front of her. Her hair was down, scattered on her shoulders. She wore jeans and a peasant blouse. She looked leaner than he remembered. And paler too. He couldn't help but stare in her direction. Emily had the unique ability to always be the most important person in the room.

"Don't you wanna go talk to Emily?" said Benny.

"In a little bit," said Nub.

"Why not right now?"

"I'm trying to blend in tonight."

"You miss one hundred percent of the chances you don't take."

"Thanks, Coach."

Benny gave a slow rally clap and shouted, "Come on, Charlie Jr.!"

"Benny," said Nub. "Don't take this the wrong way, but you're kind of embarrassing me."

"Thanks. That means a lot coming from a professional."

Leigh Ann was weaving through the crowd, moving across the bleachers. She seemed genuinely surprised to see Nub and Benny here. She was carrying a bag of popcorn, and she wore jeans that fit so tightly, Nub could read the directions on the laundry tag.

"Wait a second," Nub said as she passed. "If you're here, then who's running hell?"

"I didn't think you two ever joined the human race," she said. "I'm here to watch my daughter play trombone. Don't tell me they let you two enroll here."

"We're thinking of trying out for track," said Nub.

"You'd be an improvement to our current team."

Leigh Ann smiled at him, and Nub felt his chest get tight. Then she touched his arm. "I know Charlie Jr. appreciates you coming, Nub."

"Yeah, he's thrilled. Just look at him."

"He's a teenager," she said. "They don't have souls."

The event began with the Park Union High band playing a song at an earsplitting volume. The band finished with a Gershwin number that sounded more like a nuclear weapons field test than it did music. Then the basketball team took to the court, and everyone started howling. Park's mascot was a wild boar hog. Sometimes the whole gymnasium would break out into spontaneous oinking and squealing. A truly frightening sound.

The first two quarters of the game were uneventful. Hillcrest High School marched all over Park Union like a herd of bison. The Hillcrest fans were animated and annoying, but they were nothing compared to the communal oinking. Park came back in the second half, scoring on a few lucky shots. After the third quarter it looked like it was Park's game. Nub leaned toward Benny to announce his upcoming visit to the men's room.

"Don't break into any lockers," said Benny.

"You're hilarious, you know that?"

"I try."

Benny had barely finished his sentence when an object struck Nub on the jaw. Hard. The impact knocked Nub backward and he tumbled down the bleachers. The world turned into a blur. When Nub finally quit falling, he was three rows away from where he'd started, lying in the laps of several young men who wore Hillcrest colors. The gym had gone silent. Nobody was oinking anymore.

Nub stared at the bright mercury lights mounted on the ceiling, trying to put the pieces together in his mind. What had just happened? How had he ended up here?

But he never got a chance to figure it out. Because in a few moments, a crazed man was straddling his chest, slapping his face repeatedly.

"Don't you *ever* come near my son again!" shouted Bill Deener between slaps. "You hear me? Don't you ever touch Phillip again!"

Nub could smell whiskey on the man's breath. Lots of whiskey. Park Union's algebra teacher was three sheets to the wind. Maybe four.

"Don't you *ever* touch my son!" Bill shouted.

Slap, slap, slap.

"Get off me!" shouted Nub.

Nub threw his fist forward and connected with Deener's chin. Nub had been in enough barroom brawls to know how to give an account of himself, but his retaliation was not aggressive enough. The algebra teacher was running on alcohol fumes. Nothing was more dangerous than a guy who was drunker than you were.

Nub swung again and landed a blow to Bill's kidneys, but Bill just kept slapping Nub until his cheeks went numb. Nub eventually gathered his strength and used his boots to heave Bill off himself. The teacher fell into a flock of young women. Coca-Cola sloshed onto the bleachers. Peanuts and pretzels went flying. Soon parents were on their feet, shouting, and the gymnasium came unglued. A few men tried to break up the squabble, but Bill Deener possessed the strength of a jackass tonight. He wasn't even fazed.

"This man attacked my son!" shouted Deener.

Nub stared at him, waiting for Bill's feet to move.

"This man tried to harm my boy! This man is a child abuser!"

Nub kept his eyes on Bill's feet. You could tell a lot about how a man was going to fight by watching his feet. Contrary to popular opinion, a good fighter did not fight with his hands. A good fighter fought with his feet. You used your feet to anticipate. To prepare. To advance. To retreat. To kick. Nub could forecast most men's movements by their feet. And if all else failed, aim for the crotch.

"Your son's a lowlife!" shouted Nub. "He was throwing rocks

at his girlfriend, Bill. Where I come from, beating up on a girl makes him lower than a dog."

The algebra teacher's feet moved left. Then right. Deener lowered his head, dropped his shoulder, and charged at Nub like a bull, full steam. Nub sidestepped and watched him plow into a group of majorettes nearby—or maybe they were cheerleaders. Whichever ones carried the batons.

Down Bill went.

"Bill, I'm warning you! Stay away from me!"

"Bite me, Nub!"

"Is that a request?"

"I'd like to see you try, old man!"

Deener headed for Nub again. There was nothing Nub could do to avoid the oncoming blow, so he threw a knee into Bill's groin. Bill almost quit breathing. His face contorted in pain. He went down again. The algebra teacher roared on the floor, grabbing himself between the legs. But after a few moments, Bill sprang up and charged at Nub. Both men caromed onto the maple floor. And now it was a wrestling match.

"Don't you ever touch my boy again, you animal!"

"Get off me!"

It took four men to pull Deener off, and Nub's rescuers took their sweet time doing it. Before they removed Deener, the man had loosened one of Nub's incisors and given him not one but two black eyes.

Bill shouted, "This man is a child abuser!"

Nub shouted back, "Your son is a girl beater!"

"That ain't no girl!" Deener was restrained by many arms. "That girl's a freak. Sorry white trash, just like you! My son deserves a *lot* better."

Nub flew forward and popped Bill in the mouth. The two men were soon entangled in a mess of arms and fists again.

Two deputies broke up the fight. Deener made a show of storming off the court, shouldering past everyone, heaving open the heavy doors, and stomping into the inky darkness.

Nub used his shirttail to wipe blood from his nose. He could feel everyone looking at him, especially the redhead in the stands. A lone figure in the bleachers began to rally clap. "Let's show some hustle, Charlie Jr.!"

"Shut up, Benny," said Nub.

Emily followed Nub into the parking lot. She trotted through the gridwork of parked cars until she caught up with him in the darkness. The light from the parking lot lamps caught her copper hair and made it look almost purple. When she found him, he was leaning against the truck, dabbing his face with a handkerchief. He knew he must look pretty bad because of Emily's reaction when she saw him.

"Oh my God," was all she said.

"Mine too."

"You look awful, Dad."

"I had ugly parents."

He could see her breath in the neon glow of the moon. Snow was falling again. Or maybe it was sleet. Whatever it was, the coldness of the precipitation felt good on his bruised face. He thought Bill might have broken his nose.

"Dad, what just happened in there?"

"Does it matter?"

Emily took the hankie and started dabbing his face. He winced beneath her touch, but it was the first time he'd been touched softly in a long time. You don't often think about how badly you miss human contact until you don't get any for a few decades.

"Where did he get you?" Emily asked.

He spit blood onto the pavement. "Get me? Hell. Where *didn't* he get me?"

"You need to see a doctor, Dad. You're still getting over the car accident. You had a pretty bad head trauma, the doctor said."

"I live with head trauma."

"Still."

"I hate doctors."

She cleaned his face for several minutes using the moisture of the falling snow. And for several minutes he had a front-row view of his baby girl. It was the closest they'd been in years, physically speaking. He just watched her. His daughter was too young to be a widow. She was in a kind of limbo. Her marriage hadn't been all bad, but Nub never got the sense that she was happy either. But then, none of that was her fault; she'd never known what a real marriage was supposed to look like.

She wiped his lower lip and it stung. "Is it true what he said?"

"Yes. It's true. Your father is sorry white trash."

"I meant what he said about you beating up the Deener boy."

"You think I would harass a high school kid for no reason? Phillip Deener was taunting his ex-girlfriend, sweetie. He threw rocks at her, hit her in the head. She was bleeding. I did what any good citizen would've done. I stepped in and took care of business. That boy deserves to be locked up."

"What girl are we talking about?"

"Minnie Bass."

"I don't know her."

"You wouldn't. She's a dropout. Her family lives in Ambassador. They're snake handlers. Her mother just killed herself."

"What?"

"Never mind. She's going through a lot right now."

"What does any of this have to do with you, Dad?"

Nub wanted to explain himself and the connection he felt to that child. But he didn't. "You should have seen her, Emily. Deener's friends were dancing around her, calling her names. I wanted to whip every last one of them."

"Dad, they're kids. The cardinal rule with kids is you can't get involved."

Nub yanked the hankie from her hands. "I wish everyone would quit saying that they're just kids. Kids can be hateful when they want to be. Phillip Deener is a little snot."

Emily stared at him and didn't speak for a few moments. But Nub could feel it coming.

"Have you been drinking, Dad?"

And there it was.

This was how things always went. The great paradoxical question. *Have you been drinking?* He was on thin ice. If he admitted he had been drinking, he was the devil. If he denied he had been drinking, he was lying, and he was still the devil. You couldn't win here.

"Is that why you came out here?" he said. "To give me the fifth degree?"

"It's *third* degree. And yes, that is why I'm here. It's not every day I see my father try to beat up the algebra teacher before the entire high school."

"He coldcocked me."

"You beat up his son."

"Now you sound just like him."

"Answer my question, Dad."

Nub laughed bitterly. "Didn't you see what just happened? That man almost took off my head, and now you're going to browbeat *me*?"

She folded her arms across her chest. "How much have you had to drink?"

"You should've seen what those boys were doing to her, Em."

Emily just stared.

They could hear the game going on behind them. The cheers from the full gymnasium were muffled by the thick brick walls of Park Union High. The crowd's voices were happy and light as though nothing had just happened.

"Why do you always do this?" she said.

Nub climbed into the truck and slammed the door. He looked at his daughter. She was slender and drawn. Her face looked older somehow. Sadder. He turned the key and the Ford hacked to life. He looked at his daughter again.

"What's going on with you?" he said. "You don't seem like yourself lately."

"Don't make this about me," she said.

"Why'd you call me the other night?"

Emily didn't answer.

They were soon enveloped in a cloud of blue auto exhaust.

"I've been racking my brain," he said. "Wondering what on earth is serious enough that my prim-and-proper daughter would break down and call someone she hates at three in the morning."

"I don't hate you, Dad."

He worked the gearshift into first and gunned the engine. "Well, give it time, sweetie. Everyone eventually does."

Sixty-eight miles away in Birmingham, at 3:00 a.m., Minnie Bass was on her knees, hugging the toilet, puking her insides out. She placed her head over the bowl and tried not to make too much noise, but it was impossible. She heaved again. A few children were now gathered outside the bathroom door, staring at her in the darkness.

Sister Mary Josephine shuffled through the gaggle of nosy kids and into the stall. The old nun remained observant and quiet, watching Minnie carefully. The other kids were laughing at Minnie's short nightgown, which had hiked up and was exposing her bare backside.

Minnie's nausea finally came to an end. She was out of breath and sitting on the cold tile, head leaned against the stall divider. She wiped her mouth and mopped sweat from her drenched forehead with toilet paper.

"What's wrong with you?" asked the sister.

"I'm sick."

The sister moved closer and placed a hand on her forehead.

"Just an upset stomach, ma'am. Must be something I ate."

Minnie felt her stomach churn again. This time was worse than the first. She fell to the toilet and continued emptying the contents of her stomach.

"We all ate the same thing," said the nun. "And nobody else is sick."

Minnie spoke into the toilet bowl. "Maybe it's the stomach flu."

Sweat was dripping down her cheeks and face. She felt dizzy from vomiting so intensely.

The sister squatted onto her heels and held Minnie's hair back as she heaved into the toilet again. Minnie let go of everything she had ever eaten.

When the bout of nausea passed, the sister asked, "When was the first time?"

"First time what?"

"The first time you were sick like this."

A cool realization settled on Minnie; it was as though someone had poured a pitcher of cold water over her head.

"I don't know," said Minnie.

The nun's eyes were like knives. The old woman rose and nodded sagely.

"Oh, I see."

❦ 16 ❧

The terms of Sugar's parole required that he obtain gainful employment. His parole officer reminded him of this weekly. But jobs in a small town were hard to come by. Impossible, even. The paper mill wasn't hiring. And there weren't many jobs for Explosive Ordnance Disposal Specialists in the civilian world, and there weren't many places of business interested in hiring a convicted felon. The parole officer recommended that he look for a job closer to Birmingham, where the job market was bigger. But Shug wasn't interested in leaving Ash County and being away from his daughter. So he just kept pursuing the want ads in the *Advocate* in earnest. He begged for jobs, but nobody would have him.

Shug walked along County Route 19 with the newspaper classified ads rolled up in his hand. He wore a cheap blue chambray shirt he'd bought at the hardware store, along with Levi's dungarees. His outfit wasn't all that different from his prison blues, but he felt comfortable in these clothes. They suited him. He was institutionalized, of course. Before prison, he'd been a military man. Which wasn't all that different from prison in many ways. In the military, he had become accustomed to living in a world where people told him what to do. He knew how things worked in that world. Prison was much the same. You knew what to expect in prison. You knew the rules. You hated it, but at least you knew where you stood.

Shug paused at the four-way stop and trotted across the street into the parking lot of the IGA. He purchased a current newspaper from the vending machine. The headline read "B-52s Continue Strikes on North Vietnam." He felt a flash of a memory return to him. He remembered coming back from overseas, flying into the Baltimore/Washington airport with a plane full of wounded servicemen, all wearing army drab, carrying rucksacks. He remembered the young men on his flight who were missing limbs and eyes. He remembered one passenger beside him. A young soldier who had been a prisoner of war. He weighed ninety pounds and couldn't speak because he had no tongue. Sometimes Shug remembered too much.

He scanned the parking lot and saw the white Cadillac easing into a parking space. The men remained in their vehicle, staring. The passenger-side man rolled down his window and draped an arm out. The men held their glares.

So did Shug. Finally, Shug turned and walked through the pneumatic sliding doors of the IGA. His heart was racing as he thought about the men following him. They had been following him for weeks now but had never made a move. He remembered hearing stories of what The Organization did to those rare few who screwed them over.

Shug asked to speak to the manager. The manager was a young man with freckles and a cheap haircut. The kid wore a necktie and a name tag that said his name was Carl. Shug cut straight to the chase. He pointed to the "Now Hiring" sign on the door and inquired about the position.

Carl smiled and welcomed him back to his office. The young man was at least twenty years younger than Shug, and yet he talked down to Shug as though Shug had just graduated from middle school yesterday. A long time ago this might have bothered Shug, but he'd spent the last fifteen years being spoken to like a Labrador by COs and wardens. It was no big deal.

The meeting began with Shug telling Carl up front that he had been in prison. Carl folded his hands across the desk and tried not to act surprised by this, but clearly he was. Maybe even a little frightened. Still, the kid played it cool.

"Why did you go to prison, Mr. . . ."

"Bass. Clarence Bass."

The kid made a note.

"May I ask what your crime was, Mr. Bass?"

Shug did not hesitate. He explained his story. He started from the beginning and told the man about nearly everything except the money. He'd learned in prison that true freedom was found in honesty. When he got to the part about the gun going off and the man dying, Carl's face winced.

"You *shot* that man?" said Carl, whose voice sounded much younger now.

Shug looked down at his lap. "It was an accident, but yes, I did it."

A heavy silence filled the room.

This was not the way you wanted a job interview to go.

Shug stared at a framed piece of embroidery on the wall behind the manager's desk that read, "For we must all appear before the judgment seat of Christ." A small portrait of Jesus hung beneath the words, "What will be the outcome for those who do not obey the gospel of God?"

Finally, Carl spoke. "Tell me something, Clarence. Have you accepted the Lord Jesus Christ as your personal Savior?"

Shug looked around the room and wondered if this was really happening. "I'm sorry, what?"

"Are you saved?"

"From what?"

"Are you born again? Are you filled with the Holy Spirit?" Shug waited a beat. "Are you serious?"

Carl stood and walked around the desk. "Do you know what it means to be filled with the Spirit, Mr. Bass? Do you know what it means to love the Lord?"

Shug wasn't sure what to say here, so he just smiled.

"The Holy Spirit is responsible for miracles, Mr. Bass." The kid began to speak in a recitation voice. "'And these signs shall follow them that believe; in my name shall they cast out devils; they shall speak with new tongues; they shall take up serpents.'"

"Uh."

"Do you speak in tongues, Mr. Bass?"

"Tongues? No."

Carl presented his hand. "Would you pray with me, Mr. Bass? Let's invite the Holy Spirit into this room. Let us pray with unction and yearnings too deep for words."

"I don't know if this is such a—"

"Let us ask the Lord Jesus if you should be a team member at the IGA."

"Okay."

"I ask God for guidance in all my ways, Clarence. I seek him in all circumstances. Scripture says he is a light unto our path. He's Jehovah Nissi. Jehovah Shammah."

"What does that mean?"

"Honestly, Mr. Bass, I don't know, but it must mean something good, because it's another language."

Carl took Shug's hands. They stood facing each other, like two people about to exchange wedding vows. The young manager cleared his throat. "Dearest heavenly Father . . ."

Whereupon the young manager began speaking in tongues. At least that's what Shug assumed he was doing. It was either that or the young man was having a brain seizure.

The kid really let it fly too. As he prayed, he rocked forward and back on his toes, half shouting at the ceiling.

"We come humbly before you, God, and ask for your wisdom. We are your children; you are our hammalah shammalah sippy dippy bing bing!"

Carl paused. He squeezed Shug's hands. Shug felt the bones in his hands creak.

"Mr. Bass?" said the young manager, eyes still closed tightly.

"Hmm?" said Shug.

"Do you have anything you'd like to say to God?"

Sugar was at a loss. "Not really."

"No. You may speak freely, Mr. Bass," said Carl. "That is what it means to be one of the redeemed. The Spirit is listening to you. Tell him what's on your heart right now. He can perform miracles, both great and small."

"Miracles?"

The kid nodded with a punch-drunk grin. "Miracles, Mr. Bass."

Sugar didn't have anything in particular on his heart at the moment, so he just spoke frankly. "Dear God," Shug began, "it's, uh, it's me again. Hopefully you're doing pretty good."

"That's right, Mr. Bass. Tell it to God."

"Uh, I'd surely be grateful if you'd let me work at this IGA."

"Tell it! Mr. Bass, tell it all!"

"And, God, if you are up there, and if you're listening, please watch over my daughter. I love her so much."

He got the job.

Nub stood in the lobby of the Montgomery County Courthouse and checked his watch. His interview was in fifteen minutes. He wore his one and only tie. He had splashed on a generous helping of Old Spice. Three handfuls. Benny had bought him Old Spice aftershave for Christmas. Which was a coincidence, because that's exactly what Nub had purchased for Benny. They did this every year. Then they ate a Swanson TV dinner. Merry Christmas.

"Mr. Taylor," said the woman behind the receptionist desk. She handed him a clipboard of paperwork that was roughly the same thickness as a James Michener novel.

"What's this?" he said.

"These are the application forms I told you about."

He thumbed through them. "But I already filled out an application."

"That was for Child Services." She smiled. "This is for the Department of Child Protective Services. I'll also need three kinds of identification."

"Three? I was told I only needed two."

The woman smiled again, but not with her eyes. "Just give me what you have, please."

He dug into his wallet for the ID and birth certificate, then started filling out thirty miles of documents. One sheet after another. The forms asked detailed questions. Meaningless questions. "What color is your hair?" "What is your annual income?" "How many bathrooms are in your residence?" "Do you have any outstanding warrants for your arrest?" "What's the hypotenuse of the triangle in figure B? Please show your work."

He ate a fistful of Doublemint gum to mask the smell of his breath. He completed each field on the application. He turned in the papers, then waited for nearly forty minutes until a woman came clicking into the courthouse reception area. Her silver hair was piled atop her head. She wore thick glasses with gems in the frames. When she smiled, it was a fake smile, a bureaucratic grin with no warmth behind it.

"Mr. Taylor?" said the woman.

"Present," he said.

They shook hands briefly.

She looked at the rainbow of bruises on his face for a beat too long. "What happened to you?"

"Cut myself shaving."

She looked a few moments longer and let her eyes drift to his scandalous necktie.

The woman turned and began walking toward her office. He assumed he was supposed to follow her.

Her office was small and dank and smelled like old coffee, nothing like the opulent marble waiting room outside. Nub guessed that there wasn't much money being piped into Alabama's Child Services these days.

"Please, Mr. Taylor, sit." The woman flipped through a multipage document and cleared her throat. "Minniford Hazel Bass," the woman began, peering over her glasses.

"Hazel?" he said. "Really?"

The woman looked at him.

"My grandmother's name was Hazel."

The woman was about as enthused by this information as she would have been about, say, elective surgery. "Yes, well, Minniford was in Birmingham Catholic Children's Home, but she's been moved."

"Why?"

She dropped the document and steepled her fingertips. "She's at the Maranatha Home for Unwed Mothers."

The news was not lost on Nub. He leaned back in his chair.

"Unwed mothers," he muttered.

"It says here the urine analysis just came back. She's expecting."

Nub shook his head. This was all happening too fast.

"When can I see her?"

"Right now we need to talk about *you*, Mr. Taylor. Not her."

"Okay."

"I still need to look over your application, and you still need to attend classes and obtain your certification before you can go any further." The woman tossed the clipboard onto the desk. "This will take some time. I hope you're not in a hurry."

"Can I see her?"

"Not until you're registered and certified as a foster parent."

"I can't even *see* her?"

"Is there an echo in here?"

"She's fifteen. She's not in prison. She's in an orphanage, for heaven's sake. She's allowed to have friends, isn't she?"

"It's not an orphanage. It's a home for unwed mothers and their children. These young women are treated like adults because they *are* adults now."

"For the love of Mike, that child is not an adult. I just want to see her. What kind of law is that anyway, not letting them have visitors?"

She drew in a long breath and let her eyes fall to his hula tie. "It's not about laws, Mr. Taylor. It's about manpower right now. Group homes are shutting down every day because the state wants to move to foster homes instead of institutional homes. We're short on labor. We're racing to keep up."

"How about the phone?" he said. "Can I speak to her on the phone?"

The woman shook her head.

"I can't even call her?"

"Phone privileges are not granted to mothers younger than sixteen without approval. But you can submit a formal request for a phone call. It will take some time to verify, bear in mind."

"This is ridiculous." Then Nub swore.

"I'll ask you not to use that kind of language in my office."

Nub swore again.

With that, she rifled through her desk and handed him another form. He took it. His hands were trembling something fierce. Her eyes lingered on his quivering hand. He withdrew it and placed it in his lap. It had been a few hours since his last drink.

"Mr. Taylor. Applying to be a foster parent is the first step on a long road. As an officer with the State of Alabama, I take this sort of thing seriously. It's not an expedited process. You're not buying a Volkswagen."

The woman took a few more minutes gathering appropriate forms, then presented a new stack of paper to him. "I'll need you to fill these out before the next visit."

He sorted through the pages. "What is all this? These look like the ones I just filled out. Two times already."

"Third time's a charm."

Nub lowered his voice to a reasonable tone. "Can you at least tell me if I have a shot at being approved?"

The woman raised one eyebrow. "I'm sorry, I can't do that."

"Please. Just tell me if I have a chance. Man to man."

"Mr. Taylor . . ."

"I'm not asking you not to do your job; I'm begging for help. Listen, I know I'm not a prime candidate. I know there are a hundred folks more qualified than me. I don't have anything going for me. But I want to give this kid a second crack at life. Do you want me to get on my knees? Because I will."

"Mr. Taylor."

Nub Taylor got on his knees.

"Get off the floor."

"Please, ma'am. Let me help this kid."

The woman lifted him from the floor, then gave him a long look. He could see her hard exterior crumbling slightly. She was laughing at him beneath her hard facade.

"If I were you," she said, "I'd get my spare bedroom in order."

"Thank you," he said. "God bless you, ma'am."

Then she gave him the world's tiniest smile. Nub dusted off the knees of his trousers and felt his heart nearly explode. They ended their meeting, and he thanked her so profusely that he almost French-kissed her.

He headed for the door, but she called out to him.

"Mr. Taylor, I do hope you're prepared for this. This is going to be a long-standing commitment. This is a human life we're talking about. You can't just change your mind when the new-ness wears off."

"No, ma'am. I won't change my mind."

He turned to leave, but she stopped him.

"Oh, and something else, Mr. Taylor?"

He faced her.

"You might want to chew a little more gum next time."

"Are you out of your mind?" said Emily.

Nub was making the bed in the spare bedroom, hospital-folding the corners the way his mother showed him long ago. He had never even hospital-folded the corners on his own bed. In fact, he hadn't actually made his bed since he was in his early twenties.

"I can't believe they're letting *you* adopt a kid," she said.

"Not *adopt*," he said. "*Foster*. Big difference."

"She's a girl, and you're a man."

"So? A lot of single guys have foster kids these days. It's not unusual. Get with the times, kid."

"You're not a *single guy*. You're a sixty-two-year-old man. You're old enough to be her grandfather."

He stopped fluffing a pillow and looked at her. "You know what, you're absolutely right. Should I crawl into my casket now, or should I wait until after you leave to keel over?"

"This isn't a joke, Dad."

"She's fifteen years old, sweetie. She has nobody. She's living in a place that might as well be prison."

They had spent the afternoon doing this. Talking in circles. She hadn't been to his house in years, and he had been thrilled to have her there. It had felt like old times. But now she was reminding him of her mother, and the knock-down-drag-outs of yore.

"This is insane, even for you, Dad," Emily said. "You shouldn't be doing this."

"I've done a lot of things I shouldn't do."

"And you did them longer than most."

"What's your point?"

"My point is, this can't happen. Your life is a mess. You're a drunk."

Nub ignored the remark and inspected his bed-making skills. He knew his daughter was only telling the truth; she wasn't trying to be hurtful. He *was* a drunk. This was no surprise.

"I know what I am," he said. "But I would really appreciate your support. I know you don't like this idea. Your objection is noted. But I've made this decision, and it's happening."

"You never even say two words to Charlie Jr. He's your grandson. Why is this girl so different from your own family?"

"Charlie Jr. doesn't like me. Your mother has poisoned him against me."

"That's not true."

"Your son can't stand me."

Emily said nothing.

"You don't know what those group homes are like," he said while fluffing more pillows. "Nobody gets adopted unless they're cute little toddlers missing front teeth. Minnie would probably stay there until she aged out. After that, according to statistics, she has a one in three percent chance of being homeless."

Emily furrowed her brow. "One in three percent chance? Do you even know what math is?"

"You know what I mean."

"No, I'm not sure I do. And *toddlers* don't lose their front teeth. First graders do. You might know that if you had been around when I lost my teeth."

That hurt.

Emily left the room on that note.

Leaving the room on a high note had always been her mother's argument strategy. Always walk out on an argument before the other person could retaliate; that was Loretta's rule. The walker-outer would thereby gain valuable argument points, which could be exchanged later for prizes. He heard Emily's feet clopping down the steps toward the kitchen.

He followed her and found his daughter standing by the sink, washing a pile of dishes that had been there since the end of the Spanish-American War. She was crying. He knew this because he could hear her sniffing her nose. He could feel the ambient temperature in the room change beneath the weight of her tears.

"When was the last time you washed a dish in this stupid house?" she moaned. "These plates have some kind of fungus growing on them. You live like a slob, Dad."

She slammed a pan onto the counter. The noise was so loud that it scared Nub's cat, Wyatt, who leaped out of the room posthaste.

"I know you're upset . . . ," he said.

She slammed another plate and cut him off. "Do you? Do you know?"

"Emily. Please."

She started counting on her fingers. "First you assault a high school student. Then you get into a fistfight at the place where I work, and now you're adopting a kid. What's next? You want to put on a clown nose and go to the nursing home to wax the steps?"

"Calm down, punk."

"Don't call me that!"

She wiped her face with a dishrag. Her makeup smeared. "I've dealt with the fact that you're not meant to be a parent. Some people just aren't. I've dealt with the fact that you drink too much. But this is different. I can't watch you screw up someone else's life like you did mine."

"You're being unfair."

"Don't talk to me about fair."

Tears were dripping off her chin. He wanted to hold her, but he was afraid she'd brain him with a skillet.

"You never even asked my opinion about this, Dad. I thought we were at least friends. You could've asked me what I thought."

"You would've just told me it was a stupid idea."

"It *is* a stupid idea."

"I rest my case."

"What about *me*? You want to raise a stranger's daughter, but why didn't you want to raise *me*? What's wrong with me, Dad?" She threw the dishrag at him. "You're a pigheaded idiot. You know that? You are everything Mom says you are. Selfish, ignorant, and stupid. You're a jackass, Dad. You know that? That's what you are. A jackass. All you do is hurt people, you self-centered, unreliable, good-for-nothing jackass!"

"Sweetie, please. You don't have to be so gentle with my feelings."

He sat down at the dining table. Several minutes went by, the two of them maintaining various bouts of eye contact but not speaking. Emily was breathing heavily.

"I know it sounds crazy," he said, "but I'm ready for this. I've learned a lot about kids. We covered a lot of ground in my foster certification course."

She crossed her arms. "You took a class?"

"Yes."

"*You* took a class?"

"That's right. About raising kids."

"Lovely. You're about forty-two years too late."

He looked at his hands. "Go ahead, beat me up, Emily. I deserve it. And if hurting me makes you feel better, I'm not going to stop you."

"Okay," she said, pulling out a chair from the table and sitting across from him. "Tell me something you learned in your class. I genuinely want to know."

Nub drew into the recesses of his mind, searching for some tidbit of knowledge he'd picked up in the class, but he had never been good under pressure. All he could get out was, "Girls use twenty thousand words more each day than men."

She exploded with a laugh. "Well. Now there's a real gem. Yes, I'd say you're ready, Dad. You'll make a great father to this kid. She's lucky to have you. Maybe you'll actually come to this girl's sixteenth birthday party."

She knew how to cut him.

Nub remembered Emily's sweet sixteen party all too well. He remembered driving to Loretta's house and seeing his replacement, Daniel Barnes, stepfather extraordinaire. Daniel was playing the part of Emily's happy suburban daddy, and he was everything Nub wasn't. When Nub had pulled up to the curb, the esteemed accountant had been stocking briquettes in his brand-new, state-of-the-art charcoal grill. Daniel wore a lemon-yellow polo shirt and penny loafers.

Penny loafers.

Nub's gift to his daughter that year was to be a travel fishing rod. When he placed it on the gift table, Loretta handled the wrapped package in her hands like she was touching a jar of warm sputum. Whereupon they got into a fight. A big one. She criticized Nub for buying a fishing rod for a sixte-year-old girl. Nub reminded Loretta how much Emily had loved to fish, but his words fell upon deaf ears. *"She fished when she was five!"* retorted Loretta. Things escalated. Loretta told him to leave. He remembered throwing his truck into gear and obliging her. He remembered the rest of the night had been a 50-proof blur.

"What do you want out of me, Emily? I'm trying to do something good for a change. Trying to do the right thing."

Emily leaned onto the table and got in his face. "You don't know what the *right thing* is. What *feels* right isn't the same thing as the right thing, Dad. Do you understand that?"

He dug a pack of Luckies from his shirt pocket and wedged a smoke between his lips.

"What will you do when she won't come out of the bathroom?" said Emily. "What will you do when she can't tell you what she needs to buy from the drugstore because she's too embarrassed? What's the *right thing* to do in that situation?"

He had a brief flashback of Emily locked in the bathroom when she was twelve years old. She had been staying at his house for the weekend. A rare occurrence. He remembered Loretta rushing over to his place and taking Emily away in a frenzy, refusing to tell Nub what had happened. All she had said was that his daughter had become a full-fledged woman.

Nub clicked his lighter shut and kept quiet.

"I'll tell you what you'll do," Emily said. "You'll call me."

He had to admit this was a distinct possibility.

"You'll expect me to drop everything and come over to fix your problems. And I'll have no choice but to come over here and pick up the pieces like Mom's been doing for forty years."

He exhaled a cloud and inspected his hands. "Emily, you don't have to yell."

"And what about that piece-of-crap truck you're driving?" she said. "It's not even yours. Do you even have a license? Does Benny even have that thing registered? What happens when it dies? What if you wreck again?"

"That truck has nothing to do with this."

"No? How are you going to drive her to school if you don't have a car? How are you going to take her to band practice? How are you going to carry her to extracurricular activities? How's she going to get to church?"

"Band practice? Church? I didn't realize this kid had such an active social calendar."

Emily mock-laughed. "So what's she supposed to do? Stay here? Locked in this house? She doesn't get to have any fun outside of this pigsty, full of fungal dishes? You're going to teach her how to drink Miller High Life and break wind at the supper table?"

"Well, I'm glad you brought all this up," he said. "See, I've been working on some of those things lately."

"What things?"

"Well, I know it's hard to believe, but it's been a couple weeks since I drank. I'm still working on the smoking part, but I'm taking it slow. I'm down to one pack per day." *And one pack per night*, he thought.

Emily scalded him with her fiery gaze. "You're just telling me what you think I want to hear."

"I'm telling you the truth, sweetheart."

"Truth. Right."

"Go ahead, mock me. But I'm making some big changes. I'm trying to make you proud of me. I want to quit drinking. I really do."

She squinted, long and hard. It was a look that he knew so well he could have painted a picture. It was the look Loretta gave just before she threw something heavy across the room.

"You're not drinking?" she said. "Hand to God?"

He held up his hand. "Not drinking."

"Swear?"

"I swear."

"Then how come I saw your truck at the Legion last night?"

"Emily, a man has to eat. Leigh Ann feeds me dinner. A man can only eat so many peanut-butter-and-mayo sandwiches."

"So you're telling me you didn't drink *anything* last night?"

"Right."

"Nothing at all?"

Nub was quiet.

"Answer me, Dad."

He drummed his fingers on the table. "Just a social drink."

She erupted. Emily slid from her chair and stood; she was crying again. "I don't have time for this!" Then she swore. Emily never swore.

And then something happened. Emily's tears overtook her in a way Nub had never seen happen before. She doubled over onto her knees and sobbed like a little girl, face to the linoleum floor. He jumped up and wrapped his arms around her, but she pushed him away.

"Get off me! I hate you!"

He stumbled backward but came to her again. This time she hit his midsection with her fists. "I hate you! I hate you! I hate you!"

He did not shy away.

"I know," he said.

"I hate you so much!"

"I know."

She shoved him away from herself. And all he could do was stare at the smoldering ashtray on his table, shaped like the great state of Florida. He bought the ashtray in Panama City Beach on his and Loretta's honeymoon. Just before he joined the navy. Just before Loretta wrote to him and told him she was pregnant. He remembered the cigars the guys gave him aboard the USS *Oklahoma* as soon as he learned he would be a father.

He cried tears of joy that night in his bunk. A child. Heavens. He was having a child.

"I'm sorry, Emily." Nub was weeping now. "I really am."

"I'm forty-four years old, Dad."

"I know, honey."

"Forty-four. Look at me. It's not supposed to be like this! I'm supposed to be in the prime of my life. You've missed every birthday I ever had. You didn't even see Charlie Jr. until he was three years old. You are nothing to me." Then she screamed it. "You are nothing!"

Nub made no reply.

"I'm sorry, Em. God help me, I am."

She sniffed her nose. "Yes, you're right about that. You are *sorry*. Sorry white trash."

With that, she left his kitchen and slammed the door behind her so hard a framed picture fell from the wall.

Always walk out on an argument before the other person has a chance to speak. That was her rule.

CHAPTER

⚘ 18 ⚘

The time was 11:39 p.m. Deputy Gordon Burke was making his rounds. The weather forecast had said it would be lightly snowing. Although *icing* would have been the more accurate term. Ice was coming from the sky. The ice lining the roads was a lacquer finish. Ice was so unusual in this town that none of Park's residents knew how to navigate the conditions. Which meant a lot of disasters. Nine traffic incidents had occurred within the last twenty-four hours. A new record for Ash County.

Burke was on patrol, sipping tepid coffee from the substation Bunn machine, listening to Red Sovine on the Toyota radio. Dispatch chatter was light tonight. Dispatch chatter was light every night. This was Park, not Chicago.

His vehicle cruised at an easy twenty miles per hour. He was making more of a courtesy loop than anything, just to let people see their taxes on parade. Hardly anything ever happened in this city. Hardly anything ever would. Everyone knew it, which was a blessing and a curse. A blessing because Park was safe. A curse because he had spent thirty years doing the most skull-numbing job known to the human race.

He turned off Elwood and onto Andrew Street. Andrew was dotted with newish homes, some currently being constructed.

The new designs looked out of place in this old town. They all had flat roofs, with modern brick and square picture windows. The shrubs were geometrically cut. Park was Rockwellian. Split-level ranches had no place on a *Saturday Evening Post* magazine cover. And yet here they were.

He turned onto Seventh Avenue. On Seventh, they were breaking ground for a new restaurant called Pizza Hut behind the dry cleaners. People expected the joint to be a big hit. Just like the Kentucky Fried Chicken over in Ambassador. The food at the KFC wasn't even good. It was just commercialization. Plain and simple. The homogenization of the United States. Franchises with preordained color schemes and uniforms. It made him sad.

When he passed the Ash County Waterworks utility station on Eleventh Avenue, he noticed something. A tiny pin light, bobbing around the water tower in the midnight darkness. Burke stopped the Toyota and peered upward through his windshield for several minutes, trying to figure out what he was seeing. He stepped out into the chill air, removed his Stetson, and craned his head back.

The water tower stood high above the world like a sentinel. Like a mama hen, keeping watch over her chicks. He could see a large, dark shape dangling from the scaffolding, and the pin light kept dancing in the air.

A man was up there.

Patrol cars gathered beneath Nub, lights flashing. He was suspended 140 feet off the ground, like a dead fish on a stringer. He wasn't sure how he had fallen off the water tower scaffolding, but he was grateful he had worn the suspension harness. He looked at the blinking red lights on the cars below the water tower and marveled at them. Tiny red lights moving in meandrous patterns, the way fireflies do. This made him laugh.

The sound of a bullhorn carried into the night air.

"Just hang on, Mr. Taylor," the bullhorn voice said. "Help is on the way."

Nub kept singing.

"Can you hear me, Nub? I said, just hang on."

This made Nub laugh until he choked on his own saliva. "Hang on to what? My butt?" He laughed again. Then he reached for the half-pint bottle in his coat pocket, unscrewed the cap, and took a big swig.

More people gathered beneath him, like tiny insects. Some came by car, others on foot. But everyone had come to see the show. Whenever he glanced upward at the water tower and laid eyes on his newly completed R, he felt satisfied. No longer did he live in PAPK; now it was PARK once again, just the way God and the Ash County legislature had intended. He had corrected his mistake. Thus, no matter what happened next, no matter what the punishment, no matter what kind of ribbing would follow, Nub had righted at least one wrong within his messed-up life.

He heard another loud siren wailing. A fire truck. He could see the distant lights spinning, cutting between the trees. The truck didn't belong to Park's fire department. This truck had a huge ladder. Park's department didn't have a ladder that big. They didn't need one. The tallest building in Ash County was the bank, and it was about the size of a water heater.

The bullhorn spoke again. This time it was a female voice. "Dad?"

Nub tried to ignore the voice, but he was too drunk. He started to weep. The weeping came from a place deep within his chest. Somewhere far beneath his heart. He was weeping for more than just his daughter. He was weeping for his own life.

"Get her out of here," Nub mumbled.

"Dad?"

He swore at the top of his voice. "Someone get my daughter out of here!"

It took four hours to get Nub down from the water tower in the ice and snow and driving sleet. When he reached the ground, he was hungry, tired, and severely dehydrated. And his privates hurt badly from the harness straps that had been supporting his 149 pounds for several hours. He was promptly hoisted by fire medics into the back of an ambulance and given an IV drip.

Emily was standing beside him the whole time. She gripped his hand with both of hers. His were like ice. Hers were warm. And soft. He was still crying, of course. Because all drunks cry. It's part of the deal. They cry for many reasons, but the tears come freely. Sometimes the booze is the only thing that can loosen them.

He looked into his daughter's eyes and spoke with a slack tongue. "You used to love to fish."

"Dad. What?"

"You were my little fishing partner."

"Just try to relax, please, sir," said a medic.

"What are you talking about, Dad?"

"You. I'm talking about you, Emily. We used to fish together. You were my little fisherwoman. And I loved you for it."

"Okay, yes. I remember that."

He held her hand and kissed it. "You do?"

"Yes, we fished in Granny's lake. All the time. I remember."

He squeezed her hand and wept onto her knuckles. And

as they loaded him into the ambulance—for the second time in thirty days—he said, "I'm sorry, Emily. I am sorry for what I've done to you. I'm sorry I hurt you. God help me, I am. I am so sorry."

The doors shut.

"So am I, Dad," Emily said. "So am I."

Shug arrived at his motel just after midnight. The Scotty's sign featured an illustration of a little black dog with pointy ears, a beard, and overgrown eyebrows. The sign was outlined in yellow neon light. "Free Color TV."

Whoopee.

He entered the breezeway, reached into his pocket, and dug around for spare change. He bought a Coke from the vending machine. He started on his way up the stairs and passed some of the other full-time residents who lived at Scotty's Motor Inn. People living at the Scotty were either on the skids or heading directly for them. The woman from room 29 was smoking in the breezeway. She smiled a weak smile at him. The kind that looked forlorn.

Shug fumbled for the key in his pocket while simultaneously removing the red IGA apron from around his neck. When he got to his room, he slid the key into the door and turned the knob. He opened the door and was momentarily taken aback.

Shug's room had been trashed.

Lamps were smashed. The mattress was lying on the floor. Sheets were strewn about. The television screen was shattered. Piles of confetti glass shards peppered the floor. The bathroom shower curtain had been yanked from the rod. His rucksack had been emptied. The corpse of a headless chicken was bleeding in the middle of the room. Blood was everywhere. White poultry feathers were everywhere. And a message was written on the bathroom mirror in what looked like red lipstick.

YOUR DAUGHTER IS NEXT

BOOK
2

CHAPTER

~ 19 ~

It was raining. Nub was sitting alone in his truck. He was parked in the parking lot of an old Methodist church, watching the water pelt his windshield. A crisscross of designs streamed down the glass, making a kaleidoscope of colors. More cars pulled into the parking spaces of Blanchard United Methodist Church, one by one. He watched people jump out of their cars and rush through the rain toward the door.

Tonight would be Nub's first meeting.

He didn't want to admit it, but he was nervous. He'd been sober for almost three weeks, since he'd been rescued while painting the water tower. It had been one of many wake-up calls in his life.

He knew tonight would be painful. He knew it would be awful. He knew it meant that he would have to stop drinking forever. He knew it meant that he would have to face the jaggedness of life without alcohol to round its edges.

He kicked open the truck door, then walked through the blinding rain into the church building. He shook off his seed hat and hung his jacket on a hook with several other dripping jackets in the vestibule.

The meeting was in the basement. It was a quintessential church basement. Dank. Stinky. A fellowship hall that smelled like decade-old Folgers and a million spaghetti dinners gone by. Linoleum floors. Popcorn ceiling. Faux-wood paneling. An upright piano sat in the corner. A drinking fountain. A water-closet-sized bathroom barely big enough to sit down in. In the center of the basement were the obligatory gray folding chairs, positioned in a circle. Maybe ten or twelve. Stragglers were still filtering in, plodding down the staircase into the basement. They had wet hair. Wet clothes. They consulted the almighty caffeine machine. They laughed with each other. It was clear that most of these folks knew one another. They'd all been in this basement before. They were genial and lighthearted. Friends even. He did see, however, a few outsiders like him wading on the fringes of the room. He could tell they were outsiders by the way they lingered against the walls. Silent. Cautious. Nervous.

He was startled by a voice.

"Hi there," said a young guy with a black beard. He was dressed like a cowboy minus the hat. Big belt buckle. Square-toe boots.

Nub pumped his hand. "Hello."

"I'm Stan."

"Pleased to meet you, Stan."

Nub did not give his own name.

It was a lot like the first day at a new school. As a boy, after Nub returned home from the psychiatric hospital, his mother moved him from his old grade school in the country to Park's city school. She'd hoped there would be fewer questions for Nub to answer in a new school. ("Why'd your daddy shoot his own self?") Nub would never forget that first day in a new class-room. It was horrifyingly uncomfortable. Turned out, everyone knew. They all looked at him as though he had the plague. On the first day in a new school, you don't know anyone; you're a foreigner. The jargon is different. The inside jokes are different. The routines are different. It's unsettling in every way. When you're the new guy, and everyone knows your father blew out his own brains, it's considerably worse. Tonight Nub was an alien all over again. But he pressed onward. He knew he had to save his own life.

Nub approached the circle of chairs and chose a seat. And although he was sober, he stumbled over one of the chairs and nearly fell flat on his Blessed Assurance. The woman who reached out a hand to brace his fall was brunette, and alarmingly familiar. Nub couldn't have been more taken aback if he'd woken up with his face sewed to the rug.

"What in the name of Job are *you* doing here?" he asked.

"I was about to ask you the same thing," said Leigh Ann.

He sat in the seat beside Leigh Ann. "What, you come to these things for occupational training?"

"Not quite."

"You work in a bar, for heaven's sake."

She shrugged. "It's called cue exposure therapy."

The meeting started with a prayer and a few traditional readings. Nub looked around the room as one man read the preamble from a blue book about how there were no judgments here, no preconceived notions. As the man read, Nub took stock of everyone in the room. They all had something in common, and it wasn't just the booze. He'd seen the license plates in the parking lot as the cars were pulling in. They were all from outlying little hamlets. Other counties, even. They met here in Blanchard to remain unknown and nameless.

Anonymous.

The man read about how there were no dues for membership and they weren't part of any particular denomination or political party. Nub sipped his coffee. It was the color of weak tea. He could see all the way to the bottom of the paper cup. It tasted even worse than it looked. Leigh Ann touched his knee. It was not a romantic gesture but a supportive one. She gave him a reassuring look.

She must have thought he was scared. And she was right. The last thing he wanted to do was to be here with people who had *real* problems. He knew he had things to deal with in his own life, but he didn't want to talk about these things in front of strangers. He didn't want to whine about his daddy issues. Neither did he want to delve into how he started drinking when he was thirteen years old, at Filcher's dance hall in 1924, during the throes of Prohibition, where the beer was free for musicians. He didn't want to open his mouth at all.

The chairman opened up the floor and asked a few people in the group to share. The first man identified himself as Peter. The man was friendly. Well spoken. Funny.

Peter told his story. He had been sober for four years, going on five. Peter had two sons who were both grown now. Peter had been absent from their lives. He had missed every major event in their childhoods. And even the events he hadn't missed were a blur to him. One of his sons didn't even invite Peter to his own wedding. Nub listened very closely.

"I think I am finally accepting responsibility for what I did," said Peter, "but I'm done punishing myself for my sins. I'm just trying to act right; that's all I can do. Act. I think I've finally learned that you can't think your way into the right action but you can act your way into the right thinking."

A round of support came from the circle, but no applause. Only affirmative nods and smiles. Nub was still thinking about Peter's little catchphrase when Leigh Ann told her story.

She did not look at Nub during the telling. Not once. She was telling her tale to the group, although Nub had a feeling she was aiming her story at him. She talked about when she started drinking in the morning, after her first son was born. And about how her ex-husband hit her. About how the judge deemed her an unfit mother. Nub felt embarrassed for her, but Leigh Ann showed no shame in the telling, only honesty and vulnerability.

The next person stood and identified himself as John. The man was young. Midthirties. Blondish hair. He told stories about picking up his children from school and being wasted while he drove them home. About running his car into a telephone pole. Nub looked into his lap and thought about his own string of automotive mishaps. He had wrecked exactly seven vehicles in his life. It had become a running joke among his friends and family, a joke he realized wasn't all that funny.

More people shared, and Nub was starting to feel less freakish. These people had problems just like his. Some of these people had been sober for decades. Some weren't sober at all and freely admitted it. Others remained silent.

Nub was surprised that nobody called on him to speak. Nobody asked him to join in any readings or recite heartfelt prayers. The only thing anyone asked of him was whether he was a newcomer, and he answered yes. He realized that this in and of itself was a kind of first step.

When the meeting was over, Leigh Ann gave him her contact information, just in case he ever needed her. "I already know how to get ahold of you, Leigh Ann."

"That's not what this is about," she said. "This is me telling you that I'm here for you, Nub."

Three more people did the same thing. They gave him their numbers and asked sincere questions about him. They did not probe, but they seemed genuinely interested in helping him. He told them nothing about himself. And they didn't press him.

Instead, everyone clapped his shoulders and encouraged him on his "journey." Never once did he sense these people were trying to get him to join an organization or convert him to a cult. He didn't get the sense they were after a new recruit. They were just offering to be his friend.

He chatted with people for a few hours, until the church janitor kicked everyone out. By then, the rain had stopped. The parking lot was mud. The sky was deep black. He saw Leigh Ann sitting on the church steps, stargazing.

"Welcome to AA," she said.

"Proud to be here," he said.

Minnie sat in the classroom of the Maranatha Home for Unwed Mothers along with ten other teenage expectant mothers. An educational film was playing. Her head was down because she was embarrassed just like everyone else was. Several of the girls were making ribald remarks to stave off the awkwardness. Others looked like they were trying to disappear.

The short animated feature was entitled *The Miracle of Childbirth*. Only the film did not depict many miracles but instead dealt with horror. The misery involved was astounding. How did the female race endure such suffering?

"Shh!" said Mrs. Beiderbecke to the girls. "Everyone pay attention. Eyes on the screen."

The old woman had shushed the class a million times, but it did little good. She had a four-foot-tall beehive hairdo that defied gravity and the personality of a communist dictator. She stood poised in the rear of the classroom, operating the projector, her glasses slung low on her nose, her eyes scanning the classroom for troublemakers.

The colors of the film were messed up and faded so that everything looked sickly rose-colored. It was narrated by a voice that sounded not unlike a male game show host.

"The fascinating story of childbirth begins with the wonderful miracle of menstruation . . ."

All the girls giggled.

"Menstruation begins with one particular gland at the base of the brain called the pituitary gland, and as a girl grows up, moving from playing with dolls to being interested in boys, this gland sends messages to the human body, messages that transform a young woman's body into a biological machine capable of childbearing."

Minnie lowered her head in embarrassment.

Playing with dolls to being interested in boys? This was pure agony.

The film featured animated illustrations of the female anatomy, complete with happy little cartoon character body parts that had faces. Currently the screen showed a cartoon of various hormones circulating through a female's bloodstream. The hormones looked like little flower petals caught in an updraft as they traveled throughout the limbs of an animated circulatory system.

"When a young woman begins menstruating, she undergoes the most poignant experience of her life. Her body and mind will be forever changed by the process of sexual reproduction and, eventually, the wondrous journey of motherhood."

The film's adventurous soundtrack played the sort of music that might have been more fitting for a Lewis and Clark documentary. Minnie learned that the *wondrous journey of motherhood* started with a tiny blastocyst. The cyst developed into a primitive placenta, which then turned into an advanced embryo, which then, ultimately, became a cartoon baby that looked like Casper the Friendly Ghost. After five weeks, the narrator said, a woman's breasts would become tender and fatigue would set in. All the girls in the classroom laughed at the word *breasts*.

Minnie touched her chest absently.

By seven weeks, the film said, the uterus would double in size and nausea would be experienced. By nine weeks, a woman's waist was already getting thicker and she was hungry all the time. By ten weeks, the baby had organs and was already a recognizable human being. So far, the film was dead-on. She had experienced all those things.

"*. . . You have a tiny person inside you.*"

Good Lord. A tiny person. She hadn't actually thought of it in those specific terms before. She had a *person* inside her. A real person. A person with ideas and desires and dreams and favorite foods and personality. It was both a terrifying and exhilarating thought.

By fourteen weeks, the film said the fetus would weigh one and a half ounces. By fifteen weeks, a baby's ocular abilities would be developing and the infant could already sense light and darkness. By sixteen weeks, the baby would begin doubling in weight, its skeleton thickening, changing from cartilage to bone. At nineteen weeks, a baby's auditory senses were emerging and the baby was capable of hearing sounds from outside the womb. At twenty-six weeks, the baby was already inhaling amniotic fluid, which was a dress rehearsal for breathing. At forty weeks, at least 280 days of pregnancy, the baby was born. And a human being emerged from the birth canal.

The animation showed a simplified depiction of childbirth. Minnie began to smile. Until now, she had only felt dread and sadness at the idea of being pregnant. All she could remember was Phillip Deener pressuring her into doing it and believing that she would be a selfish person for turning him down.

Moreover, Phillip swore that he loved her. And even though his declaration seemed phony, she bought it because she wanted to. For nobody had ever truly loved Minnie Bass. Phillip Deener made her believe—even if only for a few minutes—that he truly cared about her. He was going to protect her. He promised he wasn't just going to make love to her; he was going to make a *life* with her. His promises made Minnie's brain conjure visions of a little house with shutters and a dog. Minnie had cried bitterly when they finished making love, because she knew it hadn't been love. Not at all.

But right now, right here, she was having the thrilling realization that real love was indeed in her future. Not fake love. Not promises of love. Real love. She was going to have a child who would love her. And she would love her child. She already did. Also, Minnie was finally going to have a true purpose in life. And she would have a chance to give this child something she'd never had.

> *Love before her,*
> *Love behind her,*
> *Love above her,*
> *Love beneath her.*

Minnie was excited until the film depicted a baby-like object, about the size of a nine-pound bowling ball, passing through a vaginal channel that was roughly the size of a sippy straw.

Everyone in the classroom winced in unison.

Two young women had to excuse themselves. They left without even asking permission. Minnie, too, felt her stomach drop. She left the room before she retched all over the floor. She crashed into the bathroom, but the feeling of nausea, thankfully, had passed before she reached a stall. She leaned over a sink and splashed cold water onto her face. Then she stared at herself in the mirror for a few minutes.

Goodness. She was going to have a baby.

After several minutes, Minnie left the bathroom and went back to the classroom. She sat at her desk and finished the animated film, all the way until Casper the Friendly Ghost grew up to become Wally Cleaver. Mrs. Beiderbecke followed the film with question-and-answer time. The girls had hundreds of questions. Minnie asked several of her own.

How will it fit through the opening? What is a C-section? How will I know when my milk has come in? What is a breech? Will my doctor be a man or woman? Will I ever go back to the same size I was before? How long does it take to lose weight after I give birth? How can I tell if my baby is healthy? After that, the class was dismissed for supper. Minnie was on her way out the door when Mrs. Beiderbecke stopped her in the hallway.

The old woman smiled at her and said, "Minnie, I have some exciting news for you."

Minnie felt her heart sink. There was no such thing as "exciting" anything in this place. This home was a place for scared expectant girls, for doctor exams, for educational films. "What news?"

Mrs. Beiderbecke said, "You're going home, honey."

Minnie was stupefied. "Home?"

The old woman nodded. "You're going home. On Friday. You'd better start packing your things."

"But how?" Minnie furrowed her brow. "Ain't got no family. Ain't got no home."

Mrs. Beiderbecke placed a hand on her cheek. "Apparently you do."

CHAPTER

≈ 20 ≈

The oldest and biggest tree in Alabama was a live oak. It was two for the price of one. The tree was located in the town of Comb, Alabama, which was an hour north of Park. An itty-bitty town. Population 304. The tree was called the Old General, though nobody knew why. One theory held that Confederate General Bragg passed here during the Civil War and hung three of his own men from its branches. Another theory was that General Lee was smitten with the tree when he first laid eyes on it in 1864 on his way to Mobile.

Emily's junior biology class visited the tree every year because Emily loved it here. Not just the Old General but all the other twisting and turning live oaks on the property. She glanced out the window of the school bus as they neared the state park. The roadway was dotted with signs leading through the forest. The text carved in the brown wood read, "Four Miles to the Old General." She could see the field of writhing oaks in the distance, like circus contortionists.

Emily had been visiting this tree since childhood. Her father first brought her here when she was a toddler. She thought about this as the bus bucked and jumped over each divot in the road. She sat in the front seat, keeping her eyes on the highway so she wouldn't get motion sickness, but it was too late. Cheryl, the psychotic bus driver, was taking every bump as though she were auditioning for a Winston Cup Series. Emily gripped her seat, rocking and jerking from side to side until the bus stopped. Emily took a few deep breaths and tried not to puke.

She made a little speech to the class about what the day would entail. Emily told students where to empty their bladders, what their assignments were. She put them into groups and reminded them that the consequence for misbehavior was lethal injection. The usual stuff.

The class got off the bus, scattering in different directions. The troublemakers tried to sneak away from her line of sight. The studious kids brownnosed. The lust-crazed students who wanted to grab each other's hindparts found ways to evade her.

The Old General stood in the middle distance like a relic. The tree was close to six hundred years old. Maybe older. A *Quercus virginiana.* Older than America itself. At nearly eighty feet tall, the oak's gnarled bark was thick and scarred. The lime-green host ferns sprouting from the bark's surface made it look like a furry monster. The longest branch on the Old General was 129 feet long, snaking outward, plunging into the ground, where it made contact with the soil and grew right into the earth. Many of the branches were suspended by steel cables to prevent their own weight from tearing them off. The Old General had lost two branches recently. Large chunks were missing from the torso of the tree, where the amputations had been performed, the wounds tarred over by tree surgeons.

Each time she visited, Emily was always struck by how badly this tree had suffered during its lifetime. To be a tree was to suffer. That was part of the deal. The Old General's hardships were visible on its skin, and you could feel its distress with each scar. Lightning strikes. Floods. Droughts. Vehicles had struck the tree not once but three times. Heaven knows what other disasters visited this tree that had not been recorded. Thousands of children had probably climbed it and kicked it. Dead men had hung from its boughs.

A little plaque near the tree made of bronze, in bas-relief, bore the Alabama state seal and said something about how Andrew Jackson had once visited this oak in 1818. The plaque also told of how Roosevelt's daughter held her honeymoon here.

"Everybody form your groups!" Emily shouted.

The students congregated around the base of the Old General. Their duty today was to first calculate the age of the tree by measuring its girth. Emily had not told them how old the tree was. She had covered the informational plaque with a towel. Her class measured the base of the Old General using string and then multiplied the tree's circumference by 2.5, which was the average centimeters of growth per year. It wasn't rocket science. It was basic dendrology.

Next, the kids were charged with measuring the height of the tree by using sight and angles. The kids paced away from the trunk, pausing now and then to bend forward and look beneath their legs until they could see the tree's tippy top through their britches. They would mark this point on the ground where they stood, then measure the distance between themselves and the tree, which gave them a fairly precise height of the tree. Easy. And fun.

Emily sat on the lowest branch of the Old General and watched her students perform simple calculations while she replayed her own life in her head. She went scene by scene. Month by month. She had never known until now that she was filled with such a sense of regret. How could a person not know this about themselves? If you had asked her long ago, before her diagnosis, whether she had any regrets, she would have told you she had none. And she would have believed her own statement. But now she realized she regretted lots of things. Too many things to count.

She regretted not traveling to San Francisco. She regretted not eating more pizza because she didn't want to get fat. She regretted not ordering that extra glass of wine because she was afraid she'd turn out like her father. She regretted not cutting loose more often and not eating more chocolate. She regretted not taking more time off to do things she loved, like hiking. She regretted not making an effort to spend more time with Charlie Jr. She regretted not pursuing a meaningful relationship with an eligible man after her husband died. She regretted every moment she had ever spent doing cardiovascular exercise. She regretted not going fishing more often than she did, which was never.

Above all, she regretted the pitiful friendship she had with Jeremiah Lewis Taylor, a man who lived less than six miles from her front door but who had become only a casual acquaintance. For crying out loud, she was closer to her cleaning lady than she was to her father.

The relationship with her father was a strange thing. Through the years the relationship had festered and bubbled like a sore. At first, she had ignored her father out of spite. She made him a foreigner to punish him for not trying to be more a part of her life. *You don't want to see me?* she thought. *Fine, then I don't want to see you.* But over time, this neglect grew into something else. She convinced herself she didn't like him. But it wasn't true; she didn't hate him. He had problems, yes. But he also had qualities. He was whip-smart, for starters. And he was heart-stoppingly sincere. Even in dire circumstances when it would have served him better to be disingenuous, Nub

Taylor was sincere. His greatest quality, however, was that he had the audacity to be himself, for better or worse. Something she could never do. She was too busy being other people.

Emily regretted not emulating some of his better traits. She regretted not learning to play an instrument like him. She regretted giving her late husband so much ownership in who she became. She could have been teaching dendrology. At Auburn maybe. Or Troy. Or UAB. She could have become a tree surgeon. A conservationist. An ecologist. Instead, she had let it all go. For a man. And now there were no more chances for her. Now it was game over.

Funny. She had always thought she had more time. And that was what she grieved for most. Time. That was the lie she had grown up believing. She thought she had plenty of time. When the sour truth was, she didn't even possess the minutes she had right now. No one did.

One of the sophomores approached her. "We're all done, Mrs. Ives," said the eager female student.

Emily accepted the girl's paper and gave it a once-over. "Thank you, Crystal."

"What do I do now?" the student asked.

Emily studied the paper again, then shrugged. "You're finished."

The girl remained before her. "Can I do something for extra credit?"

Emily laughed. "No. You're through. Go look around the park; there are some really great trees here. Have some fun with your friends. We still have a few hours."

The studious girl's face fell. Crystal reminded Emily of the student she had been. The girl could not comprehend the esoteric concept of fun. She only understood goals. She understood hard work, achievements, and success.

"Get out of here, Crystal. Go talk to your friends. Go have some fun."

The girl hesitatingly said, "Okay, Mrs. Ives." Then the young woman walked away, her youthful ponytail swishing behind her. She soon joined her friends. Eventually, Emily could see them laughing and horsing around.

"Have as much fun as you possibly can," whispered Emily. *While you can.*

The man was sitting in the easy chair inside the dingy mobile home. The home—if you could call it that—was perched on 1,239 darkened acres of corn and cotton and alfalfa. The moon was high outside. The man was large. Not fat, but big. The Organization only hired big men to do the sorts of jobs he did.

He was watching *The Waltons* on a small black-and-white television. John-Boy was entering a writing contest, working on an essay with the help of his attractive teacher, Miss Hunter. John-Boy had the hots for Miss Hunter. Poor kid. It was a recipe for heartbreak. The episode was a late-night rerun. The man had seen this episode once before when it originally aired. He rarely missed an episode of *The Waltons*.

There was a rap on the trailer door before it swung open.

It was his partner returning with supper. KFC again.

He was sick of fried chicken.

"Oh boy," said the big man. "Kentucky Fried Rooster. Again."

"Listen," replied his Jersey-accented partner. "You wanna be in charge of dinner? Be my guest."

The big man showed full surrender. "I's only saying."

The men pulled up their chairs to the dinette. The trailer

was so small the two large men could hardly fit around the table without busting out windows with their shoulders.

"And it's not *dinner*," said the big man, reaching into the bucket. "How many times do I have to tell you, we say *supper* in this part of the world. *Dinner* means lunch."

His northern partner helped himself to a wad of coleslaw. KFC had crappy coleslaw. "I don't care what you people call it. It's the same thing."

The big man shook his head. "It ain't *you people*. It's *y'all*."

His coworker rose from the table and started fumbling through the kitchenette drawers for utensils. "I almost forgot," said New Jersey. "I got news from Bobby today."

"What news?"

"Shug's daughter's coming back this week."

The big man spoke with a mouthful. "Coming back? I thought she was in that state home."

"She was. But the state is sending her back here to live with somebody."

"You find out who with?"

His coworker removed a pitcher of iced tea from the tiny refrigerator and filled an acrylic glass. "Yeah, some old guy who owns a big farm outside of town. Not far from here. We'll go check it out after dinner."

"Supper."

"Whatever."

The big man nodded, then took another bite of his chicken. He watched his partner take a slug from his iced tea glass and wince in disgust.

"Sweet Jesus," said the Jerseyan, "this tea has sugar in it."

The big man shook his head. "Yankees."

Phillip Deener and his friend Craig were stealing beer from the coolers at the bowling alley. They were breaking into the kitchen, which wasn't very hard. All you had to do was pick the padlock secured to the back door. They had done it a bunch of times.

It wasn't that Phillip and his friend didn't have the money or the fake IDs to buy beer; it was that stealing the beer was more fun. Stolen stuff just tasted better than paid-for stuff. Plus, it was something to do.

The padlock clicked open. Phillip opened the rear door to the kitchen.

The boys crept into the galley and found the cooler in the back of the room, next to the three-compartment sink and the popcorn machine. Craig started horsing around and threw a handful of pretzel salt at Phillip. The salt hit Phillip in the face and stung his eyes. He swore loudly and socked his friend in the stomach. And he threatened to do worse.

Craig doubled over and gasped for air. "I was only kidding, Phil."

"You idiot. They'll find our mess tomorrow morning."

"So what? Nobody will know it's us."

Phillip's friend was a complete mouth breather. Phillip smacked him. "Use your head, dork. If there's a mess here tomorrow morning, what's going to happen next?"

Craig just stared at him. Phillip could swear he saw drool coming from the corner of his mouth.

"I'll tell you what will happen," said Phillip. "They'll start locking these doors with better locks, then they'll start watching the place to see if anyone breaks in. And then we can't get in here and take any beer."

"Okay. Jeez. I didn't think of it like that."

"Clean this mess up," said Phillip, who had always liked the way his voice sounded whenever he barked orders. He had big aspirations of someday maybe going into middle management.

Craig set to cleaning up the salt from the floor when he broke the news. "Did you hear Minnie Bass is coming back to town?"

Phillip stopped rummaging around in the cooler.

Craig went on. "My mom works at the courthouse on Wednesdays. She said she heard them talking about the Jolly Green Giant. She's coming back."

"Shut up. You're lying."

Craig shrugged.

Phillip thought about Minnie Bass. He should have known better than to mess around with a girl like her. Minnie was a deadly combination. She was a virgin and she was ugly. You give ugly girls like that a morsel of attention and you'll never get rid of them. They get clingy. They start talking about marriage and stuff. But then, Minnie had been so easy to conquer. And it had always been tough for Phillip to resist low-hanging fruit.

"But she doesn't have any family here," said Phillip. "Where's she going to live?"

Craig shook his head. "She's staying with that guy."

"What guy?"

"The old guy your dad beat up."

Phillip's friend wore a smirk. Craig was enjoying this a little too much.

"And that ain't even the best part," his friend said, staring right at him. "The best part is, Minnie's carrying your baby."

≈ **21** ≈

Minnie Bass sat sandwiched between Nub and Benny, a small suitcase on her crowded lap. She hadn't said a word since they had picked her up in Birmingham. The crud-covered F-100 rumbled past the little town at dusk. Past the IGA, the dry cleaners, the bakery, Killigan's Insurance office, Jerald's used car lot, the Chicken Shed, and the Best Little Hairhouse in Alabama beauty parlor. They sat at the train crossing, waiting quietly as steel-bodied boxcars clacked across the tracks, moving at turtle speed. The barricade arms held traffic at bay, inconveniencing the throng of impatient Dodges, Fords, and Chevys. Nub felt as awkward as he'd ever felt in his entire life. He had no idea what to say to this child.

He looked at Minnie. "You doing okay?"

He'd already asked this five times before, each time hoping for a more loquacious answer from the girl.

She nodded. "I'm good."

Silence in the Ford.

"Well," Benny said, "so am I. I'm good too."

The girl looked out the window again.

The train barricades lifted, and Nub kept driving.

The fields moved past the truck windows like a dead person's EKG. The road to the Taylor farm was a long, twisting, boring one. All dirt. Benny tried a few more conversational starters that all died quick deaths. The kid didn't want to talk. So Nub and Benny quit trying. When they reached Miller's Hill, Nub flicked his cigarette butt out the window and began to wonder if this was all a big mistake. Was it presumptuous of him to think this child wanted to live with him? Yes. The answer was yes. It was presumptuous. Incredibly presumptuous. They didn't know each other. They might not even like each other. He was an old man. She was a young girl. This was stupid, that's what it was.

They drove onward.

Six miles outside the city limits, within the hinterlands of central Alabama, sat Nub's two-story farmhouse. The home was positioned on a low hill amid a world of tallgrass and jimson weed. The chipped and faded home was built in 1879. The white siding had gone grayish brown. The formerly green tin roof looked black and rusty with corrosion. The shutters were crooked. The deceased porch swing was hanging by only one chain. His mother's old flower gardens had gone to seed. The old barn leaned sideways and had holes in it. A few outbuildings that were once used for tobacco curing back in the twenties were now home to North America's largest collection of wasp colonies.

The truck moved up the winding gravel driveway slowly. He looked at Minnie through the corner of his eye, gauging her reaction to his homeplace. Minnie's posture changed slightly when the house came into view.

"This is your house?" she said.

Nub stared at his family home and felt slightly embarrassed. "Is this a trick question?"

Nub's granddaddy bought this land after the war; his family built the home with their own hands. Nub's great-uncle bought the house from the Sears and Roebuck catalog for three hundred bucks. The builders used only hammers and nails. No handsaws were needed; all the boards were precut. All the workers had to do was put the puzzle together. The home had come delivered in a septillion pieces to the Birmingham Terminal Station. There was no rural mail service to Ash County in those days, so his father and uncles had to carry the shipment here from Birmingham one load at a time using a buckboard and mule. An arduous process that took about as long as earning a PhD.

"Just y'all two living here?" Minnie said.

"Y'all *two*?" said Nub.

She looked at Benny. "You and Mr. Nub?"

Nub laughed. "You think we live together?"

"Shoot," said Benny. "If I had to share a toilet with Nub, I'd move to Canada."

Nub parked the truck. He unloaded her luggage and gave her the grand tour of the ugliest house known to civilized man. There wasn't much to it. A parlor, a kitchen, three bedrooms, transom windows over each door to keep the air moving. No A/C, no central heat. He had a fireplace that housed many happy families of squirrels. He had ancient plumbing. Chipped plaster walls. Warped pine floors. And, of course, he had Wyatt the cat, who was currently serving a third term as president of this household. It wasn't much to offer the girl. But it was something.

"You'll be upstairs," said Nub. "Complete privacy. Never even have to see me if you don't want. You'll have your own space up there. Your own bathroom and everything."

"For reals?"

"For reals," said Benny.

"My own bathroom?"

Nub shrugged. "Eat supper in the shower if you want."

They went inside and he took her upstairs and introduced her to said bathroom. He flicked on the light. The white-tile room had seen better days, although he had just cleaned it. On the bathroom counter was a host of girly products, all the toiletries and makeup that a girl might need. Leigh Ann had purchased things from the hair-and-beauty section of the Kmart. There were smell-good soaps and fragrant lotions and brushes galore. Leigh Ann had told Nub to give her a hundred bucks and to ask no questions. And a few hours later, Leigh Ann showed up to his house with enough feminine beauty products to stage a beauty pageant.

"What's all this?" Minnie asked, touching a bottle of moisturizer, or lotion, or whatever the heck it was.

"That's, uh, skin stuff. Or it might be for your shoes. I don't really know."

"It's moisturizer," said Benny. "To treat dry and damaged skin."

"Is it for me?"

Benny laughed. "Well, it ain't for Nub."

Nub removed his cap to reveal a bald spot dotted with liver spots.

"It's all yours," said Benny.

She whispered, "For reals?"

Then Minnie placed a hand on the shower knob. "You got hot water here?"

Nub and Benny exchanged a look. "'Course we got hot water."

She turned the knob. Water came rushing out of the shower head, strong enough to take the skin off a chicken. She placed her hand in the spray and smiled. Nub was thinking maybe he had scored a point by paying his most recent water bill.

"Use all the hot water you want. It's on the house."

"Yeah," said Benny. "Nub never uses it. He only showers on leap years."

At the end of the tour, they stood in what was now Minnie's bedroom, which overlooked the front pasture. Nub watched the girl take in the surroundings as though it were the first time she'd ever seen a bedroom. The room had originally been the master bedroom. It was spacious, with a pitched ceiling. The centerpiece of the room was a stained glass picture window overlooking the Taylor farm. Minnie was drawn to the multicolored window. Everyone always was.

Minnie stood before the tinted panes and ran her finger along the welded lines between them. She stared at the acreage below them through a prism work of colors.

"My mama," Nub explained, "she loved stained glass. She made my father buy it for her. She said this window made her feel like she was in church."

Minnie didn't respond.

"Anyway, this place kind of grows on you."

"Sort of like athlete's foot," Benny said.

Minnie gazed out at the lonesome prairie. After a few minutes of quiet, Benny broke the stillness. He tapped on the windowpane.

"Looks like you got a visitor," he said.

All three of them looked out the window. A cloud of dust was preceded by a gray car speeding up the driveway. It was Emily's Buick Skylark. Her headlights were slicing through the air like flaming balls of fire. Her engine whined in the far off, rushing toward the home.

"Here comes Custer," Benny said.

"Who?"

"Your new sister," Nub said.

Emily was inside Nub's kitchen before he could get downstairs. She had bags of groceries with her too. Lots of bags. The brown IGA sacks rested on every flat surface, brimming with celery stalks, lettuce heads, banana bundles, and canned goods. She was already unloading the bags and placing items into their respective cubbies, slamming cupboard doors as though she lived here, when Nub entered the kitchen. She had also brought a casserole. A big one, in a blue cornflower casserole dish. She tossed open the oven door and slid the foil-covered supper inside.

"Make yourself at home," said Nub.

"I brought food," said Emily, closing the oven door with her butt. "Everyone get washed up. The casserole takes about thirty minutes to cook."

"Who are you, and what have you done with my daughter?"

Emily adjusted the oven dial. "Well, I didn't want her first meal in this house to be pork and beans with ketchup."

"That's not fair. We were going to have Hamburger Helper."

Emily smiled. "You don't have any hamburger."

"Usually Benny and I just eat the Helper."

"Why am I not surprised?"

"Why are you being so nice to me?" he asked.

"I'm not. I'm being nice to her. Big difference."

Nub rifled through a grocery bag. "Okay then. Why are you being so nice to her?"

"Because it's what I do, taking care of kids."

He decided not to mention anything about Minnie's pregnancy. He was already under enough scrutiny from Emily Ives as it was. She would learn of the girl's condition soon enough.

"I thought you said this was all a stupid idea."

"It is."

He opened a jar of newly purchased mustard and sniffed it. "You don't have to do this."

"I know."

"Then why do it?"

"Because I can see how important this is to you, Dad."

Nub swallowed the lump of clay in his throat. He did not deserve this young woman as his daughter. He never had.

"What would I ever do without you, sweetie?"

"I don't know, Dad, but you're going to have to figure it out."

Minnie was stuffed. Dinner was a lemon chicken casserole, finished with chocolate chess pie. Minnie had never even heard of chess pie before, but it was delicious. The whole meal was exquisite. Miss Emily had outfitted the table with pressed napkins. Yes, she *ironed* the napkins before you wiped your mouth on them. Minnie had never heard of such a thing. Minnie ate three slices of pie. She could have eaten six or seven, but she was trying to be ladylike. They even used special forks, which Emily called cake forks; they only had three prongs and looked like they were for Barbie dolls.

Afterward, everyone sat around and talked. Minnie took in the house one piece at a time as the conversation ebbed and flowed around her. There were 2,319 separate floorboards, not counting the closets. Twelve windows—three in front, two upstairs, one in each bathroom, five in the back. Nineteen interior steps and eight exterior steps, making for a total of twenty-seven, the perfect number. Maybe it was a sign.

That night she took a shower—in her own personal shower.

She let the hot water run all over her face and body until the water went cold, then she got out, dried off, and after waiting an hour took another one. It was almost too much greatness to bear. When she finished, she slipped on her nightgown and crawled into bed. Her bedsheets had roses printed on them. The sheets smelled like laundry detergent, the greatest smell on earth.

Minnie lay on her rose bed and closed her eyes. She actually fell asleep, to her surprise. A nice, restful sleep. Ever since her mother died, sleep had been elusive. The state psychologists and caseworkers said this was all normal. Plus, she was going through intense hormonal changes in her body. But tonight she slumbered like a slab of granite.

Until something woke her.

It was a faint noise, but it had stirred her from her sleep. She wiped the crust from her eyes and glanced at the clock in the corner. The short hand was just past the two. The sound was a faint ticking noise on the windowpane of her new room. The noise was so muffled she almost missed it. Now that she was awake, she could clearly hear the sound over the drone of the night insects.

Tick . . . Tick.

She rubbed her eyes. It took a moment to remember where she was.

The sound again.

Minnie tossed off the covers and padded toward the window. She tugged on her nightgown so that it covered her backside. She edged toward the glass and looked through the panes.

Tick, tick, tick.

In the darkness below, on the lawn, two figures were throwing pebbles at the window. It was too dark to see any characteristics on these figures, but they were clearly male. She could tell that much. She could not tell whether they were grown men or teenagers. She couldn't see their hair color or their facial features. The men, apparently, could see that Minnie was watching them, because the next rock sailed through the stained glass window and shattered it. An explosion of multicolored shards sprayed onto the floor along with a rock the size of an egg.

Minnie scrambled backward and huddled on her bed. The next rock was even bigger than the previous one. About the size of a baseball. Another window shattered. She felt a surge of icy fear overtake her, followed by confusion, followed by a host of other emotions for which she had no names.

She curled into the fetal position. She pressed her knuckles so firmly into her open mouth against her teeth that her knuckles were bleeding.

Welcome to Papk.

CHAPTER

≈ 22 ≈

Nub shot upright in bed and looked at the alarm clock. It read 2:17 a.m. The sound that woke him was coming from the kitchen. Nub swung his feet over the edge of the bed and rubbed his eye sockets vigorously. He tugged on his jeans and staggered down the hall in his bare feet. On his way, Wyatt leaped in front of him, speeding around his oncoming feet in a valiant attempt to break Nub's neck. Wyatt landed atop the grandfather clock and resumed his feline perch.

When Nub entered the kitchen, the room looked empty. Until he found Minnie huddled against the refrigerator, crouched, clutching a large kitchen knife in both hands, like she was going to decapitate him.

He blinked.

"I take it you're not a morning person."

"I heard someone coming. I didn't know it was you, Mr. Nub."

He looked around himself. "Do other people live here?"

She was trembling.

"What's wrong with you?" he said.

She wouldn't answer. Her nostrils flared with each inward breath. He eased close to her and rubbed her shoulders, but she was shaking violently. He led her to the table. She was still clutching the knife with both hands.

"You want to tell me what the knife is for, Mr. Ripper?"

"Don't worry. I ain't going to kill you."

"I'm touched."

He waited for more explanation, but she did not add anything. So he walked toward the stove and began the coffee ceremony. The percolator on the range was filled with three-day-old cold Folgers. Just the way he liked it. He poured a cup of cold brew, then returned to his seat across from Minnie. He massaged his cheeks and lit a morning Lucky. Minnie pushed the ashtray toward him, which was a nice gesture. Normally Nub never thought about ashtrays until the ash grew to three inches long and started burning his vitals.

He tapped his ash. "So what *are* you planning to do with the knife?"

"Someone was here."

He exhaled a cloud.

"I'll bite. Who?"

"I don't know. But they broke a window."

"What?"

"In my room. The pretty colored window. They broke it."

"You're kidding. I didn't hear any windows break."

"You were snoring pretty loud."

"I don't snore."

"Well—"

Minnie was about to say something when they were interrupted by a crash. The window beside the kitchen table shattered. A waterfall of glass shards filled the room. A heavy brick hit the floorboards and skidded among broken pieces.

"Get down!" he shouted.

He threw himself at Minnie and placed her body beneath

his. They waited on the floor for a while until he was satisfied nothing else was going to happen. Nub Taylor's temper flared like powder in a flashpan. He grabbed the knife from her hands.

"Stay here."

Nub rushed outside. The prairie behind the Taylor home was vast. In the 1920s, everyone in Park farmed tobacco. These fields were once loaded with fragrant shade tobacco, the kind of tobacco used for the outside wrappers of cigars, which turned a decent profit in the olden days until the tobacco market changed and moved operations to South America, bankrupting a lot of good American men. Today the pasture was just a bunch of fescue and tallgrass.

"Who's out there?" he shouted, still gripping the knife.

His wind chimes rattled in the slight breeze. He stepped off the porch and looked around the yard. He saw nothing but bits of old garbage. An old muffler dead in the weeds. A bicycle that had belonged to some faceless child from the past who might have been him. A dead stack of Goodyears.

He looked inside the old chicken coop but found it empty. He checked the woodshed. Next he opened the large slat door to the barn and it creaked open with a loud whine. The barn smelled of gasoline and dirt. The unique smell of all car barns. In the darkness, he could make out his old '20 Packard sitting beneath the rafters, covered in corrosion. The Packard he'd taken to the *Opry* when he was a young man.

"Who's in here?"

The faint creaking of the barn door in the light breeze.

"I said, who's in here?"

Nothing.

"You're going to pay for my windows."

He waited, listening for movement or breathing.

"You got a lot of nerve, whoever you are."

After a few minutes of waiting, he decided the barn was indeed empty. He was about to leave when he heard something. A clatter in the corner. Nub felt his blood pressure spike into the danger zone. He squeezed the knife handle tightly and held it outward. Something darted past him. Something small. It was Wyatt. The cat shot out the open door and into the darkness. He could see Wyatt's little yellow eyes, like demonic reflectors in the dim light. Men have had strokes under less startling circumstances.

Crickets were singing outside. The moon was visible through a slim gap in the barn roof. He gave the barn a thorough search, just in case he missed something. He climbed up the ladder and looked into the haymow. He inspected the corn crib. Then he opened the front door to the Packard and saw one of his mother's old quilts that had been stored in the barn. The blanket was lying on the vinyl seat, along with a throw pillow. There was also a large, human-sized divot in the vinyl upholstery. He placed his hand on the divot. It was warm.

Nub closed the Packard door.

He noticed a collection of footprints in the dirt beneath him. They were leading toward the rear of the barn. He followed the prints outside and toward the back door. He exited the barn and followed the trail to an old path that led into the woods.

He called into the night, "I know you're out there."

He could hear the sounds of footfalls in the brush. Someone was running away from him. Quickly. He gave chase for exactly ten seconds before he was overtaken by a coughing fit. He crouched over to catch his breath and realized that his daughter had been absolutely right.

He was not even remotely ready for this crap.

After Nub cleaned shards of glass from the floor of the kitchen, Minnie showed him the broken window upstairs, and he made her stay in the kitchen while he cleaned up that mess too. The windows would cost an arm and a kidney to replace. He didn't have that kind of cash. The window in his mother's bedroom had been the kind of antique glass you couldn't afford to have replaced unless you had a few roman numerals after your name. He fashioned window covers out of duct tape and garbage bags for each broken window, which really dressed up the house, then he sent Minnie back to bed.

When he was finished with his makeshift repairs in the kitchen, he showered and changed for work. He drank three more cups of coffee, did the crossword puzzle, then read through the *Advocate* twice, trying to get his mind off the adrenal experience of the morning. Finally, he looked at his watch and called to Minnie.

Minnie wandered downstairs with her new book bag on her back, clutching another knife in both hands.

"Where do you keep getting knives?"

She shrugged. "From your drawers."

He held out his hand. "You're going to have to give me that thing before you go to school, you realize that. They're kind of funny about taking cutlery to school."

He had enrolled her a week earlier per the state's requirements. Well, technically, Emily had enrolled her. Actually, it was Emily who filled out the paperwork, then bought school supplies and an entire wardrobe for the child. Minnie was wearing a blue dress that fit her perfectly. The dress went nicely with her red Converse.

She placed the blade into his hand, handle first. "I'm afraid they'll come back."

"Who's *they*?"

"I don't know. All I know is there were two of them out there."

"Was one of them Phillip Deener?"

"I don't know. I couldn't see who they was."

"You'd tell me if it was him, wouldn't you? You wouldn't try to protect your boyfriend or anything like that, would you?"

She shook her head unconvincingly.

"How did you get mixed up with a mule-brain like him?"

She looked at her shoes. "He came into Waffle House one night with his friends. He was nice to me."

"That kid knows how to be nice?"

"He said he loved me."

"And you believed him?"

Minnie was embarrassed.

The sun was finishing its climb in the eastern sky. After Minnie ate a big bowl of Cocoa Puffs, they exited the house and got into the truck. Wyatt had followed them into the truck, much to Nub's surprise.

"What do you think you're doing?" Nub said to the cat.

"He keeps following me around," said Minnie.

Nub had never seen his cat try to get in the truck before. He tried to shoo the animal away, but Wyatt wasn't moving.

"Can he come with us?" Minnie asked.

The black cat sat between them, staring at the windshield, as if to say, "Let's get this show on the road."

"I'm sorry, sweetie," said Nub. "Wyatt has chores to do here at the house." He reached for the cat to pick the animal up. Wyatt bit him violently.

Nub swore loudly.

"See?" said Minnie, suppressing a laugh. "He's protecting me."

Nub licked his finger. The cat had drawn blood.

"Yeah, well, who's protecting me?" Nub said.

Wyatt just looked at him and dared him to try again.

"That cat is possessed," he said.

The truck was dead, so he had to roll-start it by pushing the heavy vehicle down the driveway and leaping inside the rolling automobile at precisely the last moment. The truck engine fired to life just before the vehicle careened into his mailbox. They began their drive toward school, riding in silence.

He had picked one helluva time to stop drinking.

"You're late," Emily said.

When Nub pulled to the curb of the school, Emily was waiting for him. The dutiful little biology teacher. She looked impatient, upset, and so very lovely.

"You're late," she said again, approaching Nub's open window and tapping her wrist even though she wore no watch.

"How many times are you going to say it?" He rubbed his tired eyes. "I'm dandy, by the way. Thanks. How are you?"

"Dad, Minnie is already going to have enough trouble catching up as it is. Being late only makes things worse for her. This can't happen again. I need you to promise me."

"I swear, *mein Führer*."

"Dad."

"Hey, I thought I was on my own with all this stuff. I thought you didn't want to help."

She stared at him.

He held his hands up in mock surrender.

"You think this is all a joke?" she said.

"Heavens, no." Nub dug a carton from his pocket. "You never joke." He clicked his lighter shut and released a cumulus of blue fog. "Truth is, we had kind of a weird morning at our house."

"What's that mean?"

He looked at Minnie, who was still in the seat beside him. "Why don't you go on into school before Miss Emily has a coronary right here in front of us and we have to call the paramedics."

"Yes, sir, Mr. Nub," Minnie answered.

"And don't call me sir," he said. "Or Mister."

"Yes, sir."

Minnie jumped out and slammed the door. The door's hinges squealed shut like a dying dog. She walked into the school the same way one might walk into their own memorial service. On her way into the school, none of the other students spoke to Minnie or even acknowledged her.

"What is all this about?" Emily said.

"You're not going to believe me when I tell you."

Emily crossed her arms tightly.

"Someone threw a brick through my kitchen window. Threw rocks at Minnie's bedroom last night too. Broke three windows. Broke the Tiffany glass in your grandmother's bedroom."

"What?"

"I woke up and found Minnie in the corner, holding a kitchen knife, like she was going to castrate me."

"Dad. What?"

"That ain't all. Someone's been sleeping in my barn. Sleeping in the old Packard. I don't know who it is." His eyes followed

Minnie as she entered the school building. "Someone wants to either scare her or scare me. Or both."

"You think it's Phillip?"

"I can't think of who else hates me more. Except for maybe his old man. Or perhaps your mother."

Emily began chewing her thumbnail, a habit she had started as a child. A habit her grandmother had tried to break her of by dipping her thumbs in Christmas-scented candle wax. It never worked. Emily's teeth were always pine-green as a kid, and her breath smelled weird.

"I tried to warn you, Dad. This poor girl's got issues you aren't equipped to deal with. This is above your skill level."

"These aren't her issues, sweetie. This is some jerk harassing her. This ain't her fault."

"What are you going to do?"

"I have no idea."

"Well, you'd better work this out, Dad."

The bell rang. The clanging sound transformed her into Teacher Emily. Now she was all business.

She turned back to him. Her voice was more serious this time. "How are you doing lately?"

He knew what she was getting at, and he knew what she wanted to hear in response.

"Sweetie, your father is the best customer Coca-Cola has ever had."

"How long has it been?"

"Twenty-one days since my last."

She made no remark. No congratulations. He didn't blame her. He didn't deserve praise. He didn't want praise. He just wanted her to know where he was.

She said, "Have you talked to someone about what happened this morning?"

"Like who? United Way? I'm talking to you about it right now. It just happened. I haven't had time to sort it out."

"You need to call the police. Call Gordon Burke."

"My favorite guy."

The bell rang for the final time.

"I don't care what you do, Dad. Just do something. I don't have time to deal with your problems *and* mine. I'm finished cleaning up your messes. I need you to understand that, okay?"

He looked at her and yanked the truck into gear. "And to think I was glad when you learned to talk."

CHAPTER

23

Nub called the sheriff's department, but nobody was around to answer any questions except Mae Beth, who was old enough to own an autographed Bible. She was his mother's second cousin. Nub cracked open a bottle of Coca-Cola and took a pull while Mae Beth talked at great length about her daughter's recent shoulder surgery. After that, she talked about her grandchildren, which took even longer, as Mae Beth had given birth to three quarters of Ash County. She and her husband, Arnold, had taken the command to be fruitful and multiply personally.

After the long introduction, he got around to telling her what had happened this morning. When he finished telling the story, Mae Beth was silent for a beat.

"Well, that certainly doesn't sound good," she said.

"I couldn't agree more, Mae Beth."

"You think it could be some school friends of hers?"

"She doesn't have friends."

"She was Phillip Deener's girlfriend. I'd call that friends, wouldn't you?"

"How old is Phillip?"

"Same age as the girl. I think he's a freshman."

"What's he like?"

"Who, Phillip? Oh, he's a real charmer. We picked him up once for beating up Jeremy Tyson. He had to spend the night in the clink. His daddy wasn't happy about that."

Jeremy Tyson was a young man with a speech impediment who used a cane to walk. Anyone who picked on Jeremy Tyson was a kid with problems.

"So he's a bad kid."

"Your words, not mine. You might have bitten off more chaw than you can chew with that girl, Nub. She comes from a screwed-up family."

"Don't we all."

"Not like her. Her father's doing life in prison."

Nub sighed. Mae Beth went on, "Look, it's probably just high schoolers horsing around on your property. I'll send Gordon out there tonight to check things out if it makes you feel better."

"Yes. Thank you. It will be so nice to see Gordon again."

"If anything else happens, you call us back. Or like we always say around here, you can always call Smith and Wesson. It ain't like Phillip Deener doesn't have it coming. I mean, don't kill him; just shoot him in the leg or something. But you didn't hear this from me."

"You're all heart, Mae Beth."

After he hung up with her, he called Glenn Barker, city councilman. Nub's boss. He told Glenn he was sick and unable to make it to work today.

"You're bailing out on me today?" said Glenn. "I need you. You're supposed to be painting the fence at Reynold's Park."

"I'm sorry, Glenn. I've got a fever." He coughed for effect. The coughing fit started out fake but immediately became real. Nub Taylor had been smoking unfiltereds since he was sixteen.

"You're really sick?"

"As a dog."

"Okay, what's your temperature?"

Nub hesitated. "One hundred and . . . and one."

"You're lying. You got the brown bottle flu again is what you got."

"No, Glenn. I've been trying to quit all that."

"Bull."

Nub gave no reply.

He heard Glenn groan in disgust. "Well, I guess that means Tonto won't be coming to work either?"

"Actually, I'm Tonto. Benny's the one who gets to ride Silver."

"I doubt that very much. Does this have something to do with that girl you adopted?"

"I'm sick, Glenn. This has to do with me being sick."

"Whatever." Then he hung up.

Nub crawled into the Ford, drove into town, and picked up Kemosabe. Then they drove out of Park, heading north, toward Ambassador, following the soupy roads of mud that cut through the foothills of southern Appalachia.

"Where are we going?" asked Benny.

"We are going to see an old friend."

Emily had taken a sick day at school. She drove through interstate traffic until she reached the doctor's office in Reed City. The brick medical building. The doctor's office was located on the fourth floor. The elevator had windows in it so you could feel your bowels drop into your feet as you shot upward.

She checked in, and the receptionist told her to have a seat in the waiting room, then judiciously avoided eye contact with

Emily for the next hour. The doctor's waiting room is a misery unto itself. It's a room where your thoughts and fears run free, horsewhipping you into a full-blown panic. The waiting room is worse than the actual appointment by far. Emily had this sinking feeling that she shouldn't be here without her mother. Or Charlie Jr. Or someone to support her. Even her father would have sufficed. But the last thing she wanted was to let her family in on this. Cancer was her secret.

If Emily Ives was going to die, she was going to do it her way.

She patted her thigh out of nervousness. A few times she attempted to read a *Highlights* magazine but found herself too preoccupied to even focus on the pictures. Part of her Type A-ness was anxiety. She knew this. Angst came with the territory. But she had never experienced anxiety this crippling before.

The doctor appeared in the waiting room doorway. Her thigh-patting stopped. He called her into his office.

Emily rose. She took in a breath. She entered the doctor's den and sat across from the desk. The room smelled of disinfectant and cheap cologne. The obligatory leather-bound volumes rested on the shelves. Did doctors actually read those things? There was a pipe in his ashtray. A window overlooked several nearby rooftops in Reed City. The doctor shut the door behind him and allowed her a few moments to take in her surroundings.

He sat behind his grand desk and folded his hands. Emily could tell by the look on his face that this second opinion was not going to be a good one.

The doctor forced a smile. "How do you feel today, Mrs. Ives?"

She shrugged. "Can we just get to the point?"

He nodded. "You wrote down in your history that you've lost some weight. Is it lack of appetite? Do you notice that you're not hungry?"

Emily frowned. "Maybe a little."

The doctor made a note and nodded. He put down his pencil and removed his glasses. "The weight loss could be from stress. How are your stress levels?"

"Well, let's see. They told me I'm dying, so . . ."

He removed a large X-ray film, then he drew in a large inhalation and heaved it outward, like he was getting ready to do something he didn't want to do. "I'm not good at words, Mrs. Ives. In my experience, I've found that just coming out and saying it is the best way. For your benefit. For everyone's benefit."

And he did.

His words hit like a brick. His diagnosis was worse than the first. She could only look out his window when he finished speaking. She could only breathe in and out.

"So I'm dying."

"The problem is," he began, "breast cancer is almost always diagnosed too late. We have a real deficit in our health-care system for this sort of cancer. We have the tools to diagnose it, but we don't. There are no excuses."

She closed her eyes. "Treatment options?"

He took another breath and looked at his hands.

"I'm sorry, Mrs. Ives. I really am so sorry."

Benny asked where they were going for the fifth time. Nub gripped the steering wheel tightly, too lost in thought to answer. The truck bucked over each pothole on Route 4 and felt like it was about to rattle apart into a collection of bolts and nuts. The scenery changed from open pastures to thick woods, to a forest that was more black than it was green.

Deadly straight longleafs lined the roads, suffocating all remnants of daylight. The truck struggled to breathe as it ascended hill after hill into mountain country. They exited Ash County and crossed the line into Blount County. Soon they were in a remote place where residents had to mail-order sunshine from Montgomery Ward.

"Are you going to tell me where we're going?" said Benny.

No answer. Nub was too busy thinking. And fuming.

They spent nearly thirty minutes stuck behind a John Deere that was driving approximately two miles per hour. The road was clay, top-dressed with gravel, and had been turned into a giant National Co. washboard by recent snows and rains. The truck bounced so hard Nub's jaw hurt.

The kid driving the Deere was bundled in a Carhartt and a watch cap. He kept waving his arm, motioning for Nub to pass. But Route 4 was too narrow for passing, with cavernous drainage ditches on either side that were begging to swallow a midsized Ford. So they loped gently behind the Deere for several bumpy miles, listening to Hank Senior sing about cheating hearts and Tanya Tucker sing about Delta Dawn wearing flowers.

When the tractor finally pulled off, Nub draped an arm out the window and gave the driver the two-fingered wave. The farmer waved back because everyone waves in the country.

Don Gibson's voice came onto the radio and began singing "Give Myself a Party." And this song triggered something inside Nub, who wished he was drunk.

"You ever play guitar anymore?" asked Benny.

"No."

"You ever think about playing again?"

"Never do."

"Really? You never miss playing with the fellas?"

Nub stared forward.

They finally arrived at a craftsman-style home in the middle of the woods. The house looked like it was falling down. The front yard was a shoulder-high sod farm. A footpath led past a graveyard of dead appliances, dry-rotted toys, a dead swing set, and a Studebaker on blocks. Nub took a few steadying breaths, leaped out of the truck, and left it idling.

"Who lives here?" said Benny.

"Just wait in the truck."

Benny shrugged. "Call my name if you run into any trouble."

"That gives me such peace of mind, Benny."

Nub knocked on the door with a friendly tap. Nobody answered, so he beat on the door again. This time it was no *tap, tappity, tap.* This time it was *boom, boom, boom.* The door opened, and a kid stood before him. He was tall, skinny, with crow-black shaggy hair. He was wearing pajamas, like he just woke up. Nub had expected to talk to the kid's mother; he expected Phillip Deener to be at school. But sometimes the universe smiles on you.

"Hiya, Phil. Remember me?"

The kid rubbed his eyes. "What do you want?"

"Is your mother home?"

"No. Nobody's home but me."

"How about your dear old dad?"

"He's at school."

"Well, how about that."

The kid's face drooped and he took one step back. Nub hung in there.

"I want to ask you a few questions, Phillip."

"About?"

"Oh, I think you know."

"Know what?"

"What'd you do last night?"

Phillip glared at him.

"Did you know Minnie Bass is pregnant?"

The look on Phillip's face told the whole story.

"So? What's that got to do with me?"

Nub leaned in. "Do I need to explain how the birds and bees work?"

The kid broke eye contact just long enough to imply guilt. "It's not mine."

"So it was immaculate conception. You trying to start a new world religion, Phil?"

"Did Minnie say it was mine? Because if she did, she's lying. She's been with tons of guys; it could be anybody's."

Nub bent down and picked up an orphaned roller skate lying on the porch. A leather shoe with orange wheels. Nub lobbed it through the front window. The window shattered beautifully. He had the kid's full attention now.

"What'd you do that for?" Phillip said.

"Effect."

"You're crazy."

"Correct."

Phillip tried to close the door, but Nub placed a boot in the way. He kneed the door open. Phillip fell backward on the floor, and Nub stepped inside. He picked up the roller skate that was lying in the middle of the pile of shattered glass.

"You broke our window. My dad's going to be mad."

Nub weighed the skate in his hand. "Were you at my house this morning?"

"What?"

Nub took a few more steps forward until he was standing over the kid. "I'm going to ask you one more time, Phillip, and then I'm going to get very mad. I'm not mad yet. *This* isn't mad. Do you understand me? Mad is very bad. You don't want mad."

The kid nodded. "Okay."

"Were you at my house this morning?"

Phillip didn't answer the question, so Nub took the roller skate and aimed it at a console television playing in the corner. The TV practically exploded.

"Hey!" shouted Phillip. "Quit it! I'm calling the cops. You're already in enough trouble after what you did to my dad."

Nub grinned. He was nose to nose with the kid.

"Go ahead. Let's call the cops. In fact, I'll even dial the number for you. Let's have a nice long conversation with the police. Let's get them over here and talk about what the law says about child support and paternity tests. What do you say?"

The kid didn't move.

"It's not mine."

"If you come near my house again, if you mess with Minnie, you will go down, Phillip Deener. Nod once if you understand me."

The kid nodded.

Nub patted his head. "Good boy. Now, get off the floor. I think you need to change your trousers."

Nub returned to the truck and slammed the truck door.

"How'd it go?" said Benny.

Nub threw the Ford into Reverse. "It went."

They rolled along the miles of county dirt, acres of golden stubble passing by like a smudged Thomas Cole painting. The ash trees were poised against the powder-blue sky and the sun was unobstructed. Nub waited for his blood pressure to lower, but it didn't. It had been a long time since he'd felt the hotness of his own anger without alcohol to dull its spiked edges.

He pulled the truck into his long-winding dirt drive, then

threw the truck into Neutral to check his mailbox, which was full. Junk, junk, and more junk. He drove up to his lonely house, tires crackling on the gravel. And something was wrong.

"Look," said Benny, pointing.

The front door to his home was wide open.

Nothing in Nub's house appeared to have been disturbed. A cross breeze blew through the rooms. The back door and front door were both open. Nub and Benny stood in the kitchen, stock-still. But something was wrong. Someone had been inside this house. The air was different too. Nub could feel someone in here.

Nub pointed upward to the ceiling.

Benny nodded and mouthed, "Upstairs?"

Nub nodded.

They kept their eyes on the ceiling as though it were going to reveal some important clue. They entered the den together. Slowly. Trying not to make clopping noises on the floorboards. The sound of the grandfather clock's pendulum was the only other noise in the home.

Wyatt sat atop the clock, staring down at them, whipping his tail, looking very much like Satan. They climbed the stairs. When they reached the top step, Wyatt was already entangling himself around Benny's lower legs. Benny hated cats, which made Wyatt love him all the more. It was a cat thing.

Nub inspected the upstairs rooms but saw nothing amiss. He flipped on the light to his mother's old sewing room. When he opened the closet, he felt Benny's breath on his neck and turned to see Benny standing behind him, holding a baseball bat cocked over his shoulder.

Nub looked at him. "Where'd you get that thing?"

"Found it downstairs."

"Well, back up a little. You're scaring me."

"I'm protecting you."

"That's what scares me."

They walked into Minnie's room next. It was immaculate. Her bed had been made. The new clothes he'd bought her had been folded squarely in her closet.

Nub was about to speak when he heard a faint noise on the staircase, as though someone was tramping down the stairs. How this person had managed to get past him was a mystery. He must have been hiding in the closet.

The two old men raced down each step as fast as two in the final quarter of their lives could move. The kitchen screen door was wide open. Nub tore out the open door and jogged into the tall grass for a better look, but there was nothing to see. It was just prairie.

He rubbed his face and tried to get his blood moving, tried to catch his breath. He swore.

"Who do you think it was?" said Benny, breathless from exertion.

Nub doubled over to breathe. He felt like he was going to puke. His lungs burned. His head was spinning and he was dizzy. He did not have the stamina to even answer his cousin.

They walked back to the house. Although *limped* might be a more accurate way to describe it. When he got into the kitchen, there were three crisp hundred-dollar bills on the kitchen table.

Nub and Benny stared at the money.

"I'm too dang old for this," Nub said.

"For reals," said Benny.

CHAPTER

～ 24 ～

Minnie's first week of school was nearly over and it had been difficult. Very difficult. Worse than she had expected. Nub had been called into the principal's office three times. At this point, it was a rarity when he *wasn't* called into the office.

Minnie usually sat outside the offices during these conferences and listened to her teachers explain to Mr. Nub why Minnie was getting harassed. They had all sorts of reasons to explain the problems, but Minnie knew that some kids just got picked on more than others. High school was a dog pack. Dogs went after the weak.

Minnie could hear Mr. Nub and Miss Rhonda, her homeroom teacher, speaking through the thin walls. She heard Mr. Nub say, "How can kids be so cruel?" She heard Miss Rhonda answer, "I don't think the students are trying to be cruel, Mr. Taylor. I think they're just experimenting with their boundaries."

On the second day of school someone put a snake in Minnie's locker. There was another incident when someone stole Minnie's clothes during PE class and she had to borrow clothes. She had to finish the day wearing skimpy shorts and a T-shirt that was too small. That got a lot of laughs.

During a music class yesterday, Phillip Deener had pinched her backside and called her a terrible name. She couldn't believe that someone who had claimed to love her was now filled with so much bitterness and hatred for her. Minnie threw a wooden marimba at the boy. The marimba splintered on the floor, and the school made Nub pay for it. Mr. Nub was thrilled about that.

She was thinking about this when Phillip Deener himself came walking past the offices. He was with his friends; they all wore team jerseys.

She avoided eye contact.

As one of the young men passed by, he called her a very bad name.

The other boys smirked at her. These were toadies who did whatever Phillip did. If Phillip ran headfirst into a stone wall, his pals would draw straws to see who got to sprint into the wall next. Not an original thought in their stupid heads.

One of the boys told a dirty joke as they passed by. The other boys laughed even though they probably didn't get it.

And it was all she could take.

Minnie stood up, drew in a deep breath, and positioned herself in the center of the hallway so they couldn't pass. She was staring over their heads like an adult in the kiddie pool. Minnie could feel her whole body trembling with adrenaline.

They just stared at her.

"What?" said one kid.

"Tell your little joke again. I want to hear it."

The boys all looked at each other. More snickers.

"Why are you so obsessed with me?" said Phillip. "You're not my type, Herman Munster." Then he called her a bad name.

"I'm carrying your child."

"You're carrying someone's bastard," said Phillip. "But it ain't mine."

Minnie did not think. She just reacted. She reached outward with both hands and pinned Phillip's arms to his sides.

"Get off me!"

With both arms clamped to his sides, Phillip was defenseless against her. He shouted as he kicked his feet. Minnie carried him, kicking and screaming, toward the door.

"Stop!" came the voice of a teacher. It was Miss Rhonda. Miss Rhonda and Nub were running from the office. The two adults raced down the hallway.

"Put him down right now, Minnie!" said Miss Rhonda.

Minnie hesitatingly did as she was told. Phillip's feet hit solid ground. His clothes were askew. His hair was disheveled. He shoved Minnie as hard as he could in a feeble attempt to salvage his threadbare pride.

"I can't believe you would do such a thing, Minnie!" said Miss Rhonda. The woman's voice was quavering with righteousness. "This is appalling. I'm shocked at you. Shocked at you all."

The woman was yelling now.

"I can't understand what's gotten into all of you! And I'm *especially* disappointed in you, young lady. You ought to know better than this."

Nub touched Miss Rhonda's shoulder. "Don't be so disappointed, sweetie. I think Minnie was just exploring her boundaries."

Nub placed his groceries onto the IGA conveyor belt. Minnie stood beside him, silent as a stump. She hadn't said much since the incident at school. Benny stood near the magazines, reading a *Cosmopolitan*, thumbing through the pages, looking at the pictures. The conveyor belt ushered Nub's grocery items toward the register. An extremely tall man with faded hair and a gaunt frame was bagging their groceries.

"There is no way one man eats this much pork and beans," said Miss Janet, the cashier, punching numbers on the register. "Does Emily know how poorly you're eating?"

"Emily's not my mother."

The old woman looked over her wire-rimmed glasses at him. "Well, someone ought to be."

Nub transferred the remainder of his items from the basket to the belt. There were sardines packed in ketchup sauce, two loaves of bread, four packages of Oscar Mayer bologna, a package of Limburger cheese, six cans of Vienna sausages, two cartons of Lucky Strikes, and a bag of cat food. He yanked the *Cosmopolitan* magazine from Benny's hands and threw it onto the conveyor belt too.

"Happy Hanukkah," Nub told him.

Miss Janet zeroed in on the girly magazine with serious eyes. Miss Janet was the oldest surviving member of the Primitive Baptist Church in Park. She had also been Nub's and Benny's fifth-grade teacher. Nub still remembered when she would grip her lectern like Billy Sunday, educating the class on the key points of predestination and everlasting hellfire. Theirs was the only class in Ash County that had altar calls.

Miss Janet read the headline aloud. "'How to Get Him to Love You Like a Mistress'?" The old woman stared at them both without moving a facial muscle.

Nub jingled the change in his pockets.

Miss Janet slapped the magazine onto the belt. "Shameful."

"Benny's a growing boy," said Nub.

Behind them was Georgianna Rodgers. Georgianna was tall, elegant, and wearing a small pillbox cap even though it was an average Saturday night and nobody had recently died. Her buggy contained enough food to compromise the integrity of the supermarket's foundation. Her toddler granddaughter was sitting in the cart, dutifully picking her nose.

"That's a lot of beans," said Georgianna.

"So everyone keeps telling me," said Nub. "I didn't know so many people cared about my dietary fiber consumption."

Nub watched Georgianna's little granddaughter dig into her nasal cavity. The kid was up to her elbows. "Cute kid."

Georgianna was old money. She was the kind of woman who did not leave the house—not even to check the mail—without wearing pearls, pumps, and a prodigious dusting of bath powder. She gave Minnie a look that was supposed to be maternal, he supposed.

Nub introduced them. Georgianna gave a plastic smile. "Oh, I already know this young woman, Nub. Her mama used to work for us, a long time ago. And I think it's very Christian what you're trying to do here, opening your home to this child."

"That's because you ain't seen my home," said Nub.

"We can all imagine it," said Miss Janet.

Georgianna placed a jar of mayonnaise on the belt. Miracle Whip. You had to worry about a person who used Miracle Whip.

"How is Emily's fever?" Georgianna said.

The words hit him out of left field. He knew nothing of a fever. He only knew about the fever he himself had faked earlier that week.

"Emily's fever, or mine?" he said.

"Mary Finlay told me Emily had a fever. She said Emily wasn't at school today. Said her fever was pretty bad."

"Oh, that fever. She's doing much better," said Nub. "I'll tell her you asked about her."

Georgianna looked back at Minnie and changed the subject. "And how are you settling in, darling?"

"Very well, ma'am," said Minnie. "Thank you."

"That's good, dear." Georgianna batted her eyes and scanned Minnie's outfit. "You know, your mother used to bring you to work when she'd clean our house a long time ago. You're probably too young to remember that, but I loved your mother. Your mother was always such a nice girl. She had such a wonderful air about her."

Nub noticed how strategically Georgianna avoided using Minnie's mother's name. "What was her mother's name?"

Georgianna looked at him. "I'm sorry?"

"You just said you were friends. You knew her. Tell us her name."

Georgianna gave a laugh. "What on earth do you mean? Of course I knew her name."

"Great. Let's hear it."

The air became awkward and heavy. Minnie looked like she wanted to shrink into a ladybug and fly away.

"What on earth has gotten into you, Jeremiah?" said Miss Janet. "She was just making conversation and being polite."

"Tell me what her mother's name was."

Benny touched Nub's elbow and tried to get him to calm down. Nub yanked his arm away. His blood was hot enough to boil cabbage. Minnie had pulled her jacket over her face.

Georgianna put her hand to her chest. Aghast. But she uttered no names. "You astound me. You know that?"

"Jeremiah Taylor," said Miss Janet. "What are you trying to prove? Why're you always stirring up trouble? Can't you just be agreeable for once in your wretched life?"

Georgianna lifted her granddaughter from the cart. "Maybe I should just leave. I'll come back and buy groceries some other time."

"Maybe you should," said Nub.

"You need to calm down, Jeremiah," said Miss Janet. "You're making a mountain out of absolutely nothing. So what if she can't remember the woman's name? That's not a crime."

The man bagging the groceries spoke. His voice was a rich baritone.

"Celia," the man said.

Everyone fell silent.

The tall man went back to bagging groceries.

"Thank you," Georgianna said. "There. You see, Nub? Celia, that was it. I grieved for that woman when she died. I love all people, rich or poor. I'm not going to stand here and be ridiculed by the town drunk."

"Nub ain't the town drunk," Benny said. "Plenty of drunks worse than him."

"Thank you, Benny," said Nub.

With that, Georgianna left the store.

Miss Janet was shaking her head at Nub. "You were out of line. You shouldn't go around acting like a blamed fool all the time."

"A fool?" said Nub. "'The fool doth think he is wise,' Miss Janet. 'But the wise man knows himself to be a fool.'"

Miss Janet punched open the cash drawer. "Heavens. A literary reference, from Jeremiah Taylor, in my presence? As I live and breathe. I wonder if you remember who said that."

"'Course I do," said Nub. "You did. All throughout fifth grade."

After they dropped Benny off at his house, Nub and Minnie drove toward the Kmart in Ambassador. Wyatt rode curled up on the dashboard. The truck loped across the long fields and cattle pasture. The night was obsidian. The moon was nearly full. Minnie sat beside him, staring out the passenger side, watching a big world whip by her window. And Nub was trying to coax his blood pressure down yet again. The people in this town were enough to drive a man to drink.

"I'm sorry about losing my cool before," he finally said. "I never should've put you through that. It wasn't very nice of me."

She shrugged. "It's okay."

"No, it's not. I'm not setting a very good example for you. Don't people like that woman make you mad?"

She shrugged. "Not really. Just how some people is."

He looked at her. There was more beneath her words than even he understood. He knew what it felt like to be blackballed. He knew what it felt like to be the butt of every joke. He knew what it felt like to survive suicide. But this child had it worse than he ever did.

"I'm sorry for what you're going through, Minnie."

Shrug.

When they reached the intersection of County Route 19 and I-65, a series of misfiring sounds came from the truck. He shifted gears to see if that helped. It didn't. The truck sputtered melodramatically. Then the wheel went slack. The needles on the dashboard flicked left in unison. The Ford veered to the ditch.

The truck was dead. Long live the truck.

They sat in the stillness among the miles of table-flat range lining both sides of the highway, far from home. The sound of crickets filled the night.

"What just happened?" said Minnie, petting the cat.

He turned to look at her. "What happened is we're gonna get plenty of exercise for the evening."

Minnie kept stroking Wyatt.

They raided their grocery bags and got ready to dine on the tailgate of the deceased F-100 while they watched the stars play above them. Angus in the nearby meadow lingered near the fence, watching them curiously. The truck battery still worked. So did the radio. So Nub treated her to WSM 650 AM, Nashville. Jim Reeves was singing "Is It Really Over?" like only Gentleman Jim could. Wyatt ate cat food straight from Minnie's hand while Nub prepared a pork-and-bean sandwich. He opened the can of beans with his P-38 can opener, which had a permanent home on his key chain ever since Pearl Harbor. He scooped beans onto the white bread, doused the bread in Heinz and Tabasco, and clapped the two sandwich halves together. He handed the soupy mess to Minnie.

"What's this?" she said, wrinkling her face.

"Food." He winked.

She took the sandwich cautiously. Wyatt sniffed it.

"It's called a Po' Nub sandwich. It will bless your heart. Try to keep an open mind."

"A Po what?"

"My own creation. Go on, eat. It's getting cold. Get away from that food, Wyatt."

The young woman looked at the concoction. She turned it in her hands. Beans spilled from the slices of bread, all over her thighs. She hesitantly took a bite. In a few moments, she began fanning her mouth.

"It's hot. My mouth is burning."

"Tabasco sauce. Key ingredient."

"Why you make it so hot?"

"Ain't my recipe."

Over the next few bites, the sandwich seemed to grow on her. She finished her first Po' Nub sandwich and ate a second and a third. Then a fourth. He was thrilled.

History's first Po' Nub sandwich happened when Emily was six years old. He had been babysitting her on a rare weekend that Loretta had deemed him fit for fatherhood. Emily fixed her father a sandwich in his kitchen using the only ingredients he had available in the fridge. Emily had been so adamant that her daddy eat her homemade sandwich in front of her. She called it a Po' Nub. It became a thing between them.

"Miss Georgianna called you a drunk," said Minnie.

He touched a fresh cigarette to the end of his dying one and puffed it to life. "Yeah, well, Georgianna's a serial monogamist, so there."

Minnie said nothing.

"And to be fair, Georgianna's right about me. I am a drunk. But I'm working on that."

She took a bite of her sandwich. "You mean you ain't going to drink no more?"

"I mean I'm taking it one day at a time."

"But if you don't drink no more, then how come you got beer in your refrigerator?"

"Hard to say goodbye."

"And you got a lot of whiskey under your kitchen sink too."

"What are you, the Southern Baptist Convention?"

Minnie fixed herself another sandwich, pouring the cold beans onto slices of bread, adding the condiments, then smooshing it all together. She had the recipe down pat. Wyatt played on her lap, rolling around like he was having blissful convulsions.

"My mama drank too much," she said.

He nodded. "Yeah, well, try not to blame her." He looked off at the cows who were looking back at him. "You and I have more in common than you think we do."

She did not respond so he just kept looking at the cows. Their big bovine eyes had always seemed so intelligent to him.

"My daddy shot himself."

Minnie was silent.

He nodded. "I was eleven. I found him in the closet. I've never seen that much blood."

"You found him?"

Nub was numb. "I didn't know it was him because his face, it was . . . gone."

Minnie was quiet for a long time. The sounds of the night swelled around them. Finally, she said, "When someone shoots themself, they kill a lot more than just them."

Truer words were never spoken.

CHAPTER

~ 25 ~

They walked the moonlit dirt roads toward Kmart, which was the closest landmark. Home was fourteen miles away; Kmart was only eight. Their feet made scuffling sounds on the dust and gravel. Minnie wore her school backpack and held Wyatt in her arms. Nub carried two sacks of groceries and suffered from a bout of emphysema that nearly killed him. After only ten minutes of walking, he was winded and he could see spots in his vision.

"Should we take a break, Mr. Nub?" she said. "You look pretty pale."

"I'm pale because you walk so dang fast."

"I do?"

"Yes, you do. Hell. We didn't walk this fast in the navy."

He dug a carton from his shirt pocket, wedged a smoke between his lips. "I have to sit down and breathe. Give me a moment."

He staggered to a cattle fence and sat on a nearby stump. He removed his seed cap and used a sleeve to mop the perspiration from his forehead. Minnie pressed her nose into Wyatt's fur and hummed softly in the cat's face. She paused her singing and looked at Nub.

"Do I look like Herman Munster?"

"Who's that?"

"Never mind." She went back to petting Wyatt.

"Well, I never heard of him, but old Herman must be a strikingly attractive young woman."

He could almost hear her eyes roll.

"Sing something for me," he said.

"Sing?"

"Don't give me that. All you ever do is sing. Give a dying man his last wish before he joins the heavenly majority."

She looked at the ground. "You ain't want to hear me, Mr. Nub."

"You're stalling."

So Minnie Bass closed her eyes and sang a song that seemed to originate deep within her breast. A song that laced the night with such immense sorrow, such deep-seated pain, that Nub's own earthly troubles paled in comparison to what this child was feeling. It was more than music. It was more than a song. It was a sacred melody of the heart. A human being spends most of his or her life hiding behind things, hiding behind their own words, pretending to feel ways they don't really feel, trying to convince themselves that everything is okay. But if you want to know what's truly on someone's mind, what's eating them inside, you pay attention to what they sing about. The truth always comes out in music.

Nobody knows the trouble I've seen,
Nobody knows but Jesus,
Nobody knows the trouble I've seen,
Glory hallelujah.
Sometimes I'm up, sometimes I'm down,
Oh yes, Lord.

Sometimes I'm almost to the ground,
Oh yes, Lord.

When she finished singing, he gazed at her through glassy eyes. He could not form words. Not at first. It took him a few moments to find them. Her song had penetrated a part of his spirit he'd forgotten was there. He lost fifty years and became a little boy. He was a child who had stumbled into the closet to find his father, lying crumpled on the floor, in a puddle of red. His father's face missing. And the rifle's trigger guard stuck to his big toe. That's who Nub Taylor was tonight. A child. And in fact, that was all he'd ever been.

The insects of the night were chirping. And Nub was crying.

"You're probably the best singer I've ever heard," he said.

"No."

He wiped his face. "I mean it. Your voice is incredible."

She shook her head. Her face wore the blush of youthful embarrassment. "I ain't nothing."

Nub approached her. He touched her chin and stared up into her dark eyes.

"Don't you ever say that again, sweetie," he said.

When they arrived at the Kmart, Nub had blisters on his heels. His knee was complaining. His lower back had seized. And his heart felt like it was going to rupture. But other than that, he was okay. Minnie, on the other hand, was pregnant and carrying an obese cat, but hardly winded at all.

Ah, youth.

He told her to sit on the bench outside for a moment. Nub walked into the Kmart and went to the manager's desk. He asked to use the phone. The manager reminded him that there was a pay phone outside. Nub told him he had no quarters, although this was an express lie. Nub lifted the receiver and dialed a familiar number.

The female voice answered. "American Legion. Where serving you is always a pleasure."

There was music in the background, along with the sound of clinking glassware and laughter.

"It's me."

"Hmm. I don't know anyone by that name."

"Got a second?"

Leigh Ann shouted over the din. "All our agents are busy helping other customers, but your call is important to us. Please stay on the line and a representative will be with you shortly."

"How long is shortly?"

"We're about to close. Can I call you back?"

"No. I'm not at home."

"What's up? Make it quick. Jerry Peters is threatening to take his pants off."

"You feel like giving an old man a lift tonight?"

He could hear her shifting the phone to her other shoulder and going someplace quieter. Her voice grew serious. "Are you in trouble?"

"Um. Sort of."

"Are you drunk?"

"No, thank God. But I wish I was. I'm just broke down. The truck died, and I have a kid in tow. And a cat."

"Where are you?"

"Leigh Ann, you're a lifesaver."

"I haven't agreed to anything yet."

He told her he was at Kmart. He told her what had happened. He told her about the Po' Nub sandwiches.

"That sounds disgusting," she said.

"You haven't tried one."

"And I never will. Listen, I have to drive Randy Atkins home first. He's been severely overserved."

"Who's to blame for that?"

"Probably his third wife. Then I have to close this place down. So I'll be about half an hour getting to you. Hang tight."

"Leigh Ann, I can't thank you enough."

"No. But you could at least try."

The Kmart closed. The lights turned off, and the last employee locked the front doors. The employees bid Nub and Minnie goodbye and offered to give them rides to wherever they were going, but Nub assured all the well-wishers someone much prettier than them was coming for him.

Soon the parking lot was empty. Nub and Minnie waited in the stillness. Minnie held Wyatt in her lap, and the cat was purring loudly. Eventually Minnie's head fell sideways from exhaustion, lying firmly on his shoulder. And she was out like a candle. He liked the feeling this gave him, the feeling of being trusted by a child. It had been a long time.

She was soon snoring lightly.

Nub looked at her and thought about his own father. He hadn't spoken of his father in years the way he had tonight, when he told Minnie his story. He was never that direct. He was never that honest. Because that is the cardinal rule about suicide. You don't talk about it.

But you never forget. Nub remembered the way the world changed after his old man's death and how his mother let the house go, let everything go, really. His mother crumbled after she lost her husband. She quit trying. She quit living. She quit bathing. She sent Nub away to an asylum, not because he was crazy but likely because she couldn't deal with him. She was incapable. His family lost everything. It lost its core. It lost its soul. He had more responsibility than a boy his age ever should have had. He began working because his mother lost her mind. He didn't have a chance to grow up slowly. He became a man overnight. And the strange thing was, in all his growing up, he never truly had a chance to mourn his father.

A faded yellow Chevy Silverado pulled into the Kmart parking lot. Leigh Ann parked before them, killed the engine, and walked around the vehicle.

"Hi there, pops."

Nub shushed her, then pointed to the sleeping kid on his shoulder.

"You'll wake the baby."

Leigh Ann came closer to the child. Minnie's mouth was gaping open and saliva was dripping down her chin.

"How many miles did she walk?" Leigh Ann whispered.

"More than you and me."

Wyatt flicked his tail when he heard Leigh Ann's voice.

"You travel with a cat everywhere you go?" she said.

"That cat is an agent of the devil."

Leigh Ann sat beside Nub and leaned her head on his other shoulder the way Minnie was doing. He was sandwiched between them. A real-life Po' Nub sandwich. He could smell Leigh Ann's perfume. He felt his insides get all squishy.

He turned to face her. He was looking at her lips. She was looking at his.

"You really are a lifesaver," he said.

Leigh Ann smiled and pinched his chin. "Takes one to know one."

Shug had been sleeping in the Taylor barn. He'd been caught unawares when a couple of guys threw rocks at his daughter's bedroom window on her first night here. He couldn't be sure it was the men who had been tailing him, but he wasn't willing to take any chances. Either way, there were no excuses for not being prepared. The number one rule in the army was: over-prepare. He had overheard his new boss talking to some of the cashiers about Shug's daughter coming back into town. It was pure chance he'd been present for such a conversation. Or maybe it was Providence. But he had still been taken unawares. It wouldn't happen again. He was ready for them now.

It was so cold tonight he could see his breath.

Shug had been keeping close tabs on Minnie day and night, watching the old farmhouse like a hawk. He divided his night watches into one-hour shifts. Each hour he would get up, stretch his limbs, and take a walk around the perimeter of the Taylor farm. Sort of like they did in Korea. Hourly patrols. Hour naps. Purgatory, the privates called it.

The men had quit tailing him whenever he walked to work; he had not seen the white Cadillac in two days. Their disappearance was an intimidation technique. He was familiar with it because he had used it before. Let your victim know you're there, then disappear. It plays with their minds. It makes them jumpy. And eventually, it makes them less vigilant and causes them to do something stupid.

Shug stretched his lanky, six-eleven frame. He heard his joints crack. His lower back was killing him. He removed his watch cap and ran his fingers through his hair. He began his patrol behind the barn. He made his walk around the perimeter in the darkness, looking for anything out of the ordinary.

When he had finished his third lap around the circumference of the farm, he stopped to light a cigarette. He clicked open his lighter and heard something behind him. Footsteps in the brush. He didn't even have time to turn around.

"Stop right there," said the voice.

Shug did not answer; the flame of his lighter was still glowing.

"Hands behind your head," said the voice. "Get down flat on the ground. Now."

Shug held up both hands, cigarette dangling in the corner of his mouth. He dropped the lighter and laced his fingers behind his head. He took a big chance and turned slowly to face the voice behind him.

It was a man in a deputy uniform. The deputy thumb-cocked his weapon. "You're not very good at following instructions, son."

CHAPTER

❧ 26 ❧

It happened in Cullman County, Alabama, in a little town called Baileytown, a few hours north of Park. Nub was in his early twenties. The war hadn't broken out yet, and the Great Depression was going on. Nub had been playing in the backup band called the Nose Pickers that did the annual gig for the local Rotary Club. It was a fun band. Nub was on guitar, bass, or mandolin, depending on the tune. Benny played fiddle. The featured entertainer for the Rotary gig that year was a pretty woman from Tennessee named Sarah Cannon. Sarah was a comedian. A joke teller. A budding performer still trying to figure out what her schtick would be. She was in her midtwenties. Lean and lithe. She wore a nice dress with flowers on it. Nub's main memory of her was that she laughed a lot.

Backstage that night, he tried to linger near her just so he could look at her. That same evening Sarah Cannon met a young woman named Myrtis backstage, the wife of one of Nub's bandmates. Myrtis was loud and funny. She was a bumpkin from a small mountain community outside Baileytown, and everyone loved her. Myrtis always brought bologna and cheese sandwiches and beer for the band. Sarah Cannon admired Myrtis's brand-new straw hat, which, embarrassingly, still had the price tag on it. Minutes before showtime, before Sarah went onstage, she asked Myrtis if she could borrow the hat.

Myrtis removed the hat and said, "This old thing?"

On opening night, Sarah Cannon took the stage in Myrtis's hat, price tag and all. Cannon opened the show by saying to everyone, "I'm just so proud to be here in Baileytown, Alabama, tonight!"

The words were off the cuff, but they would be solidified in the collective consciousness of all rural Americans. And Nub had witnessed this fortuitous moment.

He thought about that night now as he was pulling the drain plug and drying off his newly shaven face with a towel. He could hear his Minnie singing a song in the other room that he didn't recognize. She had been singing a lot lately. It was amazing what a few words of praise could do for a child's self-esteem. Everyone in this world has self-esteem issues, Nub had learned long ago. Those who pretended they didn't had them worst of all.

He looked out the tiny window of the bathroom at the dark pasture below. The moon was out, and the thin stripe of the Milky Way was on full display. He turned out the bathroom lights when he noticed something else outside.

He moved closer to the window. For a moment he couldn't believe what his eyes were telling him. Two figures were slinking slowly across his backyard. Nub blinked a few times to make sure he was seeing things correctly. He pressed his nose against the window and squinted into the darkness.

Yes. He was seeing it right. Two men. On his lawn.

One of the men had a pistol aimed at the other.

Nub was ready for the brats this time. He flew down the stairs in his stocking feet, retrieved the rifle from the coat closet, then opened the front door and tiptoed onto his porch. He made no noise. He had the element of surprise on his side this time. Before, his visitors had taken him unawares. But now the advantage was Nub's.

He craned his head around the corner of his house and saw the figures sprinting across the dark yard toward the highway. Nub knew he had them. The question was, did he want them? One of them had a gun.

He leaned against the side of his home and reviewed his options. He would be no good to anyone injured or dead. He walked inside his kitchen, lifted the receiver, and dialed three numbers on the rotary dial.

"Ash County Sheriff," said the voice of Mae Beth.

He was whispering. "Mae Beth, I need someone at my house. And fast."

"Someone? You mean someone else?"

"What?"

"Gordon is up at your place right now, Nub. He just radioed in."

Nub paused, then glanced out the window.

"Gordon? Here?"

"Yes. Gordon just saw some guy prowling around your place and he called it in. He's on foot."

Nub peeked through the curtain again and saw the two figures heading toward the east pasture. One of them was definitely Gordon.

"Well, send someone else to back him up, Mae Beth. He's a little long in the tooth to be chasing these boys."

"Someone's already on their way."

Then he heard gunshots.

Nub tore into the open field and jogged through the tall weeds in his socks. His eyes hadn't fully adjusted to the darkness yet. His feet sank into the muddy ground with each step.

"Where are you going?" Minnie called to him, standing on the porch. Her voice reverberated through the chill air.

"Stay in the house!" he yelled back.

He held his rifle like a soldier, with two hands out before him. He paused to catch his breath and saw red droplets on the trail beneath him. Someone was bleeding.

He followed the trail. He could hear faint movement from the brush ahead. A *whoosh, whoosh* in the grass. He chased after the sound. His lungs were burning when he reached a cow path. He was getting near the highway. Adrenaline made his body cold, and he was already choking for air. Nub stopped to breathe and lowered his head between his legs. Then he heard the rustling in the underbrush again.

He started running after them. He veered right and found the old wagon trail that led to the highway. It was a shortcut, a towpath from the old tobacco days. The boys wouldn't have taken this trail because nobody even knew it was here. But this trail was a straighter shot to the highway. He could beat them there if he hurried.

His breathing was getting worse now. He was nauseous from exertion. His ribs hurt. His thigh muscles felt like they were going to tear. Then he stopped and vomited a little. Nub forced himself upright and willed himself to keep breathing. To keep running.

Finally, Nub burst through the thicket onto the gravel highway. He was breathing so heavily, stars were dancing in his eyes. But he had done it. He could hardly believe it. He

had beaten the runners to the highway. They would be plow-
ing through the weeds at any moment, aiming straight for
him. He assumed a stance, braced himself, cocked his rifle,
and listened to the oncoming whooshing in the grass ahead
of him.

They were heading right for him.

He steeled himself and saw the grass part.

Two men emerged from the brush. One of them was
limping; it was Gordon. Nub attempted to shoot the one who
wasn't Gordon, but he was too weak from running to hold the
gun steady. The report of the rifle nearly knocked him off his
feet. The runner careened straight into Nub and knocked him
backward.

Nub dropped the rifle. He lay on his back, flat in the dirt.
His assailant had the rifle now, but the man wasn't aiming it at
him. The man was tall and bone-thin, holding the weapon like
a bat, gripping the business end. The man had it cocked behind
his head, ready to swing for the fences.

"I know you," said Nub.

The figure did not move.

"You're from the IGA," said Nub.

"What?" said the figure.

"You're the man who was bagging our groceries. What are
you, seven foot tall? Not many guys like you around these
parts."

There was no answer.

"What do you want with her?" said Nub.

Again the tall figure was quiet.

"Well, you're going to have to kill me," said Nub. "I won't let
you hurt that precious girl."

"You don't understand," said the man. "You don't know
what you're talking about."

Nub glanced at Gordon, who was lying on the ground, holding his leg. He shouted, "You okay, Gordon?"

Gordon only moaned.

"Who are you?" said Nub.

The tall figure in the darkness did not relax his stance. The man towered over Nub like the Chrysler Building.

"I said, who are you? Are you the one who broke my windows?" said Nub.

"I don't want to hurt you," the man said.

"I wish I could say the same to you, son. But you just shot a police officer."

"He'll be okay."

"Yeah," said Nub. "He looks terrific."

"I didn't shoot him."

Nub felt his temper surge. It was a fight-or-flight thing. A burst of energy came from an unknown place within his exhausted and asthmatic body. He was going to take this man down or go to Hades trying.

Nub bounded up from the dirt and ran toward his attacker, screaming a rebel yell. But he was no match for the man. The man jabbed him in the groin with the butt of the rifle so hard that Nub nearly passed out. Agony ripped through Nub's entire body. He hit his knees and went down under the power. Next, the figure used the bat to tap Nub from behind, just enough to knock him down. The man tossed the rifle into the dirt and spirited away.

Nub watched his aggressor dart into the night. The whole world looked cockeyed from his prone position. He had never been in this much pain in all his life.

"Gordon," he said, "are you okay?"

"I'm okay. I'm hurt. I tore my Achilles. But I'm okay."

"I saw blood. Are you shot?"

"No. But he is."

Emily Ives sat in her living room, listening to her mother tell a story she had heard at least 1,298,821 times. Maybe more. She felt her face turn to wood as her mother reached another of her story's false climaxes. Emily's stepfather, Daniel, sat beside his wife, sipping his whiskey. He'd heard this story before too. Many more times than Emily had. But Daniel knew that you did not mess with Loretta midstory.

Charlie Jr. sat on the sofa with his chin in his hands, akin to Rodin's *The Thinker*. Emily wanted to fade into the wallpaper and never come out.

She was absently thinking about the American chestnut tree. She had spent the entire morning at the tree with a young student, a xylology major from the State University of New York. The girl had traveled all the way to Park just to see the tree and to volunteer. They had a nice conversation. The young woman had the world by the tail, which made Emily mourn the passing of her own youth.

That's when she made the decision to tell her family about her illness. It was the adult thing to do.

And that's what tonight was supposed to be, in fact. It was supposed to be about Emily. She had gathered her family together to share her horrible news. But it was clear that her mother suspected nothing; therefore Loretta considered this to be a normal family dinner. So, as usual, she dominated all social discourse.

Somehow the conversation got around to the water tower incident, which brought the conversation around to the topic of Nub Taylor, which was never a good thing at a family dinner. And the subject of Nub Taylor only got Emily further from tonight's goal. Soon, stories were told about Nub. Bad stories.

Embarrassing stories. Loretta couldn't help herself but replay Nub's greatest hits.

So even when he wasn't here, Nub Taylor still managed to embarrass everyone.

Emily had almost invited her father to supper tonight, but she had changed her mind because putting Loretta and Nub in the same room was a recipe for atomic warfare. Plus, Nub was still too early in his recovery to be subjected to the stress of his ex-wife. Emily could only imagine how things might have gone if he had been sitting at this table. The last time she had invited her father to a dinner, he had shown up unshaven and wrinkled. His socks were mismatched. He'd been out all night playing at some no-name beer joint in Chattanooga, and he smelled like it too. He had arrived at her door carrying a pound cake purchased from a Piggly Wiggly, with several slices missing and crumbs all over his clothes.

Before the close of Loretta's arduous story, the phone rang. Charlie Jr. answered it. As her son listened, his face changed. Then he interrupted his grandmother's story.

"Mom, it's the sheriff."

"What?"

The whole dining room looked at Charlie Jr.

"He said he wants to talk to you."

Emily rose and began her walk across the room. But Loretta beat her to it and grabbed the phone from Charlie Jr.'s hand.

"This is Loretta," she said into the receiver.

Her mother's face went pale.

"What?" said Emily.

Loretta held up a finger. Her mother listened and nodded several times. She said a lot of uh-huhs and okays.

"Mama. What's going on?"

"*Shot?*" said Loretta. "Who's been shot?"

Emily felt her chest cave in.

"Mama, tell me what's going on."

Her mother said, "It's your father."

Nub Taylor strikes again.

Nub lay on the tailgate of Gordon's Toyota, covered in a wool blanket, holding his nether regions. The blow to his groin caused an ache that radiated all over his body, especially upward in his stomach, which hurt worst of all. If he'd known that crotch shots were this painful, he never would have kept them in his self-defense repertoire. He owed every one of his beer-joint victims a written apology. This was the worst pain he had ever known. Even his teeth hurt. He did not, however, regret hitting the crotch of Phillip Deener's father. If Nub could have, he would have delivered crotch shots to the entire Deener clan, dating all the way back to the Puritans.

Two squad vehicles were blocking County Route 19, lights blaring. The deputies were sitting in the front seats, chattering on radios. Nub saw a pair of headlights far off, heading straight for him, following the thin ribbon of moonlit gravel. The speeding car cut through distant trees, powering over each rise and fall of the landscape. He could see a nimbostratus of dust rising behind the vehicle.

Nub knew this car, even from a hundred miles away. It was a '66 Plymouth Valiant. A car that brought only dread and terror wherever it went.

"'Jesus wept,'" he muttered.

The car rolled in and the brake drums squealed. His ex-wife, Loretta Barnes, threw open her door and stepped out of her car, striking a pose not unlike a kaiser leading a charge into battle. Her car was roughly the size of a Shoney's. Her face was apathetic and hard.

She made a beeline for Nub.

Loretta was a force. Sort of like inclement weather. Only inclement weather eventually goes away; Loretta never did.

"Good Lord, Nub," she said with a note of aggravation. "We all thought you'd been shot. They made it sound like you'd been gunned down on the phone."

"I'm sorry to disappoint you."

"Let me take you home."

"It's okay; you didn't need to come. One of these guys can take me back to the house."

Loretta did not take no for an answer. She helped him off the tailgate. He leaned on her shoulder and winced each time his feet hit the ground. He groaned in pain with every doleful step.

"Slow down!" he shouted. "I'm tender."

"What happened to him?" she asked Gordon.

Gordon was sitting on the tailgate of the Toyota, massaging his bare lower leg. His Achilles had detached from his heel, causing his calf muscle to spring free, knotting up beneath his knee joint like a tennis ball.

"Nub sustained quite a debilitating blow," said Gordon.

"A blow? Where?"

Gordon and the other cops exchanged looks.

Nub and Loretta tottered to her car. Nub moved like a man who had just undergone an unanesthetized surgical procedure. Short steps. Unhurried movements. Nice and easy does it. He lowered his body into Loretta's front seat. He took two minutes to get his haunches situated. She closed the door after him, then she looked at Nub through the window. "Are you okay?"

"Greatest day of my life."

Loretta walked around the car to the driver's side, slid behind the wheel, cranked up the heater, and drove as slowly as she could over each bump.

"Why did they call *you*?" he asked.

"They didn't. I was at Emily's. They called her."

"Then why isn't she here? She's nicer than you are."

"We were having dinner at Emily's." Loretta somehow managed to make this remark sound like a mild chastisement.

"Well, I'm sorry I missed the family party."

Loretta took a bump with considerable speed. He moaned in anguish.

"We came as fast as we could. Emily's over at your house, with . . . that girl."

"If I told you her name was Minnie," he said, "would you use it?"

She looked at him. "If that's what you want."

"It's what I want."

Loretta shook her head. He could feel it coming. Loretta was big on monologues. "You amaze me. You already have a daughter, Nub. Did you forget? You've had a daughter for forty-four years. You can't atone for your sins by adopting some pregnant teenager off the street."

"She wasn't on the street."

"You know what I mean."

"No, I'm not sure I do. And how did you know she's pregnant?"

"Have you forgotten where you live?"

"Does Emily know?"

"There isn't anything Emily doesn't know."

"Minnie's a good kid."

"Oh yes, I'd say you've got a model teenager."

He took a few cleansing breaths; it helped with the pain.

They rode in relative silence until Nub broke the calm before the storm.

"Listen, I know I wasn't around for Emily. But let's be clear about something. That's what *you* wanted. You never wanted me around my own daughter. You made that obvious to me and to everyone else. I stayed away out of respect for you, and I regret it now. But I wasn't a deadbeat."

"Right. Let's make everything my fault. I'm a bad mother because I kept a drunk away from his child. I'm the villain. I'm the one who peed in a kiddie pool during a family reunion and sang 'I've got a river of life flowing out of me.'"

Nub fell silent. The tune had actually been "Deep and Wide."

They neared his driveway. Three county vehicles were parked beneath the carport, light bars flashing. Deputies were combing through his barn with spotlights. Another officer was standing by the back door. Loretta's Plymouth eased up the driveway slowly.

"I'm noticing a pattern here," Loretta said.

"What?"

"You're getting beaten up a lot lately." She turned to give him a maternal look. "Maybe there's a lesson to be learned in all this."

"You're absolutely right. Thanks for not letting this teachable moment slip past me, Loretta."

Emily was waiting for her father on the other side of the car door, staring through the window at him. He opened the door and Emily helped him out of his seat. Deputy Burke had been escorted to the house in another patrol car. Deputies muscled both Nub and Burke up the front steps. Loretta merely stood nearby and instructed everyone how to do their jobs.

Inside, Minnie was seated at the kitchen table with a

young-faced deputy. She was still wearing her nightgown. When she saw Nub walk in, she threw her arms around him. "Mr. Nub, I was so worried!"

She hugged him.

"Go easy on me, sweetie," he said. "I've been gelded."

"Been what?"

"Just be gentle with me."

He hobbled into the living room, where he lightly collapsed on the settee. Everyone gave him privacy while two fire medics stripped off Nub's pants. The medics looked at the injury in horror. They were both male.

"Now that's what I'd call considerable bruising," said Gordon Burke, who was staggering into the room using crutches.

"Who was that man you were chasing?" said Nub.

"I don't know, but I saw him on your property. We were fighting over my gun, and the thing went off. Shot him right in the leg. I'm surprised he was still walking."

The medics probed Nub with rubber-gloved hands and sent shock waves of suffering throughout his body.

"I hope you don't plan on having any more kids," said Gordon.

"Hey, that's pretty good," said Nub. "You should get a booking agent."

When Nub was fully dressed, a young deputy gave him packs of frozen vegetables from the freezer. Nub held a baggie of chopped okra on his groin. Emily sat beside him on the sofa, crying.

"We thought you'd been shot," said Emily. "That's how they made it sound."

He used his finger to wipe a tear away from her freckled cheek. "Well, I'm not. Although right now I wish I had been."

She cried onto his shoulder. He was moved that she would

weep for him like this, but he was concerned about where it was coming from.

"Why are you crying like this, sweetie?" he said. "I told you I'm okay."

She laughed through the tears. "Dad, I'm not crying because you're hurt. I'm crying because you're not drunk."

BOOK
3

~ 27 ~

The moon looked like a cue ball. Sugar Bass stood at the entrance of the paper mill, waiting. He smoked a cigarette and kept checking his watch. He had tried to quit smoking in prison several times because it was an expensive habit. Cigarettes were like five-dollar bills in the pen. But prison has so few vices, so few moments of respite. Sometimes a vice was the only thing that made you feel normal.

He looked at the R&T mill's recovery boiler behind him, adorned in red safety lights. He drew in a lungful and admired the panoramic sight.

A green Ford Maverick pulled into the empty mill parking lot and the driver stepped out. It was Willie. He hadn't seen Willie since they were young men, working for The Organization. Willie had aged. A lot. They embraced. Willie looked at Shug's bandaged leg. The lower half was wrapped in white gauze.

"What happened there?"

"Nothing."

"Doesn't look like nothing."

Willie moved closer to Shug's leg and inspected it. The bandage was bloody and needed to be changed. "You can't just go missing like this. They're going to revoke your parole."

Shug shrugged.

"And even if they don't," Willie went on, "we're probably going to die anyway. We've pissed a lot of people off. The only reason they haven't killed me yet is because they can't find me. But I know they're looking; they're always there."

Shug stepped on his cigarette. "Did you find what I asked for?"

"Yeah, I found it. Just where you said. I was careful handling it." Willie looked around at his surroundings. "This is a weird place to meet, Shug."

"They have security here, cameras and everything. They won't tail us into a place where there's security cameras."

"Security cameras could bust us just as easily."

"I snipped the wires."

They walked to the Ford Maverick and Willie popped the hatch. In the back was the army box with the stenciled letters. The label read "Explosives."

"I drove as gently as I could. Jeez, Shug, I was scared I'd hit a bump too hard and end up on the nightly news."

"It doesn't work that way. You don't have to be gentle with this stuff."

"We never should've taken their money. These guys don't even care about the money; all they want is to get even. We won't survive this if they find us."

Shug ran his hand along the box. It had been a long time since he'd handled explosives. But it all comes back to you. You never forget. Just like riding a bike.

"You know these guys," said Willie. "They don't let any-thing go. We should just give the money back while we're still breathing. Is it still in the same place?"

This was an odd question for Willie to ask. Willie knew perfectly well where it was. Shug's radar went up.

"It's too late to have a change of heart, Willie."

"For mercy's sake, Shug. Sometimes I think I can hear someone breathing on the other end of my phone. Let's give it back. Let's be done with this."

"It doesn't work like that, Willie."

"We could at least talk to them."

"That money belongs to my kid."

"Half of that money's mine, you forget. I was there that night, right beside you when the gun went off. You don't get to make all the decisions. I want to get rid of it. I want to be finished with this."

"You can do whatever you want to with your half, Willie. You know where to find it."

"I don't want my half. I can't spend a dime anyway. Cripes, Shug. They'll break my neck the moment I buy a new car."

Shug shrugged. "Your choice. My half belongs to my girl. That's nonnegotiable."

"That kid's never even met you, Shug. She don't even know you're alive."

Willie placed the explosive case into Shug's arms. It was heavier than it looked. The size of a small steamer trunk. Drab army green. It even smelled familiar to Shug. A common myth was that C-4 explosives smelled like almonds. But the truth was they smelled like motor oil, or tar.

"What are you going to do with this stuff?"

"I appreciate the help, Willie."

"I wish you'd rethink this."

"See you around."

"You can't beat these guys at their own game, Shug. That money is our bargaining chip. You give your half to the kid; they won't need you anymore. You heard what they did to Randy's whole family?"

"Randy? Randy Chandler?"

Willie looked at the ground. "His wife and his kids. All gone. These guys don't mess around, Shug. They're going to come after *your* kid."

Shug looked off. "Yeah. They will."

Willie closed his trunk hatch and they embraced again.

"I hope you know what you're doing, Shug."

"Watch your back, Willie."

"Who's watching yours?"

Shug lifted the heavy case and disappeared back into the woods from whence he came.

He wore his Sunday best to church this morning. Minnie walked beside him into the church. She had donned a brand-new Kmart maternity dress; purple, with little white dots. Her sticker-covered Chuck Taylors didn't match her outfit, but she loved them. Her belly was getting bigger every day.

Two ushers stood at the front door. The male usher was old with white hair. The woman looked old enough to remember when they invented rocks. When Nub walked through the front door, both ushers reached their hands outward and grabbed both of his. It was a six-handed handshake. The kind of welcoming handshake you get at church, shortly before they start feeding you.

"Hello, Nub," the old woman said. Then she gave him a kiss.

"Hello, Miss Heather." He kissed her back.

Nub and Minnie had found a home in the Mount Lebanon Church of God. This church was never full. Even so, Nub liked this place. He liked it because Minnie liked it, and that was enough reason for him. And these were good people. They'd do anything for you.

Each week Minnie would disappear into the back choir room and get ready to join the choir onstage. It was the highlight of her week, singing with this little group. There were only four people in the church choir, but they sang four-part harmony, and they were pretty good. They practiced shape-note singing each week. Someone from the church would swing by Nub's house on Wednesday nights and take Minnie to each practice. Nub helped her work on her parts. Nub couldn't read music, but he knew harmony by ear, and he knew how things should sound.

Church had never been Nub's thing. After his father's end, he had grown to hate church. To Nub's people, suicide was a nonstop ticket to hell. So church people *never* talked about suicide. They pretended like it never happened. Church to Nub was just a bunch of people who were all wound up tighter than fish rectums. They believed that anything fun was a sin. If it felt good, it was wrong. And he wasn't crazy about how church people always casually quoted Scripture in daily conversation. Everyone was always talking about how they were "led" to do this and that, and how their cups were always runnething over.

But lately, he'd come to feel differently about all this. Something in his life had shifted. He couldn't explain what. He was going to AA meetings three times a week with Leigh Ann. And in a way, those meetings were a little like church. He was participating in the AA readings. He was saying AA prayers for the group. He was beginning to believe certain things he had never allowed himself to believe before.

He believed, for instance, that everything that had happened to him, no matter what it was, was a good thing. Before, he had believed that life was a random collection of BS. Nothing had any rhyme or reason. You dealt with whatever junk happened, but there was no deeper meaning to it. Part of living in a fallen world. Then you died. Maybe you went to a sort of heaven. Maybe you didn't. End of story.

But in the months that he'd been caring for Minnie Bass, he'd felt the hand of an unseen entity clearing the way for him. He had no name for this entity. You could've called it God, he supposed. But it was bigger than three Latin letters. Much bigger. So why call this entity anything at all? Any word would be too small to embody this great thing.

Minnie took to the altar and the piano began to play. The guy at the keys beat out a few chords with an ascending gospel bassline. Minnie sang with an intensity that could uproot boulders. It was a song she had been working on all week. "Didn't My Lord Deliver Daniel?" If there was a dry eye in the room, it was made of glass.

Lately things had been happening that could only be explained as minor miracles. Sometimes he wasn't sure there would be enough food to make it until the next stipend check. But then someone would deliver groceries to his porch. And ever since the first hundred-dollar bills had been left in his house, an anonymous person had been leaving more big bills on his doorstep.

And then there was his sobriety. He had been sober for months now. A lifetime record. He couldn't believe it. Still, he couldn't take credit for his own sobriety. It wasn't him. Something bigger was involved here.

His relationship with Leigh Ann helped him stay sober, sure. She called him every day. Sometimes three or four times a day. Sometimes they talked for hours. Sometimes she visited him at his maintenance jobs around town, keeping him and Benny company while they worked painting buildings or repairing electrical fixtures in the courthouse. Sometimes Leigh Ann picked Minnie up from school and they all went out for hamburgers. Leigh Ann was fast becoming his link to the Greater Good. But it wasn't her that was keeping him sober. And it wasn't Minnie. It was the unnamable entity.

AA was big on this concept of a higher power. In fact, one could argue that AA was not about alcoholics at all but about the higher power. That was the whole basis for the community. AA was about putting your faith in this power and realizing that this higher power is the key to everything. You can't get sober by yourself. You can't rebuild your life by yourself. You can't do *anything* by yourself. You are totally, wholeheartedly, painstakingly powerless. In the twelve-step program, the term *higher power* could mean anything you wanted it to mean. The name didn't matter. You could give God a Jewish, Greek, Indian, Catholic, Christian, or American name. But the fact remained the same: whatever it was, it was a lot bigger than you.

Minnie sang another song.

An older man next to him in the pew was missing most of his teeth. His hands were ragged. He had a crown of dandelion fuzz around his bald head and sinewy muscles. He probably weighed a buck five and he looked tough from a lifetime of labor.

He started crying as Minnie performed her solo. Nub marveled at this. Minnie's ability to draw tears. On Nub's other side was a young woman and her husband. She was pretty. Her husband was handsome. She wore a big hat and he wore a nice suit. They, too, were weeping. So were others in the congregation. Minnie had them all sniffing.

The child had a talent even he didn't understand. Another song began. All the people stood. Minnie Bass led the singing.

Her belly was large and bulbous but there was no shame here. Not in this room.

Nub opened a hymnal and sang along.

Minnie had been coming back to life in his house over the last months. Bit by bit. It was a slow process. But each day he saw new pieces of her personality emerge. Sometimes she could be silly. Other times she could be quick-witted and sassy. She could make him laugh. She could make him feel—really feel— things. And her memory. The girl could remember everything. Her mind was prodigious.

Minnie's appearance had changed over time. Her cheeks were rounder. Her hair was shinier. Her eyes were brighter. She was getting close to her due date, and the bit of extra weight looked good on her. She carried a healthy glow with her. When she smiled, her face became so round and full that Nub's heart started to hurt.

Sometimes he wanted to tell her how much he loved her; he wanted to tell her that he found her to be one of the most incredible people he had ever known. Sometimes he wanted to tell her how much she had helped his heart heal wounds that had been present in him ever since the death of his old man. But he wasn't there yet. It was hard for him to say everything he felt. He was working on it, though. One day at a time. That's what Leigh Ann always said. One day at a time.

When the hymn was over, the preacher took the platform. Minnie joined Nub in the pew. When she sat, the whole pew creaked like it was going to cave inward.

The people became wildly animated during the sermon. Old men stood for no reason at all and shouted, "Amen!" People nodded in affirmation and clapped intensely. Old women pumped their hands at the ceiling. Minnie hooked arms with Nub. She put her head on his shoulder. He kissed her hair softly.

"Great job," he said in a whisper.

"Thanks."

Another kiss.

For most of his life, all he had been able to think about was himself. Used to be, all he ever thought about was what *he* was feeling. It wasn't just thoughts about drinking. Drinking was just what he did. It was that he was always thinking of *his* current state of being. *His* life. But now he was someone else, thinking about the current state of another.

He draped an arm around Minnie. She smelled like the perfume he'd bought her. The preacher invited anyone who wanted prayer to come to the altar. Nub was surprised to see that Minnie was among the first to stand. She walked to the front of the church and knelt at the altar in that careful way that pregnant women move. The preacher laid his hands on her shoulders and prayed for her in a voice that was clear and strong, originating from deep in his chest.

When the prayer finished, Minnie opened her eyes to see that Nub was kneeling beside her. So was the entire congregation. Everyone in the room was touching Minnie Bass. Old women had rested their hands upon her back. Children had placed their hands on Minnie's head. People who couldn't reach Minnie had their hands upon those who could. It was a giant spiderweb of arms, with Minnie in the center. He told Minnie he loved her.

She repeated it back to him.

His cup ranneth all over the place.

CHAPTER

28

The bell dinged over the door to Tacky's Pawn. The pawnshop was a dump. Junk was hanging on the walls. There was no rhyme or reason to the organization of the place, just a lot of castoffs piled atop more garbage, piled atop more junk. Schwinn bicycles dangling from the ceiling. Stacks of girly magazines predating the Triassic Period. A large basket filled with riding crops. Life-size wooden carvings of Native chiefs selling boxed cigars. A lone statue of the Blessed Virgin holding a tin of cigars. Weird stuff.

Nub and Benny approached the counter and Benny rang the service bell. They waited. Benny rang again. Benny had a thing for bells.

"Keep your pants on," came the grizzled voice from the back.

The curtain of beads parted, and an old man shambled forward, wiping his mouth with a napkin. "Well, if it ain't Abbott and Costello," said Tacky. "You caught me during lunch break."

"It's eight o'clock at night," said Benny.

"Late lunch."

They all shook hands.

"Buying or selling?" the old man said.

"Selling," said Nub.

240

Tacky folded his hands as if to say, "Let's get this going."

White hair was growing out of the old man's nostrils like tusks. His drawling accent was so thick he was almost speaking another language. Nub made no move at first. Namely because he couldn't believe what he was about to do. There were some things a man did not do. Hawking heirlooms was one of these things. His family had so few of them. All his life, they had been cherished. Like the bones of saints.

"Well?" said Tacky. "Sometime in this century?"

Nub reached into his pocket and unwrapped a linen cloth to reveal a pocket watch. It was sterling. He had spent half the evening polishing it to a reflective shine.

"This belonged to General Hood," Nub said.

The little old man frowned. "Proof of that?"

Nub reached into his pocket and removed a sandwich baggie containing a crinkled letter. The script on the parchment was from another era. The signature was General Hood's. Tacky fetched a loupe from beneath the counter and placed it over his eye. His overgrown eyebrow tightened over the lens as he adjusted the focus. "I'd have to have this authenticated, you understand."

"Of course."

"Could take a while."

"Sure."

"Months maybe."

"I don't have months."

The watch had been given to Nub's grandfather before the Battle of Nashville. The story went that his grandfather, a private in the Confederate army, was taking a leak in the woods when he heard footsteps in the brush. It was an ambush. Before finishing his business, his grandfather drew fire and nailed six Union men with his trousers still undone. In a few minutes, his grandfather was joined by his comrades in gray. A full-scale dogfight ensued. Nub's grandfather had accidentally averted one of the greatest ambushes orchestrated by the Union army preceding the Battle of Nashville. With his pants down. Had the Union succeeded in the ambush, the Battle of Nashville might have gone very differently, which in the end turned out to be a moot point because the Union won one of its largest victories at the Battle of Franklin. But still.

The pocket watch was given to Nub's grandfather by General Hood in the absence of a medal, only days before the famous battle. Hood removed the watch from his own pocket and pinned it to Nub's grandfather's shirt. For years thereafter, Nub's grandfather gave toasts at holiday dinners cheerfully commemorating his own bravery with a poem.

> Friends may come, and friends may go,
> And some may peter out, you know,
> But I'll forever be thy friend,
> Peter out, or peter in.

Tacky popped open the watch face and looked at the inscription, which read "I am my beloved's and he is mine." The inscription was signed by Anna Marie Hennen. Hood's wife. Dated 1831.

"I've heard about this watch," said Tacky. "Why did you bring this to me?"

"Times are tight."

The old man looked at him again. "So get a job."

"I got one."

Tacky turned the watch in his hand. "They have banks for that sort of thing."

"Not for guys like me."

The man clicked off the desk light and pushed the watch across the counter.

"You don't want to sell this, Nub. I grew up with your dad. He'd kill me."

"Daddy ain't here no more."

Tacky sighed. "This is family, Nub. I don't take heirlooms."

"I need a car, Tacky. I got a kid depending on me. Leigh Ann has been driving me everywhere. I'm about to have two kids. I need a car. I got doctor visits to drive her to and prenatal vitamins to buy. And I'm about to be neck-deep in diapers. Help me out here."

Tacky looked at them both. He tucked the loupe in his chest pocket.

"I don't do business this way, Nub."

"This is the only way you do business."

The old man shook his head. "It's too desperate. Feels wrong."

The old man was full of bunk. Quick negotiations were how this trade was done. And this was how negotiations were always started, with a mock refusal. This man was not just an expert at the art of haggling; he was an Arabian horse trader. "I'm just not looking to spend this kinda money right now," Tacky said. "You understand how it is. The recession and all."

"Give me a price."

The old man looked through the window, past the sign with the pawnbroker's symbol of the three balls. He was playing the part of the reluctant buyer to a T. He heaved another sigh.

"It's a nice piece. I'll give you that. But I don't want to insult you."

"Insult him," said Benny. "He's used to it."

Tacky named a price.

Nub felt his heart shrink. Not only was the offer not enough to buy a car, it wasn't even enough to buy tires for a car. Nub countered with a higher number, an offer that would have at least gotten him a piece-of-trash used Chevy with transmission problems from the classifieds. But the old man shook his head again, his signature move. He came back with a number that was higher than his last offer, but still not enough to say grace over. They went back and forth for a few minutes.

"Jeez, Tacky," said Benny. "This watch could go to auction and bring you a fortune, and you know it."

The old man nodded. "You're probably right, but that's all I can give you."

Tacky had him by the short hairs now.

Nub countered. Tacky only raised his price by nano increments. There came a point when a man knew he had gone as far as he could go. Nub was at that point. He was about to give in when Benny pointed to an instrument hanging behind the old man's head.

"How about you throw in that guitar?" Benny said.

The old man turned to look at the gaggle of wooden instruments lining the wall behind him. There were guitars, banjos, fiddles, mandolins, cellos, and dulcimers of every shade and hue. Blonds, brunettes, electric reds.

"Which one?" said Tacky.

"The Gibson," said Benny.

The man folded his arms in a kind of protest. "That's a sixteen-hundred-dollar guitar."

Benny picked up the watch. "This is worth a whole roomful of them, and you know it."

Tacky held his gaze.

The old pawnbroker removed the jumbo guitar from its hook and tuned it, cocking his ear to the ceiling as if trying to hear a distant song. He handed it to Nub. It had been nearly thirty years since Nub had touched a guitar. And he had never touched one this nice.

"I don't want a guitar," said Nub.

Benny said, "Take it before this idiot changes his mind."

Nub balanced the instrument against his chest. It was the smell that got him first. All stringed instruments had smells that were entirely their own. Spruce and hide glue. Rosewood and ash. Fragrant bits of wood glued together to make art. Not unlike fine pieces of furniture with strings.

He adjusted the E string and began to pick "In the Garden." Next he played "Old Folks at Home," a song that most people knew as "Swanee River." Then "Wildwood Flower."

"Okay," said Tacky. "I'll throw in the Gibson. Because it's you, Nub. But I'm losing money here."

They shook hands.

"There's a special room in hell for you, Tacky," said Benny. Everyone laughed.

Tacky placed cash in Nub's palm. They walked out of the place and Nub felt a weighty sense of self-disgust sweep over him. He had given away the most important object in his father's and grandfather's lives in exchange for a small pile of government paper. One of the last heirlooms of his father. Tacky was right: his father would have killed him for doing something so foolish.

Then again, Nub's father was in no position to judge.

The guys in the Legion applauded when Minnie finished singing. They gave her a standing ovation. Nub made a final flourish on his old mandolin. Benny played a closing tag on the guitar. Nub's fingertips were raw. His left hand ached from gripping the neck of a stringed instrument that looked as though it had been sized for Tom Thumb. But he felt gratified.

This was the first time he'd been in the Legion in months. The place seemed dingy and dark to his newly accustomed eyes. Whereas once this place had seemed so bright and cheery, now it was ugly and dim. He wasn't quite sure what he'd once seen in this place. It used to be his favorite spot on planet Earth. But this place was just a sad, stinky room of tired old men.

It was also the first time Minnie had performed somewhere other than the church. The big child sat on a stool, clutching her pregnant belly, singing country songs about lost love, wayward romances, pickup trucks, trains, honky-tonks, and Jesus. Nub had been eager to see people's responses to her silken voice. Their reactions were perfect. Genuine surprise and delight. There was nothing these old soaks at the Legion loved more than beautiful singing and beautiful girls. And this kid was both.

Minnie began her musical set by singing "Half a Mind" by Ernest Tubb. Then she sang a few Jean Shepard numbers. She sang a gospel tune. She closed with "It Wasn't God Who Made Honky Tonk Angels," à la Kitty Wells.

She killed.

People whooped and hollered. Nub's mandolin solos were garbage, and Benny played okay. But Minnie's voice was a treat to the ears. If you closed your eyes, she sounded like a cross between Mavis Staples and a Brahms symphony.

After they finished their first set, Nub propped his mandolin in the corner. His arthritic hands ached and he massaged the life back into his left hand. He could overhear the remarks from the oldsters in the joint. "That kid can sure enough sing." "Sounds better than any kid I ever heard." "What a set of pipes." "Nub looks good. Has he lost weight?"

Nub sat at the bar and ordered a Coke. Leigh Ann placed it before him and watched him drink his benign carbonated beverage with a great smile on her face.

"Don't make me say it," she said.

"Okay. I won't."

"I'm proud of you, Nub Taylor."

He shushed her. "Don't jinx me, evil woman."

Leigh Ann nodded toward the back of the room. "Too late."

In the doorway of the room was Loretta Barnes. He almost choked on his Coke. His ex-wife was heading straight for him. She looked as though she had come directly from work, dressed to the nines. But then, Loretta always looked like that.

He looked at Leigh Ann. "See what you did? You cursed me."

Leigh Ann threw up her hands.

Loretta ordered tonic water from Leigh Ann. "And, miss?" added Loretta. "Could I have two lemons in that water?"

Leigh Ann smiled. "Yes, ma'am."

Loretta slid onto a stool next to Nub.

"Hey, baby, what's your sign?" he said.

"Dollar signs."

"Least you're honest."

Loretta squeezed lemons into her water. "That girl is very talented. I'm not surprised you two found each other."

He nodded. It was rare for Loretta Barnes to pay a compliment. He wanted to remember it. "That child is probably the best singer I've ever heard in my life. Wait until you hear her sing gospel. We've been invited to sing at First Baptist for Easter Sunday. She's going to blow their underpants off."

She raised her eyebrows. "You? In a church? Where's Chicken Little?"

Nub remained silent.

Nub took a sip from the Coca-Cola and looked at her again.

She was a stunning woman. Always had been. Lean, with bird-like features. Her hair turning silver hadn't hurt her appearance a bit. In many ways, she was more beautiful now than she ever had been. Her edges had softened with age. Nub noticed Leigh Ann from the corner of his eye. She was watching him.

"You're drinking Coke," Loretta said.

"Bad habit. I started young."

"I didn't think you had it in you."

He set down the Coke. "That actually means a lot coming from you. Thank you."

"I'm sure it's killing you not having a drink."

"Weirdest part about drinking Coke is, subconsciously you keep waiting for a beer buzz. But there is no buzz. Only the joy of Coke."

Loretta nodded like she completely understood. Loretta was a know-it-all. It was her most annoying habit. *The problem with know-it-alls*, Nub thought, *is that they make life difficult for those of us who actually do.*

"So you've quit drinking for good?" she said.

"I'm taking one moment at a time."

She took a sip and dabbed her mouth with a napkin. Dainty. He nodded toward Minnie. "Band sounds pretty good, huh?"

"How old is your singer again?"

"She'll turn sixteen in a few weeks."

"And how far along is she?"

"Eight months."

Loretta kept her eyes on Minnie. "So very young."

"We go to OB-GYN appointments more often than we go to the grocery store. The doctor's office has become my second home. I'm thinking of moving in."

Loretta brought her knifelike green eyes to face him. "Why are you doing this?"

"Doing what?"

"Helping some young woman who isn't even yours?"

"Because I can."

He marveled at her. Growing up, they had called Loretta a tomboy, on account of she sort of looked like a boy with her pageboy haircut. She wore overalls from birth to age twelve. She used to be a rural person, just like him. Now she was sophisticated and urbane. And he was still white trash.

"How's Daniel?" he said.

"It's tax season." She said this as though it explained everything. And he guessed it did.

He sipped again. "Tell him I said hello."

Loretta shifted in her chair and gave him a strange look. "Can we go somewhere and talk alone?"

He furrowed his brow. "We are alone."

She glanced at Leigh Ann. "I mean *alone* alone."

"Trust me, honey. You're never more alone than you are when you're sitting at this bar."

She sighed, then started to say something, but they were interrupted. Minnie stood before him and reminded Nub that break time was over. Benny was already on the stage, tuning his guitar. Minnie took him by the hand.

"Hold that thought, Loretta. The boss lady is calling."

Nub and Minnie took the small stage and sang a few more tunes. Nub played fiddle on a few. Minnie's voice was pure and unrestrained, full of power. It was the kind of voice that contradicted her meek personality. It was muscular and vibrant. Proud and confident. The voice that belonged to someone who has never doubted. She sang a song her mother taught her.

> *Hush, hush, somebody's callin' my name.*
> *Hush, hush, somebody's callin' my name.*

Oh, hush, hush, somebody's callin' my name.
O my Lord, O my Lord, what shall I do?
What shall I do?

Sounds like Jesus. Somebody's callin' my name.
Sounds like Jesus. Somebody's callin' my name.
Oh, sounds like Jesus. Somebody's callin' my name.
O my Lord, O my Lord, what shall I do?
What shall I do?

I'm so glad trouble don't last always.
I'm so glad trouble don't last always.
Oh, I'm so glad trouble don't last always.
O my Lord, O my Lord, what shall I do?
What shall I do?

After the song, the audience paused slightly before their applause. The crowd in the Legion hadn't recognized this spiritual, and they weren't quite sure what to do with it. Most didn't know whether to clap or cry.

He could see Loretta in the back of the room. She wasn't clapping or crying. She just looked at him wearing a sad face. The trio played several more songs, and Nub kept his eyes on his ex-wife, who was consuming enough tonic water to sink a small barge. Something was wrong.

On the next break, Nub took Loretta into the parking lot to show her his brand-new Gremlin. The squatty 1970 AMC Gremlin was parked at the curb. It was low to the ground, with tiny tires, about the size of a bowling shoe, only with less legroom.

"Where's Benny's truck?" said Loretta.

"Dead."

"I never would've visualized you in this kind of car."

"Can't a self-respecting cowboy drive a compact car?"

"Where's the self-respecting cowboy?"

She walked around the tiny car and ran her hand along the striped trim. She inspected the windows and touched the tail-lights. Many automotive enthusiasts regarded the Gremlin to be the ugliest car of all time. And to be fair, it was. But she pretended like it wasn't, which was sweet. And frighteningly uncharacteristic.

"Take me for a ride," she said flatly.

He couldn't have been more shocked if she had hit him with an overdue library book. He searched her eyes for signs of sarcasm. "A ride? I thought you wanted to talk."

"We can talk in the car."

"What's gotten into you? You hate it when I drive."

She crawled into the passenger seat and buckled her seat belt. "I'm waiting."

They motored out of the parking lot in reverse. Loretta gripped the chicken handle with both hands because she didn't like to be the one who wasn't in control.

He drove around Park, and she kept remarking that she liked how the vehicle "handled." She probably heard that word on television. She was only being polite; he knew that. But he was grateful she wasn't being critical. He drove along every side street, back alley, dirt road, and even the empty stretch of County Route 19 to show her how fast the car could go on open highways. He was surprised at how good it felt to have her close to him like this. It was almost like the old days.

Almost.

Nub did not feel romantic feelings toward her, not at all.

But he felt nostalgia, and nostalgia can feel almost the same. They had been two idiot youngsters who accidentally created the prettiest redheaded girl to ever live. You can't forget stuff like that.

"What's going on here?" he finally said.

She didn't answer.

"Loretta? Talk to me."

She looked at her hands. This woman was normally so tightly wound she made squeaking noises when she walked. She was not the kind of person who afforded herself many opportunities for silence. But not tonight; something was different.

"It's a nice car, Jeremiah."

"You didn't come here to talk about automobiles."

He turned onto the main drag and approached town proper again. He tapped the brakes at the caution light on Clairmont. He idled at the light, waiting for her to speak. Loretta looked through the windshield at the water tower in the distance. She wore a pained half smile.

"Papk," she said softly. "People are still calling this town Papk, even after you fixed it."

"It's Russian."

"What?"

"It's the Russian word for folder."

"What does that have to do with anything?"

He shrugged.

She laughed. "I don't know how you do it."

"Do what?"

"You drink, you cuss, you fight, you say whatever's on your mind, you care only about yourself, but you have two girls in your life who love you to death."

He looked at the caution light. The halo of yellow humidity surrounded the old traffic signal. The yellow caution light blinked like a metronome.

"Do I?" he said.

She nodded. "And if I'm being honest, I love you too. In a different way than I used to. But it's still love. I'll always have love for you, Nub."

"That's just the tonic water talking."

"It's been a long time since I've ridden in a car with you."

"What would Daniel say?"

She smiled. "He'd probably be glad to get rid of me. We're on different planets. We live different lives."

Nub could only imagine.

Loretta gazed out the passenger window. "All I ever wanted was to have the kind of life you read about in magazines. I wanted to have enough money to dress cute and be able to afford some of the things I wanted. Is that so bad? I just wanted more than what my parents had when they were growing up."

"Lo, what's wrong?"

She began to weep. It was a low-pitched, throbbing kind of cry.

"I was with Amanda Ruark yesterday," she said. "She kept asking me how Emily was doing."

Loretta blew her nose quietly.

"There was something about the way Amanda kept asking about our daughter that seemed all wrong. Amanda told me Emily had been missing school a lot lately. Said she'd been out sick a lot. I could tell there was something off."

Nub nodded. Amanda Ruark was Dr. Ruark's wife. Dr. Ruark had delivered half the town. He had been Emily's physician from childhood. Ruark the Stork, they called him. He was an ass.

"I had to drag it out of her," said Loretta. "I had to beg

Amanda to tell me. She was so embarrassed, like she was breaking the rules. She kept apologizing because she said she thought I already knew."

His heart felt like it quit beating.

"Already knew what, Loretta?"

CHAPTER

≈ 29 ≈

Hank Senior's music was playing in the clunky headphones on Minnie's ears. The headphones were attached with a long, woven cable to the record turntable. She lay on her bed, listening to Hank sing "I'm So Lonesome I Could Cry," while absently reading an *Archie* comic book. Williams was brilliant, she thought. And Archie was an idiot.

She turned a page.

Minnie felt sort of helpless. Phillip had been leaving threatening notes in her locker. And sometimes she worried that he'd come back to the house to taunt her. Moreover, she wondered what would happen when she had the baby. Phillip would have a right to be part of the child's life, wouldn't he? Did Phillip legally have to stay in contact with her? Did she have to remain in contact with *him*? She hoped Phillip wouldn't want anything to do with her. She wished he'd forget all about Minnie and her child. She had a family with Mr. Nub now.

She quit reading when she felt the flutters in her stomach beneath the taut skin of her belly. She sat upright in bed and placed a hand on her tummy, and the tiny pulses got stronger.

Minnie had been feeling the baby kick for a while, but it never got old. Each time was a reminder that she was growing an actual human inside her. She wondered whether it would be a boy or a girl. Sometimes she could make out a foot or the baby's butt as it rolled around. The baby's hiccups were the best. Like little bubbles in her gut.

She removed the headphones from her ears and placed them onto her belly so the child could hear Hank Williams's anthem to the spurned. The flutters in her belly became a little stronger with the music.

"You like that?" she said aloud.

She couldn't believe it. Maybe the baby could actually hear the music. When the song finished, Hank sang another song. The shrieking fiddle intro played and the baby was soon kicking to beat the band. Literally. Minnie started to laugh out loud, but covered her mouth so as not to wake Mr. Nub. When Mr. Nub didn't get enough sleep, he was a grouch.

Her heart had never felt quite this full before. She had never smiled quite this big before either. Eventually, the child in her womb calmed down and the kicking faded. But Minnie clutched her midsection, stuck in a kind of reverent glow. Because it had immediately occurred to her.

She wasn't lonesome anymore.

Cornstalks. Shug was walking through cornstalks. Barefoot.

The stalks rose above Shug's head so that he couldn't see where he was going. He used the small compass embedded in the handle of his Bowie knife to guide him. It was the only way to get through this serpentine cornfield without getting lost.

A cornfield was a dangerous place to be. Most people did not regard things like cornfields as being dangerous, but they are. City mice saw them as pretty scenes on postcards. (Greetings from Nebraska!) But a cornfield could be deadly. A person could get lost in a cornfield for days and die there. Happened all the time in the Midwest. Motorist breaks down on a highway. Driver decides to hoof it through the cornfield toward a distant farmhouse on the horizon. How hard can it be, right? But the corn blocks your vision. You get confused. You lose your orientation. The cops find you six days later, dead from dehydration.

But it was the perfect place to hide.

Shug was moving barefoot tonight because he could move better without shoes. Also, he made less sound this way. Plus, it was how he was raised. He owned shoes as a child, but they were only for special occasions like Sunday school and funerals. Depression-era kids in Ambassador, Alabama, grew up unshod. Their feet were so calloused and toughened that shoes only gave them foot problems.

He carried the heavy satchel over his shoulder. The strap was digging into his collarbone. He carried another bag over his other shoulder. This bag was brimming with a rat's nest of copper wires and detonators. He brushed past stalks of corn and followed the compass dead east.

He emerged from the cornfield to see a single-wide mobile home before him. The old trailer looked as though it had at one time been brown but was now faded tan. There were lights on inside. He could see shapes moving in the windows.

A white Cadillac was parked in the driveway.

Shug reached into his bag and removed a block from the satchel. The block was shaped like a giant stick of butter covered in brown paper with warnings printed on the labels. When you took off the wrapper, you were left with what looked like a bar of wholesale cream cheese. Plastic explosives. The way America won World War II. The British developed the substance first, known as Composition C. Then it was developed into C-2. By the end of the Korean War, it had been redeveloped into C-4.

In a strange way, sometimes he missed being in the military. He didn't miss the bad food or the grueling hours spent outside. But he missed having a real job. He had been good at his job. And there was a certain pride in being good at what you did. You rarely got that kind of pride working at steel mills. You certainly didn't get that kind of pride working for the depraved men in The Organization.

He crawled onto his belly and scuttled beneath the Cadillac.

During the war, Shug used C-4 on an almost daily basis. They used it to demolish bridges, tunnels, tanks, enemy strongholds, and key buildings in the Taebaeksan region of North Gyeongsang. It was a tool of his trade. It was his art. Some men worked in oils or clay. Shug Bass worked in explosives.

Shug pressed a lump of clay onto the chassis of the Caddy, near the gas tank.

Then he heard vehicles approaching.

It sounded like a motorcade was pulling into the driveway. Shug saw a train of headlights. He huddled into a ball beneath the car and tried not to breathe.

He heard car doors open, then slam. He heard men get out. Shoes shuffling in the dirt. He could see their feet from his angle beneath the Caddy. He was only inches away from their shoes. Nice shoes. Several of them. Too many to count. And all the shoes were accompanied with trousers that were cuffed. Expensive slacks, probably.

The many pairs of feet lingered outside the vehicles. He heard men's lighters click open. He heard their voices, laughing and carrying on. He recognized some of the voices as old coworkers, but most of the voices were new to him. He recognized one of the voices as a boss in The Organization. A key man. A man with a lot of blood on his hands.

After a few minutes, the conversations died. He saw a dozen

cigarette butts fall to the earth. He watched nice shoes step on each butt. Then the pairs of feet walked inside the trailer home.

And Shug's heart finally began beating again.

He shimmied from beneath the Caddy. He almost couldn't believe what he saw. A parade of cars sat parked in the driveway. A cavalcade of luxury vehicles with lots of chrome and blemish-free, white-walled tires. Cadillacs, Lincolns, Mercuries, and Buicks. He couldn't believe they were all gathered in one place like this.

He checked the contents of his satchel. He had enough C-4 to take care of a small country. He had hit the proverbial jackpot. Maybe luck really was on his side. He crawled beneath the mobile home and spent two hours rigging up C-4 on the floor joists. He spent a half hour stringing long copper lines hundreds of yards into the distance. He took cover in the cornfield. And when the clock struck the top of the hour . . .

He blew them all to perdition.

CHAPTER

⊰ 30 ⊱

The sun was rising over the tree line of Park, Alabama. The portrait of farm-town life at its best. And its worst. The brick buildings were framed by the orange glow of daylight. The faint smell of manure was in the air, a smell that visitors found repulsive but residents were unable to detect.

Nub was parked in the redhead's front yard.

He was seated on the hood of his little Gremlin. He was smoking. It was the first cigarette he'd had since he'd quit last night. There were some battles you could win; others you couldn't. That's what AA taught. You did what you could. You took it one step at a time. Most people at AA smoked like freighters. Nobody judged you for it.

Emily came out of the house and shut the door behind her. She didn't lock the door since nobody in Park locked doors. If ever any thief came through town and wanted to pilfer through the belongings of Ash County, all he would have had to do was pick his favorite house.

When Emily saw him, she stopped.

They just looked at each other. She was dressed for work. Her school clothes were smart. Her blouse was cream-colored and she wore a blazer over it. Pearls. Slingback heels. Her hair was pulled behind her in a tight French roll. Unlike any biology teacher he ever had. He bet the high school boys paid very close attention during her lessons. He could tell she'd lost weight.

"Dad?"

"I've been called worse."

"What are you, a stalker?"

"Maybe."

"I thought you quit smoking."

"I'll quit tomorrow."

"You make it sound so easy."

"Quitting smoking is easy. I've done it thousands of times."

She ignored him and walked to her Buick. She tossed open the door and threw her bags into the back seat. She was a bag person. Wherever she went, she carried bags. Not just purses but canvas bags with lots of stuff. Loretta was the same way. They carried bags containing half the contents of the known universe. God help the man who asked for a strip of bubble gum from Emily or Loretta. It usually tasted like old perfume and purse dirt.

"Let me give you a ride to school," he said.

"No thanks. I'm okay."

"Are you?"

She gave him a look.

"Move your car, Dad. You're blocking me in. And I'm running late."

He smiled at her. "Let me give you a ride to work. Pretty please? With cherries on top?"

"What is this?"

He shimmied off the hood and opened the door to his microcar. He made a gesture like a man welcoming a queen into his carriage. "Your transportation awaits, m'lady."

Emily was not amused, but something in her face changed. They had a short standoff before she relented. "I don't want a ride, Dad."

"And I don't want to have to kidnap you. But we all do what we have to do."

Her voice broke. "Get out of my driveway and let me go to school, please."

The petulant teenager, digging in her heels. Nub was not exactly father of the year, but he knew one thing that always worked with petulant teenagers who dug in their heels.

"I will give you fifty bucks if you get in this car and let me drive you to school."

"Dad."

"Seventy-five."

"You can't even pay your light bill."

He removed his wallet and shook it at her. "Tell that to Benjamin Franklin."

"Please get out of the way."

"*Two* Benjamin Franklins."

Emily sighed. She jerked open the door to her Buick and removed her bags. She transferred them into Nub's back seat, then climbed in and slammed the door shut. He stepped into the car and sat beside her. He turned over the engine.

She held out her hand. "Pay up."

"That's my girl."

When Emily realized they weren't going to the school, she flipped out. When Nub told her he had called Principal Anders and gotten her the day off from work, she was livid. It was a kind of anger he had rarely seen before. It was existential anger.

It was the kind of anger that had nothing to do with him. Nub recognized the tone. He knew it well. She would get over it.

With his prisoner in the passenger seat, he passed all the little outlying towns and drove past the wide pastures of summer fescue and alfalfa. The foraging grass was being cut for silage. He took the cutoff that led around the county perimeter and found himself on the interstate, riding alongside Peterbilts and Mack trucks with wind currents powerful enough to sweep his miniature car off the road. They were heading toward Greenville, which was two hours south of Park. Plenty of time for her to simmer down. Plenty of time to talk.

"Who told you?" she finally said.

"You just did."

She gazed out the window. He saw her wiping her eyes. "How long have you known?"

"Not long."

"Does Mama know?"

"Amanda Ruark told her."

They were quiet for a long time. Until he took the off-ramp. He rolled to a stop, then turned at the stop sign. They arrived in Greenville proper. Also known as Camellia City. He eased into the parking lot and killed the engine. Before them was a simple restaurant with a shingled rooftop. The place sat perched thirty miles south of Montgomery in Lowndes County. A place that started in 1923 when Willie Claude and Helen Bates received nine turkey eggs as a birthday present from Willie's aunt Marie. The turkeys got the farming family through the Depression. The restaurant was the result of that. Bates House of Turkey. A national institution. God bless America.

"What are we doing here?"

"Girl's got to eat."

"I'm not a girl anymore."

"You will always be my little girl."

They walked inside and the bell dinged over the door. Bates House of Turkey was a place with brown tile floors and Tammy Wynette singing overhead. A deli case was up front. McDonald's-style menus on the walls. A few men in seed hats were in the dining room, sipping coffee. Relaxing on the axis of the Wheel of Life. A throng of customers gathered before a register. They joined the line. Emily took her time reading the menu. So thorough. So diligent. His daughter did nothing half-way. He, too, glanced at the menu. But only half-heartedly. He was too busy watching his little girl.

"What're you going to order?" he asked.

"I don't know."

There was a lot to choose from. Turkey salad, turkey legs, turkey thighs, turkey dressing, turkey pie, turkey noodle soup, hickory smoked turkey, pecan smoked turkey, mesquite turkey, barbecued turkey, and the Gobbler, a signature sandwich served with a tomato slice and lettuce piled atop a fluffy white bun that was big enough to be used in pillow fights.

Nub ordered a Gobbler. Emily ordered the smoked turkey. They both ordered large iced teas. The tea came from a machine and was sweet enough to break your jaw. They sat outside at a picnic table. Traffic whizzed by on the interstate nearby. He was overwhelmed at how fast vehicles traveled now. Nub had grown up on a tobacco farm, during an era when the fastest a vehicle could go was however fast the mule pulled it. Now there were semis the size of small continents doing ninety. The world was leaving him behind.

He looked at the young woman before him. She was quiet. Sullen. He had screwed up her life; this never once escaped him. Not once did he forget that he was the source of her pain.

Not once did he forget all the missed birthdays and the broken promises. He could recite his failures one by one.

Emily stole Nub's pickle. She snapped into it without saying anything, a hanging offense in some parts. But he let it slide because he liked the offender.

"What're you thinking?" he said.

"I'm scared," she said. "That's the emotion I can't get rid of. I'm afraid all the time. Every moment. It never goes away."

He pushed his plate away. "Okay, what are our options here?"

"There are none. The doctors say they can't do anything for me."

"Doctors don't know everything." He looked at her. "Have you had a second opinion?"

"Yes."

"How about a third?"

"And waste what little time I have left?"

"You're a science major; I don't have to tell you that small-town bumpkin doctors don't know squat. Have you tried UAB? That's where all the rich people go. You're rich, you know."

"I don't see the point."

Nub studied the parking lot behind them. It was steadily filling with vehicles. Families in station wagons. People in Volkswagen vans. People from six counties were visiting this place. It was *the* place to be.

"What exactly did the doctors tell you?" he said.

"That it's spreading."

"Spreading."

"That my breasts have multiple tumors. That we caught it too late. That I'm dying, Dad. I'm dying."

"Have you told Charlie Jr.?"

Her eyes were bloodshot now. "You're the only one who

knows. And I guess Mama. And I'd like to keep it that way. For now. I'm not ready to tell anyone."

His little girl began to cry. The child whose life he had ruined. His mind was filled with one hundred gallons of regret. His heart was filled with several thousand watts of pain. He had missed her life because he had refused to fight for her. Because he was too drunk to be present.

He said, "You have to tell Charlie Jr."

"Please don't tell me how to be a parent. You of all people."

"I want to help, Emily."

She touched her mascara with her pinky. She laughed. "*You* want to help. Perfect."

"What do you need?"

"I don't know what I need anymore."

"What do you want, then?"

She stared at her sandwich. She was in some kind of daze, gazing at it long and hard. "I don't want to die, Daddy."

And the floodgate opened. His baby was four years old again. She was the same child who had fallen on the gravel road and busted her chin open. The same little girl who once accidentally ran a fishing hook through her finger. The same child whose boo-boos he used to kiss away.

He reached both hands across the table. She held his hands with hers.

"I love you, Emily."

She did not answer; she never did.

They pressed their foreheads together but didn't speak for a long time. He wanted to bawl alongside her, but he knew his daughter needed strength right now, not commiseration. They listened to the tributary of interstate traffic scream by. He could think of nothing else to say, so he said the first thing that came to his mind.

"How about we go get some ice cream?"
She sniffed. "Okay."

Nub and Emily drove to Comb, Alabama. To Swan's Ice Cream Shoppe. A kid in line ahead of them got blueberry and chocolate scoops. Classic mistake. Chocolate and blueberry clashed. Chocolate was not the correct foundation for a blueberry partner. It was like trying to build a brick house on sand.

When it was Emily's turn, she ordered one scoop of chocolate and a second scoop of caramel. Then she topped it with crushed toffee. A seasoned pro.

Nub selected a scoop of vanilla, a scoop of orange sherbet, and a scoop of lemon ice cream.

They loaded into his car and drove out toward the Old General. They arrived in the empty gravel parking area. They had the tree all to themselves.

Together they sat on the lowest branch, watching the onslaught of spring erupt all around them. They licked their cones at their own paces. She had stripped her jacket off so that she was wearing only her blouse, which was stained with streaks of melted brown ice cream. She looked so skinny that he lost his appetite.

For a moment in time, she was his little girl and he was her youthful father. For a moment in time, they were fishing buddies. For a moment in time, she was pigtails, freckles, and missing teeth. They talked about average things. People in town. People who annoyed them. Funny stories involving distant cousins. Things involving Loretta. They didn't ignore the topic of disease, but they didn't wallow in it either. She cried a lot. He cried some. They held each other. She leaned on him the way she used to. He kissed her hair the way he used to. He reveled in the smell of her shampoo.

When they finished their cones, they took the long drive back to Park. Although the drive wasn't nearly long enough. He wished it would take days. Years even. He wished it would take them decades to get back home so they could be together forever. He didn't want today to end. But it had to end. All good things did. Minnie would be home from school. And the world would resume its normal pace. Things needed to be done. Chores needed doing. His foster child needed her clothes ironed for the upcoming Easter service next week. Supper had to be made. Minnie had homework. He had bills to pay. His life revolved around stacks of laundry that were roughly the size of subtropical continents. It was the first time in his life he had lived for another person. He regretted that he hadn't lived life for the person in his passenger seat.

He pulled into his daughter's driveway and tugged the parking brake. He wriggled his body out of the car. It was hard getting out of a Gremlin; the car rode so low to the ground you couldn't have rolled a baseball beneath it without getting it stuck.

He removed his daughter's many bags from the back seat.

"I can get my own bags," she said. "I'm not dead yet."

He handed them to her and smiled. "Okay."

She left him and walked toward her home. Away from him. She waved goodbye weakly, then shut her front door.

He stood there for a while, in her driveway, looking at the opulent place where she lived. The pillars. The wide porch. The sun was getting lower over the tree line. The crickets were so loud they hurt his ears. And he wanted to hate God, but he was too sad to hate anyone right now.

Finally, he was about to get into America's smallest car

when he heard feet scuffling on the sidewalk. He turned. Emily was jogging toward him. Without saying a word, she threw both arms around him and squeezed. She hadn't hugged him like this since she was eight years old. So openly. So unashamedly. He spoke into her ear. The words just came from him, without thought, without preparation.

"Lord, please grant my daughter the serenity to accept the things she cannot change, the courage to change the things she can, and the wisdom to know the difference."

≈ 31 ≈

Easter came with all the triumph of a royal wedding. The trees were blooming. The forests that had once been dead and barren were fragrant and viridian. Nub, Minnie, and Benny arrived at First Baptist Church on Easter morning carrying instrument cases. First Baptist always had big to-dos for Easter. They always hired visiting musicians to perform for Easter Sunday since Easter was when the church had the most prospective clients. And this year Minnie had been invited. Several other musicians had as well. A gospel quartet from Leeds; an all-sibling blue-grass group from Franklin, Tennessee; a one-woman band from DeFuniak Springs, Florida, who could play "All Hail the Power" on the piano while using her left foot to play a hi-hat and her mouth to play the jaw harp.

The church lawn had been transformed into a veritable camp meeting. A large white tent sat perched on the lawn, the kind of tent traveling revivals and circuses used. A main stage had been erected inside, with an amplification system that was big enough to stage a Who concert.

"Looks like the Ringling Brothers came to town," said Benny.

Nub was dressed in pastel attire. Benny wore enough Old Spice to suffocate a toddler. Minnie was wearing a red-and-white maternity dress. Leigh Ann had come to Nub's house that morning and spent an hour altering Minnie's dress, and another forty-five minutes on her hair. Forty-five minutes.

"I'm nervous," said Minnie.

"Don't say that," said Nub. "Never say that."

"Why?"

"It's an old vaudeville superstition."

"What's vaudeville?"

You had to worry about today's youth.

The band entered the tent and placed their cases on the stage. They were greeted by a tall woman with silver hair. Miss Linda Currington. She welcomed them and thanked them for coming. The old Baptist woman was about as warm and fuzzy as a frozen banana.

"Happy Easter," said Nub.

Miss Linda gave a curt smile, glanced at Minnie's belly, then walked away.

"What was her problem?" said Minnie.

"Not enough Metamucil," said Benny.

"Didn't anyone know I was pregnant?"

Nub held out a hand and rocked it back and forth. "Some did."

"But they still invited me?"

"Not *they*. Carolyn Winters invited you."

"Who's she?"

"Carolyn is a liberal feminist who burns bras and doesn't shave her armpits."

"She's kind of an activist," said Benny.

"What's that?" Minnie asked.

"Someone who yells a lot."

They were led to the fellowship hall, which was serving as a sort of dressing room for all the visiting bands. The musicians gave Minnie strange looks when she entered. Like Miss Linda, their eyes would flit from Minnie's eyes to her belly. It was a wonder they weren't dizzy.

"Hello, Nub," said Brad Walker, the church usher, pumping Nub's hand.

"Hello, Brad," Nub said in his overly social voice. "Why, I haven't seen you since . . ." Nub drew a blank.

"Since you rear-ended me last year."

"Right."

"I was at the caution light on Clairmont."

"Uh-huh."

"I was at a standstill. You rammed right into me and totaled my Plymouth. And then you didn't have insurance, so I had to take you to small claims court."

"Yes, that's it. So how's your wife?"

Brad promptly walked away.

Benny and Nub began unpacking their instruments. Nub began tuning his mandolin with an upright piano in the corner. Benny replaced the high-E string on his Martin.

Carolyn Winters entered the room and started shaking all the performers' hands. Carolyn was strangely dressed in a peasant's dress. She was tall. And richer than Jesus' aunt. She dressed like Joni Mitchell and talked like Elly May Clampett. She was sponsoring the musicians this morning, and letting everyone know it. Nub wondered whether her armpits were as hairy as a man's.

Old money. Park was full of old money.

Carolyn shook Nub's hand with a man's grip. When she pumped Minnie's hand, Carolyn's eyes went directly to Minnie's midsection.

"So she's trying to prove some point by having me here?" said Minnie.

"No," said Nub. "She's paying us three hundred dollars."

"It's not worth it," said Minnie.

"It is when you're the one buying all the Hamburger Helper."

"Don't take it personally," said Benny. "These people are about as much fun as hepatitis. They don't even like themselves. That's their real problem." Benny tapped a finger against his temple. "It's called psychology."

The trio ran through their tunes in the fellowship hall standing in the corner. Minnie was prepared to sing three songs. She would open the service with "Christ the Lord Is Risen Today." Then she would sing "Peace in the Valley." After which she would finish with "In the Sweet By and By." Nub would play fiddle on the last tune, although he hadn't played fiddle since FDR was in office. They rehearsed all three songs until they hated each melody. Because that's how you practiced, Nub often reminded her. Once you hated the song, you were ready. That's what Nub's banjo-playing grandfather taught him.

They strummed the final chord, and Benny whistled in appreciation. "If that don't light your fire."

"Okay," said Nub. "How's everyone feeling?"

"I'm really nerv—" She caught herself. "I'm doing okay."

"Attagirl."

Minnie's ankles were a little swollen; she needed to get off her feet. Nub found a folding chair for her and helped her sit. Minnie looked nervous. The other performers moved around the room, speaking to each other, but they refused to say a word to Minnie. They didn't look her in the eyes. There were no "Happy Easters." No "He has risen indeeds." They didn't acknowledge her. They moved around her like she wasn't there.

"Nobody's talking to me," she said to Nub.

"Beautiful girls intimidate ugly people, sweetie."

"Is it because I'm . . ." She touched her distended tummy.

Nub squatted before her and held her hand. "One cold morning a long time ago, a girl not much younger than you came into town riding a donkey. She had a baby, and that boy went on to change the entire world."

"You mean Jesus?"

"Jimmie Rodgers."

When it was closer to performance time, Nub slipped out the side door to scope things out.

The monstrous church tent began to fill with bodies. Baptist churches always fill up the same way: back to front. He felt the familiar performance butterflies dancing in his stomach. It had been a long time since he'd played music before a large crowd. He was exhilarated and a little worried that he'd make a mistake.

He felt someone breathing on his neck. It was Minnie.

"I really am nervous," she whispered.

"I told you not to say that."

"Look at me, I'm shaking."

"No, you ain't."

"Yes, I am. And I've had to pee five times already. And I think I have to pee again."

"Well, step away from me then. These are my new shoes."

The crowd kept getting bigger. Soon the church tent was at capacity. People were sitting cross-legged in the grass. Boys were relinquishing folding chairs to older ladies. Children were sitting in their parents' laps. Kids were seated in the grassy aisles. The outskirts of the tent were overflowing with piety.

"Remember," Nub told her. "Just like I told you. Visualize everyone naked if you start to get anxious."

"Even the old men?"

"Especially the old men. That'll sober anyone up."

Nub checked his watch.

Eight minutes until showtime.

He wanted to puke.

Nub wedged the fiddle beneath his chin to warm up. He re-tuned it for the eighth time. Benny was using a dishrag to wipe his guitar; the spring humidity was causing condensation to appear on the lacquered finish. Benny picked through a few bars of something slow and mournful. Nub played along on the fiddle. Nub was impressed at how his cousin, with a half-paralyzed face and body, could still do anything on a guitar. It had been at least half a century since these two men had performed such tunes, and yet Benny sounded the same as he always had. One of the church ushers milling around back was watching Nub bow his fiddle.

"That's a mighty nice violin," the usher said.

"Ain't a violin; it's a fiddle."

The usher smiled. "What's the difference?"

"Nobody cares if you spill beer on a fiddle."

The event began. Nub could hear the preacher speaking through the large amplification system, kicking off the service with an opening prayer. The sound of his devout words vibrated throughout the whole of Ash County. Then everyone sang a few opening hymns. The congregation exuded about as much enthusiasm as a graveyard.

Leigh Ann met Nub backstage. She was wearing a white dress. It was formfitting.

"Hey, you," she said.

"I didn't think you came to church," Nub said.

"There's a lot you don't know about me." She placed a small

white rose in his lapel and patted his cheek. "I just wanted to wish y'all good luck."

"This is a Baptist church, Leigh Ann. They don't believe in luck."

"Okay, well then, break a leg."

"This crowd would like to see me break my arm too."

In only moments, the trio was announced. The people applauded. Nub and his cousin and Minnie took the plywood concert stage like guests on the *Ed Sullivan Show*. The congregation fell bone quiet as Minnie absently rested a hand on her large midriff. Nub had been expecting a mixed reaction from the crowd, but he was not prepared for what happened next.

The audience began murmuring among themselves. Truthfully, Nub couldn't blame them. It wasn't every day the town drunk took the platform at First Baptist Church alongside a pregnant teenager. He watched the ripple of muttering trickle through the congregation and he felt his temper rise. People craned their necks. Others leaned over and whispered to their neighbors. Nub took to the mic and introduced the band. As he spoke, two people in the crowd got up and walked out. Nub knew the people who were leaving. Another man ushered his wife out of the tent. Then a few more left the service. Followed by a few dozen more. Then several more. Nub felt naked on that stage.

"What's everyone leaving for?" whispered Minnie.

Nub said nothing.

A young couple left. Then two middle-aged couples. Then more older people. These were people Nub Taylor had known his whole life. People he'd gone to school with. People he'd grown up with. People he said hello to on the street. People he had worked with.

When the crowd had thinned somewhat, Nub's heart was

in his shoe. He addressed his audience with a soft voice. He wanted to dog cuss them all, but when he looked at Leigh Ann, standing in the wings, he remembered how he had gotten here. He was here because of the endless AA meetings, the endless cups of cheap coffee, the midnight talks with Leigh Ann, and the tears shed with his sponsors.

He spoke into the mic. "I suppose the last place anyone expected me to be on Easter Sunday morning was right here." His words reverberated through the air. "I bet you think it's pretty odd, seeing me here. Mainly because most of you know me. Most of you know who I am, and *what* I am, and what kinds of things I've done. And to be quite honest, I'm pretty embarrassed right now."

Nobody in the audience breathed a word.

Nub looked at Emily, who was seated in the front row. She had steepled her hands together and wedged them beneath her chin. Leigh Ann was smiling.

"But you know what?" Nub went on. "I'll get over my embarrassment. Because if there's one thing I've learned, it's that you can't save your ass and your face at the same time."

The preacher flatlined.

But to Nub's surprise, a few on the church lawn began applauding his words. And this applause slowly grew into a swelling roar. A few congregational members even started a standing ovation. Soon, the remainder of the crowd was on its feet applauding one pregnant child, one stroke victim, and one drunk.

When the applause trickled out, the music began. Nub picked his mandolin. Benny strummed his Martin. And Minniford Hazel Bass blew everyone's faces off.

CHAPTER

≈ 32 ≈

Minnie Bass had never been a celebrity before. But she was today. At least that's how she felt. After the Easter service, people were swarming her. Members of the First Baptist congregation were competing for the chance to meet her, hug her, shake her hand. Minnie was supposed to sing only three songs, but the crowd cheered for encore after encore, so she ended up singing for nearly forty minutes before the other performers had a chance to play the first song. Mr. Nub called it charisma. He said Minnie had it. And he told her you couldn't teach charisma. He told her charisma was like having a cleft lip: either you were born with it or you weren't.

And so Minnie found herself caught up in the most wonderful morning of her entire life, there in the parking lot of First Baptist. It was the best day of her existence, hands down. Because there were so many people fighting for the chance to meet her. She hugged endless rivers of people. She posed for a few photographs. She had never felt so unalone before.

After pressing the flesh and glad-handing, Mr. Nub and Mr. Benny and Miss Emily and Miss Leigh Ann whisked her away from her flocks of admirers.

They plodded through the parking lot toward the Gremlin,

parked at the far end, past an Atlantic of cars. Miss Emily went on and on about how great she did. Miss Leigh Ann told her how beautiful she looked. Mr. Benny kept replaying the performance and picking out his favorite moments. Mr. Nub wore a face that looked like he'd just discovered teeth.

Minnie was tired and a little overwhelmed, but glowing all over. She could feel her heart beating wildly from all the social interaction and conversation. The pregnancy was taking a toll on her energy levels. She was depleted and tired and her feet were so swollen she could hardly walk. But she drew a different kind of energy from her success.

"You were amazing, Minnie," said Miss Emily. "I can't believe your voice. I've never heard anyone sing like that before."

"Thank you."

"I'm not sure you understand how good you are," said Leigh Ann.

"You have real talent, sweetie," Emily went on.

"My favorite part was when Nub said *ass*," Benny added.

When they got to the Gremlin, Newton's third law demonstrated itself to be true. It was something Minnie had always known was true. Every action had an equal and opposite reaction. Every up had a down. Every high had a low. You couldn't trust any peak, because a valley would soon follow. It was a mathematical principle. And you could not break mathematical laws.

A crowd of churchgoers was gathered around Nub's car. They were all covering their mouths. Mr. Nub pushed his way through the clot of onlookers. He froze in his steps.

The Gremlin's windshield was shattered. The hood was smashed. Both bumpers had been ripped off and were lying on the pavement. The tires were slashed and airless. The doors had been kicked in. Windows broken. The antenna ripped off. And the upholstery torn apart.

Minnie ran away weeping.

Minnie blew out the sixteen candles atop her cake. The party was small but fun. Just the five of them. Miss Emily, Benny, Nub, Leigh Ann, and the birthday queen. It was not a small cake, however. Emily called it a "chocolate death" cake, and it was about the size of a basketball court. The cake sat on the table. Ten layers. When Emily cut into the center of the cake, an ooze of molten chocolate came gushing out, akin to a primordial pit. The doctor had told Minnie to watch her sugar consumption.

"Gestational diabetes does not exist tonight," said Nub.

"Oh yes, it does," said Leigh Ann. She turned to Minnie. "Just one piece."

Nub plated Minnie's nine-pound wedge of cake with a wink.

For supper, they'd eaten barbecue ribs and pulled pork. Mr. Benny had been smoking pork all day behind the barn. The meat had been a little spicy for Minnie's preference, but delicious nonetheless. Benny said his spicy sauce was a special family recipe. Two parts melted butter, three parts ketchup, and sixteen thousand parts black pepper.

After the meal, Minnie moved to the sink to do the dishes like she did almost every night, but Nub wouldn't allow it. Not on her birthday. He sent her into the den where they opened gifts. Emily had bought her lots of nice clothes; none of them were from Kmart. Leigh Ann gave Minnie a basket of beauty supplies. Benny bought her a scented candle called "Parisian Rendezvous."

But the apex of the evening came from the box that was tucked in the corner, behind the settee. Mr. Nub told Minnie to go fetch it. She opened the large, oblong box to find a big guitar with a blond finish.

"The fretboard has mother-of-pearl inlay," said Benny, pointing it out.

The headstock read "Gibson."

Minnie had been learning to play with Benny's old guitar for months now. She had been practicing each night after Nub went to bed. She could play several chords and accompany herself pretty well.

Minnie strummed on the new guitar and began to sing "Amazing Grace," then followed it up with "Hey, Good Lookin'," a song she remembered her mother singing long ago. And as Nub did dishes in the other room, he called out that she should play more country music, since country music was more marketable, and didn't she want to be famous one day and make a lot of money and have a nice house and manservants who would empty her trash and such.

So she played country music for him. She adjusted the guitar on her large belly and began to sing one of Nub's all-time favorites: the 1953 hit by Kitty Wells, "Will Your Lawyer Talk to God?" In the song, Kitty Wells asks her wicked ex whether his divorce lawyer will talk to God and defend him on that final judgment day. The song was supposed to be somewhat humorous, but whenever she played it, the melody seemed to touch Mr. Nub in a deeply spiritual way. Next, Minnie played "Back in Baby's Arms," a tune by Patsy Cline. She played "I've Been Everywhere," because it had taken her weeks to memorize the lyrics. But it was during her rendition of "Just a Closer Walk" that something in her stomach began to happen.

Minnie stopped playing. She lurched forward. She placed

the guitar on the sofa. At first, she thought it was just the baby kicking again. But it soon proved to be more.

"What's wrong?" Emily said.

Minnie gripped her abdomen. There was the pain again. It felt like a bowel movement, sort of. A strong pressure was coming from her back and stomach, radiating through her upper thighs and her butt. The pain got worse.

"What is it?" Emily said.

"You're going to think it's gross," Minnie said.

"No, sweetie, I won't think it's gross."

Minnie sucked in a breath through her clenched teeth. "It feels like I'm going to have diarrhea."

"Dad!" Emily shouted.

Nub appeared in the den with a dish towel in his hands.

"What is it?"

"She's having her baby," Leigh Ann said.

Dark meadows whipped by Emily's Buick, which was moving as fast as it could travel. Minnie was doing her best to keep breathing like Emily and Leigh Ann were constantly telling her. She was in the back seat with Nub and Leigh Ann. Emily was driving. Benny was in the passenger seat instructing Emily how to drive, which was ticking Emily off. She threatened to throw him out of the car at least twice.

"Just keep breathing, dear!" Emily shouted as she stared at the road. "Breathing is key! In and out!"

Minnie did her best to follow Emily's advice, but it was hard to remember to breathe beneath all this pain. Emily and Leigh Ann had told her the same thing all the books said: with enough conscious breathing, the pain could be managed. Not eliminated, but managed. The books, with all due respect, were full of crap. No amount of breathing was reducing the nuclear pain of childbirth Minnie was undergoing right now. There was an ache in her pelvis that felt as though her bones were about to break. A strange pounding feeling was moving across her belly. Like the muscles were about to tear themselves.

The car hit a bump in the road. The passengers were momentarily airborne. Everyone came down onto their seats with a crash.

"Uh-oh!" Minnie screamed.

"What's uh-oh?" Nub said.

Minnie shouted, "I think I'm peeing myself."

"You're what?" Benny said.

"Miss Emily, I think I'm ruining your car."

"You're not peeing," Leigh Ann said. "It's your water breaking. It's okay. Emily's car will survive."

"But I won't," Nub said. "I'm all wet."

She could hear the fluid splatter on the floorboards.

"I'm so sorry about this, Mr. Nub," Minnie said. "I'm sorry about your car, Miss Emily."

"Quit worrying about her stupid car," Benny said. "Emily's loaded."

"I think I'm having another contraction," Minnie said.

The doctor had spoken at great length about contractions at her appointments. He told her how the contractions would feel and how they would be spaced several minutes apart to begin with, but then the intervals would get smaller and smaller.

Emily looked at her in the rearview mirror. "What are you feeling?"

Minnie howled in pain. She was closing her eyes tightly, clutching her stomach with both hands. "Feels like my stomach's going to rip open!" Minnie shouted with agony again. The pain was so great, she could hardly breathe.

"I'm scared," she said. "Mr. Nub, I'm so scared."

"It's okay, darling," said Nub. "Women have been doing this for thousands of years. Nothing to be worried about."

Leigh Ann held her hand tightly.

Minnie was crying now. "This is all my fault. I'm so sorry for all the trouble I've brought on everyone. I'm so sorry for everything. This is all my fault."

Nub patted her hair. "Hush that."

Minnie screamed again. This scream had a different ring to it, even to her own ears. She had to push.

"Emily!" shouted Leigh Ann. "Pull over!"

CHAPTER

❧ 33 ❧

Eight miles away, Shug was seated before a campfire, braiding together strands of fishing line. He had been staying in this holler for weeks now. He'd been sleeping in the woods. He knew this place so well, he felt at home.

Several weeks ago he'd quit reporting to his parole officer. And after he'd been recognized by Nub Taylor, he'd quit going into work at the IGA. He'd decided to go into permanent hiding; however, he did so after removing several Organization members from this earth. He stayed out here and kept eyes on the Taylor house. Twenty-four seven. Well, almost.

He caught rabbits and squirrels and lived on those. He built his campfires in pits so he could cover his tracks. He never stayed in the same location twice. It was the kind of life he'd craved when he was inside an eight-by-five cell. Out here, he felt as though he'd been born again. He'd been trapped in a cage for fifteen years, eating the same food, looking at the same painted block walls. He'd been having the same stupid conversations with his lawyers, week after week. The entire time, all he had wanted to do was be outside. He wanted to sit beneath an open night sky like this. He wanted to smell the immobilizingly sweet smell of pine trees. He wanted to sweat. He wanted to be miserable from mosquito bites. And ticks. He missed them all.

He had missed nature. In prison, the only nature you got was head lice.

He heard the sound of footsteps in the grass.

He stood.

He had nothing but a pair of pliers nearby. But pliers would work in a hand-to-hand situation. The things you learn in prison. He'd seen a spoon used in a prison fight once. It was startling what men could do with a spoon when properly motivated.

"What're you going to do?" said his visitor, stepping through the brush. "Take out my teeth with pliers?"

"I didn't know it was you."

They embraced. Brant Simms clapped Shug on the shoulders. Shug had known Brant since they were four-year-old snots, playing cowboys. They shot their first deer when they were ten. They bagged their first turkeys at age fourteen. They stayed close until Shug had strayed from the path. But Brant was a good man. He worked at the paper mill, had a wife and three kids. His family lived on nothing, but somehow Brant made it work. For which Shug respected him greatly. Shug had not been able to do the same.

"Anyone know you're out here?" said Brant.

"Just you."

Brant stabbed the fire with a stick. Sparks flew into the night. He was wearing clothes with holes in them. His shoes looked old and worn. He was a family man now.

"Don't you think it's a little gutsy, having a fire? Someone could find you out here. Someone might hear the racket. What are you making?"

Shug inspected his braided trip line. "Arts and crafts. Did you get the safety deposit box?"

"Yes, I got it. It was easy." Brant dug into his pocket and

handed Shug a small key. "She'll have to show ID before they'll let her in there."

"Good." Then Shug felt a cool wave of fear come over him. If Brant was out here at this hour, something was wrong. They hadn't planned to meet until a few days from now.

"Why are you out here this late?" said Shug.

"Well, let's see, I'm here because you killed eight of the most dangerous men involved in organized crime within the Southeast. I'm here because you have an entire police department looking for you. Jeez, Shug. Aren't you worried?"

"The Ash County Sheriff's Department isn't exactly the few and the proud. I'd rather take my chances with them than with gangsters."

"They're not just gangsters, and you know it. These guys are mercenaries. And I wouldn't call the sheriff's department nothing either. That deputy shot you."

The truth was, Shug accidentally shot his own leg. It happened during the struggle over the cop's gun; the pistol went off. It was nobody's fault. The bullet went straight through the top portion of Shug's quadricep and burned like the dickens. At first, he thought he had mortally wounded himself, but it wasn't as serious as it could have been. Shug had seen enough gunshot wounds in his career to know that he was lucky. A wound like this would take time to mend, yes, but it would heal.

Brant stabbed the fire again and sat on a log. "They're going to kill you, you know that, right? You've become their number one priority. I remember you telling me what it was like when you and Willie worked for them. These guys have multiple orgasms over revenge kills."

A few moments went by. Both men were solemn.

"The state is going to put you away if they find out what

you've done, but maybe if you turn yourself in, they'll go easier on you. You saw what they did to Willie."

Shug shook his head. "What happened to Willie?"

"Oh, you didn't hear. Jeez, I'm sorry, Shug."

Shug stared into the fire as Brant described the way Willie had been removed from this world. It was not pretty.

After a few more minutes of Brant trying to convince him to turn himself in, Shug finally looked at him and used a sharp tone. "Are you going to tell me why you're out here?"

Brant tossed the charred stick into the woods. He stood and dusted his trousers. "Well, for one thing, I wanted to see my best friend. Isn't that reason enough?"

"Not under the circumstances, no. You have a family. They could have followed you."

Brant smiled. "I know these woods too well."

Shug waited for the other shoe to drop.

Brant said, "I came to give you some news." He reached into his pocket and removed a walkie-talkie. He tossed the device to Shug. Shug just looked at the radio.

"It's a police scanner," said Brant. "I've been listening for weeks, looking out for you after you killed those guys."

The radio squawked quietly.

Brant nodded to the device. "It's your daughter, Shug. A call just came in about fifteen minutes ago. She's having her baby."

It was the first time Shug Bass had cried in fifteen years.

CHAPTER

≈ 34 ≈

Life can play tricks on you. Life can be funny. Not funny ha-ha. Funny weird. The thing is, you *never* know what's happening in life. The only thing you really know about life is that it *is* happening. You thought you knew how today would go, but you were way off base. You thought you had everything figured out, but you couldn't have been more wrong if you had been born a pineapple.

Because, you see, life is about variables. And variables, by definition, vary. That's one thing you learn when you are a math nerd. Factors are subject to change.

That's what Minnie was thinking as she crawled out of the Buick and hobbled into the ditch at eleven o'clock at night to have her child.

Emily and Leigh Ann helped Minnie squat, there in the darkness, beside the Okyeha River. Nub held her hand. Benny paced, smoking cigarettes.

"It's coming!" shouted Minnie.

"Push!" shouted Emily.

The highway was empty tonight. The Buick was parked behind them in the ditch near the shallow creek bridge. The same bridge where Minnie had caught her first fish with Mr. Nub a few weeks ago. It was the first time she'd ever held a fishing rod in her hands. Nub cleaned the catfish and they ate it for supper.

"Push, sweetie!"

"You can do it!" Nub shouted.

"You can do it, sweetheart," said Benny.

"Push!"

Minnie looked at the sixty-two-year-old man who crouched beside her in the darkness. His face was lined from too much living. His hair was white fuzz, sticking out from beneath his ball cap. His eyes were tender and warm.

With her left hand, she braced herself against the hard ground beneath her. With her right hand, Minnie held his hand tightly.

"You're doing it!" he said.

Minnie bore down. She pushed so hard the circulation in her head momentarily stopped. Her mouth was making no sounds. She was gritting her teeth. She was locked in a muscular effort of the ages. She was getting tired. She wanted to quit.

"I can't do it!" Minnie shouted.

"Yes, you can, sweetie. Push again for me."

Minnie sat up slightly and drew in a sharp breath. She looked at all four of these people gathered around her. They were rooting for her. They were here for her. They loved her, heaven only knew why.

She pushed. As hard as she could.

"I can see the head!" said Leigh Ann.

"I'm so proud of you, baby!" shouted Nub.

But Minnie had to quit pushing. She didn't have the stamina to continue. She breathed in. She breathed out. She leaned back into Nub's arms and tried to catch her breath.

"I need one more push," said Nub. "You're almost there, darling. I know you're tired, but you can do it."

"I can't."

"You can, sweetie," Nub said.

"You can do it, baby," Emily said.

"No, I can't."

"I think I'm going to puke," Benny said.

And then . . .

Time stopped.

All sound stopped.

All emotion stopped.

The head came out first.

The shoulders came next.

Then the torso.

Then the rest of the infant slipped from the canal, just as easy as you please. Leigh Ann shined a flashlight on Emily. Her hands were a mess. In her arms was a child who wasn't moving. Minnie started to panic.

"What's wrong with my baby?"

Emily handed the child to her father. Mr. Nub used his finger to scoop mucus from the infant's mouth. He did this little move so casually, it was as though he'd been delivering babies all his life. In moments, the baby began to cry. And the forest was overcome with the sounds of music. The infant's complexion changed to a healthy color.

"You have a daughter," Leigh Ann said.

"A daughter?"

"You had your child on your sixteenth birthday," Emily said.

"Ain't too many people can say that," Benny said.

"She's beautiful."

"A daughter? I want to see her."

"Hold out your arms, sweetheart. You have to support her little head."

Minnie held her baby. The infant smelled like flowers. She

wasn't sure how that was possible, not after all the fluids that had just come from her body. How could a child smell floral? But that's how this child smelled. Like a freshly picked bouquet. Minnie kissed her daughter's head.

"Do you want to hold her again, Mr. Nub?" Minnie said.

Nub Taylor held the child against his plaid shirt. For once in this man's life, he seemed to be at a loss for words.

"Say hi to your granddaddy," Minnie said.

Salt water began to roll down the old man's cheeks. She watched tears fall onto the baby's naked torso.

"Hey there," Nub whispered.

"What're you going to call her?" Leigh Ann asked.

"I'm going to name her Bun," she said.

"Is that a family name?"

"No," Emily said. "It's Nub spelled backward."

Shug sat huddled near his campfire, nestled in the deep woodland of Ash County, listening to a police scanner. For the last hour, he had been listening to occasional chatter between officers apparently on patrol, waiting to hear news of his daughter. Sadly, their conversations were not about anything important. Just idle talk among coworkers. He heard one officer talk about his kid's Little League team and how the coach was a complete boob. He heard another officer discuss his personal views on which female in town had the most exhaustive collection of anatomical giftings. He heard one of the officers trying to recall the words to "I Love a Parade" by Bing Crosby. The officers spoke with country drawls so thick you could have used them to pave county roads, and they seemed about as intelligent as dishwater. Finally, one of the deputies made the call Shug had been waiting for.

"I'm here," said the officer. "I just got here. I can see them now up ahead."

Static.

"What's your twenty, Danny?" said dispatch.

Static.

"I'm a couple miles from the Taylor place, not far from the cutoff for County Route 19, just before you cross the river."

Static.

"What do you see?"

Static.

"Well, it looks like something has happened. Everyone's standing outside the vehicle. Out in the ditch. Wait. Here comes someone. It's a woman. It's Emily Ives. Stand by, dispatch."

Static.

Minutes passed. Several arduous minutes. Shug held the radio with both hands, staring at the device as though he were holding precious gems. He heard the occasional chatter of other officers on the frequency and wanted to get on the radio and tell them to shut up.

Finally, the radio squawked to life again with the voice of the officer who found Minnie.

The officer spoke. "She's had the baby. They want to go to the hospital."

Static.

"You're kidding. She had a baby on the side of the road?"

Static.

"Guess so. Poor kid."

Static.

"Ten-four. What's the status of the mother?"

Static.

The officer sighed into the radio. "Oh, I'd say she looks pretty tired. They're putting her in my vehicle now. Kid's been through a lot tonight. She's got the baby in her arms."

Static.

"Copy. And the baby's okay?"

Static.

Long pause.

"Yeah, the baby seems okay. Got all its fingers and toes. Breathing real good. It's a baby girl, so there's that. Anyway, I'm taking them over to Baptist Memorial now. The family's going to follow me over there."

After a short hiss of static, the radio went silent. Shug stared at the glow of his campfire in the suffocating darkness. He listened to insects erupt around him like a choir. He wiped his face with his sleeve.

It was a girl.

CHAPTER

≈ 35 ≈

Before there was the King of Rock 'n' Roll, there was the King of Country Music. And that man was Roy Acuff. Hank Williams said of him, "He's the biggest singer this music ever knew. You booked him and you didn't worry about crowds. For drawing power in the South, it was Roy Acuff, then God."

Roy Claxton Acuff started his career in medicine shows, playing fiddle alongside banjoists and spoon players. Then he started making records for the American Record Company. Records were a paltry business in the thirties. Being in the record business wasn't even that big of a deal, sort of like being in the coloring book business. The world was going through a Great Depression. Dust bowls in Kansas were sucking the Midwest off the map. Only a scant few Americans had record players. Nobody was buying albums anyway; they were all buying groceries. But Roy had a startlingly clear, sharp voice that could cut through static and low-fidelity speakers. He sounded great on the radio. Acuff auditioned for the *Opry*. The powers that were turned him down. He was too bland, they said. Too vanilla. So Roy went back to playing skating rinks, retirement parties, and funerals.

Until one fateful Saturday night in 1938. One of the fiddle players on the *Opry* cast got sick. They needed a substitute, so they called Roy's band, the Smoky Mountain Boys. All they wanted was for him to play fiddle, nothing more. Just play your fiddle and shut up, boy. But Roy played second fiddle to no man. Roy was looking for a job. And although Roy was a passable fiddle player, he could sing like a mother.

When the radio show began, instead of waltzing up to the microphone and playing his fiddle, Roy went rogue. He sang "Great Speckled Bird," and he brought the house down. George Hay signed him to a contract, and Roy Acuff became the face of the *Opry*. It was Roy and Minnie Pearl. In that order. Never let anyone tell you it pays to follow the rules. Rule-followers do not make history.

Things had changed considerably, however, since the 1940s. Roy was gray-headed now and looked like your granddaddy's dentist. Minnie Pearl was matronly and wore spectacles. Roy's music was outdated according to the younger generations who wanted a shirtless Jimi Hendrix kicking in amplifiers. The world had fallen in love with a less sedate form of country music championed by hippie cowboys and Hank Junior, who played in tank tops and shades. Crowds of young women, wearing skirts short enough to be classified as belts, who called themselves country music fans, gathered before concert stages, swooning like they were at Woodstock. Roy Acuff was considered about as exciting as a routine tonsillectomy.

By 1973, Roy was playing small concerts, folk festivals, and the occasional used-car dealership grand openings. He was popular with the older crowd, who still came out to hear him, clad in their western-wear regalia and hearing aids. But that was about the only crowd he drew anymore.

Which was why when Roy Acuff's RV pulled into Park, Alabama, nobody was there to greet him. Nobody really knew who he was. Fewer cared. He was acutely aware of this, and it didn't seem to bother him. In fact, people close to him said he liked the peace and quiet. Which might or might not have been true.

Roy's bus found the American Legion Post 120 parking lot at quarter till noon, a few hours behind schedule. These were the first pangs of summer, a few months after the serendipitous birth on the side of the road. The world was a florid mess of blooms and birds. At the time, Leigh Ann was doing inventory behind the bar, making sure she had enough Budweiser for tonight's onslaught. Younger people didn't drink beer on tap anymore. They wanted longnecks, which was fine with the Legion, because they could charge more for bottles.

"The bus is here, Leigh," said one of the waitresses.

"They're late," Leigh Ann said.

The waitress shrugged and went back to prep work. "Don't shoot the messenger."

Tonight was the annual barbecue and pool players tournament. The tournament had become a big deal in Park. When the tournament first started, nobody really participated in the festivities except other pool players. Certainly no locals from Park cared much about it. But over the last few years, word had gotten around the Southeast. Players from other towns started entering the contest. Then a few vendors got involved. The vendors started erecting tents and selling their wares. And each year more vendors signed up. There were leathercraft vendors. Guys selling heirloom tomatoes and squash. Boiled peanuts. Funnel cakes.

The event became the annual highlight of Park's official inauguration of summer. Bands came to town and provided music. Good bands too. One year there was a Cajun band from Slidell. One year they had a rock-and-roll band from Huntsville that sounded like the Allman Brothers Band. One year they had been able to get the Statler Brothers.

The Legion parking lot was overrun with people performing various tasks. Caterers. Cooks. Servers. Volunteers. John Danson was outside, manning a smoker, preparing 286 pork shoulders and 104 pork butts for the event. "That's a lot of butts," the *Advocate* remarked.

Eighty-some amateur pool players were filing into the hamlet of Park, Alabama. The Scotty's Motor Inn was booked. The overflow stayed at the new motor inn recently built in Ambassador. Others came in custom RVs, so you knew they were serious players. You had pool players from Tennessee, Georgia, Kentucky, Illinois, Missouri, Arkansas, and Ohio, all coming down to Ash County with their artisan-made pool cues, ready to strut their stuff and win the kitty.

Leigh Ann watched Nub and Benny use an electric drill to mount two large speakers over the main stage that Roy Acuff would soon be playing on. She was sitting at one of the tables up front, under a tent, doing paperwork, thinking about Nub and the great change that had overtaken him. She was signing checks, sipping from a bottle of Mountain Dew. Stealing glances at him. Now and then she would stop writing because she had a feeling. She had always believed that you could feel it when a man looked at you that way. It was an energy thing, a tingly feeling in your stomach.

Occasionally she looked up from her checkbook to find Nub glancing at her. When she made eye contact with him, he would tuck his head and pretend to be doing something else. It was cute.

"Hey!" shouted Benny to Nub.

"What?" Nub said.

"You almost dropped the speaker on me, you big idiot. Would you keep your eyes on what you're doing?"

When the two men finished installing the speakers, they

ran twisted masses of electrical wire through the parking lot, all the way to the soundman, who was operating a soundboard that was roughly the size of the starship *Enterprise*. Nub walked past her and she could feel him watching her.

"Would you like something to drink, Nub?" she said. "Pretty hot out here."

"Sure."

"How about a Dr Pepper?"

He wiped his face with a handkerchief. "I wouldn't use Dr Pepper to get oil stains off my driveway. Coke, please."

"The Real Thing?"

"So they say."

She reached into the cooler by the sound booth. The bottles of Coke were stacked atop each other like artillery cartridges. She placed one before him on a tall table. With a flick of her wrist, she had the cap off. She slid the green hourglass bottle to him.

"Take a break," she said. "You're sweating."

He took a pull on his bottle and thanked her.

She had always found Nub to be a vulnerable personality. Even when he'd been blind drunk. He was a big talker, yes. He was animated, sure. But she always got the feeling that these things were part of an act of sorts.

She knew it must still feel odd for him to be drinking Coca-Cola at the Legion. She could tell by his mannerisms. They were rigid and awkward. He wasn't used to this. He would never be used to this.

Being here at the Legion made him think too much about an old way of life. She could tell sometimes that it embarrassed him to be the only guy without a drink in his hand. And if he was anything like her, and most alcoholics were, the old way of life never stopped calling. It never would. The danger was in thinking that maybe, just maybe, you could tolerate one or two drinks. That was the delicious lie you had to resist. Constantly. Forty-eight hours a day. Because once you went down that path, you lost decades from your life.

Nub placed the Coke on the table. She watched him and noticed that he was looking more fit than normal. His skin color looked golden now that summer was in full swing. He was loose built, like a man who was comfortable in the company of hard work. He was the kind of man who, you could tell, was at home out of doors.

"How've you been doing?" she said. "I mean, *as of late*?"

"I'm okay."

"You'd tell me if you weren't?"

"I would."

"You'd tell me if you felt like drinking?"

He nodded.

"What about Phillip Deener?"

"He has a tiny brain and he pees sitting down."

"No, I meant, have you heard any word from him or his family? Have you had any more strange visitors in the middle of the night?"

"No." Nub used a knuckle to rap on his own temple. "Knock on wood."

He looked off at the tour bus pulling into the parking lot.

Leigh Ann's eyes followed the bus. "Nub, meet Roy Acuff. Roy Acuff, Nub."

He laughed. "I wonder what he's like."

"I heard he can be a little bit of a jerk."

"Yeah, well, not everyone can be as warm and charming as me."

She went back to filling out checks. She felt him looking at her again, but she didn't mind it. She liked having him watch her. And she liked watching him in return. He was nothing like the other guys in her life. He was approachable. Real. Nub knew what he wanted. He knew what he didn't want. It was that simple.

"I appreciate your help with all this," she said. "I wish you'd let me pay you."

"I won't hear of it. You practically delivered my grand-daughter."

"It's not hard to deliver a baby. You just catch it when it falls out."

"Little more to it than that."

Nub Taylor had been sitting at her bar for a long time, but she had not seen him the way she had been seeing him lately. He had changed. He was less of the shabby older man somehow. Or maybe—and she couldn't rule this out—maybe *she* had changed. Maybe helping someone through the process of finding their own way had altered her. Helping others was the foundation stone of recovery. It was what kept you rooted in real life. That's what AA believed.

"You seen those stupid Coke commercials on TV?" she said.

"Commercials? I didn't think you watched TV."

"I got two teenagers at my house. The TV never goes off. There's this commercial where everyone is standing on a hillside and singing about how they want to buy the world a Coke."

"I've seen it. I have a teenager too."

"Well, sometimes I feel that way about my new way of life. About your new life."

"How do you mean?"

"I wish everyone knew how it feels to get a second shot at being alive."

Nub nodded thoughtfully and drained his Coke. "Are we having a moment here, Leigh Ann?"

She could feel herself blushing.

"That's what I thought," he said.

Leigh Ann had spent her previous life in a blur. She got married at age seventeen. She started having babies with a man who treated her like garbage. And then he left her for a woman ten years her junior. Since then she had struggled to keep going. Struggled to feed her kids. Today they were doing well in school. It was no thanks to her ex. No thanks to her either. It was all a testament to divine providence. God looks out for children and fools.

"You know," she said, "you're different."

"Yeah, they've been saying that to me all my life."

"No, I mean, you've really changed."

"Are we having another moment?"

They were interrupted when a few of the guys from the American Pool Players Association entered the Legion. They looked like military men with high-and-tight haircuts. They carried toolboxes, levels, and hand trucks. They were here to adjust the pool tables and make sure things were up to snuff.

Leigh Ann paused her conversation and said, "I'll be right back, Nub."

"I hope so."

She smiled, then started to leave to talk to the pool player guys. They wanted her to show them where to set up their gear. As she walked away, she had that tingly feeling again.

Roy Acuff was a slight man. Lean and polished. He was pushing seventy. Or maybe he was pulling it. But he looked good for his age. When he took the stage, Minnie watched with an outsider's admiration. Not because she knew much about him; she didn't. She knew only what she'd heard about him. She admired him because this man was very important to Nub, although she couldn't see why. He wasn't playing the fiddle much, and he spent more time balancing a bow on his nose to whip the crowd up. Even so, Nub had all his records and knew the lyrics to all the man's tunes.

The whole town had showed up to the concert. Minnie scanned the crowd and found Phillip Deener in the audience, drinking from a large foam cup. He kept looking at her. His expression was one of repulsion. She had the feeling he'd come just to ruin her day.

She knew she wasn't very attractive with the post-baby weight still clinging to her already large body, and this made her self-conscious. Earlier Phillip had roughly brushed past her. Bun was fast asleep at the time, and she had nearly dropped her. She almost coldcocked Phillip, but he was already gone when she turned around.

Roy Acuff continued to sing. His silver hair was lacquered to his head, styled with the perfect finger wave. His suit was bright red, with western scrollwork on the sleeves, scrollwork down the stripe of his trousers, and a bolo tie. He wore boots the color of chili peppers. He was playing a fiddle that looked like it had some mileage on it.

Minnie rocked her two-month-old in her arms and surveyed the impressive audience. Leigh Ann said there were 881 adults here today, which was a prime number. It had taken her nearly five minutes to factor 881 to discover it was prime. It took so long because she was distracted by all the confusion going on. Roughly a third of the adults in the audience had brought their kids, totaling 293 children, including Bun, which was also a prime number, if you could believe it. Two prime numbers. This brought the total up to 1,174 people altogether, which was not a prime number. Its square root, not that anyone cared, was 34.263 and some change.

Minnie bounced Bun and asked Nub, "Have you ever seen him in concert before?"

He nodded. "First saw him when I was in my twenties. At a show in Opelika. Long time before you were born. He was a great showman. Still is."

It was getting late and the sun was getting low when Roy Acuff took a break. He turned the stage over to another band who kept the crowd engaged. People were sweating through their clothing. Minnie's shirt felt like onion skin on her back. Nub's white shirt had gone to be with the Lord hours ago. He was dripping like a faucet. The bandleader announced that Roy was returning for another set, and the crowd went nuts when Roy came to the stage. The applause finally died down and a silence fell over Park, Alabama. Roy Acuff was about to speak to the crowd when someone interrupted him. Someone on the side of the stage was bending his ear.

It was Benny.

Minnie turned to Nub. "What's Benny doing on the stage?"

He shrugged and wore a sheepish grin.

The conversation between Benny and the King of Country Music went on for a few minutes. Roy listened to everything Benny had to say, nodding now and then. Then Roy scanned the crowd and found Minnie. Roy Acuff smiled.

"Uh-oh," said Nub. "Someone's looking at you."

Minnie felt her chest get heavy.

"Ladies and gentlemen," said Roy to his 1,174 admirers. His voice was loud and clear enough to be heard all the way in Canada. "It has come to my attention that we have a young woman in this audience today who can sing a magnificent rendition of our national anthem."

Minnie looked at Nub with wide eyes. "You didn't."

He was grinning. He reached over and took Bun from her arms and gave her a shove toward the stage. "Don't embarrass me," he said.

People began cheering.

Something had shifted in Park since the Easter Sunday disaster. People in town had chosen sides when it came to the subject of Minnie Bass. People admired her talent and her resilience. Once, someone even purchased Minnie a month's worth of groceries in the IGA anonymously. If you lived in Park, you were either a Minnie admirer or you suffered from a severe case of fundamentalist hemorrhoids.

The people here today loved her. And there is nothing small towns love more than cheering their own. The deafening fanfare of Park's people rose to inexhaustible heights as Minnie made her way to the stage. She wandered through the masses, moving toward the platform, and people patted her on the back as she passed. She felt so embarrassed with this many people cheering her that she had started to shake.

Minnie took the stage, and Roy Acuff gave her a sideways hug. The band asked her what key she wanted to do "The Star-Spangled Banner" in, and she hummed a few bars. When the guitarist began to play, she approached the microphone and stared at the massive audience.

And then she started singing.

She finished the first verse, and the crowd was so stunned they could barely respond. She rounded into the second verse, a verse nobody ever sings, a verse so rare Francis Scott Key had probably forgotten he wrote it. But when she got out the first few words, a foam cup sailed through the air toward the stage. The cup struck her on the face. It splattered all over her. She could smell the stale, yeasty liquid as it ran down her face and all over her dress. Before she fully realized what had happened, another cup struck her.

In a few minutes, a small riot was taking place in the audience, with Phillip Deener and his henchmen at the center. The demonstrative young men were subdued by a flock of Minnie's admirers. They came from all corners and gave the boys what for. And as the rowdies were taken away, Minnie was suddenly aware that she was standing before a massive crowd of people who, for some inexplicable reason, believed in her.

She was wearing beer-stained clothing that clung to her chubby body. And everyone was looking at her. Someone started applauding. Then everyone followed suit.

"Oh, sweetie," said Roy Acuff. "Keep singing."

So that's what she did.

Emily was not at the concert.

Currently she was naked from the waist up, sitting in an exam room at the University of Alabama at Birmingham. The room was cold, sterilized, and white. The lights above were so obscenely bright, they were giving her a headache. The doctors looked young. Like belonged-at-a-frat-party young. Or a skating rink. The lead doctor had shaggy hair and acne scars on his face. His colleague beside him looked even younger and wore an open collar beneath his lab coat. They were in their late twenties, maximum.

"I don't mean to be blunt," Shaggy said, "but I'm just going to cut the crap and speak frankly with you, Mrs. Ives." He tossed his clipboard aside. Then he leveled his gaze on her. "We can cut them off."

She heard the hum of an air conditioner kick in.

"But I thought my cancer had . . ."

"Metastasized? It hasn't. Not yet. You have a relatively slow-moving cancer, although I can see why your doctors thought there were no treatments available for you. They're probably using an outdated playbook."

The younger doctor added, "They're making predictions based on old methods; they're doing it the way they did in the forties. This is a different world, medically. You're still in the early stages, technically. You could still beat this."

"But I've been losing weight."

"Stress," said Shaggy.

"Stress?"

"Sure. You think you're dying."

She was afraid to even utter the words. "And . . . I'm not? Dying?"

Shaggy smiled. "Not according to me. Your previous doctors, no offense, don't know what they're talking about, ma'am."

The other doctor added, "They probably still think castor oil cures the hemorrhoids."

"It's localized," the doctor said as he examined her breast. "The scans aren't unhopeful. This can be dealt with. But it should be done quickly."

"You're kidding," she said. It was as though someone had removed a great stone from her shoulders. "This can't be . . . You mean I'm going to . . ."

Shaggy replaced her paper gown and covered her. "I can't

see the future, Mrs. Ives. But I think you've got a real shot here."

She stared at the plain walls. Why are all the walls in medical places always white?

"Listen," said the doctor, "I realize this is a big decision to make. But it's a no-brainer. A radical mastectomy will give you your life back. We do them every day with cases much worse than yours."

Her head was in her hands. She was sobbing.

"It's a simple surgery," the younger doctor said. "There's not much to it."

Then the doctors outlined exactly what they would be doing and how they would do it. Step by step.

"There are prosthetic brassieres," the doctor added. "You could get breast implants. The point is, you have a lot of options once the procedure is done. We're not in the dark ages anymore. We're making huge strides in the field of breast cancer. Twenty years ago, a mastectomy wouldn't have even been an option for you. They would have written you off as a casualty. They weren't even thinking this way back then. It's an exciting time to be alive. We're saving a lot of people."

"Cut off my breasts?" she said vacantly.

Both doctors looked at her.

"Mrs. Ives. My job is to keep you alive. For your family. For your kids. And I'm really good at my job."

When she was a teenager, all she had wanted was for her breasts to develop. She had been anxious about it. She had been shorter than the other girls, a late bloomer compared to her friends. Then, one day in the tenth grade, everything happened. She developed. Just like her mother said she would.

Emily glanced down at her chest. A part of what made her

a woman. She wondered what she would look like when it was over. Then she felt the weight of death being lifted from her. And the answer was easy.

"Okay," she said. "Cut them off."

The doctor nodded. "Let's compare calendars."

CHAPTER

~ 36 ~

The only information Sugar Bass knew about his daughter had come to him in the form of letters he received in prison. Celia wrote to him every week. She missed a week now and then when she went on drinking binges, but she always made up for it with extra letters.

What he knew was that Minniford Hazel Bass was born on February 28, 1957. When she first came into this world, she weighed fifteen pounds and two ounces, roughly the same weight as a General Electric mini fridge. The doctor remarked that he had never seen an infant so large, not in all his career. The nurses nicknamed her Minnie, to be cute. The name stuck. Shug had come up with Minniford, which he thought sounded more sophisticated, and he sent this to Celia in the mail. Celia wrote the name on the birth certificate.

Minniford.

Celia and Shug agreed to tell their daughter that her father had been killed in Korea. That he died a hero. Celia souped up the lie until it had become ridiculous. She told the girl that the president had mentioned her father's name on a national radio broadcast. She said Minnie's father was a secret army agent. Shug was against this, but there wasn't much he could do from a cell. He had become invisible.

The letters documenting his daughter's life were the only real possessions he had in Draper. They covered every major moment. And every small one too.

Minnie was a happy baby and a good kid. He could tell by the letters. Her mother said she was mild-mannered and gentle. But kids teased her a lot because she was different. To be different was to extend an invitation for commentary from fools. Shug knew this intimately.

In Minnie's fifth-grade music class, her mother once wrote, a young man named B. J. Steadman kept calling Minnie "Jolly Green Giant." Shug wanted to tear through his cell doors and march down to Park Elementary and confront the kid. Another time a dreadful girl named Charlotte Waters indicated that Minnie's face resembled human buttocks. Charlotte had drawn an illustration to accompany this remark.

Minnie rolled over and took the abuse. It was a Bass trait. Shug was the same way. Minnie was just like him. A mostly sedate person with a strong tolerance for the stupidity of others. She was optimistic, almost heedlessly so. She loved *Batman* and *The Jetsons* and *Looney Tunes*. Especially the Road Runner. Shug had never heard of most of these TV shows, but he liked knowing her tastes just the same.

She was perpetually cheerful and she was too trusting. Also, Minnie was obsessed with counting things. Minnie's mother said her counting was an unhealthy obsession, a habit Minnie could not stop. Her mother said that wherever they went, Minnie had to know how many windows were in the house, how many steps on the staircase, how many lamps in the home, how many floorboards. She counted designs on area rugs, on wallpaper. She counted numbers on dials. She counted seams on sidewalks, leaves on trees, bricks on buildings, louvers on doors, spots on the ceiling. If she got hard up, she would count the little hairs on her arms.

Above all, Shug knew that Minnie loved to sing. "She could crack your skull with her loud voice," her mother once wrote. When Minnie was eleven years old, she auditioned for school choir. She sang "Up the Lazy River," followed by "This Little Light of Mine." After her audition, the choir director claimed Minnie's voice was so loud that it had given her a headache and she had to lie down. Shug read this in his cell and wanted more than anything to hear his daughter's voice. But he could only imagine it.

Her life was hard, and it was his fault. This fact never escaped him. Not once.

When Minnie turned thirteen, her mother lost her job cleaning because of an injury. Her letters became sparse. She was drinking more often than normal. From the scant letters that came thereafter, he discerned that Celia had checked out emotionally. Minnie was doing what she had to do to survive.

Minnie dropped out of school. She helped her mother pay rent. Her first job was working for a local farmer in Ephesus. She picked cotton all summer until her hands were bloody. The last letter he received stated that Minnie had gotten a job at Waffle House. It seemed wrong that his artistic and mathematically talented daughter should be slinging hash for truckers.

But then the letters stopped. One day one of the guards brought the news. Shug collapsed on his bed. He did not grieve for Celia. He did not grieve for himself. He grieved for Minnie.

Shug loved his daughter more than his own life. To love someone you had never met was its own form of torture. It was the agony of being unseen. It was the pain of never having a single smile offered to him personally. It was never hearing "Dad" or "I love you."

Shug was thinking about his girl as he strung a trip line around the perimeter of the Taylor house. It was sunset. The sky was pink lemonade. The trip line was only an alarm device; if anyone came close to this property beneath the cover of darkness, he wanted to know about it. If the line were tripped, a small wind-up alarm clock would begin to clatter and ring and someone would have a very bad day, courtesy of Sugar Bass.

He used a hammer to beat nails into nearby trees and various structures, then tied the line around each nail until the wire was banjo-string tight. It had been a while since he'd laid a trip wire.

Once the entire device was strung up, he disengaged it. He would engage the alarm system when Minnie and the others were safely inside the home. And if anyone came within rock-throwing distance of the Taylor house, Shug would be all over them like butter on a sweet potato.

He heard an automobile approaching, rolling up the driveway. He finished his work quickly and disconnected the trip line. He dropped to the ground, then commando-crawled on the dirt until he was beneath the front porch of the Taylor home. He shimmied toward the edge of the home so he could get a better look at the passengers exiting the vehicle.

It was his daughter.

Minnie was carrying the baby in her arms and she was drenched. Nub Taylor was consoling her because she was crying. The baby had a pink bow in her hair. The baby's head was topped with a shock of red hair. Everything within him wanted to burst forward into the glorious light of day and hold his two girls. *Everything* within him. But he remained still. He remained silent. Stoic and unmoving. Invisible.

CHAPTER

≈ 37 ≈

The rock crashed through the bedroom at three in the morning.

Nub had been ready for it this time. He had been waiting for it, ever since the boys threw their drinks at Minnie onstage. He had been on full alert after that. In fact, he rarely slept. It was just like when he stood watch in the navy. You ate, slept, and breathed the possibility of attacks. You spent so long within this state of readiness that when the attack finally came, you were almost grateful for it. You were looking forward to getting it over with.

So when the rock hit the floor of his bedroom and glass sprayed all over him, he was not surprised. He was not shocked. He lifted the rifle from the bed and moved with precision. He was sober. For once. With a plan.

He thumb-cocked his Remington, then lumbered onto his steady feet. Reaction timing was of paramount importance here. Speed of response was the key, not accuracy. He wanted his presence to be known to his offenders. That was what mattered. He wanted whoever was out there to listen up and know that he was not going to be calling the police. Not this time.

He aimed his rifle out the busted window and shot above the tree line. The report of the Remington was loud. He pumped the lever and shot again. Each rifle kick was so hard it knocked him back a few feet.

Next he slid on his boots and tramped down the hallway, bounding through the front door. He stepped onto the porch wearing only boots and boxer briefs. Rifle held before himself. Nub fired over the trees again to show the man he wasn't afraid. He saw a shape in his yard. It was a man. A single silhouette standing in the grass.

"You're about to get shot!" he shouted to him.

But the man didn't move. He simply faced Nub squarely. Like a sentinel. It was a stare down.

"You hear me?" shouted Nub. "I said get off my land, or I'll remove you myself!"

The man was carrying a gasoline canister. Nub felt his insides become watery when he noticed the flickering glow coming from the back of his home. Within moments, the glow became stronger, until it had crept across the lawn and up the siding of his house. The man with the canister tossed the gasoline container onto the porch. The container clanged like a bell. And the man walked away.

"Tell Sugar we said hello!" the dark figure shouted.

Nub fired, and the rifle let out a crack.

But the man kept walking.

"Stop right there!"

Crack! Crack!

But the man was already gone. Nub sprinted inside to wake up Minnie. The flames were already quickly licking up the sides of the home. Tongues of fire crawled upward a few feet every second. The man must have been saturating his house with fuel for the last few hours.

He could hear Bun crying. He jogged upstairs, clearing two stairs at a time. He rushed through the house, boots pounding loudly on floorboards, but he couldn't find Minnie.

This confused him. She wasn't in her room. But there was

no way she could have left the house so quickly. She wasn't downstairs. And he could no longer hear Bun crying. He called her name, but there was no answer.

"Minnie! Where are you? We have to get out of here! Now!"

He could already see the flames outside the bedroom window, lapping onto the eaves like breakers on the shore.

"Minnie, sweetie! Answer me!"

Nothing.

He could hear the popping of the fire. It was gaining intensity, and fast. He kept going through the rooms, looking for her under beds and in closets, but he couldn't find her. Wyatt was sitting on the windowsill in his room, anxiously whipping his tail. Nub lifted the cat into his arms. Wyatt clawed his skin, then shot free and tore down the stairs, out of the house.

"Minnie! Sweetie! Where are you? Answer me!"

He opened the linen closet in the upstairs bathroom and found Minnie huddled in the bottom of the closet, beneath the towels, crying.

"We've got to get out of here!" he shouted. "The house is on fire!"

Minnie was rocking back and forth. She was catatonic. He tried to remove the baby from her arms, but she beat him away.

"Minnie," he said, tugging at her clothing. "Please. We have to go. Right now. Get up!"

She kept rocking. "Gunshots. I heard gunshots."

"Yes, I know sweetie. It was me."

He could feel the floor beneath him warming up, and smoke was filling the upstairs like a heavy fog. He began coughing. He peeked out the bathroom door to the top of the stairs. He could see his kitchen was already in flames. He returned to the bathroom closet.

"Minnie, please. Sweetie. Please snap out of it!"

He squatted to her level. He touched her head. He stroked her hair. "Darling, listen, we have to get out of here. Do you hear me? Please. We're going to be in trouble if we stay any longer. You don't want Bun to get hurt, do you?"

He coughed.

But it was already too late. The smoke was getting too thick. He could feel his throat burning something awful. And he was getting dizzy. He was losing his grip with consciousness. Soon the air was pure white. He knew he'd never get her out of this house. Not in the state she was in. So he staggered to the window and tore it open to ventilate the room. He heard glass breaking downstairs from the heat. He heard wood snapping. He heard things falling. He heard the house bellowing and creaking from the strain. The house was coming apart.

"Minnie, we've got to go," he said weakly, choking on the thick air. "Please."

Then he fell face forward and passed out.

CHAPTER

~ 38 ~

Anna Lee Broussard loved revivals. Evangelists used to come through Park every summer for revivals and the whole town would show up. People went crazy for revivals.

"You don't have to advertise a fire!" the preacher would shout to the reprobates and heartless sinners as they filled his tent. And he was right. If you are on fire for the Lord, you don't have to tell people about it. The fire will practically burn your clothes off and be seen by all heathens who have given their lives to drinking and fornication and playing bingo. At least that's what Anna Lee Broussard was remembering at this particular moment when she saw the fire truck clanging past her house.

Anna Lee stepped to her window and scanned the night horizon with her eighty-seven-year-old eyes. She could see a cumulus of smoke rising in the distance. She got out her binoculars.

"Oh dear," she said aloud.

The first thing she did was call Cynthia Lindsey. Cynthia lived north of town, and she would definitely know what was going on. Cynthia was hooked up to the pulse of Park like a heart monitor. The woman knew everything about everyone.

Cynthia answered her phone quickly.

"Cynthia, it's Anna Lee."

"What is it, Anna Lee?"

Cynthia was obviously awake already. Her voice was fresh and dry.

Cynthia told Anna Lee she had already talked to Boyd Lovelace, who said he had talked to Vance Woods, who had gotten word from Mae Beth at Ash County dispatch, who had just called to tell her that it was Nub Taylor's house on fire.

"Nub Taylor," said Anna Lee. "Have mercy."

"It's always something with Nub Taylor."

"Bless him."

"I feel sorry for his family."

"Poor Loretta. Can you imagine being married to someone who pees in a kiddie pool at your family reunion?"

"I caught Harold peeing in our sink once, but thank heavens he'd taken out the dishes first."

And so it went.

When the conversation ended, Anna Lee quickly threw on her pink robe and shuffled across Belleville on her old feet, using her aluminum cane for support. She moved as fast as she could without compromising her newly installed steel hip. She beat on the door of the largest house in Park. She could have called, but news like this deserved an in-person delivery. When the door opened, Anna Lee said, "I'm sorry to wake you up, Emily. But your father's house is on fire."

Shug smelled the fire before he saw it. He sat bolt upright, roused from a deep sleep by the scent of burning wood. He looked at his campfire pit. The fire had been extinguished for many hours. The fire wasn't his.

He sniffed the air. This was fresh smoke. Acrid and new.

Biting and pungent. He wiped the sleep from his eyes, crawled from beneath his quilt, stood, and stretched. He hadn't meant to fall asleep. He didn't even remember falling asleep. But the days of constant vigilance and surveillance were catching up with him. He looked at the tiny alarm clock perched beside his foot. The bell that was attached to the elaborate series of trip wires he had activated after the lights had gone off inside Nub's house. The alarm was inert and unmoving. He looked again into the night sky and saw the plumes rising above the trees.

His device had failed.

Shug raced through the thicket toward the farmhouse. When he saw the home in the middle distance, he could already hear the crackling of wood. And then he heard someone scream.

Minnie watched Nub pass out before her on the floor. He lay totally still. It took a second to sink into her traumatized brain what had just happened. The image of him there on the floor. Unmoving. She was in shock. And getting very dizzy. She knew she wasn't thinking clearly. When the gravity of the moment finally hit her, she fought off the drowsiness from the smoke and called his name. But Nub made no movement. He was totally out.

"Mr. Nub?"

Nothing.

Bun began to cough. Minnie's throat was already raw, like it was bleeding. She couldn't stop hacking. She wet a rag and held it over Bun's face, but she was afraid she would suffocate her daughter. She had to get out of here or Bun's little lungs would never recover. They would all die.

The bedroom was filled with white fog. Finally the mother-hood instinct kicked in. Her childish panic was driven away by a sense of protectiveness all mothers have. Minnie stood and felt her fear fade into a cool realization of what she must do. She walked to the open window and considered jumping out. But she could easily drop Bun. And what about Mr. Nub? She stuck her head out the window. The roof was on fire. She wondered whether the stairs were on fire too. But it didn't matter if they were. There weren't any other routes out of this place.

She went to Nub, who was still inert on the floor.

"Get up, Mr. Nub!"

The old man coughed but did not open his eyes.

"I'm sorry, Mr. Nub. I don't know what was wrong with me. We have to go."

He hacked so hard that his body curled into the fetal position.

"We have to get out of here, Mr. Nub. Please."

His eyes opened for a brief moment. "Get that baby out of here."

CHAPTER
❦ 39 ❦

The roofline was an inferno, sunken sideways. The porch was already destroyed. The framework beneath the porch had been burned so that the platform sagged, which would soon bring down the porch's support structure. Overhangs and soffits were about to start detaching and falling. The whole house of cards was tumbling. Rafters fell inside. Beams collided with the floor.

Shug arrived in time to see splinters of charred wood crash onto the porch. The windows were gone. The interior beams were exposed, bright white with flames. The house was intact, but not for long.

A fire truck sat parked in the front yard. Men in fire-retardant gear were scrambling in all directions, manning miles of hoses. Shug couldn't believe what he was seeing. He couldn't believe how badly he had failed his daughter.

"Minnie!" he screamed.

The diesel engine thrummed and shook the earth, drowning out his voice. The hydraulic pump was roaring. Men in helmets screamed while training the blast of the hose at the fire. A man in a helmet used a ram to beat the front door. The door flew inward, as though it were made of balsa wood. Shug ran forward.

"Isn't someone going to go in?" he shouted.

"Sir, step back," the fireman said.

The firefighters were hacking at the wood, swinging axes wildly.

"Someone's got to get inside!"

"You need to step back, sir."

"Minnie! My God, Minnie! Someone needs to go in there! Right now, dammit!"

The man was shoving Shug back now. Restraining him. Shug fought the man, straining against his grasp. He was already trying to charge into the house, but five or six men were holding him back, tearing his clothing.

"Minnie!"

He screamed her name until he lost his voice.

Minnie heard someone call her name. A wave of something cool ran through her body. Something clicked inside her. An internal light switch. The knowledge that her loved ones would die if she didn't do something. Now. And she had seconds to do it. She looked at Bun, cradled in her arms. She looked at the old man on the floor.

Her heart made a pact with her body. She would die trying to get out of here. The odds were against her; she knew this. But she had to try.

And this knowledge replaced the fear. Or maybe it drowned out the fear. Or maybe it just distracted her. Either way, her internal voice was all she could hear at that moment. The voice of reason. Or maybe the voice of complete insanity.

She squatted onto her heels. She slung the old man over one shoulder. She slung her daughter over the other shoulder.

And she ran.

Emily arrived in a panic, but the firefighters would not allow her any closer. She looked at the old farmhouse in the distance, where she had been born, and she collapsed in the yard. She fell to her knees and watched the glow of the fire in rapt anguish.

"Daddy!" she shouted.

Her whole body went numb. This could not be real. This was all just a bad dream.

She could see through the windows. The kitchen was ablaze. Her mother had not wanted her to be born in this house like sorry white trash. Civilized people went to the hospital to have babies. That's what Emily's mother wanted. But her mother did not get her wish. Emily had been born in the kitchen of this old Sears, Roebuck & Co. home. The table had been covered in a rubber tarp her father bought from the hardware store. When the birthing was over, her father said it looked like someone had dressed a deer in their kitchen. Emily watched flames enshroud the room of her birth.

"Daddy!" she shouted until her voice broke.

Then . . .

Emily heard one of the firemen shout. The mighty blast of white water was diverted from the front door. Men in leather-head helmets gathered around the front of the home.

"Look!" shouted another fireman.

A silhouette came through the flames, moving slowly over the debris. The silhouette crawled over the splintered porch, carrying a grown man over her shoulder and a baby in her arms. The silhouette was tall. Broad-shouldered and stately. She emerged from the infernal Gehenna wearing a blackened nightgown. Barefoot. She stumbled onto the lawn and dropped the body of Nub Taylor onto the grass. She carefully placed Bun atop Nub's body. Then Minnie collapsed in a coughing fit. She coughed until she vomited. Minnie kept pointing to her throat as if to say, "I can't breathe."

CHAPTER

~ 40 ~

When Minnie's eyes opened, she saw a white light above her. A curious light. What was this light? It was an enveloping light. Not like a light at all but more like a world of its own. The light transformed from an encompassing brightness into a smaller, more focused, circular orb of light, hovering above her. The little ball of light moved back and forth. Side to side. Up and down. It was a tiny light, but bigger than a firefly. Her weary eyes followed the bouncing light.

It was a man with a flashlight. A man in a helmet. The man was asking her to tell him her name, but she couldn't speak. Neither could she figure out what her name was. She was too confused. She couldn't make her mouth form the words. Her voice was gone. Her lungs were numb with pain. Her eyes kept going blurry. She had a strong desire to sleep. It was the strongest urge to sleep she had ever felt in her life. It was pulling at her. Gnawing at her. It was making her vision blurry.

"Don't close your eyes, miss," said the man.

She tried to speak, but she coughed instead. The coughing never stopped.

Minnie closed her eyes and gave in to the sleep.

"No, ma'am. Don't close your eyes. Stay with me."

But it was too late. Minnie was asleep. Although it was

restless sleep. She saw her mother in her dreams. The woman was wearing a green dress. She was standing in a wide-open field. Her dress was whipping in the wind. Her face looked years younger than the tired face Minnie had come to know. Minnie wanted to speak to her mother, but her voice wouldn't work. She saw her father too. He was wearing a yellow shirt. Short sleeves. He was young. Handsome. At least she assumed it was her father. She'd never laid eyes on him before. He looked like what she'd imagined.

Her eyes opened again.

This time she saw two men over her. Men dressed in blue, wearing badges. And her world was twisting sideways. As though she were being sucked through space and time. Or transported on a stretcher.

"What's happening?" she tried to say.

She closed her eyes.

It was the world of white again. She saw her mother looking down at her, leaning in to her face. Beaming. Minnie wanted to tell her mother how sorely she missed her. How life had been since she went away. She wanted to tell her all about Nub and Bun and Benny and Emily and Leigh Ann, and all the new things she'd been doing since she'd made these new friends. But only coughs came out of her mouth.

Her eyes opened.

She was still in an all-white place. Heaven, maybe? Definitely not the other place. She heard beeping. Machines, perhaps? Were there fluorescent light bulbs and beeping machines in heaven? Nurses and doctors were gathered around her, using medical supplies, and the strong smell of disinfectant was filling her nostrils.

"Minnie," a man's voice said to her. "Can you hear me?"

She closed her eyes again. It felt so good to close her eyes.

She heard the voice of her mother. The voice of her late grandmother. The voice of a man. The voice of her baby crying.

"Minnie," said a voice. "Can you hear me?"

She coughed hard but could not get a full breath.

"I need the pulse oximeter, stat!" the dreamy voice said.

It was a strange thing for someone to be saying. What was an oximeter? What did *stat* mean? What was going on?

"Her pulse is below forty! Oxygen is sixty! We're going to have to bag her. Get me the bag!"

Her life had been so beautiful. It hadn't been perfect. But it wasn't supposed to be. It all made sense now. Only imperfection is beautiful.

"Pulse is down to thirty. Dropping, dropping. Bag her! Now!"

Everything vanished into a miasma. The medical men. The voices. The image of her mother. The world of white. All gone.

"I'm losing her!"

CHAPTER

~ 41 ~

Park Baptist Memorial Hospital was a squatty brick building on Phillips Avenue made of tan brick and ugly bulbous windows. It had a flat roofline, no landscaping, and the whole place adhered strictly to a style of architecture that could be loosely defined as Adult Correctional Facility. The place had been built in 1947 out of pure necessity. Park residents got tired of traveling to Birmingham whenever their kids broke a bone or stepped on a rusty nail. The McDaniels family spearheaded the project. They fronted $680,000 to break ground on the hospital and started the proverbial ball rolling. The McDanielses were staunch Freewill Baptists. Ergo, the place was Baptist.

Nub had worked on the hospital construction crew along with hundreds more grunts from around town. A lot of guys who worked at the paper mill built this place. They even let Nub man an earth mover when the lot was being leveled. Greater thrill hath no man than to operate heavy machinery. To ride atop a 205-horsepower machine with 460,100 pounds of operating weight is bliss of the most primal variety.

The hospital was always busy. Not just with patients. The cafeteria at Park Baptist Memorial got most of the action because they were famous for their fish sticks. People raved about them. Although Nub wasn't sure why. There was nothing special about Canadian-caught whitefish, deep-fried in Baltimore, flash-frozen, delivered via freezer truck to Atlanta, then shipped to a Jacksonville food supplier before riding eight hours in a hot truck to rural Alabama.

Nub was eating his fish sticks while lying in a bed in the Baptist Memorial burn unit. Leigh Ann sat near the bedside, feeding him one stick at a time. *Little House on the Prairie* was playing on the television above him. Laura Ingalls was running through a meadow that was supposed to be Minnesota but looked more like a sun-scorched Hollywood back lot.

"It never snows on this stupid show," said Leigh Ann.

"Hmm?" he said with a mouthful.

His jaw hurt to move, and his chest hurt to breathe. The smoke had done a number on his lungs. He had also broken his collarbone when he fell. He was in a torso cast, so he looked like a pantomime, frozen midroutine. They said Leigh Ann had spent forty-four hours at his bedside. They said she held his hand for two whole days. She had friends bring her food. She slept here. She had not showered. She had not changed. She only left to use the bathroom.

"It never snows on this show," she said. "My uncle lived in Minnesota. He said it snows all year long. But on this show it's always sunny and bright, and everyone is suntanned."

Nub forced himself up in his bed. His collarbone felt like it was going to snap in two. But it was worth it for the view. Leigh Ann looked soothing to his scalded eyes.

"What are you still doing here?" he said.

"The better question is, what are *you* still doing here?"

"I come here a lot," he said. "This is my home away from home."

She smiled. "You're very lucky to be alive."

He could tell by the pallor of her face that she'd been crying.

Leigh Ann placed another fish stick in his mouth. He was more than capable of feeding himself, of course, but he let her feed him and pretended to be a little worse off than he actually was.

After a few minutes, Leigh Ann was replaced with two Ash County deputies. They were not nearly as nice-looking as his caregiver had been. They wore khaki uniforms and square-toe Ropers. They removed their Stetsons to reveal matted hair.

Deputy Gordon Burke was the older of the two.

"We ought to quit this charade and move in together," said Nub.

"You'd get sick of me," said Burke. "I don't put the toilet seat down."

"I never even lift it up."

"We were hoping to get a statement, Mr. Taylor," said the younger deputy. "Do you feel up to telling us what happened a couple nights ago?"

"Sure," he said. "Someone set fire to my house. Tried to kill me. Tried to kill three of us. I almost died. Any questions?"

The younger of the two removed a notepad from his chest pocket. "Do you have any idea who this arsonist was?"

"I know exactly what you know."

The two deputies looked at each other.

"Anything you can tell us might be helpful," said Burke.

"Okay. Deer mice are the most common mammal in North America."

Gordon pulled a chair beside Nub's bed. "What's the last thing you remember?"

"I remember seeing a man on my lawn, holding a gas can. He called me Sugar."

"Sugar?"

"That's what he said."

The young deputy made a note. "Any idea who he could've been?"

"Just making a wild guess here, Officer Junior, but I'd say he wasn't with the local Rotary Club chapter."

The young notetaker made a note.

"Are you actually writing that down?"

The deputy looked embarrassed.

"Did you see the man's vehicle?" said Gordon.

"I didn't see a vehicle at all. He must have walked."

The kid scribbled more notes.

The younger deputy spoke. "Is there anyone with a grudge against you? Anyone who has been making threats?"

"Half the county has a grudge against me, kid. Give it time; you will, too, one day."

The two deputies looked at each other again.

"Look," said Nub, "I don't know who it was. Maybe start with Phillip Deener. And let's not rule this out—his dear old dad tried to kill me at the basketball game."

The young deputy shook his head. "Nope, it wasn't Bill Deener. He was at a game in Prattville. And Phillip was at the movies with a girl. Several witnesses saw him."

Nub felt his vision blur slightly from the heaviness of the medication taking effect. It was not an altogether unpleasant experience, but it also made him a little nauseous.

"Nub," said Gordon, "I realize you've been through a lot. But before we go, is there anything else you can remember?"

Nub leaned backward in his bed. The world started to spin around in that opiate haze of marshmallow weightlessness.

He muttered, "I love you so much it hurts . . ."

The deputies cleared their throats. "Nub? Stick with us for a second longer."

"I can't stand that dreadful little Nellie Oleson . . ."

"Mr. Taylor?"

Nub laughed to himself, eyes closed.

The deputies sighed. The younger deputy shook Nub by the shoulder to bring him back. But Nub was already fading.

"It never snows on this stupid show."

CHAPTER

≈ 42 ≈

Two days later, Minnie awoke.

Nub was sitting next to her in a wheelchair. The right side of his torso was wrapped in a plaster cast. Surprisingly, he was still mobile. His arms were burned and he looked like a man who had been rolled in bruises. But he could still get around.

"Sign my cast?" he asked.

She blinked and struggled to sit up.

"Easy," he said. "You're gonna be just fine. You're not burned, amazingly. Just a little bit of smoke inhalation. And, hey, I've been suffering from smoke inhalation since I was thirteen years old."

"Where's Bun? Is she okay?"

"Emily's got her. By the end of the day, your daughter will own seventy thousand pairs of cute shoes."

Nub notified the nurse that Minnie had awoken by pressing the little button no fewer than several hundred times.

Minnie rubbed her head. "I don't remember what happened."

"I can't help you there."

"I just remember the gunshots."

Nub wheeled his chair to her other side. "That was me doing the shooting."

Minnie closed her eyes again. A machine in the room was beeping every few moments. The beeping noise was like the sound from the arcade game they had at the roller rink. Pong, the game was called.

"Why did this happen?"

"I wish I knew."

"Why do people hate me?"

Nub wheeled his chair to her window and used his fingers to separate the blinds. He looked out. "What makes you think it's about you? I've pissed off more people in ten minutes than you have in your entire life."

Just then Emily walked through the door with her arms full. She was carrying a tray of food from the cafeteria. Mashed potatoes. Creamed corn. Collards. Yeast roll. Fried whitefish sticks aplenty. Bun was in her other arm, resting against her shoulder.

Minnie's face ignited.

So did Emily's. "You're *awake*," Emily said. And she began to weep. "Are you strong enough to hold Bun?"

Minnie stretched out her arms.

"Here's Mama," Emily whispered to the sleeping babe.

Minnie accepted Bun from Emily's arms. She held her child and rubbed her own cheeks against the baby's skin, speaking softly to her.

"Are you hungry?" Emily asked, placing the platter of food before Minnie. "I brought Dad fish sticks, but you look like you need them more than he does."

Minnie accepted the food, lifted one of the fish sticks, looked at it, and took a bite. The fish had a weak flavor, but she was starving. In a few moments she had eaten all four fish sticks and was asking for more. So Emily flagged down the nurse in the hallway, and Nub went back to looking out the window. A man was seated on the bench outside, chain-smoking.

He was one of the largest men Nub had ever seen.

Burke and Roger had been with the Ash County Sheriff's Department for a combined total of thirty-one years. Thirty years for Burke. One year for Roger. Roger was ambitious. At age twenty, he was still basically a teenager. Not even old enough to drink. But he was eager to learn all the right things, so he was welcome in Burke's Toyota. Burke's own kids didn't idolize him the way Roger did. Roger had been with Burke for exactly one week and he was starstruck with the old lawman. This made Burke feel more alive than he'd felt in a long time. Burke was doing more than training the kid. He was passing the torch.

Burke and Roger drove along County Route 19 looking for anything unusual. Burke's gut was telling him to check out the Taylor farm again. Back at the hospital, Nub told them someone had been on the lawn with a gas can. There were no vehicles nearby, Nub had said. So it only stood to reason that this person had been close by, since there were no residences around for miles. He would have either been camped some-where or had his car parked near the Taylor home. And if that was the case, wouldn't there be traces of a campsite? Or maybe they'd find where the perpetrator's car had been parked. It was a long shot, but one never knows, does one?

They rolled along the gravel road before sundown, tires popping on the rocks. Lights on. Burke told Roger to keep an eye out for places where the underbrush parted. Roger nodded respectfully.

They roamed the periphery of the Taylor farm, looking for anything out of the ordinary. Burke tapped on the brake when he saw a place where the thicket was disturbed.

"Bingo," said Burke.

"What do you see?" said Roger.

"Let's you and me go for a walk, Roger."

They hiked through the woods together, holsters unsnapped. Burke used his flashlight to follow the dim path that led through the greenery. It might have been a cow path or a footpath. Either way, Burke's gut told him to follow the trail. It might have been a dead end. But it might not. Boot prints were visible in the patches of mud. Fresh footprints. They followed the prints until they came to a small cleared area. A pit was filled with charred wood. There was a matted grassy place where someone had been sitting on the ground, or sleeping. And there were bed linens, folded nicely.

"Maybe we could get prints from some of this?" said Roger.

Burke laughed at the rookie's enthusiasm. "From what? Bed linens? Smoldering logs?" Burke shook his head. "You watch too much *Hawaii Five-O*. What we need here is what the textbooks call methodical deduction."

"No, I wasn't talking about the linens," the kid said, pointing to an empty military crate marked "Explosives."

Burke's eyes found the box. "Oh, that."

"I learned something else," the kid said, removing a notepad from his pocket. "Did you know that Minnie Bass's father was in prison?"

Burke turned to face the kid. "Uh. No, I didn't."

The kid flipped through the first several pages. "Yep. I made a few calls. Found out her old man was in for manslaughter." The kid met Burke's eyes. "He killed a man. A guy with a history in organized crime."

Burke pushed his hat brim back onto his head. "Okay."

"Her father's name is Clarence." The kid closed his notepad and tucked it back into his shirt pocket. "But everyone calls him Sugar. He's skipped parole. Nobody can find him."

Burke made a mental note to start watching *Hawaii Five-O*.

Shug was sitting outside Baptist Memorial on a bench as the sky's last flicker of sunlight fell. He was on his twentieth cigarette. And he was thinking about how this was the very hospital where his daughter had been born sixteen years earlier. At the time he had been stuck in a cell no bigger than an area rug. Celia had sent only two photographs of their child. He taped these two photos to the wall of his cell and greeted every morning with them. Shug had Minnie's face in his mind. He had memorized every curve and rise.

A red Impala turned into the hospital parking lot.

Shug watched the vehicle pull into a parking slot and saw a man step out. He was middle-aged, wearing a dress shirt and a pair of slacks. This was the man he'd been waiting for. He didn't recognize him, but when you were paid to rough people up, it did something to your mannerisms. The man walked around his car, reached into his back seat, and pulled out a Colt .45. The man checked the barrel of his weapon, then slapped it shut and shoved the pistol in the back of his pants.

Shug watched the man enter the hospital through a side door near a dumpster. The cafeteria maybe. Or the laundry room.

He crushed out his cigarette, then took a few deep breaths.

The adrenaline was coursing through his blood and made his body nearly frozen. He walked past the pneumatic sliding doors of Baptist Memorial, and he said a silent prayer. Asking for a miracle.

CHAPTER

❦ 43 ❧

The main thing you learn when you are dying is that the number one emotion is disappointment. Yes, there is anger and all the other stuff too. But the foundation of those other feelings is disappointment. It's as though you were reading a book and before you got to the final scene, someone yanked the book out of your hand and turned off the lights. A close second emotion is embarrassment. Which is a weird feeling to have under the circumstances. There isn't anything to be embarrassed about. But you feel ashamed just the same. Dying is humiliating. Nobody ever tells you how degrading it will feel. To die is to admit defeat. And we're programmed to resist defeat. At times Emily had felt as though her impending death was due to some kind of weakness on her part. As though she couldn't cut the mustard. She just wasn't strong enough.

She had expected to feel relief and excitement about her upcoming mastectomy. And she *did* feel those things. Sort of. But the main emotion she felt was wonder. As though she had been shot out of a cannon and she was flying, looking at the world beneath her, seeing the world for the first time.

Emily had left the hospital briefly to go home and shower and change and feed Bun but was back now. She parked in the space reserved for clergy because it was one of the only free parking spaces left. She threw open her vehicle door and removed Bun's baby carrier from the passenger seat.

"Are you ready to go see Mama?" she said to the baby.

The long walk across the parking lot felt good. The sunlight felt good. The taste of summer was everywhere. Life felt hopeful again.

She found her father parked outside his room in a wheelchair, smoking a cigarette.

"Should you really be smoking after suffering from smoke inhalation, Dad?"

"Thanks for the inquiry, Oral Roberts."

"I'm glad I caught you alone, Dad."

He looked at her. He stabbed out his cigarette on his shoulder cast. "You have my attention, sweetie."

She smiled. "How do you feel?"

"High as a kite, since you asked."

"Are you in pain?"

"How could I be? My body is a chemistry experiment right now. The doctor says my collarbone took the brunt of my fall like it was supposed to. Like a circuit breaker. Says my body was just doing its job, looking out for me. I told him it was a good thing the collarbone was looking out for me, because my brain gave up trying about thirty years ago."

He wheeled closer to her. "What did you want to talk to me about?"

She looked at him. Ever since her teenage years, she had been hesitant to show Nub Taylor any public affection. The few times he dropped her off at school, she had tried to pretend not to know him. She hadn't wanted her friends associating her with a drunken fool. As a grown woman, not much had changed. It was hard to hurdle old obstacles.

"I went to UAB a few days ago."

Nub struggled to sit upright in his chair. "And?"

"And they checked me out."

Without meaning to, she started crying before she had even broken the good news. She had promised herself she wouldn't cry, but all bets were off.

"My God, darling. What did they tell you?"

She couldn't speak. She couldn't get the words out. Because what if it wasn't true? What if the doctors were wrong? What if she was only hoping for something that would never come to fruition?

"Sweetie, what did you find out?"

She opened her mouth to speak, but she didn't have a chance to get the words out.

Because that's when they heard gunfire in the hallway.

⁓44⁓

Burke and Roger had just finished eating at the KFC. Burke had ordered the three-piece chicken dinner. Roger got the eight-piece because he had the metabolism of a hummingbird. He could eat whatever he wanted and finish out the day like a caffeinated hamster. They paid their bill, and Burke visited the little colonel's room. He splashed water on his face to revive himself. He was already feeling like a sedated grizzly after consuming Mr. Sanders's eleven unique herbs and spices. They left the restaurant and waddled through the parking lot.

They were halfway across the pavement when a call came on the radio. Burke could hear the radio voice squawking inside the Toyota through the closed windows. He could tell by the cadence that it was serious. It was a "shots fired" call.

In his three decades with Ash County, there had been only a few shots-fired calls. They were almost always harmless—everyone in the county had a gun. Even members of the clergy. But after the eventful week he'd had, he knew this was different. Burke jogged to the car. When he got there, he was out of breath. He fiddled with his keys and opened the door, then slid into the seat and keyed the mic.

"This is Burke."

Static.

"Shots fired. Shots fired. All units."

Static.

"Tell me where, Mae Beth."

Static.

"Baptist Memorial. We have one man down. Shooter is active. Shots fired. All units."

Static.

CHAPTER

❧ 45 ❧

The sounds coming from outside the door of Minnie's room sounded like firecrackers. Pops. Not like the sounds of gunfire in the movies. Emily was in the corner, holding Bun against her chest. Nub was parked by the window. Lying beneath the bed were a nurse and a janitor. And Benny. The door was locked.

Minnie moved toward the door, which was thick oak with a wire-framed window. She stared out the door's window but saw nothing. Then she heard the sound of more popping in the hallway. Like a cap gun. Only louder.

"Get away from that door, sweetie," said Nub.

The popping was louder. Closer.

Nub asked the janitor, "Can we get out through the window?"

The janitor shook his head. "Can't. That window don't open."

"We could always break it," said Benny.

"Pretty steep drop," said the janitor. "We're about twelve feet off the ground."

"Hard to jump twelve feet with a baby in your arms," said the nurse.

Nobody said anything to that.

Minnie stared out the door's window again.

She felt a roiling anger. It was an aggression that was almost more than she could bear. She could hear her pulse in her ears. She was tired of being afraid. Something had shifted inside her during the fire. She had found some powerful piece of herself she hadn't known was there. She placed her hand on the doorknob.

"What are you doing?" said Emily.

Everyone in the room put up a fuss when Minnie turned the doorknob and eased the door open.

"Sweetie, get away from that door," barked Emily.

Minnie said, "Stay here."

"Get back in here," Nub said.

But Minnie was already gone.

The Ash County Sheriff's Department had four deputies, and only two were full time. The smallest county in Alabama also had the lowest budget, statewide. Today, all two of Ash County's units were parked outside the hospital. There were other unmarked Fords from Blount, Walker, and St. Clair too. The most patrol cars Burke had ever seen in Ash County at once.

"This doesn't look good," said Roger, slamming his door.

Nurses were standing in the parking lot, holding each other, weeping. People lingered nearby, crying, trying to walk off the anxiety that accompanies trauma. Rotating red and blue lights were everywhere. It looked like something very, very bad had just happened here. Something you never expected to happen in a town of 1,302 people. A badge approached Burke's vehicle. He wasn't one of their guys. His badge said he was from Walker County. He looked maybe twelve.

"Tell me what happened," said Burke.

"Got here as soon as we could. We have a shooter inside, a handgun best we can tell. And hostages, I guess. Shooter's unidentified. Nobody has gotten a visual. Might be more than one. But we can hear the shots."

"Who are you?" said Burke.

"Walker County. Your sheriff asked us to come."

"How many officers inside?"

The young officer looked around. "None."

Burke stepped out of the vehicle. "None?"

The kid nodded.

"How many innocents are trapped inside?"

"Best count right now? Maybe forty or fifty."

"And *nobody's* gone in?"

The kid looked nervous. "We were waiting for orders, sir."

"And nobody gave you any?"

The kid said nothing.

Burke slammed his door. He walked toward the entrance of the hospital, removed his Stetson, and peered inside Baptist Memorial, keeping a low profile. Two bullet holes peppered the laminated glass. The rounds were in random locations, which suggested either wild shooting or a struggle. Which told him that whoever was holding the gun had plenty of ammunition.

Burke walked back to his vehicle and threw open his trunk hatch.

"What're you doing?" said Roger.

Burke removed his hat and unbuttoned his shirt. "Something a guy my age shouldn't be doing."

Minnie padded down the hallway. Her gown was open in the back, and she could feel the draft on her backside. She moved through the corridor and found a trail of blood streaking across the white linoleum. She came to the end of one hallway and stood at the edge of the cool cinder block wall. She was trying to get her bearings. There were four hallways that intersected with the nurses' station. Like a four-way stop. She had no idea which hallway the shooter was in. She was moving on pure instinct.

She heard a shot. Then another shot rang out and took a piece out of the stone wall beside her. She threw herself onto the ground.

Another few shots.

Crack! Crack!

Minnie sprang to her feet and turned to run the other way, but ran face-first into a man who was blocking her path. She screamed. But the man covered her mouth. He was extremely tall. He was looking right at her with piercing eyes.

"You shouldn't be out here, Minnie," he whispered.

More gunfire sounded.

The man threw her to the ground and dove atop her, shielding her with his body. The shots kept coming. Then the man on top of her yelled in agony. It was a yell unlike anything she had heard before.

"What's happened?" she said.

"I've been shot," he said.

CHAPTER

≈ 46 ≈

In the early seventies, someone discovered that several layers of a material called Kevlar would stop bullets. Not all bullets, but some. And stopping *some* was better than none. The Kevlar was not a miracle, but it was pretty close. Before Kevlar, ballistic vests were cumbersome and heavy, like wearing a parka made of limestone gravel. Impossible for maneuvers. Your average patrolman never could have worn a Kevlar vest and conducted his duties without looking like the Michelin Man.

That all changed when a man named Richard Davis came up with a material called Zylon, which was lighter than Kevlar.

Davis's genius, however, wasn't his invention. His brilliance was that he sold his vests directly to officers, not to agencies. Droves of policemen sent checks to him, including one Officer Gordon Burke from Ash County, Alabama. Burke bought three vests for the Ash County Sheriff's Department using his own money. These were volatile times. Civil rights. War protests. Nixon. He read the newspaper.

Burke threw the vest over his khaki uniform shirt and used the Velcro straps to cinch it tight. The vest felt like wearing a refrigerator carton. The collar had no V-notch, only a flat piece that dug into your neck and gagged you when you tried to open your mouth. Roger helped him straighten the armor, but it was still somewhat awkward.

"I *really* don't think this is a good idea," said Roger.

Burke tightened the waistband. "Good thing we don't pay you to think."

They heard more shots and Shug covered his daughter with his body again.

Pop! Pop! Pop-pop-pop!

"Are you okay?" Minnie asked him.

"We need to get out of the hallway."

"You've been shot."

"Go to the nurses' desk."

"You're bleeding."

"*Now*, I said."

They crawled across the hallway on hands and knees until they reached the nurses' station. They were not alone. Also hiding beneath the desk were two young women huddled together in a tight ball. One was painted in blood. She wore a pink nurse's tunic and pink trousers. Beside her was another nurse, also wounded. They were both fighting to stay calm but were critically injured.

"Listen to me," Shug said. "I need you to focus, ladies."

The women choked their tears back and gave him their attention.

"I need you both to calm down and tell me what happened."

"A man. He came in here and started asking questions about patients. He had a gun."

The woman began to sob into her hands again.

"Where is he now?"

The nurse shook her head. "I don't know."

He clutched his wounded arm, trying to staunch the bleeding, and he tried to think.

"Now what do we do?" said Minnie.

"We pray," said Shug.

The hospital doors opened automatically.

Burke walked into Baptist Memorial. His Stetson nearly blew off beneath the air lock. The automatic doors shut behind him with a vacuum seal.

The place was stone quiet. He walked the hallway, moving slowly, his weapon held outward. Elbows locked. Muzzle leading the way. He muted the chattering radio clipped to his belt. His boots clicked on the linoleum, giving him away. He tried to step softly, but each *clack* of his soles reverberated off the halls. No one was in sight.

Three of the other officers offered to accompany him into the building, but he could see they were frightened. They weren't trained for this. And a frightened deputy is about as good as a panicked airline pilot. Once you panic, you're screwed. They taught him that in the army. He sent officers to guard each exit and told them to wait.

Burke stopped at the first hospital room. He opened the door and made a quick sweep. Nothing. He checked the next room, located on the other side of the hallway. It was a sort of break room. Big refrigerator. Small sofa. Enamel table with coffee mugs. Four women were huddled against the refrigerator. Nurses in pink uniforms. They all stared at him with large eyes. He pressed a finger against his lips.

"Is anyone hurt?" he whispered.

They shook their heads.

He mouthed, "Where is he?"

They pointed toward the rear of the hospital.

He nodded, then left the room.

Burke levitated down the hall. Light footsteps. Barely breathing. He peeked into the window of another room. Inside were sleeping patients, lying on beds. No nurses. Both patients were elderly. Eyes closed. No signs of disturbance.

When he got to the end of the hallway, he saw a trail of blood smeared across the floor. The red trail went beneath a door marked as a supply closet. He stood before the door for a few moments, listening. He heard nothing. He drew in a few steadying breaths, then placed a hand on the lever and turned it slightly. He used his boot to nudge the door open. The door swung open wide.

He made a sweep.

Nobody inside.

Burke shut the door and pressed himself against the wall and listened. He heard the occasional movement in the distance. Footsteps. The thud of bare feet on linoleum. The rustle of fabric against fabric.

He made his ears bigger, trying to locate where the sounds were coming from. The nurses' station. Someone was hiding beneath the desk. Burke eased toward the desk. In front of the desk were several folders and white pages splayed on the ground. Whatever had happened here had happened by surprise. He made a wide arc around the desk.

He trained his revolver on the people behind the nurses' station.

There was a very large man. The Bass girl. And two nurses.

He lowered his weapon, squatted, and pressed a finger against his lips. The man was clutching his arm. His sleeve was covered in red. Burke recognized this man from their previous encounter.

"You again," said Burke.

The man pointed down the hallway toward the east entrance. "I heard shots back there, on the other side of the hall."

"How many shooters?"

"Just one."

Burke chewed on his lip. He reminded them all to stay down. "Any idea what he's after?" he added.

The wounded man nodded toward the Bass girl. "He wants her."

"Me?" said Minnie.

"And he wants to make me watch," the man said.

"Why do you say that? Who is he?"

"I don't know, exactly."

"Well, who are you?"

"Name's Sugar Bass."

Burke nodded.

"Everyone stay here," said Burke. Then he rose to his feet . . . and felt an explosion hit him between the shoulder blades.

CHAPTER

~ 47 ~

Nub heard the shots.

It sounded like a toy gun. Or fireworks. Or popcorn. Gunshots don't sound anything like they do in the John Wayne pictures. You learn that right away on a navy gunboat. You hear all manner of guns: big ones, small ones, itty-bitty ones. They sound like cracking logs. Sometimes they sound like cherry bombs.

He was still hazy from the medication, but adrenaline compelled him to get out of his wheelchair. He struggled to his feet.

"Dad," said Emily. "What are you doing?"

"I'm not sitting here. I can tell you that."

Benny was standing at the door, blocking his way. He wore a firm look on his face and folded his arms. "You're not going out there."

"Get out of my way, Benny."

"You can't, Nub."

"Thank you for your concern, Benny. But I'm a big boy."

Benny clenched his fists. "I won't let you, Nub. I won't let you do something stupid."

"I've been doing stupid things all my life."

"Not today." Benny shook his head. "You'll just make things

worse. You always do, Nub. You always do something that makes every situation ten times worse than it had to be."

"But you'll let a sixteen-year-old go out into that hallway?"

"I tried to stop her, but she's younger and faster than I am."

"Benny. Move or don't move. Either way, I'm going out that door. It's your choice whether you want to keep your teeth."

They had a short staring contest. Benny finally stepped aside. Nub tossed open the door and moved into the hallway. In a few moments, he heard steps behind him. It was Benny.

"Get back in that room with my daughter."

Benny shook his head. "You're not the boss of me."

Minnie was lying with her face on the ground, her hands covering her head. The shots had been louder than she thought they would be. So loud that her ears were ringing. The man had said they were after her, and she wondered what this was about. Whatever this was, it was not about Phillip Deener; she knew that much.

The wounded man was still clutching his arm, closing his eyes tightly. She could hear him breathing heavily beneath the pain.

"Who are you? Your last name is Bass? And why did you say they're after me?" she asked.

"Minnie," he said, moaning in pain, "can you make a tourniquet?"

"A what?"

"A tourniquet."

"I don't know what that is."

"Take off my belt."

"*Do what?*"

He closed his eyes tightly and gritted his teeth. "Please, Minnie."

In seconds, Minnie had removed his belt and followed his instructions. She tightened the leather around his arm until the hemorrhaging stopped.

"How do you know my name?" she said.

More shots.

This time the shots were accompanied by an eerie sing-songy voice coming from the hallway. "I know you're in here, Shug! *Come out, come out, wherever you are.*"

Minnie peered around the desk, down the hallway.

"Get away from there," whispered the man.

She could see the officer lying flat in the prone position. His boots were not moving. She heard approaching steps on the linoleum. The next thing she knew, the gunman was standing over her.

Nub made no noise as he walked through the hospital hall. He looked around for something he could use as a weapon. A cane, maybe. A walker. Something sharp. Anything. But there was nothing. All he could locate was a small, red fire cabinet mounted on the wall. In the olden days, the cabinet would have featured a fire axe, which would have made a great tool in a situation like this. If they were so lucky. Which he never was. But he told Benny to look anyway.

Benny crept down the hall toward the cabinet. He opened the door so slowly that Nub celebrated four birthdays. Finally, Benny reached into the cabinet. It wasn't an axe. Neither was it an extinguisher. Benny removed a giant brass nozzle connected to a long fire hose reel. The coil of canvas hose spilled onto the floor like a limp python. Benny held the nozzle in both hands with a stupefied look on his face.

"Bring it here," Nub said.

"A fire hose?"

Nub motioned for him to hurry up.

Benny placed the heavy brass thing into Nub's hand. The nozzle was bigger than Nub expected it to be. The opening was about the size of a regulation baseball. This thing was designed to pump out a lot of water.

Nub leaned in to whisper to his cousin. "Go stand by the spigot. When I need you, I'll shout. Then you spin the handle as fast as you can."

Benny furrowed his brow. "This is a terrible plan, Nub."

"Wait for my signal," said Nub.

Benny reluctantly walked back to the hose cabinet, placed one hand on the circular valve handle, and gave Nub the "okay" sign.

Benny was right. This was the worst plan known to humankind. Nub held the hose like a bayonet. His body cast allowed limited mobility with his forearm. The excess hose trailed behind him. His collarbone burned like it was about to snap.

He crept down the hallway and approached the nurses' station. He saw a deputy lying on the floor. It was Burke. Then he saw Minnie behind the desk, a figure standing over her with a pistol trained on her head.

Nub tightened his grip on the hose and opened his mouth to scream.

When Burke came to, he was lying facedown on the floor, which smelled like industrial cleaner. Like every public school, church, and government institution he'd ever known. Strangely, the smell was almost comforting right now. Familiar.

He did a full body scan.

He was okay. He would be bruised from hell to breakfast, but all right. He turned his head slightly so that he could see behind himself. He almost didn't believe what he was seeing. An old man who looked a lot like Benny Taylor was standing next to a red fire cabinet. The standpipe hose cabinet door was open. The fire hose reel was strewn down the hallway, snaking through the corridor like a giant piece of linguini. Benny's hands were gripping the valve spigot. Burke made eye contact with Benny and started to say something, but before Burke could say a word, the hallway erupted with a shout.

"Now, Benny!"

CHAPTER

~ 48 ~

Your average home faucet puts out about 50 pounds of pressure per square inch. It's enough pressure to clean your dishes, but barely. A typical garden hose exerts roughly 80 pounds of pressure, enough to clean off your sidewalk if you're lucky. A commercial faucet pumps out maybe 120 pounds of pressure, which is enough to take old paint off your house. With a fire hose, however, you're looking at roughly 1,600 to 2,000 pounds of water pressure per square inch. That's enough pressure to knock down a freestanding brick wall. Enough pressure to bore a twenty-two-foot-deep hole in the ground. A fire hose also doubles in size every fifteen seconds. The hose starts out flaccid and soft, like an elephant trunk. But in under only two seconds, the silicone and canvas become granite hard. Turgid, like iron. You could park a semitruck atop the hose and the flow would not be impeded. Not only that, but the hose begins lurching in all directions, flailing around like the world's largest anaconda.

And that's exactly what was happening now.

After Nub screamed the command, the hose in his hand immediately became solid and full. And it started bucking and kicking like a wild mustang. He held the hose with both hands and immediately felt his broken collarbone move in an unnatural way. His feet were nearly lifted from the floor by the pressure. He tried to control the hose and point it at the shooter, but the hose was untamable. The nozzle shot water off the walls and bored holes into the suspended ceiling. The gunman fired straight at Nub and missed. Thank God. But he shot again. And again. Nub closed his eyes and tried to subdue the hose. He expected to feel the impact of a bullet bite him any minute. But each shot was a miss. Providence.

The gunman stepped forward and took a more careful aim. *Pop! Pop!*

This time Nub felt something rip through his upper thigh and send burning heat throughout his lower body. He screamed when he felt the object cut through his quadricep and exit through his hamstring. He felt hot blood spilling on his lower leg. He felt his leg go limp.

By now, the spray coming from the hose was full force. Approximately two thousand pounds of unmitigated water pressure slung the hose in every direction. The hose, completely beyond Nub's control, seemingly with a mind of its own, blew its spray into the gunman, knocking him against the wall. The nozzle was whipping itself through the air, randomly blasting the gunman. The thing was yanking Nub all over the place, and if he let the hose go, he had no doubt the flailing hose would brain him to death next.

"Help me, Benny!" he screamed as he flopped around like a rag doll. "Help me!"

The gunman was slipping and sliding on the ground, trying to reach the gun that had been knocked from his hand.

"Help, Benny!"

In a quick moment, both Minnie and Benny arrived at his side and clutched the hose. The gunman scrambled to his feet and lifted his gun from the floor. The man held his arm

straight, and just as he was about to aim the pistol, Nub trained
the hose onto his chest and nailed the man against the wall.

When Burke got to his knees, he found that his legs were wobbly
and his body was covered in cold sweat. He was nauseous. He
was definitely suffering from shock. He knew the symptoms.
But he managed to get to his feet and jog down the hallway,
where he found the gunman pressed firmly against the wall by
Nub Taylor's fire hose stream.

Burke raced forward and dove in front of the jet stream,
knocking the gunman to the ground. The man put up a fight,
and Burke had been weakened by the blow to his chest. Burke
was soon on his back with the gunman atop him, whaling on
his face with both fists. Water sprayed in all directions, and
he could hear Benny and Nub arguing about which direction
to point the hose. Burke struggled to land a few flimsy blows
into the gunman's midsection. He was losing this fight.

Until, all at once, the punches ceased.

Minnie Bass had lifted the shooter from the ground
and held him suspended in the air. She had him in a bear
hug, squeezing him so hard the man's face became purple.
It looked like the man's eyes were going to be expelled from
his head.

Benny killed the water pressure. The hose went slack. A
flock of officers had entered the building. They wrenched
the gunman from Minnie's arms and threw him to the floor.
When the long struggle was over, everyone was soaked and
the hospital corridor was covered in several inches of standing
water.

And Nub Taylor was unconscious.

The floor was a river of red. Blood mingled with water. Minnie shouted for someone, anyone, to help.

"Mr. Nub, can you hear me?"

"I can't feel anything, sweetie."

"What do you mean?"

"I'm cold."

"Hang on." Minnie stood and shouted, "He can't feel nothing! Help him!"

"My whole body's so cold."

"Mr. Nub."

"Sweetie, I don't think I'm going to . . ."

"Someone help him! Please!"

Nub closed his eyes.

"No!" Minnie shouted. "Don't close your eyes!"

But it was too late.

CHAPTER

❧ 49 ❧

The chopper came directly from Birmingham. Emily could hear it beating through the air above them. She stood in the parking lot of Baptist Memorial. Minnie held her tightly and wept into her shoulder.

Both women remained beside Nub, holding his hand during the flight. The paramedics didn't often allow passengers on the helicopter due to added weight. But this was different. A major artery had been compromised. A femoral artery. He was losing too much blood. The medics kept telling him to stay with them. They kept shouting his name. They kept telling him not to go to sleep.

Nub's eyes opened lazily. "Tell my daughter . . ."

"Dad, I'm right here."

But he was already leaving them.

"Daddy?" she said.

His eyes remained shut.

Emily kept her head near her father's ear. She sang to him over the din of the chopper noise. Her voice was not pretty like his, but it was all she had to give. She sang "In the Sweet By and By." She sang "When the Morning Comes" and "Oh When the Saints." She prayed for him. She placed her forehead upon his chest and prayed long and hard. But in her heart, she knew it was not going to work. A heavy weight settled on her, a coolness that told her life was not going to be the same after this. Nub Taylor would not make it, not this time.

He quit breathing twice on the helicopter journey. His blood pressure was almost nonexistent. One of the medics told her to say her final goodbyes.

The aircraft landed on the helipad of the hospital. The downdraft from the rotors nearly blew the surrounding paramedics off their feet. When the cabin door opened, the sound of the rotors outside was loud enough to rupture her eardrums.

The paramedics whisked Nub away on a roller gurney.

One medic approached Emily and Minnie and shouted over the howling motor. "Which one of you is his daughter?"

"We both are," Emily said.

CHAPTER

❧ 50 ❧

Carraway Hospital was enormous and looming. It was a massive maze of unrelated rooms and corridors, bigger than a university and twice as confusing. Emily found that she could hardly muster the energy to remain upright as she leaned against the wall and let out a gush of tears and sobs. People stared as they walked by, but there was an unspoken permission given in hospitals that it was okay to cry. When she gathered herself, she went to the vending machines and got something cold to drink and a pack of cigarettes. As she was walking down the hallway toward the intensive care unit, Charlie Jr. came running toward her. He was frantic.

"Mom! Granddaddy's awake!"

Emily dropped her can of Coke and her Pall Malls. She followed Charlie Jr. down the hallway, racing. She jogged past rooms that were filled with spaceship-like machinery and blinking lights. She sprinted past men in lab coats with notepads. She weaved by nurses who asked her to slow down. She dodged a janitor cart and nearly knocked over an old man with a walker. She reached her father's room in a breathless frenzy.

The room was a somber place. She had been living there for the past several days. They all had. Minnie was still seated beside Nub's bed, holding Bun in her arms. Leigh Ann was still holding his right hand. Benny was leaning onto the rails of the bed and talking into Nub's left ear in a whisper.

One nurse was administering fluids via an IV. Her father was intubated with a breathing tube. The sound of the breathing apparatus filled the room. Beeping. Suction sounds. The hum of a hundred tiny compressors keeping him alive.

But his eyes were open.

"Dad."

Everyone parted and made room for Emily. She leaned forward and smiled at her father. He attempted to smile back—the muscles in his cheeks tensed—but the breathing tube made it impossible.

"When did he open his eyes?" Emily asked Leigh Ann.

Leigh Ann looked like she'd been crying for ten years. "A few minutes ago."

Nub made a weak grunt at Emily and squeezed her hand. He looked even worse than he had before. His face was pinched and drawn. His cheeks were hollow. And pale. He closed his eyes again.

"Oh, Daddy."

Her own tears saturated her shirt. Emily had been living in this hospital room for three nights alongside him, surviving on vending machine food, sleeping in vinyl chairs, inhaling rivers of tobacco. Nub had been unresponsive. Emily had already been calling relatives and friends to let them know the doctors said he could pass any day now. Loretta had been by the hospital twice already.

None of the people in this room had showered, eaten a meal, or done anything but stay right here and watch him dwindle. They all wanted to be the last hands he held, the last faces he ever saw, the last voices he heard. The last presence he felt.

Minnie often held Bun close to Nub's face so that Nub's

face could touch the baby's face. Leigh Ann regularly kissed Nub, and occasionally wet his face with her own salt water. Benny never quit speaking softly into Nub's left ear, retelling elaborate stories from long ago, stories that were apparently intended only for himself and Nub.

"Mrs. Ives?" the doctor said.

The doctor asked to speak to Emily outside the room.

"What's going on?" she asked. "He's awake."

The doctor grimaced. "I wouldn't get too excited about that."

"Why not? His eyes are open."

"He's not doing well," said the doctor. "I don't want to deliver false hope."

"What's that mean?"

"I'm afraid it means the worst, Mrs. Ives. His stats keep dropping, and he's not breathing on his own. We're just keeping him comfortable until he passes."

"But he's awake."

"The painkillers might have relieved some of the pain, which helped him wake up. But it will start happening less and less."

The dam burst. She covered her face with both hands. A thousand and one childhood summers came back to her. The days when she used to sit beside her father on a shallow creek bridge, eating Junior Mints and chewing Bazooka bubble gum. Him, sitting beside her. Young and lean. Strong and healthy. Fishing rod in his hands, cigarette wedged in the corner of his lips. The perpetual young buck. Singing to her. A girl's father is the first and greatest love of her life. At least, that's how it's supposed to be.

When the doctor left, Emily went to her father again. She sat in the chair beside his bed. She held his hand. She covered that hand in her tears. And the cold reality was falling upon her. She knew this was it. This was the moment when the great love of her life would end.

"Can you hear me, Daddy?"

Grunt.

"Do you need anything, Daddy?"

Her father's eyes blinked open again, but only briefly. His eyes still had love in them. And although he couldn't speak, she could feel what he wanted to say. And she knew he was saying goodbye. Nub's tap-water blue eyes focused on her. Then they focused on Minnie. Bun. Benny. Leigh Ann. Then Emily held Nub's limp hand tightly. Her father's hand was cold. Unmoving. She squeezed his hand and pressed it against her chest.

"I love you," Emily said.

He grunted three times.

And at 8:29 p.m., the doctors of Carraway Methodist pronounced Jeremiah "Nub" Taylor dead.

CHAPTER

∾ 51 ∾

The 362-seat brick-faced Union Gospel Tabernacle, built in 1885, sat on the street corner at 116 Fifth Avenue North, in downtown Nashville, like a temple. The building was nick-named after the man who financed it, Thomas G. Ryman. Ryman was a former sailor, a saloonkeeper, a hard drinker, and a shrewd businessman, and he was considered by many sources to be a little turd.

One spring day he attended a tent revival led by Reverend Sam Jones. Ryman was drunk, staggering into the tent, shouting obscenities. You could have blindfolded him with a strip of dental floss.

His only reason for attending the revival was to heckle the Reverend Jones and cuss him off the stage. And that's exactly what he started doing. But he failed. Ryman was converted. Right there at the altar. By the end of the service, Ryman was weeping, lying prostrate before the preacher.

The same week, Ryman dedicated his family fortune to building a church downtown. The church took seven years to build and cost nearly a hundred grand—three million in modern dollars. The tabernacle opened its doors, and the city was never the same. Preachers called down fire from heaven. The lame learned to walk. Blind men saw. Desperate people found what they were seeking in this room. And even now, although this church was home to America's longest-running radio show, this place was holy. It was still a church. Of all things.

Minnie was backstage, peeking through the curtains. Hordes of people were lining the pews. The old tabernacle was stuffy and hot. She was sweating. Everyone was. Some in the crowd were fanning themselves with paper fans, but this did little to kill the communal armpit funk.

A man in a headset tapped Minnie on the shoulder. "Ten minutes to showtime," he said in a stage whisper.

The *Grand Ole Opry* was about to begin.

It was quite a night for the *Opry*, with an all-star cast. Even a former US president was in the audience. Minnie could see the president in the crowd with his entourage seated around him. He looked just like everyone else, except he was dressed much nicer.

Minnie wore a slim-fitting white dress with western fringe on the sleeves. Her hair was braided. Her boots were green. Her Gibson was strapped to her chest. A man in a ten-gallon lid stepped toward her and presented his hand. The man wore a blue sequined suit. His hat was tall and white. She recognized his smile from Nub Taylor's old record covers.

They shook hands.

"My name's Ernest," said the man.

"I know who you are."

He smiled.

Then he introduced her to a shorter man wearing a pink suit adorned in jewels. A guitar was draped from the man's shoulder. Yellow wood. The man's name was inlaid on the fretboard. He had close-cropped hair. His jaw was sharp enough to slice a watermelon.

"This is my friend Clarence," said Tubb.

"Most people call me Hank," said the man.

Minnie released his hand. "I know who you are too."

Hank strummed one chord on his guitar. "What key do you do 'Wildwood Flower' in?"

"I do it in C."

"How fast do you want to take it?" He strummed a little more.

"That's a good tempo," she said.

The men nodded.

Another man joined the conversation. It was Roy Acuff. His hair was finger-waved. His face was bright and cheery. He was looking at Minnie with a large grin. He thanked her for accepting his invitation.

"Thank you for having me," she said.

"Are you nervous, sweetheart?"

"No."

The cowboys all smiled at each other.

"That's good," said a woman nearby. "It's bad luck to say you're nervous."

The woman was loud and lively, wearing a straw hat with a price tag dangling from the brim. "Just picture the audience in their underpants, sweetie. Especially the cute boys. It won't make you less nervous, but it will make you smile ever so big."

Minnie checked her makeup in a mirror. She couldn't help but notice how much she looked like the father she had believed was dead throughout her childhood.

Shug Bass was taken into custody by Ash County law enforcement. He appeared at a preliminary hearing, and Minnie was in attendance. She was seated in the front row of the courtroom, marveling at how handsome her father was. She had never visualized him as a handsome man.

The court hearing was not all bad. The prosecution gave Clarence "Sugar" Bass leniency, and the DA offered him a plea bargain in exchange for testifying against the same racketeering organization that sought to kill him. Shug testified. The criminal defense attorneys tried to destroy Shug's credibility. The defense cited Shug's history as an army EOD specialist and talked about an ongoing investigation involving the usage of C-4 in a mob hit. Shug never moved a facial muscle. He denied involvement. Within the week, he was relocated from Draper Correctional Facility to Blanchard Federal Correctional Prison, a minimum-security prison not far from Ash County. His sentence was three months, thanks to his cooperation. His cell at Blanchard had a barless window and a full bookshelf. His door had no lock. They even had Ping-Pong tables. Minnie visited him several times. She was pretty good at Ping-Pong.

Shug got to know his granddaughter and his daughter. And Minnie got to know her father. She baked him things. He wrote her poems. One time Shug even asked if he could hold her hand. And she let him. After their last meeting, Shug gave her a small card with the name of a bank and a number written on the back.

"What's this?"

He'd told her it was the number to a safety deposit box. Then he told her where to find the key to open it. *"What's in the box?"* she had asked. Shug didn't answer; he merely suggested they play another round of Ping-Pong.

Roy Acuff stood beside Minnie Bass and placed a hand on her shoulder. "You have your encore song ready?"

"Yes, sir."

"Good. These people love their encores."

"I doubt they'll encore me."

"If they don't, I will."

That same summer, Ash County sheriff's deputies arrived at Phillip Deener's house to administer a paternity test. The kid urinated into a paper cup under direct supervision by his lawyer. Phillip's blood was then drawn by a medical technician who seemed to enjoy sticking the kid multiple times to find an acceptable vein. The results of the test found, with 80 percent certainty, that Deener was the father of Minniford Bass's child. Deener was ordered by the court to contribute child support until Bunniford Taylor Bass turned eighteen. In the event Deener defaulted on payments, the judge stipulated that Phillip's parents would assume financial responsibility for Bunniford.

The show began.

The crowd applauded.

Acuff took the Ryman's center stage to earsplitting applause. The rhinestones on his jacket caught the light and looked like a miniature solar system. He stood behind a condenser microphone poised on a tall silver rod and spoke to the audience. As she waited in the wings, Minnie thought about her life.

She was seventeen years old. Seventeen wasn't very old. Only 6,223 days old, not counting today. Most of those days her life had been filled with disappointment. But then the last year had been filled with so much wonder, it was staggering when she thought about it. She had earned a child, a sister, and a grandfather, and her father had risen from the dead.

If those weren't miracles, nothing was.

But then, life was full of overlooked miracles. And miracles never happen the way you expect them to. They are softer than a baby's breath. They are, at times, as noticeable as a ladybug. A miracle is not a big thing. A miracle is millions and millions of small things working together. But then, this didn't matter. Not really. Because Minnie had come to believe that life was not about finding miracles, or happiness, or success, or purpose, nor was it about avoiding disappointment. It was about finding people. People are what make life worth it. People are the buried treasure. People who understand you. People who will bleed with you. People who make your life richer. Your people. Your kinfolk.

The man on the stage introduced Minnie Bass to the audience. Then Minnie Pearl escorted Minnie Bass to the microphone, arm in arm. Two Minnies at the Opry. You couldn't make this stuff up.

The musicians took their places behind Minnie Bass. The crowd erupted. Minnie shielded her eyes from the powerful lights. She scanned the audience. There in the pews, she picked out her one-year-old daughter, who was sitting in Benny Taylor's lap, wearing a pink ribbon in her mess of red hair. He was bouncing the child on his knees. Benny was wearing a necktie. He had removed his cap. The liver spots on his scalp had never looked finer.

Miss Emily was sitting beside them.

Earlier that week Emily had a routine follow-up appointment in Birmingham. Minnie had gone with her and sat in the waiting room. When Emily emerged, she was all smiles. The doctors could find no traces of her cancer after the mastectomy. Although excited, Emily was afraid to celebrate, so they didn't. They just hugged, right there in the office, for maybe five minutes. And they went out for ice cream.

They agreed never to speak of ductal carcinoma again—until the next follow-up.

Next to Emily was Leigh Ann. She was wearing a sequined blouse, and she looked lovely. Before the *Opry*, Leigh Ann had helped Minnie fix her hair and makeup, reminding her how proud Mr. Nub would be of her.

And in the chair next to Leigh Ann sat a sixty-three-year-old man wearing a hula-girl necktie. He had dandelion-fuzz hair. And he was smiling directly at Minnie. The man's eyes were bright and blue, and possibly wet. When she took the stage, he applauded so hard he nearly broke his wrist. Benny handed the baby off to him, and Nub Taylor lifted the arm of the baby girl and waved her tiny hand at her mama.

Mama waved back from the stage.

The doctors had pronounced Nub dead when his heart stopped. But doctors don't know everything. Yes, his heart had stopped beating for four minutes and seventeen seconds. But his spirit had not gone anywhere. He had been clinically dead for a total of 257 seconds, and 257 is a prime number. And within those four minutes, as the overeager young doctor made numerous attempts to shock Nub's heart back into rhythm, the whole world quit moving. When the pulsometer started beeping again after the young doctor's last try, the whole room had broken down sobbing. Nub's eyes had opened. And in a moment of agony, Nub managed to move his arm. He tapped two fingers against his lips. Benny translated for everyone. *"He wants a cigarette!"*

Nub's recovery was long and slow, but he had three women in his life—four including Bun—who were there to help him find his way when he couldn't.

Minnie began to play her guitar. Softly. Just the way Nub had taught her.

With each gentle tone of the instrument, she found herself remembering how it had felt to unwrap an instrument like this one on her sixteenth birthday. A Gibson. She remembered how it made her feel, seeing something so beautiful. Something lovely, which had been intended just for her. The guitar had been destroyed in the fire. But it didn't matter. The memory of the moment was worth more than gold.

Minnie closed her eyes and felt love radiating from her family in the audience. It was tangible love. It was palpable. She felt this love all over her body. Love before her. Love behind her. Love above her. Love beneath her. Love on the crown of her head. Love on the soles of her feet. Love way down in her heart.

Minnie Bass gently wiped tears from her cheeks as she stood before 2,362 audience members and one former US president. She approached the microphone center stage.

"I'm just so proud to be here," she said.

⚞ A NOTE FROM THE AUTHOR ⚟

As a boy, my father used to listen to the *Grand Ole Opry* and drink beer in his garage. We were Southern Baptists, and Southern Baptists do not drink beer inside, only in the garage. Occasionally they smoke out there too. But only when your mother is out of town visiting her aunt.

Out in that garage I listened to 650 AM, Nashville. I heard Loretta Lynn, George Jones, Sarah Cannon, and all the greats.

If my mother happened to be home, and if she came into the garage unexpectedly, my father would quickly pass me his beer and cigarette and say to my mother, "Look at what I caught your son doing."

Foremostly, I was a kid with musical proclivity. I wouldn't go so far as to call it "talent." I was, however, allowed to sing and play piano in church.

Namely, because it was only a twenty-seven-member church, and the only other soul in our congregation who was called upon to sing offertory hymns was Mrs. Wannamaker, who many said had a voice like a Buick with a bad starter.

My father took his own life when I was eleven, whereupon I began listening to the *Opry* faithfully. Every Saturday. I suppose I was trying to keep him alive, somehow. It was stupid, but there you are.

Eventually, I grew up. Eventually, I parted ways with modern country music because I preferred a style of music that didn't involve thong underwear and three-thousand-dollar boots. I preferred my father's style of music. Blue-collar music. Tunes sung by folks who knew what it meant to work for a living. Just like my old man.

After a long, rocky childhood, and a string of failures, I fell into novel writing when I was in my thirties. I was making hundreds of dollars per year.

Still, I have been fortunate enough to produce a handful of novels. And I feel grateful for this. No, they are not highbrow novels, but I'm still proud of them.

Not to toot my own horn, but one time my work caused a well-known literary critic to generously remark, "I want the last eight hours of my life back. This guy sucks."

My writing led to speaking gigs. Which led to my performances where, before live audiences, I would perform a one-man trainwreck. My one-man show has led me around the nation as a stand-up storyteller and song-singer.

I have delivered my one-man disaster in nearly every state in the Union except North Dakota, of whose existence I am starting to doubt.

It's not a glamorous life. Mostly, I have spoken and told my jokes in VFWs, nursing homes, or at the grand openings of various feed and seeds.

At this age, I can attribute my entire career to those evenings listening to the *Opry* with my father in the garage.

And so it was, on one summer afternoon, a few years ago, I sat down to write a novel. And the premise was simple:

I wanted my book to be about an underprivileged kid, a screw-up, a suicide survivor, and a musician. I wanted this kid, my main character, to have no confidence. Just like me. I wanted this kid to feel lost and unloved. And in the end, I wanted this kid to be called up to the Grand Ole Opry.

I started writing this book, but told nobody about this manuscript. Not even my wife. I worked on these sentences every day. Weeks turned into months. Months turned into years. Nobody knew what my book was about. Not even me.

Then, one day, out of a clear blue sky, my wife got a phone call. My wife nodded a lot during this call. She said a lot of *uh-huhs*. Then she hung up the phone. There were tears in her eyes.

"Do you know who that was on the phone?" she asked.

"The IRS?" I said.

"That was the *Grand Ole Opry*," she explained. "They want you on their show."

I nearly collapsed. The novel I began writing many years ago had somehow, through a grand mystery of the universe, come true. To me.

Later, when my editor, Laura Wheeler, asked what I wanted to title this book, I told her I didn't have a title. She said, "Why don't we call it *Kinfolk*?"

Months thereafter, Laura showed up to my *Opry* performance. She hugged me after the show and we both cried into each other's shoulders. "You did it," she said.

"No," I said. "We did it."

Here's what the dictionary says about *kinfolk*.

Kinfolk: (in anthropological or formal use) a person's blood relations, regarded collectively, or singularly in the American dialect. A member of one's own family. One's own flesh and blood, a blood relative. A loved one.

This book is for all those unfortunate enough to be my kinfolk. My loved ones.

ACKNOWLEDGMENTS

And now I'd like to introduce the band. First, and foremostly, my wife, Jamie. The long-suffering, saintly woman who has, to my knowledge, never tried to suffocate me in my sleep. And to my agent Alex, without whom I would be surviving by enrollment in a government subsistence program.

To Amanda, my publisher, who took a chance on me and changed my life forever. To Laura, my editor, who has consistently prevented me from looking like Baalam's ass. And Julie, who has edited every novel I've ever written, and probably will continue doing so until either I die or she dies—for her sake, I hope I go first. To Philip, my tour wrangler, who got me on the *Grand Ole Opry*, and fulfilled a childhood dream, and transformed a fool.

And to you who, for some reason, gives a dang about me. I don't know why. But you don't know how much I love you, and I fear you will never know the totality of my affection. So I'm saying it once more, in case you missed it. I love you.

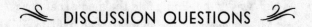

DISCUSSION QUESTIONS

1. Sean begins his story with the line, "This is the wrong way to begin a novel." How do you like a novel to begin?

2. What character did you connect with the most and why?

3. Nub and Emily's relationship is a complicated one. Did you find yourself more sympathetic to Nub or Emily? Why?

4. How did you feel about how Shug tried to protect Minnie? How Nub tried to protect her? Did you think their actions were justified?

5. Emily was bothered and hurt by Nub's relationship with Minnie and struggled to make sense of why he would take care of Minnie when he had been so neglectful of her. Did you understand Emily's conflicting feelings toward her father or did you wish she had more compassion for him?

6. What was your favorite moment between Nub and Benny? Between Nub and Minnie?

7. Did you feel satisfied by the resolution with Philip Deener or do you wish he had experienced more repercussions for his actions?

8. In what ways were Nub and Shug alike as fathers? Different?

9. What did you think of the dynamic between Loretta and Nub? What do think they truly felt about each other?

10. As Nub was dying, Emily told the medic that both she and Minnie were Nub's daughters. What all do you think had occurred that led Emily to be able to make that statement? What do you imagine Minnie felt in that moment?

11. What did the Ryman and the Grand Ole Opry symbolize in the story? What role did Minnie Pearl and Roy Acuff play?

12. In the end, "Minnie had come to believe that life was not about finding miracles, or happiness, or success, or purpose, or about avoiding disappointment. It was about finding people." Do you believe that is true? If so, how has it been true in your life? Or are you still searching for your people, your kinfolk?

From the Publisher

GREAT BOOKS

ARE EVEN BETTER WHEN THEY'RE SHARED!

Help other readers find this one:

- Post a review at your favorite online bookseller

- Post a picture on a social media account and share why you enjoyed it

- Send a note to a friend who would also love it—or better yet, give them a copy

Thanks for reading!

Beloved writer Sean Dietrich will warm your heart with this rich and nostalgic tale of a small-town sheriff, a mysterious little girl, and a good-hearted community pulling together to help her.

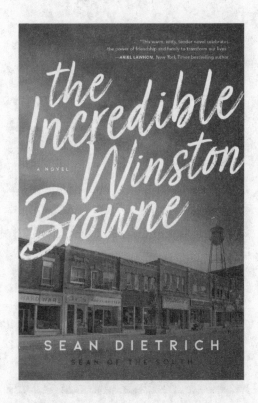

Available in print, e-book, and audio

THOMAS NELSON
Since 1798

In this heartfelt tale about enduring hope amid the suffering of the Great Depression, Sean Dietrich weaves together a tale featuring a cast of characters ranging from a child preacher, a teenage healer, and two migrant workers who give everything they have for their chosen family.

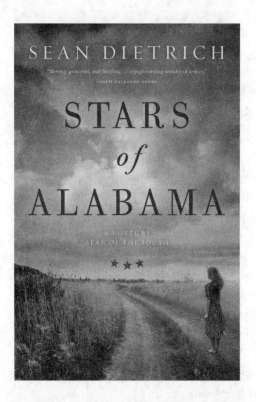

Available in print, e-book, and audio

THOMAS NELSON
Since 1798

ABOUT THE AUTHOR

Photo by Sean Murphy

Sean Dietrich is a columnist, novelist, and stand-up storyteller known for his commentary on life in the American South. His work has appeared in *Newsweek, Southern Living, Reader's Digest, Garden and Gun,* and the *Birmingham News,* and his column appears in newspapers throughout the US. He has authored fifteen books, is the creator of the *Sean of the South* podcast, and makes appearances on the *Grand Ole Opry.*

Visit Sean online at seandietrich.com
Instagram: @seanofthesouth
Facebook: @seanofthesouth
Twitter: @seanofthesouth1